HE CAME DOWN RIVER,

fighting Indians, pirates, English and Spanish agents—and he won a fortune for himself.

In New Orleans, all the luxury and beautiful women of that lush city lay at his feet. The whole world opened up before him. He felt like a king!

Then the message came. Philippa Baynton, the loveliest woman he had ever known, had been captured by the savage Shawnee chief, Chicatommo . . .

DALE VAN EVERY'S

THE VOYAGERS

Bantam Books by Dale Van Every

BRIDAL JOURNEY
THE VOYAGERS

THE VOYAGERS

Dale Van Every

*This low-priced Bantam Book
has been completely reset in a type face
designed for easy reading, and was printed
from new plates. It contains the complete
text of the original hard-cover edition.*
NOT ONE WORD HAS BEEN OMITTED.

THE VOYAGERS

*A Bantam Book / published by arrangement with
Holt, Rinehart & Winston*

PRINTING HISTORY

*Holt edition published August 1957
2nd printing .. September 1957
3rd printing ... February 1958*

Bantam edition / July 1959

2nd printing .... July 1959	5th printing . September 1967
3rd printing .... July 1959	6th printing .. February 1971
4th printing .... August 1959	7th printing .... May 1977

ISBN 0-553-10281-8

Published simultaneously in the United States and Canada

THE VOYAGERS

1

The people of Traner's Station were inclined to patronize their neighbors. They were able to feel that, for a new country, the place already had quite a history. Reflecting upon this history, it was their way to refer to any past year in terms of the principal event that had marked that twelvemonth. The year after Pontiac's Rebellion, 1764, for example, had been the year that old Nicholas Traner had located his hunting camp by the spring. The hickory pole-and-bark shack was still in use as a chicken coop, which established the station as the oldest continuously occupied settlement on the Monongahela between Pittsburgh and the river's headwaters. The next, 1765, had been the year that Abel Traner became the community's first native-born white child, a circumstance made possible by the insistence of Elizabeth, Nick's wife, on coming out with him to help put in his first corn patch. Other notable years had been 1777, the year Job Moyer started his ferry, 1782, the year of the last Indian siege, and 1783, the year old Nick had been trampled to death trying to mate one of his cows to a trapped buffalo bull. The present year, 1788, was already being accepted as the year the movers swarmed. Every spring since the end of the war with England there had been movers on their way to Kentucky; but this year, as early as February, they were pouring over the mountains in such numbers that it was something hard to believe even while watching them come in. Afterward, when events had taken on more proportion, people remembered 1788 as the year that Abel Traner left for New Orleans.

For Abel, youngest of the four Traner brothers, the day that was so greatly to alter his situation began much as any other. Before it was light he stood up in his blankets, pulled on his pants, and thrust his feet into his boots. Out of the darkness around him came the muffled drone of snores, wheezes, coughs, and mutters from the still-sleeping twenty-odd other members of the family. Eben, oldest of the Traner brothers, was, like Abel, a bachelor, but Micah had six children and Caleb eight. On the firestep along the wall, on which formerly riflemen had stood to the loopholes, children were now bedded end to end. Kate, Caleb's big, good-humored wife, had borne him a child each year of their marriage, and Selina, Micah's young second wife, was already well along with her first.

Abel's sleeping space was on the floor by the fireplace in the kitchen end of the big one-room cabin. He rolled his blankets against the wall, pulled the backlog forward over the embers, threw on a handful of sticks, and went outside. The crests of the mountains to the east were black against the paling sky beyond, as were those of the hills to the west against the afterglow of the moonset. The stars gleamed frostily. The main winter ice had gone out with last week's thaw but a new film was crackling along the edges of the river as the current kept breaking it away. He broke the ice in the rain barrel and dabbed cold water across his face. When he went back in he found Selina kneeling at the fire, shivering over a skillet of bacon and a pot of burned-barley coffee. She looked up at him half guiltily.

"Long's yer the only Traner that gits up to go to work—'pears like somebody might git up once in a while to feed yuh."

Selina rose awkwardly to her feet, her belly thrust out before her as prominently as though she were carrying a basket of clothes clasped against her slight form. Suddenly she pressed her hands to it. A spasm of panic contorted her sharp, thin face.

"He's kickin' agin. I kin feel him."

"No call to let him skeer you," said Abel. "Young uns come easy in this house."

Selina's look ran resentfully along the firestep. "Mebbe too easy. Mebbe time could come when there ain't room fer one more."

"None of us starved yet," said Abel.

He squatted and began eating the half-cooked bacon. Selina snatched a basket of cold corn bread from the cupboard and offered him some.

"I didn't aim to say nothin' agin the Traners," she said. "I ain't fergettin' I'm one now myself."

It was beginning to get light when Abel went out again. He gave another look at the sky and took the path that wound among the occasional palisade timbers still embedded in the earth around the original circumference of the stockade. Eben had sold off all the sounder members to be cut up in Job's sawmill. The nearby stubblefields and all the slopes

2

leading down to the river were white with frost except for the black spots formed by the ashes of the movers' cooking fires and the trampled circles where their hobbled stock had shifted about during the night to keep warm. The frost was white, too, on their tents and brush huts and on the blanketed huddles of those sleeping in the open. A very few of them were beginning to get up to throw fresh wood on their fires.

Under the flume at the corner of the sawmill Abel paused to whistle. Job let his dogs loose at night and they were trained to jump anybody who came near, even his hired hands. There followed the creak of Job's opening door, his answering whistle, the scrape of his feet on the ladder, and then a brief clamor of swearing and barking and chain rattling as he tied the creatures up for the day. Abel beat on the side of the sawmill to rouse Silas Mapes, Job's sawyer, who was a hard sleeper, and stepped up on the skidway where Silas built the flatboats. He had another one about ready to shove into the river. Abel jumped from the skidway to the lumber pile alongside and kept on to the new shipways where the hull of the nearly completed keelboat loomed before him. Nothing since the news of Yorktown had so stirred the community as this most recent of Job's enterprises. A flatboat, after all, was little more than a big square raft—a floating barnyard, as it were, into which a mover herded his livestock and family and drifted off downriver—but a keelboat was a real ship, seventy feet long, with the curving, molded shape of a ship, a bow, a stern, a cabin, and a mast and sail. Nothing like it had ever before been attempted in any of the boatyards along the river this side of Pittsburgh, and most people had never even seen one before. Job himself had, at first, been so engrossed in the project that he had had the keel laid almost up against the blockhouse in which he lived. Abel vaulted over the rail and stepped across the deck to the other rail to look down at Job feeding his dogs. Job was cuffing the great animals with his club, teasing them with chunks of meat, and chuckling at their growls and lunges.

"Thet pup," he exulted, "he's a-turnin' out meaner'n any the old uns. He'd have a leg off'n me was I to look t'other way long enough to spit."

The dogs were a breed of Job's own contriving, achieved by crossing mastiff and bearhound with a bitch he had brought back from an Indian campaign. He gave his pets a last playful kick and unlocked the door to the storeroom which occupied the first story of the blockhouse. Abbie and Judah came out. Abbie was a middle-aged Negress, dignified by her dual role as housekeeper and duenna to his daughter; but Job kept her locked up in the storeroom every night along

3

with Judah, the accomplished young black for whom he had paid the unheard-of sum of fifteen hundred dollars because he had been trained by his former owner on the Delaware as a shipwright. Silas and his two helpers came over from the mill to get their tools, which Job also kept locked up when not in use.

"She'll be done by noon," said Silas, jerking his head toward the flatboat.

Job grunted. "I'm takin' the pup out to let him run a deer fer a spell," he said without looking up. "Arter I git back I'll be over to auction her off."

Job climbed back up the ladder that led to his living quarters in the overhanging second story of the blockhouse. Abbie was already busy with his breakfast at the fireplace in one end of the big room. He went to the other, kicked away the pallet on the floor on which he slept, and edged aside the elkskin curtain hanging behind it which shielded the alcove in which his daughter slept. She was always there; there was no other place she could be. Often during the night he awakened to listen to her soft breathing, but it was his invariable morning custom, the moment it had become light enough to see, to look in at her.

For Esther Moyer, as it had for Abel, the day had begun as usual. She had awakened in time to watch for the night sky's first paling. She had waited for Abel's whistle and next had strained to listen during the chaining of the dogs and the unlocking of the storeroom. She had heard her father's voice and the nasal tones of Silas but nothing more from Abel after the whistle. When her father's hand dropped the elkskin curtain back into place she rose to her knees in her bed, gathered the buffalo robe around her, and applied her eye to the little triangular tear, scarcely larger than a pinhole, in the sheet of oiled paper that had covered her window since she had broken the glass pane the day that Abel had started work on the keelboat.

Judah was handing up the portable forge and the other tools over the rail to Abel on deck. Everything that had happened during the building of the boat had been just below the window and so near that she could even study the expression on people's faces. Abel walked across the plank that led from the rail of the boat to the middle of the ladder and then for a moment he was in the next room. He reappeared outside with the shovel of coals, dumped it in the forge, and shook out half a sack of charcoal over the coals.

The rising sun glinted on his red hair and freckled face. He was thin from his narrow hips to his small feet, but his shoulders, arms, and hands were thicker. Though not a much big-

4

ger man than her father, like him he gave an impression of stored-up energy as in a coiled spring. Judah had finished the bowl of mush and clabber Abbie had handed down to him and Abel was already at work. Judah was a clever enough carpenter but Abel was better at ironwork. He was making a lock and fitting it to the cabin door.

The smell of trout frying in butter drifted in from the kitchen. Last night Flourish Hyd had brought a basket of fish and three brace of wild geese. It was one of her father's crotchets that he would eat only game and his demands kept Ish, whenever Ish was around, as busy as any of the regular hands. Abbie came tiptoeing to the curtain and peered in at her. Esther drew the robe more closely about her and shook her head. Abbie tiptoed away again.

"Still snoozin' away," she told Job. "Gals her age need lots o'sleep."

Esther returned to her lookout. Her father appeared, his rifle in the crook of his arm, and stood on the plank, frowning at what Abel and Judah were doing as though that were what he was thinking about. Abel's lock-fitting took him out of sight within the cabin. Esther lay back in her bed, her smiling glance wandering about the tiny room, scarcely larger than a closet, her interest seeming to embrace even this familiar and restricted scene. Aside from the bed and the window there was the chest at the foot of the bed, the clothes hanging on the wall above it, including the three new dresses that her father had had sent out from Philadelphia for her just last month, and on a shelf near the trapdoor in the ceiling the keg of water kept ready to extinguish Indian fire arrows on the roof. It had been six years since there had been Indians this side of the river in sufficient numbers to attack a settlement, but her father remained as watchful as if they might come any night. From below came a sudden outburst of swearing and barking as he unchained the young dog. He had decided not to wait for her to get up. Before Abel had started work on the keelboat she had often gone with her father to the woods. The tap of Abel's hammer signaled that he was back at the forge and she looked from the window again. Watching his hands shape the bit of iron, her own hands began to press, convulsively, into the fleece of the buffalo robe that enveloped her body.

Toward noon Abel looked up from fitting hinges to a table so that it could be raised and hooked against the wall, to discover Selina standing in the cabin doorway. Her face was glowing and she was breathing hard.

"If that's what you come to see," said Abel, "there she is."

He indicated the bench with the lidded hole in the seat that was built into the corner of the cabin. Heber Fortiner, the Philadelphian who had forwarded to Job his urgent order for a keelboat, had included in his instructions three sheets of detailed specifications calculated to make the craft more comfortable for a woman passenger, but none of these stipulated novelties had excited more local comment than this one.

Selina, however, was not to be distracted even by this extraordinary contrivance. She pressed her hands to her belly as though more conscious of the life there than of her own. Furious words burst from her.

"I jest heered Eben and Caleb a-talkin' about sellin' Job the river bank forty."

"So they told me last night," said Abel.

"It's yourn—as much as theirn. Ain't yuh goin' to stop 'em?"

"How? That forty's already mortgaged to Job for more'n it's worth."

"So now yer givin' it away. The only fit piece o' land the Traners got left. There ain't one o' yuh got so much sense as old Ish when he's havin' one of his fits."

Abel grasped at this change of subject.

"Ish is some brighter'n you guess. When I was a boy there was four-five years him and me hunted and fished together most every day."

Selina's anger was not diverted.

"Mebbe yuh figger thet when all the land's gone then Micah and Eben and Caleb they'll have to go to work. A body couldn't blame yuh. But yuh got the stick by the wrong end. They won't never turn a hand long's yuh keep on makin' enough to feed 'em."

Abel laid down his hammer and chisel and carefully brushed aside the shavings.

"You've come to a time when it's common for a woman to fret. But the Traners have always made out. That's why there's a station here."

"Yuh don't have to tell me a family'd best hang together. But yer the youngest. Why should they hang to yer coattails? Why should yuh have to take on like yer their paw?"

"They're looking around. Eben just the other day was talking to Job about starting a store for him."

The remnant of Selina's restraint was swept away.

"Fer Job. Why allus fer Job? Kin yuh tell me thet? Job's nothin' more'n a common, low-down, ignorant old bush rat. 'Til he settled here to raise thet gal o' his'n he'd never had his nose outta the woods before. No matter how many Injuns he's knocked in the head in his time—or mebbe white folks, too, accordin' to whut some say—whut's there about thet to make people step out'n his way like he was General Washington? He don't know enough to stick his thumb in a hole. Ish feeds him, Hank Donovan rows his ferry, Silas runs his sawmill, and now you and thet nigger is a-buildin' him newfangled boats like this un. He's got nothin' to do but fool with his dogs and grease his guns and spoon-feed that little wench—while other folks make him rich. And with movers bunchin' up like they is, he'll go right on gittin' richer and richer." She sagged in the doorway, her voice failing to a hoarse whisper. "While the Traners they keep right on gittin' poorer and poorer."

It was about that same time that Ish sighted the Indian. After leaving a dozen partridges with Abbie, Ish had skirted the movers' camps, pausing occasionally to stare at some of their more singular early-morning occupations, and then had struck out for the edge of the woods. As he had rounded the corner of the Donovan cow shed he had come upon Peggy McCarty, Henry Donovan's niece, standing beside her half-filled milk pail, listening raptly to the twittering of a reed sparrow in the marsh at the mouth of Copperhead Creek. There was something less than a chance in a thousand that a reed sparrow had returned from the south so early in the year. Seeing Ish, she had hastily jumped back to her milking. Ish had plodded on into the woods and then, crawling back into a laurel thicket, had settled down to watch her with that unblinking, blank stare with which he so often contemplated the maneuvers of wild animals. Peggy had been carried off by the Shawnee as long ago as the Hannastown raid and since being ransomed the year before she had twice tried to run away. As soon as Ish was out of sight she had leaped up again, her moon face first bright with the hope that the bird call might be repeated and then sagging with disappointment when it was not. Ish had begun to circle, with infinite care, through the head-high brush that had sprung up in the burned-over stretch beyond the creek. In an hour he had made certain that there was but one Indian. But that one had been hanging around long enough to know the ground and it took another couple of hours to work him into the open.

The Indian, a lean and starved-looking young buck, broke out across the marsh, bounding from side to side like a running stag. Ish deliberately lifted his rifle and kept the bead of his front sight centered on the back of the Indian's neck, but he did not squeeze the finger resting on the trigger, even after the Indian had plunged into the river and started swimming across. Lowering his rifle, he waited until the Indian had crawled from the icy water into the sanctuary of the farther bank and then set off at a trot for the station.

7

Job had returned from schooling his dog. Several fights had broken out among the waiting movers as they disputed their rival claims to the privilege of buying the flatboat. The tension among them sharpened as finally Job came down the ladder and walked over to the platform. He was not above middle size, but when he pushed in among other men, way was made for him as when a fighting cock enters a chicken yard.

"First off," he announced, "I don't want no cows nor no horses nor no pigs nor no dishes nor no clocks. I don't want nothin' in trade. Only bids I want to hear is bids in money —hard money."

He broke off as he caught sight of Ish on the outskirts of the crowd. Nothing ever pleased Ish so much as a chance to do a friend a favor. His toothless mouth was hanging open in a foolish grin and little drops of sweat were standing out on his leathery old face. Job began shouldering his way to him.

"How many?" he called out.

Ish amended the Indian sign he was making to indicate only one but that one just across the river. The movers screamed their protest against the abandonment of the auction, but the men of the station, who had gathered to be entertained by the sales proceedings, rushed off to get their rifles. Job seized Ish by the arm.

"Git fer yer canoe and git acrost the river and git his track spotted," he directed, "so's when we git there with the dogs we won't lose no time pickin' it up."

Micah burst into the keelboat cabin where Abel was setting up the small iron heating stove.

"Ain't yuh heard?" he cried. "Ish flushed an Injun right at the edge o' Donovan's clearin'."

Abel straightened up momentarily but then shook his head.

"I figgered on helping Judah step in the mast this afternoon."

"Stuff Judah—and the mast, too. Crave to miss a chance to see can them dogs o' Job's pull down an Injun?"

"No, I don't," said Abel. "Would have suited me a sight better if Ish had saved his Indian 'til tomorrow. Because today I'm finishing this job—my way—before that feller from Philadelphia shows up to want everything changed around his way."

"Wall, she's his boat, ain't she?" said Micah.

"Not yet she ain't," said Abel.

Eben, Caleb, Macah, Silas, the two apprentices, three of the Donovans, and two of the more spirited movers crossed on the ferry with Job and his dogs. A few minutes later the baying of the hounds echoed over the river and then gradually died away in the distance as the manhunt ranged deeper into the western hills. Abel and Judah erected the mast and tightened the rigging. Esther opened the kitchen window and leaned on the sill to watch them. Abbie brought down the mattress that she had stuffed with the prescribed goose down, and it was fitted into the bunk in the cabin. Before dark the keelboat was finished, though the launching was to await Fortiner's arrival. Judah, wearied by the culminating drive toward completion, signalized the occasion by retiring to his bed in the storeroom with a bottle of Job's rum that Abbie had filched for him. But Abel lighted a lantern and for hours continued to prowl about the craft, examining, inspecting, and occasionally pausing to contemplate each detail of its construction. When at last he went home he paid little attention to the pot of catfish chowder that had been kept warm for him, and sat staring into the fire. The children, excited by the Indian hunt, were deaf to Kate's amiable efforts to persuade them to settle down.

Selina pretended to retire and from her bed uneasily studied Abel. After a while he stood up, looked around at the cluttered, half-lighted room, threw his blankets over his shoulder, threaded his way among the heaps of scuffling children, and went out. There had been times before, when his brothers sat up drinking or had neighbors in late, when he had withdrawn to the barn to sleep. But this time there was something in his manner that caused Selina to run to the door to look after him. Instead of having turned toward the barn, he was headed for the boatyard. She grabbed up a shawl and followed, keeping well back lest in the brilliant moonlight he notice her spying. But without once looking around he made a beeline for the keelboat.

For a while he wandered about the deck, staring at the rigging, the mast, the rail, the cabin, as intently and yet as absently as he had into the fire. Finally he unlocked the door and went into the cabin. Selina crept closer. She could not see what he was doing until the fire that he had started in the stove had begun to glow, and by then he was stretched out in his blankets in the bunk. He was lying with his fingers interlaced behind his head, his pleased and speculative glance wandering idly about his refuge.

Selina ran all the way home. The children had worn themselves out but Kate was still up, sitting on the hearth combing her great mop of yellow hair. In other respects she took scant care of her ample person, but she was forever fussing with that.

"Where yuh bin?" she scolded. "Yuh look like yuh bin seein' ghosts."

Selina looked around wildly. The room, now that it was dark and silent, smelled the more strongly of soured milk, pickle brine, rancid pork, sweaty clothing, and its winter accumulation of dirt.

"All he's got to do is take one step—one little step—on to one o' them movers' boats a-shovin' off downriver—the one thet's leavin' tomorrer, or the next one, or the one after thet —and he'd be shet of us."

Kate got to her feet and put a soothing arm around Selina. "Now, honey, take hold o' yerself. It's only natural just now fer yuh to have the foolishest notions. The whole week before my Benny come I was sure he was goin' to show up with a harelip. Micah ain't a-goin' to run off. He don't allus act like it, but he sets real store by his young uns—and by you too."

"Micah! Who said anything about him? And, whut difference if he did run off? It's Abel, I mean. And nobody could rightly blame him. But when he does whatever'll happen to the rest of us?"

Kate sat down and resumed combing her hair.

"A sight o' men got itchy feet. But not the Traners. They're homebodies. And Abel's the most Traner of the lot."

For a moment Selina continued to stare about her. Then she dropped on her bed and began to moan and writhe.

"Gawdamighty," said Kate. "So yer time's come this soon."

Selina bounced to her feet again. Her eyes were still wild but it was the wildness of sudden purpose.

"If I made out to fool you—then mebbe I kin fool Abbie, too."

"Yuh want Abbie? But Abbie can't come over here—yuh know thet. Not with Job away. She's got to stay with thet gal."

"Can't yuh git it through yer head? I ain't havin' the baby. I'm only actin' like I was." Selina caught up Kate's cloak. "We got to hurry. We only got 'til Job gits back." She pulled Kate after her out the door. "Now don't gawp at me—jest lissen. And see thet you do eggsactly whut I'm tellin' yuh. Nothin's more natural than fer yuh to take me over to Abbie —long's she can't git away to come over to our place. Soon's we git there I'll take on somethin' turrible—like I was goin' to have it any minute—and I'll take to the gal's bed 'cause thet's the only bed they got up there. While Abbie's in a roar tryin' to take care o' me—thet's the time fer yuh to do yer part. You ask the gal why she don't walk across that plank

10

and sleep in peace and quiet on the new mattress in the cabin on thet boat. Yuh sure now yuh understand?"

"I don't understand nothin'. Thet gal will never go nowhere —not while she can stay and watch all the fun o' yer havin' a baby."

"I keep tellin' yuh I ain't havin' the baby. And she will too go. She wouldn't stay was I havin' four. Peekin' all the time the way she does—she knows Abel's sleepin' in thet cabin tonight."

"Gawdamighty in a barrel," breathed Kate. "Mebbe yuh has got hold o' somethin'. And ain't thet Abel a deep one? Think of a man up to figgerin' out a scheme as full o' tricks as thet."

"Watch out where yer goin'. This ain't no time to break yer leg. Abel he ain't figgered out nothin'. He don't know about it—yet."

They were feeling their way around the stern of the keel-boat.

"But yuh got to tell him," hissed Kate, " 'fore we bust in up there—else what's the use?"

"No, we don't. Only give him time to back out. Best we kin do is push the gal in at him and hope some good comes of it. And don't argue. Folks git into trouble faster when they ain't lookin' fer it."

They had reached the foot of the ladder. Selina began to groan. "Don't jest stand there. Make out like yuh got to boost me up."

Abbie opened the door above and when she had grasped the nature of the emergency made them welcome with all the zest of the old midwife who realizes no human vocation can be so important as hers.

The first full-throated outcry of Selina's performance aroused Abel. He sat up sleepily and peered from the porthole. Esther, shrouded in the folds of the buffalo robe, was halfway across the plank. He leaped from the bunk, grabbed for his pants, missed them in the dark, and leaped back into bed. For she was already opening the door. She dropped the robe and advanced until the faint gleam from the stove was on her face.

"No use pretendin' like yer asleep. I heard yuh jumpin' around."

Abel pulled the blanket to his chin. "Maybe you can guess I ain't real sure I'm awake."

Esther stared down at him accusingly. "Somethin' I sure enough can't guess is whatever give yuh the idee I'd come."

Abel sat up and stared back. "I'm awake enough to do

11

some wondering myself. Whatever give you the idee I wanted you to?"

Selina screamed again. Esther jerked her head toward the sound. "I s'pose yuh can't hear thet? I s'pose she couldn't of had her brat to home? I s'pose yuh didn't come crawlin' in here first off?"

Abel looked blank for only another second. Slowly his face turned up toward the disturbance above. He dropped back on his bed, began to chuckle, and then to choke with laughter. Esther took a step nearer the bunk.

"You kin laugh all yuh want—'till Paw gits back."

"That's another thing we might try to figger. D'ye guess he'll shoot me—or whop you—or both?"

"Depends on whut I tell him."

"Does he do everything you tell him?"

"Paw he don't do nothin' nobody tells him."

"Your pa is about as hard a man as I ever see. But folks say you got him wrapped right around your little finger."

"That ain't nothin' to whut he'd wrap me around—did he know where I was this minute."

She walked resolutely to the door and picked up the robe. Abel sat up in bed again. His bewilderment had passed and the most unforeseen ideas were leaping at him. He thought of the time Ish had told him that Esther's mother had been a Frenchwoman of Vincennes who had taken care of Job one spring he had been laid up while waiting for a Miami arrowhead to work its way out of him. He thought of Eben's frequent and authoritative assertion that Frenchwomen had a very different way with them. Esther was her mother's daughter as well as Job's. Her eyes were glowing in the firelight as she looked back at him over the robe clutched in her arms.

"If it's your pa you're skeered of—he ain't going to jump right in at us. We can always hear the ferry coming back across the river. And if it's me—all you got to do is holler."

"I didn't holler when I first come in—and Abbie and Kate and Selina they all know I'm down here."

"They don't know I am."

"They was the ones that sent me."

"That's what makes it stand to reason they don't know."

"Whut yer tryin' to make out is thet the whole bizness was jest an accident?"

"What else? Nobody could have planned that Indian your pa took off after."

Esther was folding and refolding the buffalo robe.

"There still ain't no call fer me to stay."

"We might find two-three things to talk over."

12

"Sech as whut?"

"You're cold."

"No, I ain't."

"You're shivering."

" 'Tain't from cold."

"I wouldn't want to see you take a chill while we're talking."

"I already told yuh I ain't cold."

"Did you never hear of bundling?"

The robe slipped from Esther's grasp.

"Yuh mean when folks is courtin' and git into bed to keep warm—with a board atween 'em?"

"I ain't got a board but don't seem right my staying warm while you stay cold."

Esther edged back to the stove. Abel raised on one elbow and cleared his throat sociably.

"Selina and Kate were just today talking about how you're growing up."

"Is thet whut yuh want to talk about?"

"That—and maybe one or two things that might lead up to."

Esther took another half-step nearer.

"We better talk fast—'cause it might be a while before we git another chance to say much."

He threw back a corner of the blanket. For an instant she swayed, as though dizzy, but then she awkwardly crept into the bed beside him. He leaned over her to tuck in the blanket. She was still shivering. He stared down at her and shook his head.

"No good—that's what it ain't. You ain't never had the chance to learn how to look after yourself."

"Mebbe we got plenty to worry about," she whispered. "But not about thet. There ain't nothin' thet kin happen— like this, thet Abbie ain't told me about—over and over."

Across the ensuing moment of silence during which neither seemed to breathe rasped the sudden scuff of Job's moccasins as he scrambled up the ladder to the door of his home.

Job had sighted, from a distant hilltop, the lighted windows of the blockhouse. He had been in high good humor, for in the successful pursuit of Peggy's Indian suitor his dogs had proved themselves as never before. But after one glance at that faraway glimmer of light that suggested some unusual night activity in his house, he had left them with Ish and run on ahead of the party to cross the river in Ish's canoe.

Abel craned to look from the porthole. Job was framed in the glow of light as he threw open the blockhouse door at the head of the ladder above.

13

"Whut in goddam hell is a-goin' on in here?" he roared.

Selina's lusty outcries trailed away into a groan of genuine misery. Kate dropped a basin of water. Abbie backed against the wall, muttering a prayer.

"Whut ails you-all? Can't a man set foot in his own house without folks jumpin' like they's seein' a spook?"

"Mis' Seliny," gasped Abbie, pointing a shaking finger toward the couch. "Her time's come on her—an' it tuk her turrible hard."

"Why'n yuh say so in the first place? Whar's Esther?"

"She—she done gone down to sleep on the boat."

Job's grunt was completely noncommittal. He descended the ladder to the plank and jumped from it to the deck.

Esther was struggling with Abel. "Leastwise I don't aim to let him catch me in bed," he whispered.

"Yuh got to leave me talk to him first."

She ran out and confronted her father.

"I bin lissenin' fer yuh to come back, Paw."

Job leaned his rifle against the cabin and put his hands on her shoulders, as though to make sure she was again within his reach.

"Yuh know better'n to leave the house when I ain't around —but a body kin hardly blame yuh fer wantin' go git off a ways from all thet yappin' up there."

"I bin lissenin' fer yuh 'cause I got somethin' to tell yuh. I didn't come down here to git away from thet. I come down to talk to Abel."

She clutched at him frantically but he pushed her aside and tore open the door. This time Abel had found his pants but he was only half into them. Job reached for his rifle.

"Yuh call it talkin'—when a man has got to take his pants off to lissen?"

Esther seized the rifle barrel and clung to it.

"No matter what yuh call it, Paw, it was all my doin'." In that moment she seemed as strong as Job, for he seemed unable to wrest the rifle from her. "I'm tellin' yuh, Paw. If'n you shoot him yuh might's well shoot me, too, while yer about it."

Job leaned down, peering into her face. People often claimed that Job could see better in the dark than most men could by daylight.

"I bin a-wonderin' when the time'd come you'd want yerself a man."

"It's come, Paw. And I done picked him."

"Then git back in there and hang on to him. Yuh coulda looked all over Fayette County and done a sight worse."

Abel had gotten into his boots and was stumbling over the

14

buffalo robe on his way to the door. Job shoved Esther against him, pushed them both back into the cabin, and slammed the door upon them. He turned to the three women, staring, rigid with mingled terror and curiosity, from the kitchen doorway above.

"Git back to yer whelpin' and git it over and done with. We don't want nothin' gittin' in the way o' the weddin' tomorrer." The block and tackle at the riverbank began to creak as the ferry put off from the other shore. Job ran to the bow of the keelboat and bellowed, "Ish, git along back here with them dogs. Soon's it's light we're headin' crost the ridge to git us a buffler to barbecue."

Selina desperately explained to Abbie that the shock of Job's returning had put an end to her pains and slid down the ladder to overtake Kate. Thus, when the ferry landed, she was able to require Kate to share with her the privilege of breaking news of such import to the Traners.

In the cabin Abel was taking the time and apparent thought to adding a few sticks of wood to the fire that it might have cost to start a fresh one in a pouring rain. Esther sat on the bunk behind him, hugging herself and watching his every move.

"Lissen to them brothers o' yourn holler. They got a right to. They got no more worries about whar the pork and hominy's a-comin' from. Yuh bin takin' care o' them 'cause yuh had nothin' better to do, but now they know yer fixed so's they kin go right on stayin' as no-'count as they want."

Abel sat back on the floor and stared into the fire. Esther laughed delightedly.

"And lissen to Abbie sing. Thet's one reason everythin' worked out so smooth as butter—like it did. Everybody wanted it this way. Selina she wasn't havin' no baby. Abbie seen thet right off. Her—and Kate—and Abbie, too— they was all treein' the same 'possum."

Abel picked up the tongs and poked at the fire. "Everybody after the 'possum but your pa."

"I ain't so sure about him, neither. With movers comin' at us like they is, there's sure to be call fer more'n more boats. Silas and Hank they ain't much good and Judah is only a nigger. So there's nothin' Paw needs more'n a son-in-law man enough to take hold."

Abel stood up. "You've got a right good head on you—to be able to figger everything out so clear."

"I wasn't able to figger out nothin'—not 'til jest now. Ontil I come in thet door I could see how nothin' was ever goin' to come out. Where yuh goin'?"

She jumped up but he pressed her back on the bed.

15

"Stay there and rest yourself a spell. Tomorrow's going to be a long day. I got a couple of things to do."

Before she could reach the door he had closed it behind him. For a moment she stood with her hand on the latch, but then she ran back to kneel beside the bed, her arms stretched out to encircle the tangle of blankets.

Job, Silas, and Judah were rolling out a barrel of whisky from the storeroom. Abel slid over the opposite rail and kept the bulk of the keelboat between him and them. There came the squeal of Eben's fiddle from the Traner establishment. Some of the movers were getting up to investigate the untimely sounds of celebration. Abel turned up the hill alongside the flume and sat down on the ground.

Caleb and Micah came running with pails to fill with whisky. More fires were blazing up among the movers' camps and some of the movers were beginning to gather at the Traner house or about the base of supplies at Job's barrel. The Donovan women, having heard the news from their men, were rushing over to congratulate Selina and Kate. Silas, Judah, and the apprentices came out with shovels and went to work on a barbecue pit. The moon was setting and the eastern sky was beginning to grow pale.

Flames from a new fire beside the barbecue pit revealed the sleek, curving lines of the keelboat's hull, the sharp, clean lift of her mast. So short a time ago he had been trying to picture the far distances of the river down which presently she would glide. There had been times before in his life when he had had one of those same sudden flashes of expectancy, of feeling that, sooner or later, almost anything might be likely to happen to him. But there would be no more of them now. Nothing more unusual was to be waiting for him than for Eben or Micah or Caleb.

The thin, wailing note of a screech owl sounded at intervals, now near, now beyond the sawmill or the blockhouse. Ish kept on circling patiently, but for a long time Abel did not respond to the call that had been their private signal in the days he had so often been Ish's woods companion. When finally he answered, Ish trotted along the flume up to him and gave the well-remembered sign that he had something special to show him. Once it might have been a panther's den or the spawning riffle of a sturgeon. Abel listlessly got up. Ish led the way to the riverbank. There, bobbing in the shadow between the mill wheel and the moored flatboat, was Ish's canoe with the paddle laid ready athwart the gunwales. In it he had deposited Abel's rifle, powder horn, leather hunting shirt, and hatchet, together with a spool of fishing line, a pair of beaver traps, a roll of blankets, a sack of corn, and a skin of pemmican. Ish was watching him questioningly yet eagerly, his mouth open in that foolish grin that revealed the extraordinary pleasure he always took in doing a favor for a friend.

Abel looked out over the dark river which stretched away toward its union with the Allegheny at Pittsburg and on beyond. From the Traner house came the twang of a banjo added to the whine of Eben's fiddle and the shrill gabble of the women and children. Caleb, who could never hold his liquor, was already beginning to whoop.

"Ish," bellowed Job from the blockhouse. "Where the hell are yuh? Time we was gittin' arter thet buffler."

Abel poked his elbow into Ish's ribs and Ish began to cackle with smothered delight. Job's dogs were barking excitedly. Abel stepped into the canoe. With the third stroke of the paddle he had disappeared into the predawn mist rising from the water.

Toward noon Job and Ish returned with three horse loads of buffalo meat. The station that had had so festive an air when they left now appeared all but deserted. Silas, coming to the mill doorway, ducked back upon sighting Job. The Traner children, clustered in their dooryard, pointed and then darted within. Even the handful of movers, gathered in the boatyard, stared up the hill at Job and began drifting off to their camps.

Job's nostrils quivered and his little eyes glowed. Senses sharpened by innumerable experiences with wilderness disaster warned him that something which threatened him had come to pass. He dropped the lead rope and ran for the blockhouse. The sound of Esther's sobbing hit him before he had reached the foot of the ladder. He burst into the room. Clad in the white silk dress from Philadelphia, she was stretched out face down on her couch. She had never cried, even as a baby. But now she was hoarse from hours of weeping.

"Whut's she bawlin' about?"

Abbie was seated in a chair. She did not get up.

"She's shamed—thet's whut about. Fer a gal like her there couldn't be nothin' worser."

"Who shamed her?"

"Why'n nobody tole yuh? Abel he tuk to the woods long about light this mornin'."

"Which way'd he go?"

"He tuk his gear—and Ish's canoe. Folks say he could o' tuk off upriver, downriver, or crost river. Take yer pick."

Job moved over to the couch.

"No matter which way—nor how far—I'll ketch up with him."

"What good'll thet do?" said Esther and went on sobbing.

Job lunged for the door. Throughout all of a long lifetime he had measured his every physical move with the care of the born woodsman, but now in his moment of greatest trial he took no heed whatever. He lost his footing at the head of the ladder, fell backward, struck the rail of the keelboat, and pitched forward again to the ground.

After a time Abbie toiled back up to the room and stood over Esther.

"Git up," she said. "Yuh got no more time fer cryin'. Yer paw's done busted his back and cain't move nothin' but his eyes and his fingers. From now on yuh ain't got time fer nothin' 'cept lookin' arter him."

2

There might be those inclined to attach no great significance to the history of Traner's Station, but there could be none to minimize that of Pittsburgh. The town was not yet overwhelmingly larger, with its something less than four hundred inhabitants, nor so very much older, with its earliest habitations antedating Nicholas Traner's half-faced camp by no more than ten years; but Boston, New York, nor Philadelphia had provided a stage for events of more historic consequence. Figures of the stature of Washington, Braddock, Forbes, Bouquet, Pontiac, and Clark had played principal parts on this stage.

Now another figure of historic prominence had come to Pittsburgh. James Wilkinson was here on the last leg of his tremendous and dramatic journey to Natchez and New Orleans and Havana and Richmond. It was whispered that he had found a way to circumvent the Spanish blockade of Mississippi trade, and everybody was aware that if this were true it made any Westerner who owned a bushel of corn or a pound of tobacco many times richer than he had been the day before.

The feature of the great man's visit that excited the most attention, however, was his carriage, which had been dragged over the mountains from Philadelphia by the combined exertions of eight horses, six Negroes, and three teamsters. No four-wheeled vehicle, except for the army wagons of the days of the English expeditionary forces, had ever before been seen on the banks of the Ohio. Literally every inhabitant had gathered on the waterfront to watch the loading of the magnificent red, blue, and gold equipage on a flatboat for shipment to Kentucky, where it was destined to add a climactic flourish of pageantry to Wilkinson's triumphant return there. But in all that circle of elbowing gapers no one watched the embarkation with the burning attention bestowed upon it by Jasper Hedges.

19

Jasper crouched at the window in the second-floor front room of Barny Curran's tavern, from which he could look directly down upon the operation. One of his glittering black eyes was slightly cocked, which lent his scrutiny the appearance of his being capable of perceiving simultaneously the movements of individuals in all parts of the crowd. His long, pencil-thin mustaches, drooping on either side of his wide mouth, quivered like the whiskers of a stalking cat, and his long, exceptionally prominent nose pressed so hard against the windowpane that the whole end of it had whitened.

Suddenly he leaped back from the window and then with the most extreme circumspection looked again. Four men had detached themselves from the crowd. One was a very large man made to seem even larger by a bell-crowned hat and a thick stroud greatcoat. The other three looked like French-Canadian boatmen, but they carried Pennsylvania long rifles and wore knives and tomahawks at their belts. The big man seemed to be giving them instructions. Presently two of them nodded and circled through the tavern yard toward the stables in the rear. The big man and the other seated themselves on a bench where they were in a position to watch the front door of the inn while seeming to take an interest only in the to-do about the coach. No detail of this brief pantomime escaped Jasper's fixed and fascinated gaze. One or two beads of perspiration appeared on his brow and several times the tip of his tongue crept out to moisten his lips.

There came a heavy step in the hallway and a peremptory knock upon the door. Jasper ran to it and made sure that the wedge of the floor under it was firmly in place. The innkeeper's voice was lifted in angry impatience.

"Open up, dammit," shouted Barny. "I'll have no doors locked agin me in me own house."

"Contain yourself, good sir," said Jasper. "I shall find leisure to receive you anon."

He sprang to the bed, upon which his outer clothing was spread. His underclothing was so worn and ragged as to seem all but falling from his gaunt frame. Over it he hastily drew on a ruffled linen shirt, doeskin breeches, a red waist-coat, and a plum-colored coat. These garments were of expensive material and cut but the shirt was patched and no longer white, the breeches saddle-worn and out at the knees, the waistcoat lacked all but two of its gilt buttons, and the coat was faded and travel-stained. He caught up a heavy gold watch chain to which was attached neither a watch at the one end nor a fob at the other and thrust these unadorned ends into his waistcoat pockets so that the chain looped across

20

his front. His rapid movements had caused strands of his wiry black hair to escape from the string tying it at the nape of his neck, to fly about as if electrified and to add to his air of perpetual excitement. He kicked aside the wedge under the door, leaped to a seat at the table, snatched up a pen, and became engrossed in writing.

Barny once more put his shoulder to the door, it this time swung open without resistance, and he came staggering in. Jasper laid aside the pen and began folding the sheet of paper.

"Ah, my good man. A most timely entrance. Will you make the greatest haste to engage me a special post boy. Be certain to select one who commands the use of fast horses. This letter to Alexander Hamilton must reach Philadelphia at the earliest."

Barny's face turned shades redder. "Post boy. Alexander Hamilton. Philadelphia. Fast horses. And will you tell me who's to pay fer so much as the paper you write on?"

"I should expect to make a most adequate payment. It is a missive of the first importance."

Barny swung his bulk forward and leaned heavily upon the table. The stare he directed upon his guest was fierce and yet half hypnotized, as though his faculties were being taxed beyond the limits of ordinary comprehension.

"You can post yer letter in yon chamber pot. What I'm after tellin' you is this. I seen General Wilkinson."

"Ah. And did you pay him my most humble respects?"

"I passed him the word you was up here in this room."

"And how did he receive the news?"

"He said he didn't know you—had never heard tell of you—and gave niver a damn what room you was in."

"Obviously my message became garbled in some fashion. Did you take care to mention New Orleans and the palace of Governor Miro and the evening of the twenty-second of last August? Did you particularly stress that date?"

"I forked out all that. All he done was laugh. He said he'd knowed me a long time and was surprised at how easy I'd been to take in."

Jasper sat back in his chair and nodded portentuously, as though this were no more than he had foreseen. "There are powerful forces opposing me—so powerful that even a Wilkinson feels compelled to stand aside. I have dangerous enemies, Barny. Even now they lie in wait for me at your very door."

Barny snorted. "More talk. Ain't a soul in Pittsburgh knows you—or ever seen or heard of you—or got any sort of call to hold a grudge agin you. Nobody, that is, 'cept me. I ain't lissenin' to no more. On yer feet—and make for that door."

Barny grasped the table to pull it from between him and Jasper. Jasper laid a hand gently on one of Barny's.

"You grieve me, Barny. Still this immense concern with a miserable tavern bill."

"Miserable. Miserable you call it? Near two weeks you bin here. In me best room. Eatin' me best vittles. Drinkin' me best likker. And never the color o' one red penny have I seen."

"We can readily rectify that. I shall pay you here and now." Jasper reached for pen and paper.

"Don't go scratchin' up another sheet o' thet paper. Whatever you're writin' it ain't so good as a counterfeit continental. Either take yerself down them stairs on yer own two legs—or get yerself pitched down 'em on yer head. Take yer choice."

Jasper smiled reassuringly. "If you will but look you will see I am not promising to pay. I am drawing you a draft on my Philadelphia bank—and adding a hundred dollars over the amount of my reckoning—as a token of my appreciation of the exemplary care you have taken of me." His pen continued to fly across the page. "There must surely be one flicker of the gambler's instinct even in your stolid bosom. It lacks but two hours of nightfall. The draft is yours in return for my continued occupancy of this room for that two hours. Consider. Two hundred dollars for two hours. That is a high rental. For no matter how fixed your opinion, there must linger in your mind the faint apprehension that the draft might be good."

"Only part of the gamble I like is the two hours. You'll for sure take yerself off—come night?"

"Positively. Absolutely. Indubitably."

Barny turned in the doorway with one more scowl.

"Mind you—no tricks. Come night—you're gone."

"Come night, and come what may."

So soon as he was alone Jasper returned to the window and resumed his intent vigil. The coach was now on the flatboat and men, deluged with comment and advice from the onlookers, were engaged in nailing cleats and props to hold it in position. The big man was no longer in sight, though the smallest of the three boatmen was still on the bench. An object in midriver came into Jasper's field of vision. A man in a leather hunting shirt was driving a canoe with long, steady strokes on downstream past the town. No one in the crowd paid any attention to the craft a hundred yards out, but Jasper began to watch it. Suddenly the paddle ceased its rhythmic dipping and the canoeman's face was turned toward shore. He had apparently caught sight of the brilliantly painted coach in its incongruous nest on the flatboat. After a long look he took several more strokes and then drifted again while he looked once more. Before he had drifted quite past, he swung the canoe around and paddled slowly toward the waterfront. Every indication suggested a traveler on his way downriver who had had no intention of pausing at Pittsburgh but whose curiosity had been so aroused by the novel spectacle of the coach that he was making a stop to satisfy it by a closer inspection.

Jasper went to the door, made sure the hallway was empty, and gave a low whistle. Adah Metch, the tavern maid-of-all-work, came running on noiseless bare feet. Jasper returned to the window. Adah came in, shut the door swiftly, bent to adjust the wedge under it, and straightened, beaming. Her hair was tousled, her hands work-roughened and her complexion weatherbeaten, but when she crossed the room it was with the animal grace of youth and health. She came to a stand beside the bed and giggled, but Jasper did not look around. She waited, rubbing one foot against the other and then upon the floor. The faint scuffling sound was succeeded by a more obvious rustle as she seated herself on the corn-husk mattress.

"I was a-startin' in to think mebbe you'd fergot how to whistle," she observed archly.

Jasper continued to watch from the window for another long minute, but when he turned to her his smile was as warm as was hers.

"Enchanting, this past week, as I have found your hospitality, this chances not to be quite the opportune moment for dalliance."

"Oh, Mr. Hedges, I never kin make head nor tail to all them words you say—but I do admire to lissen to 'em."

"Then come here to the window and listen carefully to a few I shall endeavor to keep within the range of your perception." She ran to him. He slipped an arm around her waist and drew her back slightly. "Not too near the window. Now —do you see that young man in the leather shirt just stepping out of his canoe?"

"Yes, I do."

"Know him?"

"No, I don't."

"Does he live in Pittsburgh?"

"I wouldn't reckon so. Leastwise, I ain't never seen him before."

"Good enough."

Jasper removed one shoe and plucked from it a Spanish silver dollar.

"Oh, Mr. Hedges, I don't want you should give me money."

"Such was the farthest from my intention, my dear. I want you to take this down and show it to the young man. Show it to him—mind—not give it to him. And be sure that no one hears what you say to him. Tell him that if he will come back with his canoe and land it exactly where it is now— just at dark tonight—he can earn that and nine more dollars. Have you got that clear?"

"Yes, I have."

"Then run before he gets away."

Abel built his cooking fire on the opposite bank a mile above Pittsburgh. It had turned warmer and the south wind was steady and strong. Almost certainly it would rain or snow before the night was over. He had not counted on stopping off at Pittsburgh where there were a number of people who knew him, but that uncut silver dollar the girl had showed him was a sight almost as rare as the red and gold coach. At dusk he paddled across to the shadow of the Pittsburgh bank and drifted slowly downstream. Full darkness had just fallen as he beached the canoe before Barny Curran's tavern. Wilkinson's Negroes had built a big fire on the shore beside the moored flatboat. One of them was strumming a banjo and a considerable crowd of townspeople was still hanging around. No one seemed to notice the arrival of the canoe and Abel saw no sign of his mysterious employer.

Jasper crouched at his window, his wary glance roving from the group around the fire to the canoe. Carefully he edged the window open and leaned out to survey the area immediately before the inn. There came a scratching at the door. He hurried to it and removed the wedge. Adah slipped breathlessly into the dark room beside him.

"The big man with the scar on his chin," she whispered, "is havin' hisself a drink at the bar right by the foot o' the stairs—and the skinny one he's with him. The other two— they's a-watchin' in the cow shed by the back door."

"Priceless reconnaissance, my treasure. Now—when you can no longer see me in that window—then is the moment to open this door and begin screaming as loud as you can."

"I'll do everythin'—jus' like yuh tol' me." She clutched him. "And you ain't fergettin'?"

"Never will I forget anything about you, my blessedly insatiable nymph. In an hour I will look for you on the river-bank just below the Old Fort."

He disengaged himself from her clasp, patted her cheek, and ran to the window. For a moment his lanky figure was doubled up in it and then it dropped from sight. Adah opened the door and began to scream.

Abel saw the shadowy form hanging at arm's length from

24

the window ledge. It dropped to the ground. A second later a tall man was running into the circle of firelight and directly toward the canoe. A woman's piercing screams continued to echo from the tavern. A big man burst from the tavern doorway and also ran toward the beach. The tall man reached the canoe first and threw himself into it. Abel shoved off. The big man leaped into the water and grasped the gun-wale with both hands. Abel lifted the paddle and brought it down with knuckle-crushing force. The big man swore and jerked his hands away. Abel dipped the paddle and swung the canoe out of reach.

"Gabe," shouted the big man, "fetch me my rifle."

Abel lifted his own piece into view.

"If you got some sort of a shooting match in mind—have right at it. I'll be out there in the dark and you'll be here by the fire."

"Bravo," called Jasper from the bottom of the canoe.

Abel dipped the paddle and drove the canoe beyond the circle of firelight. Jasper raised his head and peered over the gunwale.

"Faster," he urged. "They may procure boats and set out in pursuit."

Abel shipped his paddle and let the canoe drift. "No use getting too far—if I make up my mind to take you back."

Jasper squirmed to his knees. "You who have proved my savior," he protested. "Surely you would not elect to become instead my executioner."

"What was that woman yelling about?"

"Ah," breathed Jasper. "That was Adah, the tavern maid. She is my friend. Her outcries were to cover my retreat. It may aid you to believe me if you will recall that it was Adah who this afternoon engaged your services in my behalf."

"She said something about ten dollars."

"Those were precisely my instructions. You will be paid that—and double that—the moment I am safe."

"Why was the big man chasing you?"

"You have every right to an accounting. I am Jasper Hedges, a merchant. This has been my first visit to Pittsburgh, but in New Orleans or Philadelphia or New York I should be able to furnish you with the most substantial references."

"But what was it the big man had stuck in his craw? He was real serious about catching up with you."

"I am coming to that. I am not advised what name he has adopted at the moment, but he was christened Todd Barklit."

"Never heard of him."

"You have possibly heard of Dr. John Connolly?"

25

"The Tory who tried so hard to hand Pittsburgh over to the English back during the war? Yes, I mind Pa talking some about him."

"Dr. Connolly is still an English agent. This Barklit is his lieutenant. Therefore in confounding him, as you have just so shrewdly managed, you have served not only me but your country."

"You make it quite a story."

"It is one I can enlarge upon to any extent you desire. But first may I suggest once more that our rate of progress invites pursuit?"

"Nobody's going to start chasing us tonight. It's too dark for them to see, I got head start enough so's nobody can catch up if they could see, and anyway all we'd have to do is duck into the brush on the far bank."

"I am happy to be so astutely reassured. Is that by any chance the Old Fort we're drifting past?"

"Why? That where you want I should land you?"

"On the contrary, that is one of the places I most decidedly do not wish to be landed. But your inquiry leads me to assume —and with immense relief, I may say—that you have at any rate decided not to return me to our point of embarkation."

"I ain't decided anything yet."

"If I may be so bold, may I ask what then chiefly troubles you?"

"I'm having trouble figgering you out."

"While you are grappling with that abstruse subject, may I on my part ask who you are?"

"My name's Abel Traner."

"When I first glimpsed you this afternoon, you appeared on your rather urgent way toward some quite definite destination."

"I wanted to get past Pittsburgh while it was still light enough to look for a place to camp."

"Is this a long journey that you have undertaken?"

"It's no journey at all. I'm just doing a little hunting and fishing—and sitting in the sun when the sun's warm enough."

"A salutary existence indeed, and one in which I should be entranced to join you, did circumstances permit. I take it, then, that you are at present unengaged?"

"I ain't looking for a job if that's what you mean. I had one —and I don't need another for quite a spell."

"You must have had some project in mind this afternoon when you undertook my transportation."

"I did. Ten dollars."

"That, sir, you have already earned. Is there the smallest

chance that you might elect to earn—say—fifty times that amount?"

"By doing what?"

"By continuing this delightful voyage—at a somewhat more expeditious pace, of course—on down the river."

"How far?"

"Kentucky."

"When?"

"So soon as you can get me there."

"I mean when do I get the five hundred?"

"So soon as I can see to write in the morning I will draw you a draft for the full amount."

Abel dipped his paddle and the canoe shot away downriver. A ledge of rock appeared directly ahead. With a twist of his wrist he swerved the canoe into the swirl of white water that framed the rock and straightened the craft again below. Jasper laid his fingers on the gunwale.

"Marvelous."

"I been handling a canoe all my life."

"And a rifle, too, if I may judge from your attitude when that topic came up. Todd Barklit is not a man accustomed to being treated so cavalierly."

"I didn't like the way he put his hands on my canoe."

"That was quite apparent. I can see that you are a rather abrupt fellow." Jasper cleared his throat. "By the way, you are aware, of course, that when I speak of a draft I mean a written instrument drawing upon my account in an Eastern bank and that there may be some slight delay in converting it into cash?"

"I'll take my chances on getting it out of you. I might's well have me a look at Kentucky anyway."

3

It might have been said as well of the Ohio River that had it not existed it would have had to be invented. It took a whole people upon its back and bore them on to their inheritance. The cross-section of a nation was thus borne Westward—men pursuing new opportunity, men seeking better land, men fleeing from failure, men escaping the law, men courting danger, men merely seeing the country, men of every sort, young and old, gamblers, farmers, tailors, traders, soldiers, carpenters, politicians, runaway boys, footloose wanderers such as Abel, persons difficult to identify such as Jasper, and, the few who took their toll of all the rest, land speculators such as Heber Fortiner, owner of the keelboat *Naiad*.

Naiad lay at anchor in the lee of an island five days downriver from Pittsburgh. Head boatman Fred Burd, standing second night watch, climbed up on the cabin and began taking methodical quarterturns as he peered out over the river, straining to distinguish the first indications of what the morning might reveal. The broad river was beginning its dawn transition from smoky black to slate gray to steel blue. The wooded mid-channel island, a hundred yards to starboard, and the more heavily forested south bank, three hundred yards to port, were beginning to show detail. The night-long clamor of the frogs in the bordering estuaries and ponds had begun to weaken. Drifting fleets of waterfowl became visible as they began to stir and splash. A trumpeter swan's deep, resonant blast reverberated against the hills. The now rapidly growing light picked up the red, green, and gold of the flock of parakeets clustered in a huge sycamore on the island as they began to awaken, to stretch their wings, to preen themselves, and to set up their harsh, incessant chatter. A file of a dozen buffalo emerged lazily from the upstream point of the island and waded out into the river, their progress disclosing the existence of a pattern of shoals connecting the island with the south bank. Fred regarded all this

28

pleasant and natural activity with a cold and practical eye. He was, as always at dawn, looking for Indian sign and the normal behavior of all wild life within his view was a good sign.

He dropped to the deck and turned toward the ladder that led down into the hold. Spencer, Fortiner's valet, was standing on the topmost rung, his attention fixed on the passage of the buffalo. His pale, delicately featured, lined, yet curiously ageless face was alight with an interest that amounted to fascination. Fred grinned at the Negro's childlike excitement.

"Takin' yerself yer own look-see, eh? Spot anything mebbe I missed?"

"Good morning, Mr. Burd," whispered Spencer. "Not likely. There's so much to see, and I know the meaning of so little that I do see."

He deferentially stepped aside from the head of the ladder.

"Everybody else down there still asleep?" asked Fred.

"I'm not sure about Mr. Fortiner."

"Good for him. We're a-comin' to a stretch o' this river that kin give us all somethin' to lay awake and think about."

Fred slid down the ladder into the hold. This region below deck, customarily devoted to a keelboat's cargo, had on this voyage become the sleeping quarters for the men aboard. In the more favored positions nearest the hatchway were on the one side the bed of the owner and on the other that of his guest, Rodney Baynton. Beyond Fortiner's were the mattresses of his two Negro servants, Spencer and Buck. Beyond Baynton's was the space allotted to the two boatmen. Fortiner's eyes opened and followed Fred's descent. Fred carefully circled the foot of his bed to awaken Buck, and circled back to step over Baynton and prod Ben Taafe, the other member of the crew.

"It's turned much warmer," said Fortiner.

"Turned a sight warmer during the night," agreed Fred.

Fortiner got up, but sudden as was his movement, Spencer had slipped down the ladder in time to stand beside him holding out his dressing gown. Climbing to the deck, Fortiner glanced at the sky and then moving abruptly to the rail began to study the nearby island. He was a man of forty with a touch of gray at the temples, a vigorous body and an erect, athletic carriage. His squarish, firmly molded face must have been considered handsome, were it not so hard and resolute, but it was also a face across which occasionally passed gleams of an intelligence so lively as to make him seem younger, more amiable, and less arrogant. Fred and Ben were pulling up the anchor.

"Let the anchor alone," said Fortiner. He resumed his sur-

29

vey of the narrow, mile-long island. "We'll lay over here a day."

By the time Fortiner had returned to the hold, Spencer had laid out a canvas hunting coat, heavy woolen britches, and leather leggings. Fortiner peered at this array and then, quizzically, at Spencer.

"What put all that into your head?"

Spencer met the look with one of innocence.

"It struck me as a very suitable outfit for wear ashore."

Fortiner frowned, but there was a brief twinkle in his eye.

"Isn't it something of a strain, Spencer, to try to do so much of my thinking for me?"

Spencer laughed softly. "Nobody could think that fast, Mr. Fortiner."

He tossed aside the outdoor garb and swiftly helped Fortiner into a velveteen lounging jacket, an unstarched linen shirt, flannel trousers, and a pair of rope-soled sandals. Fortiner bent over and shook Baynton awake.

"Get up, Rod. It's a fine spring day for a change. And there's a most promising-looking island alongside—part marsh, part brush, and part woods. How'd a spot of botanizing strike you?"

Baynton sat up in bed and blinked vaguely. "Island? Island?" Comprehension brought with it a stir of excitement. "Oh, good morning, Heber. Splendid. Splendid. Nothing could appeal to me more."

Fortiner went on deck and sat in a chair. Spencer brought hot water from the galley and began to shave him. Baynton appeared with his collector's kit and began eagerly to scan the island. He was a gangling, aristocratic-looking young man with the intent, introspective air of the scholar. Unlike Fortiner he seemed older than his years.

"A most promising site, to be sure," he said. "But are you certain, Heber, that you can afford this delay? I am aware of what a headlong rate we've come down the river thus far."

"That was only because the weather was so foul. And the distance we made then but gives us the more leisure now. Fred, what's your trouble? You're glowering at that poor little island as though you were seeing an Indian under every bush."

Fred jumped and turned a placating grin on his employer. "I ain't nary a trouble, Mr. Fortiner. The way them parakeet and buffalo was actin' this mornin' that island she's as clean as a whistle."

"All the same, you and Ben will take your rifles and go ashore with Mr. Baynton—and stay with him. Buck, serve Mr.

Baynton his breakfast now. I'll wait and have mine with Mrs. Baynton. Another thing, Fred—take Buck with you so that he can bring the skiff back. Spence, by then you'll have finished serving our breakfast. You and Buck can try the shallows around the island and see if you can't catch us some panfish for lunch."

Spencer took a step back and shot a quick glance out over the river.

"Don't tell me you've got a different idea?"

"A slightly different one, Mr. Fortiner."

"Trust you for that. Well?"

"There may be mushrooms on the island and—since there's nothing you like better—we might look for them as well as fish."

"Waste of time. It's too early for mushrooms."

"Do you mind if we ask Mr. Baynton's opinion?"

Fortiner's eyes narrowed for a second but he continued to smile.

"Some fungi," said Baynton, "appear very early in the spring and among the earliest are the eminently edible morsels I assume Spencer will be looking for."

"Mushrooms, then," conceded Fortiner. "But, mind you, if you don't find any—get to fishing. Don't come back without one or the other."

Spencer folded his towels and picked up the basin of water. "Never fear, Mr. Fortiner. I have a strong feeling this will be a lucky day—for both of us." He, too, seemed oddly excited.

"Speaking of shore expeditions," said Baynton. "Shouldn't I call Philippa? She's certain to want to go, too."

"No," said Fortiner. "I may bring her ashore later—after Fred and Ben have had time to have a thorough look over the island."

"Philippa's already up," called a voice from the cabin, "and about to emerge."

Fortiner got to his feet. All the others, perched on the rail or squatting on deck, were hurriedly eating, but every other head also came up and every other face was likewise turned expectantly toward the cabin door. The lock clicked and Philippa Baynton appeared in the doorway. She was smiling and outwardly poised and yet there was the faint suggestion that she had braced herself before opening the door. There seemed little enough reason that she should shrink from inspection. She was as perfectly groomed as though she had emerged from a Philadelphia boudoir rather than the cabin of a keelboat on the Ohio. A jeweled pin set off the golden sheen of her hair, the pale blue of her gown accentuated the

31

violet blue of her eyes, the froth of lace at her throat called the more attention to the beautifully modeled oval of her face.

"Good morning, Heber. Good morning, all. What a heavenly day. Just think of all that sleep yesterday and the wind and rain the day before. Good morning, darling."

Baynton rose hastily from his collector's kit and kissed her cheek.

"Good morning, dear. You are looking particularly well this morning, if I may say so." He seemed less aware than she of the eyes upon them.

Baynton got into the skiff and Ben began to hand his equipment down to him. Spencer started into the cabin with a tray from the galley.

"It's lovely here in the sun," said Philippa. "Can't we have breakfast out here?"

"There's a little wind coming up," said Fortiner. "Still, I don't know why not. Spencer, set the table out here. Fred, before you get away, will you and Ben stretch a canvas from the corner of the cabin to the rail."

Philippa watched the erection of the wind screen. "You do think of everything, Heber—and so quickly too."

"I try to."

The skiff shoved off for the island and disappeared from view behind the canvas screen. Spencer was busy spreading a cloth, laying out silver, pouring coffee. Fortiner sat down, rested his elbows on the table, and looked at Philippa.

"Forgive me if I treat myself to a good long stare," he said. "Not since we left Philadelphia have I been able to enjoy an uninterrupted look at you. Why do you frown? You are as aware as I that you are beautiful. You are as aggressively intelligent in your way as Rod is in his or I in mine."

"Intelligence can be a mixed blessing—in a woman."

Philippa glanced up at Spencer as he bent to offer her a tray upon which were small silver dishes of honey, sugar, butter, and marmalade.

"You need have no concern about Spence," said Fortiner. "As my alter ego he knows me better than I do. In any event, Buck will be back with the skiff in a moment. The two of them are about to take themselves off to hunt mushrooms. But you haven't touched your bacon and eggs. Before Spence clears out, don't you want him to get you something else?"

"No, thank you. Whether or no it represents intelligence—I am not hungry this morning. I would like some more coffee."

Fortiner touched his fingers to the coffee pot. "Never mind, Spence. This is still hot. You can get along. Wait. What all have you got in that basket?"

Spencer turned back from the rail and with smiling resignation offered the basket for inspection. Fortiner peered into it and then up at Spencer.

"The basket is for mushrooms," said Spencer. "The lines and hooks to catch fish. The knife to clean them. The flint and steel to build a fire on the beach in case it might occur to you to have lunch ashore this afternoon. The pistol is according to your orders. You have so often said that none of us during this voyage should ever go anywhere unarmed."

Fortiner laughed. "There have been kings nicknamed 'the Just.' But Spence's should be 'Justified.' He's always able completely and utterly to justify whatever he's up to. Get along with you. And when the time comes, build your beach fire. Only be sure you've something to cook over it."

He walked to the rail and watched the two Negroes row away. Returning to the table he paused behind Philippa's chair, placed his hands on her shoulders, and pressed his lips against her hair.

"No, Heber," she said.

He went around the table and sat down again across from her. His face had paled but his scrutiny was contemplative, almost objective.

"What's our trouble?"

"I'm trying to decide. I think that as much as anything it is that canvas—stretched there to shut us off from the view of our people on the island. It was such a telltale last straw. So much like—like going behind a hedge."

"Yet," said Fortiner, "back in your home—surrounded by your friends and your husband's faculty associates—you were affronted by my most tentative approach. Then it was because our situation was too much in the public view."

"That is true."

"And we were under no illusions about our expectations when we hit upon the device of this journey."

"That also is true."

"Then what—at this final moment—*is* our difficulty?"

"Perhaps it is—other illusions that I had. I imagined so many things. I imagined a different world, with nothing in it like anything I had ever known. I imagined danger—physical danger—and a wild and reckless atmosphere in which all sorts of accidental and unpremeditated things might happen to us for which none of us would be responsible. What I did not imagine was an occasion as conventionalized as this one —as carefully and furtively contrived as any assignation in a back-street rooming house."

There was a vein throbbing in Fortiner's temple and a little muscle twitching in his cheek, but he clung to his composure.

"Can you have decided that, after all, you are in love with your husband?"

"No. Once I was, with his mind; but that's a charm that can pall."

"Have you begun to fear that he suspects?"

"I'm certain he does. But I cannot say that is something I fear."

"Because you think he already suspected when he was so ready to be persuaded to embark upon this expedition?"

"He is remarkably self-centered—not in himself as a man but in himself as a scientist. However, my husband is no longer my keeper. I am."

"Which takes up back to the beginning. What then is our trouble?"

"Call it no more than a woman's whim, if you like. I'm not proclaiming a stand. Possibly I'm merely asking for time."

"Suppose I cannot consent?"

"Then I must insist."

"And I, for my part, must likewise insist. We could make no greater mistake. This entire aimless conversation has been a mistake. That first moment when I came back from the rail, had I swept you straight off into the cabin, there'd have been none of this pseudo-maidenly toying with the idea of summons and surrender."

"But the moment did pass. And now it's gone."

"I'm not at all sure."

Fortiner sprang to his feet and was halfway around the table when he was halted by the unmistakable squeak of an oarlock. He peered past the edge of the canvas screen and, with a grunt of infinite disgust, sat down again.

"Unfortunately we'll never know—about the present moment, I mean. Here comes Buck—rowing like mad. Something's happened."

The big Negro scrambled over the rail, fell to his knees, and crawled toward Fortiner. He was in an agony of fear.

"It's Spence, Mr. Fortiner."

"What about Spence?"

"He's run off."

"Get over here, Buck, where I can smell you. You've been drinking again."

"No, I ain't. Mr. Fortiner, 'fore Gawd, I ain't. It's Spence. He's run off."

"Nonsense. You just got lost. Or he did."

"There wa'n't no time to git lost, Mr. Fortiner. Soon's we come to land—Spence he run off."

34

"Whatever gave you the fool notion he was running any-where?"

" 'Cause 'fore he start off, Mr. Fortiner, he want fer me to run off with him."

"Oh, he did, did he? Why then didn't you stop him?"

"Couldn't nobody stop him, Mr. Fortiner. Nobody."

"He was playing a joke on you."

" 'Twa'n't no joke, Mr. Fortiner. When I grabbed hold o' him he lit into me wif a knife."

Buck pulled back his coat to disclose a shirt that was wet with blood. Fortiner got to his feet and yanked Buck up beside him. He stripped off the coat, peeled back the shirt, and examined the gash. Tearing a strip from the tablecloth, he bound the wound roughly.

"That'll hold it for a while," he said. "Now show me where you saw him last."

"Wait, Heber," cried Philippa. "It's just not possible that Spencer is actually trying to run away. He must be sick."

"He'll be sicker when I get hold of him." Fortiner paused, half over the rail, and looked back at her. "And you'll have to come along. I can't leave you alone on the boat—not out here in the middle of this river."

In their camp on the next island below, Jasper slept on but Abel awoke and began a desultory daylight inspection of the site which he had selected in the darkness just before dawn. Since leaving Pittsburgh Jasper had insisted upon their traveling only at night in order to run less risk of obser-vation by any of that array of mysterious enemies to which he so constantly alluded. Pushing into the fringe of brush at the water's edge, Abel surveyed the main channel and the shores of the north bank, then crossed to the other side to examine the south bank. When he caught sight of the keel-boat anchored five hundred yards upstream he came to a sudden stand and watched intently for many minutes. Finally he turned back and awakened Jasper.

"There's a keelboat anchored out there," he announced. "I'm going to go take a look at her."

Jasper leaped up in instant distress.

"I absolutely forbid any such foolhardy venture."

Abel drew the canoe out of its hiding place in a cedar thicket and carried it down to the riverbank. Jasper ran after him.

"I must remind you that I have chartered your canoe for the duration of the voyage, and I repeat that I forbid any collateral use whatever."

"Just the same I'm taking me a look at that keelboat."

"Have you any conceivable reason for such utterly irrational conduct?"

"Two reasons. One—there's something queer about her. Doesn't look as if there's a soul aboard. And two—I built her and I want to see how she's been doing."

"Has it not occurred to you that this might be a ruse, a stratagem to lure us into the open?"

"Nobody's trying to lure me anywhere, but if you're stuck with the idea they are trying to lure you, then maybe you'd better stay here."

This proposal seemed to appeal even less to Jasper. He splashed into the water and took his accustomed seat in the prow. Abel looked to the priming of his rifle, laid it across his knees, and picked up the paddle. He half circled the keelboat, keeping well off while he continued to study her. There were no signs of disaster but equally none of life aboard. He drifted closer and presently made out the name painted on the bow.

"*N-a-i-a-d*," he spelled out. "That's a funny name."

"*Naiad*," said Jasper. "Greek for 'water nymph.' Let us draw what comfort we can from the totally unexpected. The classical allusion suggests the craft has come into hands of people of sufficient education to be considered semi-civilized."

"Hey," called Abel. "Anybody home?"

There was no reply. He moored the canoe to the anchor rope and swung aboard. Jasper clambered after him. Abel came to a stop on the foredeck and stared at the table, at the two breakfasts on it, one half eaten, the other untouched, at the torn tablecloth, at the splotches of blood on the deck, and at the oddly stretched canvas. Jasper began backing into the prow, ready to bolt back to the canoe.

"If you will but take account of every eloquent detail with your mind as well as your admittedly sharp eyes," he said, "you will note the abundant evidence of a surprise attack. The keelboat's people were set upon and carried off—by Indians, by river pirates, by presumed friends, who can say? —so suddenly they had not time to start up from their breakfast. The assailants may still be nearby. I strongly recommend we do not linger in the vicinity an unnecessary moment."

"You're either seeing more than I am or thinking a sight faster," said Abel. "What I do see is them silver dishes still on the table. What I don't see is any signs of a fight—except them two spots of blood—no bullet holes, no arrows, not even a chair tipped over. And if you've got it all figgered out, will you tell me who rigged the sail that way—and why?"

"There remain, to be sure, certain anomalous features,"

admitted Jasper. He snapped his fingers. "I have it. Mutiny. And the rascals have taken their victims ashore to bury them." He peeked around the edge of the canvas at the island and again began sidling toward the canoe.

Abel picked a handkerchief from the deck and examined the bit of cambric.

"A woman's," exclaimed Jasper, running back to him. "The perpetual cause of dissension." He bent and sniffed. "Ah, and not one of your homespun wenches, but a lady."

Abel smelled the handkerchief and looked toward the cabin. He started for the door but, instead of going directly in, swung up to the cabin roof.

"While I'm seeing how things look aft, you take a look down there," he said, pointing to the open hatch.

"Invariably a most unwise policy to separate in the presence of unknown perils," said Jasper, starting to follow him.

However, in circling the hatchway he cast a dubious glance into the hold, paused to look again, and then suddenly turned back to scuttle down the ladder. Abel made a quick circuit of the afterdeck, examined the rudder, and climbed the mast to survey the island. Jasper was emerging from the hold as he returned to the foredeck.

"No bodies," reported Jasper, much more cheerful than he had seemed before, "and no evidences of strife. But beds for six. Judging by the appurtenances: one gentleman, one near-gentleman, two servants, and two bumpkins."

Abel touched the coffee pot. "Not real cold even yet. It all looks the same way. They'd anchored here for the night like most folks on the river do. This morning, before getting started, the hands and the help had their grub—sitting around there on deck and along the rail where them crumbs are. The table was set for the other two—most likely the owner and his wife. Then, just as they were starting in to eat, something happened that made everybody jump up, drop everything, and take off. It must have been in their own skiff 'cause it's gone. It don't make too much sense, for a fact." He looked toward the cabin with an anticipatory air. "Course we ain't looked in there yet."

He opened the cabin door, took a long look from the threshold, and went in. Jasper, his hands clasped beneath his coattail behind him, followed as far as the doorway. Abel, staring at the bunk, the open wardrobe, the washstand, and the general array of feminine paraphernalia, gave his first exclamation of outright astonishment since coming aboard.

"I wondered why he wanted but the one bunk and that one so narrow," he said. "After all the fuss made about fixing the place up for her, she sleeps here by herself."

"Ah," said Jasper. "The mystery dissipates. Six men sharing so cramped a craft with a lady who smells of lilac and sleeps in silk and who as yet belongs to no one of them. There you have the powder—the match—and the inevitable explosion."

Abel bent to glance from the porthole. "No matter what set 'em off, it took 'em no further than this island. You can see the end of their skiff sticking out from behind that rock."

"Then they may return at any moment," cried Jasper. "Opportunity, having sprung at us, will as soon spring away again. Rouse from your dreaming and consider the reality which has so far escaped you. By the law of the sea an abandoned ship becomes the property of the first comer who boards her. We must instantly weigh anchor and be off downriver with this one."

Jasper's excitement drew no sparks from Abel. "We're a good ways from the sea," he said, "and folks out here don't go much by laws."

He resumed his absorbed contemplation of the cabin. His eyes kept coming back to the bunk. The covers were thrown back exposing the white linen sheets. Across the foot of the bed had been flung a woman's blue silk nightgown. He touched his fingertips tentatively to the sheets and then to the gown.

"Sniffing like a young dog around a fence post," remonstrated Jasper. "Have you never been in a woman's bedroom before? What lecherous conceit can have possessed you? Do you fancy you envisage the delightful creature who sleeps there? But this solitary couch could as well suggest that she is totally undesirable. Still, if treasure your illusions you must, then sprinkle yourself with her toilet water and stuff her nightgown in your bosom—only come along. We haven't a single precious moment to lose."

Abel looked from the porthole again.

"Three of the boat's people have come down to the beach."

"Then even your groping mind must grasp the fact that our time has all but run out."

Philippa, struggling at every step to free her skirts from the snags and brambles, worked her way out of the thicket and turned to confront her husband, Fred, and Ben.

"You didn't find any trace of him?"

"He ain't no place on this end of the island," said Fred, "that's for sure."

"Where's Heber?" asked Baynton.

"I long since gave up trying to keep up with him." Philippa gestured toward the deeper woods in the center of the island. "Somewhere in there—threshing about like a wild man."

"A most singular occurrence," said Baynton. "One would not imagine that in all North America there was a slave with more reason to feel content with his position. Yet at the first ill-considered opportunity he darts off into this wilderness."

Philippa sat down on a rock and examined her battered slippers. "I'm sure, Rodney—had the import of your herborizing occurred to him—he'd have postponed his design until a more convenient occasion."

His approach advertised by a premonitory crashing of underbrush, Fortiner burst out on the beach. His thin clothing was in tatters and his face and hands covered with scratches. He had lost the sandals and his bare feet were bleeding.

"I've got to go out to the boat for something fit to wear," he said. "And you, too, Philippa. The rest of you start again at the lower end. Form a line and go slow and this time really cover the ground. Look under every stick and every stone and into every rabbit hole. Buck's watching by the pond where Spencer'll have to come out in the open if he makes a break for the other end of the island. I'll be back before you get to the thicker woods there in the middle."

Jasper had untied the canoe and drawn it amidships where it could not be seen from shore. He was crouched by the rail, shivering with impatience and exasperation.

"I agree that by now it's perhaps too late to possess ourselves of the ship," he called. "But will you gather your addled wits and come get in the canoe before it's also too late even for that? The ship's people may return at any moment."

Abel came out of the cabin. "That's what I'm waiting for." He walked to the shoreward rail and stood clear of the canvas screen. "Whatever that is you've got in your tail pocket—put it back where you found it."

"I must object to your tone. I am not a sneak thief. I have already enlightened you regarding the law of the sea."

"Two of the boat's people are coming out now. Put it back."

"You cannot know whereof you speak. What I have in this pocket—and of which I am the legal possessor unless we prove so demented as to wait until the ship's owner returns —is a purse containing some hundreds of Spanish silver dollars."

"I said put it back."

Jasper glanced behind him into the canoe as though contemplating independent flight and then back at the approaching skiff and then once more at Abel's implacable grin. "I solemnly warn you fortune invariably punishes those who scorn her favors." He moved sorrowfully toward the hatchway, but with one foot on the ladder he suddenly turned, his expression brightening mercurially with a new thought. "Bent as you appear on self-mortification, will you listen to one word of advice?"

"What kind?"

"Will you delay—at least until we may form some estimate of the situation—any announcement that you are the proud architect of this craft?"

"What for? Only reason I'm here is to find out how my boat's been doing."

"How can I say what for? Who can foresee what may be about to happen? Just for once accept my counsel. There is no better general rule than never to volunteer information."

Philippa in the stern of the skiff caught sight of Abel.

"Look, Heber, there's somebody on board."

Fortiner suspended his rowing and looked over his shoulder. He stood up angrily.

"Who the devil might you be? And what are you doing on my boat?"

"Better sit down," advised Abel, " 'fore you upset. And go back to rowing 'fore the current carries you past."

Fortiner swore but resumed his seat and picked up the oars. Abel rested his elbows on the rail and looked past Fortiner at Philippa. The skiff bumped against the hull of the larger craft and again started to drift with the current.

"Throw me your line," proposed Abel. "Save you some more extra rowing."

Fortiner swore again but threw the line. Abel pulled the skiff alongside. Fortiner clambered over the rail and stood glaring, first at Abel and then at Jasper as the latter emerged from the hold.

"I asked you a question and I haven't heard an answer."

Abel shrugged, turned back to the rail, and resumed his contemplation of Philippa.

"We noticed your ship was abandoned," put in Jasper hastily, "and naturally stopped to investigate."

Fortiner took a second look at Jasper's strange figure, his scowl half puzzled, half contemptuous, and then another at Abel. Abel's back was still to him. Irritably Fortiner grasped his arm and pulled him around. Abel took hold of the hand on his arm with a grasp that gave Fortiner a start, removed it from his arm, and let go of it. Fortiner eyed Abel swiftly from hear to toe.

"Whoever you are, young man, you look like you might know your way around in the woods. One of my servants ran off and is hiding somewhere on that island. If you'll help me find him, I'll make it well worth your while."

Without waiting for a reply he strode to the hatchway and went down the ladder.

"Meanwhile, would you mind helping me up?" said Philippa.

Abel bent over the rail, caught her by the wrists, and swung her up on deck. Like Fortiner she was immediately struck by Jasper's remarkable appearance, but also like him her attention came back to Abel.

"Thank you," she said.

He became aware of how intently he was staring at her.

"Don't mention it, ma'am," he said, swallowing.

Jasper swept her a low bow.

"May I be so bold as to remark, madam, that—having inadvertently caught a glimpse of your boudoir—a bower so entirely without precedent on this wild river—we were looking forward most hopefully to our first glimpse of its occupant —and that we have been in no way disappointed?"

"Sir, you are too kind. I had been led to expect many prodigies in this wilderness, but such gallantry was not among them."

Her ironic remark seemed addressed to Jasper, but while she was making it her glance had come briefly to rest on Abel's hunting shirt. Looking down, he discovered one corner of the handkerchief protruding from a pocket. He yanked it out and extended it to her. But she had already turned toward the cabin.

"If you will excuse me, gentlemen. As you can readily see, I, too, must change."

Abel continued to stare, fascinated, at the closed door.

"Come back to earth, my young friend," said Jasper. "That, I admit, is something very, very pleasing indeed. But it is not for you and this is no place for you. May I remind you once more that our canoe, our mission, our itinerary, and our own far from unimportant affairs still await us."

Abel merely shook his head slightly as if brushing off a fly.

"There remains, of course, one brief alternative to which I would not too vehemently object. Were we to linger only long enough for you to find his slave for him—which should not take long on yon small island—we might take with us a distinctly useful handful of those Spanish silver dollars."

Abel replied without looking around.

"Can't you see all that shoal water up there? It ain't nowhere more'n neck deep. While everybody was wallowing through the brush on the island, his nigger had plenty time to get over to the south bank."

The cabin door opened a crack and Philippa looked out speculatively, first at Jasper and then at Abel.

"Mr.——?"

"Name's Abel Traner, ma'am."

"Could you help me a moment, Mr. Traner?"

"Yes, ma'am."

Abel darted to the door. Jasper turned to take a thoughtful look toward the south bank and then with sudden and equal alacrity darted down the ladder into the hold.

Abel came to a stand in the doorway. Philippa, in underbodice and petticoat, was balancing on one bare foot while peeling a stocking from the other. As she straightened, her loosened hair fell about her shoulders and her arms came up gracefully to remove the remaining pins and then swiftly to wind it about her head again. She half turned from the mirror.

"Please don't stand on ceremony, Mr. Traner. You must overlook this appalling informality. But Mr. Fortiner will be ready to go ashore any minute and I must be ready to go with him. It happens, however, that the heavy shoes I need are in that box and I can't get it open."

Abel closed the door behind him and bent over the wooden chest. It had been rain soaked somewhere along the way and the inset lid had swollen until it was stuck in its frame. He forced the tip of his knife under one corner.

"You'd better give me a hand," he said. "Bear down on the knife handle—only not hard enough to break the blade."

She knelt beside him. An unpinned lock of hair fell down over her eyes. With both hands clasped on the knife handle she could not brush it back and he was able to take one steady, unabashed look at the smooth white arms and shoulders presented to his view in an intimate proximity ordinarily reserved to a lover. He fumblingly inserted the blade of his tomahawk under the other corner and the lid came open.

"Oh, thank you," she said.

He straightened and looked, as she still knelt before him rummaging through the chest, at the curve of her bosom under her bodice, at the gleaming silkiness of her hair, and at the graceful movements of her hands. When she rose he did not look away in time and their eyes met. Her quick frown was as quickly succeeded by a half-smile.

"I have to remember that this was a tableau of my own contriving."

She turned back to the mirror and resumed doing her hair.

"I surely didn't aim to mortify you, ma'am," said Abel. "But there ain't no use my trying to make out like I'm blind."

The door flew open and Fortiner came in, followed by

Jasper. Abel whirled guiltily. Fortiner's deshabille was even more informal than Philippa's, for his change into heavier clothing had proceeded only so far as a suit of red flannel underwear. His concern for the moment, however, was no more with his own or Philippa's attire than it was with Abel's presence in her room.

"How do you know he got over to the south bank?" he demanded.

"I don't know," said Abel. "But the water's shallow enough so he could have. And it stands to reason, if he had spunk enough to make a break at all, he'd have had enough not to squat on the island waiting for you to come up with him."

Philippa, brush in hand, joined the conference.

"Spencer must have completely lost his mind," she exclaimed. "He can't have the faintest idea what he's about. He'll be as helpless in the wilderness as I'd be. Likely as not the poor soul will stumble straight into the hands of the Indians."

"That's what your 'poor soul' is counting on," said Fortiner. "Every runaway black knows that if he can keep going until he runs across Indians he's in clover. Indians are always glad to take them in."

Philippa looked questioningly at Abel.

"That's a fact," said Abel. "But not much chance his lasting on that shore until Indians find him. A hundred to one by now he's going in circles 'cause he's already lost and wearing himself out so's he'll starve that much sooner. Nothing in the woods to eat this early in the year. Could be, of course, as he begins to peter out the wolves will pull him down."

"Oh," said Philippa, "there must be some way to find him."

"This fellow," said Fortiner, indicating Jasper, "says you're an expert woodsman and well able to track anything that walks—through any kind of going."

"I also pointed out," amended Jasper, "the manifest perils of the undertaking, including not only the risks connected with Indians and wild beasts but the circumstance that the fugitive is certain to resist. Mr. Fortiner is prepared, therefore, to pay you a hundred dollars in the event you succeed."

Abel shook his head. "When a man—even a nigger—wants this bad to get away, I don't aim to be the one to bring him back."

Philippa clasped Abel's arm. "But, Mr. Traner," she begged, "you mustn't think of it that way. Spencer is Mr. Fortiner's favorite and most pampered servant. Whatever possessed him—it was without reason or forethought. What

43

we're really asking of you is not to capture him but to save him. You will, won't you?"

Abel looked down at the hand on his arm and then into her eager, flushed face.

"Yes ma'am," he said. "I will."

"Good," said Fortiner. "Give me two minutes to get some clothes on and I'll be with you."

"I'll go alone," said Abel. "I'll want to move fast—and quiet."

"Maybe so. But that won't do. I have to be there when he's taken."

"Then you go after him."

Fortiner's eyes glittered. "You leave me not even the poor comfort of resenting your insolence. Let's hope you are as ready to press an advantage if you come up with him. Remember, he has a pistol."

"He's lost it by now—or wet his priming. He'll make me no trouble, 'less he's too tuckered out to walk back."

Fortiner accompanied Abel to the rail.

"I presume your expert eye will enable you to tell right off when you reach the south bank whether or not he actually did cross?" Abel nodded. "Then make us a signal so I can call off the hunt on the island."

Abel paddled upriver a half-mile and turned in to shore. Philippa stood beside Fortiner, watching. Abel had barely landed before he waved his hat. Fortiner ceased to scowl for the first time since Buck had crawled to him across the deck.

"Scarcely the sort of day we anticipated, my dear, except possibly for this curious stage of undress. Mine, I confess, must look far from fetching, but I have never seen you in a more effective costume."

"You can be a brute in so many different ways, Heber. If he is brought back, what will you do to him?"

"Such fair shoulders to bear so many woes. Some sort of discipline is obviously indicated, but there will be no rude spectacles to offend your sensibilities."

"I should think yours—and his—were more to be considered."

Philippa turned abruptly and went into her cabin. Fortiner started down the ladder and paused to look back at Jasper.

"I don't believe I caught your name."

"Jasper Hedges, your most humble servant, sir. And yours, may I ask?"

"Fortiner."

"A name I have many times heard in Philadelphia. Though I do not recall we ever had the privilege of meeting."

"Nor do I," said Fortiner. "Can you handle a skiff?"

"It chances that I am fairly adept at the management of anything that floats, except that devil's own instrument, the canoe."

"Then, to save time while I'm dressing, will you go get my people on the island? I think they'd better all be aboard— just in case your partner's chasing my nigger through the woods stirs up some kind of hornet's nest on the mainland."

"Gladly, sir. Though you need have no fears for Abel's acumen. He is remarkably sagacious for one so young. Your affair could not be in safer hands."

The overloaded skiff eventually put out again from the beach. Fortiner was waiting at the rail for Buck.

"Let's have another look at that," he said, pulling back Buck's coat.

"If you will permit me, sir," said Jasper. "I at one time served as acting surgeon on the privateer *Gamecock*."

He examined the wound with a professional air, pronounced it but superficial, and redressed it. As he tightened the bandage, his eyes were already wandering to Baynton's absorbed sorting and arranging of his specimens.

"If I might be so bold, sir," said Jasper. "Are you not tying a sprig of *Salix pumila* to one of *Salix capreoides?*"

Baynton looked up in astonishment.

"You are a botanist?"

"Only a passing hobby with me. My principal subjects at Yale were Greek and Divinity."

"You, Fred, and Ben—and you, too, Hedges," said Fortiner. "Get your minds off everything but one. Watch those woods. I can't tell you what to watch for. Look for anything you can see—any change—even in the way the birds fly over it."

The three moved to the stern and sat with their legs dangling over the rail, each keeping watch in his own way on the wilderness beyond the river. Jasper speedily overcame the boatman's initial prejudice with the aid of a fund of ribald stories of extraordinary novelty, and then cemented their regard with an infinitely detailed and personal account of the year he had been a captive of the Barbary pirates and had at length been made gatekeeper of the bey's harem. But even this tale had an end, and as the afternoon wore on he became less and less able to sit still.

"Have no idle doubts of Abel's capacities," he kept declaring. "I who know him well have none."

For all aboard the keelboat the waiting had become a trial. Fortiner paced the foredeck, furiously smoking an endless succession of cigars. Philippa took up her post on the roof of

45

the cabin and stood, hour after hour, her gaze fixed on the wooded hills that rose beyond the river's edge. Buck kept coming to the galley door to peer out and to finger his several charms. Even Baynton from time to time laid aside his tweezers and vials of alcohol and went to the rail to look. No one once called out in alarm or excitement. There was nothing to see. The wilderness remained mysterious and changeless. Though bathed in sunlight, it also remained dark and forbidding.

Jasper, more and more restless, finally sought out Fortiner.

"This servant of yours," he inquired. "Is he practiced in the use of a pistol?"

"No. But he has been taught to shoot. Let us hope your man does not underestimate this as much as it seems his habit to underestimate most difficulties."

"There is not the slightest cause for anxiety," said Jasper, wetting his lips. "I assure you that his is not the overconfidence of ignorance. He is not one to walk blindly into danger. He is a true denizen of the forest—as tireless as the wolf, as stealthy as the panther."

"He may need to be all that you say. I have discovered my pocket compass is missing. Instead of wandering aimlessly, Spencer can have set off upon a straight line into the hills—which can very considerably prolong the chase."

The sun set. The shadows deepened. The wooded hills to the south became more enigmatic than ever as night settled over them. Fortiner climbed up beside Philippa.

"Getting a bit chilly," he said. "Or can't you tell?"

She obediently slipped her arms into the cloak he was holding for her.

"Thank you, Heber. Yes, I can tell. I've been cold for the last hour."

"Are you shivering more for the young man or for Spencer?"

"A little for the young man. I can't forget I persuaded him to go. But much more for Spencer. I can't help thinking—perhaps, as usual, too much. And this time possibly too late. Anyway, I can't decide whether I hope he's brought back or not. Even if remaining free means the death of him. He was so desperately determined to get away. Heber, have you no inkling why?"

"None. Never has a nigger had an easier time. He's never had anything harder to do than polishing my boots. He's always been my personal boy. He was born the same year I was and we grew up together. His mother was my mother's maid. We learned together to ride, hunt, fish, read. When tutors were brought into the household he shared my les-

46

sons. When I went to the university he went with me. I've never gone anywhere without him."

"Something must have driven him to this. What?"

"Your guess is as good as mine. The smartest niggers are full of fool ideas. Could be he pictured himself cutting a wide swath among the Indians—you know—better first in a wigwam than second in Rome. Another possibility. He's never to my knowledge had any truck with women. Maybe his imagination has been overrun by bevies of Indian maidens. But what's the use of speculating? We can't tell what notions possessed him—or how to cure him of them—until we get hold of him again."

"Do you think punishment will cure him?"

"Well, I don't propose to kill him, so we'll have to try some sort of cure. But, look, it's so dark you can't see a thing. Come sit down. What you really need is something to eat."

Philippa permitted him to help her down to the foredeck.

"You men back there," Fortiner called. "Supper. Buck, let's have it."

Buck placed on the deck a tray of baked ham and two bottles of whisky, but nobody reached toward the offering. Fortiner scowled as though he considered the general uneasiness in some way a reflection upon him.

"Here, Fred," he said, irritably, extending one of the bottles. "Might be what you need is a bracer."

"Jest might, at that," said Fred. He took a long drink and looked from the bottle to the platter of meat. "Everything all set now—everything it takes for a wake."

"Everything, possibly, except the body," said Baynton. "Or bodies, as the case may prove."

"What the devil's come over all of you?" said Fortiner.

Ben's voice, disembodied in the gloom, came down from above. "I kin tell you what's gittin' under my hide. Jasper there he's likely frettin' about what's happened to Abel, but me, I never laid eyes on Abel. I'm a-thinkin' about that nigger. No matter where he winds up, he's been a-poundin' out a real hard run fer hisself."

Fortiner laughed harshly. "A most painful dilemma for the squeamish. Well, we live in a democracy. Come, let's take a vote. Who prays for the survival of the white man and who for the runaway black one?"

"Something's comin'," said Ben.

There was the splash of a paddle alongside. No one moved or spoke. Ben leaned out to look but said no more. A pair of hands reached from below into the light, groped, and clasped the rail. Spencer heaved himself wearily up, sprawled on

47

the deck, got to his feet, and stood, shoulders slumped, head down. He was doubly naked. In whipping his clothes from him the wilderness had also whipped from him his spirit. Abel swung over the rail, the canoe's mooring line in his hand, stood his rifle against the cabin, stepped over Fred's and Jasper's outstretched legs, and tied the line. No one else moved. Every eye was fixed on Fortiner. His calm, dry voice ended the waiting and the silence.

"Buck, take him below. He's your boy until morning. And if there're any more tricks between now and then, it'll be your gizzard that pays for it."

"Yes, *sah*," said Buck.

He took Spencer roughly by the arm, pushed him to the ladder, and followed him down it. Philippa rose suddenly and turned toward her door. Her shaking outstretched hand missed the latch. Abel sprang to open it for her, but Fortiner shouldered in front of him.

"The day been too much for you?" he asked, peering to read her expression in the shadows.

"Apparently," she said, averting her face.

She went in and closed the door. His hand returned to the latch, as though he were about to follow her, but after a second's hesitation he faced around to Abel.

"I take it you had your troubles. But we did some sweating of our own while we waited."

"I had some," said Abel. "Never knew a man to travel so fast through bad brush as he did for a while. But along toward night he got bogged down in a swamp."

"Anyway, it was a good job." Fortiner drew from a pocket a leather purse that clinked as he extended it. "Here, take it. Take it. No reason to squirm. You've earned it."

"Give it to Jasper," said Abel. "He made the deal."

Fortiner shrugged, tossed the purse to Jasper, picked up one of the whisky bottles, and looked again at Abel.

"What's your choice? Eat first or drink first?"

"I've got a saddle of venison in the canoe. I reckon I'll just push off ashore and cook some of it. Come on, Jasper."

"Suit yourself," said Fortiner.

Jasper had nothing to say until the canoe had been beached and, while Abel was kindling a fire, he had completed, by fingering the coins in the darkness, his count of the dollars in the purse.

"An even hundred. And, most happily, at the cost of no more than a single day's delay. It is not quite clear to me why Fortiner's bread would have stuck in your throat. Was it because you felt guilty about catching his slave or about coveting his woman?"

48

Abel finished, with great care, trimming the venison roast and impaling it on his ramrod. "She might be married to him but she's not his woman."

"There you are doubly deluded, my friend. He undoubtedly escaped your notice in the darkness, but among the ship's company is a young professor of botany who chances to be her husband—at least in name."

Abel dropped the venison in the sand. He carried it down to wash it off in the river and returned to set it over the fire.

"You're crazy," he said.

"We all are—at times. But at the moment I am spectacularly rational. Aside from deductions that could be made almost at a glance, you must realize that all those hours you spent hounding the fugitive I spent in sociable intercourse with the crew."

"It still makes no sense. Fortiner was the one who ordered the boat built. Three months ahead he knew what was coming and had everything fixed up special for her."

"But pursue that trail with half the perspicacity you follow Spencer's today and it will lead you to a similarly inevitable conclusion."

"You're worse than crazy. To begin with, no man married to her could be that much of a polecat."

"It is not a pattern entirely without precedent—a young and beautiful wife, a wealthy and powerful suitor, and a husband who is complacent because he is poor and ambitious."

Abel made a sudden move. Jasper eyed him but Abel, his brow furrowed with thought, was merely throwing another stick on the fire.

"I still don't believe it. I don't reckon I know too much about women. And for sure I ain't never before seen one even the least little bit like her. But I have now. And I don't believe it."

"The eyes of innocence are occasionally clear as well as wide. My informants aboard *Naiad* confirm your intuition. They agree that, while Fortiner has been laboring most assiduously in the vineyard, he has as yet to harvest the first fruit."

"The more you talk the less sense you make. This Fortiner might be a son of a bitch but he's no fool. Whatever scheme he had up his sleeve in the first place, it wouldn't have been the one you claim. With seven people cooped up on that one boat and, besides, somebody always standing night watch, he'd have known he never could get within ten feet of that cabin without everybody on board knowing about it."

"There innocence betrays you. For such a man as Fortiner the want of privacy might but add zest to the game."

"Will you shut up, for God's sake. I'm getting sicker and

49

sicker of all this gab, gab, gab, about something we neither of us know the first thing about."

Jasper subsided. They ate, put out the fire, and spread their blankets. Then, in the darkness, it was Abel's sheepish voice that reopened the subject.

"You know, Jasper, what the funniest thing about the whole business was? When I first saw her there in the skiff—I saw right off how much out of the ordinary she was—but I wasn't surprised. It was like I knew ahead of time what she was going to look like. I can't understand that."

"It's always easier to assume clairvoyance after the fact. There is another explanation. Every man has special and peculiar weaknesses. I take it your ideal of female beauty has always been tall, blue-eyed, high-bosomed, golden-haired."

"I don't know about that. I ain't been more partial to one kind than another. Most the towheaded girls I ever noticed struck me as more apt to get sunburned in summer and runny-nosed in winter, and the year round it was easier to tell their hair needed washing. No, what I think was what got me so set up was this: I built that cabin and the bed and everything else in it. And all the time I was working on it I kept wondering what the woman who was going to stay in it was going to turn out to be like. I left before she showed up, so I thought I was never going to find out. Then when I went in the cabin again today—with her things all around—the dent in the mattress where she'd been sleeping—her nightgown right where she'd taken it off and dropped it—all of a sudden it was almost like I could see her. Even that lilac smell was like something I expected. I can guess how simple maybe this sounds, but that's the way it was."

"No simpler than sunlight or the law of gravity," said Jasper. "I am beginning to fear that your case is a very sad one, indeed. Before every normal young man there loom many unavoidable pitfalls. But the net chance has spread for you is intricate indeed. Do you mind my making one or two very personal remarks on this topic?"

"Be no way to head you off if I did."

"That may well be. For I perceive you stand in the most painful need of advice. You can make no more grievous error than to take a fancy to a woman who, by whatever quirk of feminine reasoning, considers herself of a higher order than you. The occasional beautiful woman, such as Mrs. Baynton, takes such tribute for granted, but it is easy for almost any woman to imagine that she is bestowing an incalculable favor by her mere condoning of a man's attentions. The man who encourages this ridiculous posture is a fool. Now do not be misled. I am not suggesting continence. Far from it. To the

50

whole man, woman is a necessity. So by all means look about you. Look constantly and indefatigably. But look always below you—never above or beyond. Remember that what you most require from a woman has little to do with her face, her station, or her intellect. Remember that the world is filled with prepossessing, robust, and hearty chambermaids, farm girls, seamstresses, nurses, laundresses, older sisters, plainer daughters. Discover for yourself the reward in a situation in which it is you who are bestowing the favor. Now, I realize that it will be an instance without precedent in the history of man if one of your age and experience pays the slightest heed to this priceless counsel, but nevertheless I am obliged out of my affectionate regard for you to offer it. Ah—I apprehend by your gentle snore that you have not so much as listened."

Abel had not been listening but he was only pretending to snore. Never had he felt less like sleep. The image of Philippa hovered between him and the stars. He was not seeing her as the flesh-and-blood woman kneeling before him by the chest but as an unearthly figure of porcelain and gold, so mysteriously delicate and fragrant and perfect as to seem a visitor from another world. It had become suddenly apparent to him that it could have been this other world that, without knowing it, he had set out to find.

With the first slant of dawn down the open hatchway Fortiner was up and dressing. Spencer lay flat on his mattress, his vacant stare fixed on the stanchion immediately over his head. He gave no sign that his master's awakening had meaning for him. But Buck, squatting alongside, watched Fortiner's every move, his bulging bloodshot eyes intent on every flicker of expression, every garment lifted, as though the most obscure detail of Fortiner's behavior this morning had for him untold significance.

"Put some clothes on him," said Fortiner.

Buck leaped to obey. Spencer submitted with inert limpness. Fortiner turned to the foot of the ladder with a curt gesture. Buck jerked Spencer to his feet. Fred and Ben, sitting in the bow, ceased their whispering when they heard the scuff of feet on the ladder and watched with morbid curiosity as Fortiner and the two Negroes appeared on deck.

"Put him in the skiff," Fortiner directed Buck.

The cabin door opened and Philippa came down. Her pale, drawn face suggested that she had not slept. She looked down at Spencer and Buck in the skiff and then at Fortiner with one leg over the rail on his way to join them.

"Are you taking him ashore to hide from me what you propose to do?"

"What I propose to do can concern nobody else, you included."

"But it does concern me. It is necessary for me to understand. Will you answer one question? What do you expect to prove?"

"I expect to prove to him who he is—and who I am—and that there is a difference."

"You mean that he has challenged you and you are compelled to take up the challenge."

"If you like."

"But that the selection of weapons you use when resisted is better kept from me?"

"Put any construction on it you choose."

Fortiner dropped into the skiff. Buck picked up the oars. Philippa watched the craft's shoreward progress, her hands tightening on the rail.

The squeak of the oarlock aroused Abel. He sat up in his blanket. Fortiner stepped out on the beach and strode off toward the wooded middle of the island. Buck followed, prodding Spencer before him. Jasper awakened and leaned on one elbow. The three disappeared from view in the woods.

"Justice takes its inexorable and immemorial course," murmured Jasper.

"Abel," called Philippa from the keelboat. "Abel."

Abel jerked on his moccasins and shirt, clapped on his hat, and launched the canoe. When he backed water alongside *Naiad*, Baynton was expostulating with Philippa.

"I forbid this incredible stupidity," he was saying. "It is not your place to attempt to interfere. He is our friend and our host."

"Yes, I know," said Philippa. "And you are my husband."

She pulled away from him and leaned over the rail toward Abel.

"Take me ashore," she commanded.

Abel stood and swung her down into the canoe. She knelt in the prow with her back to him.

"Hurry," she said.

The canoe touched the beach. She sprang to land and set out swiftly for the woods. Abel trotted to overtake her. She was breathing hard.

"I have to see," she said. "I have to see with my own eyes."

"He's flogging his nigger," said Abel. "Is that what you want to see?"

For a moment she did not reply. "It's not possible," she said. "It's totally inconceivable—as inconceivable as his flogging me."

"Then that's what you think, too? That Spencer's his own

52

brother I—mean, that they had the same father? Anybody can see they got enough of the same look."

She shook her head vaguely, not so much in negation as in a kind of refusal to grapple with the idea. Suddenly she came to a stop.

Ahead of them, past a fringe of rhododendron bushes, was a forest glade with a fallen sycamore lying across it. Buck was tearing off Spencer's clothes. Spencer was making no attempt to resist. His gaze was fixed on Fortiner's face. Each time Buck jerked him this way and that Spencer's head turned to maintain that inscrutable gaze. Buck climbed over the tree trunk, leaned back, grasped Spencer's wrists, and pulled him, face down, over the log, exposing his stretched bare back in a rigid arc. Fortiner had a six-foot length of peeled inch-thick hickory sapling. Taking it in his two hands, he swished it experimentally through the air.

"Want I should stop it?" asked Abel.

Again Philippa shook her head vaguely. "I have to see," she breathed. "I have to see with my own eyes."

Fortiner's manner was calm and businesslike and his voice was carefully matter-of-fact as he asked, "Ready, Buck?" He planted his feet, lifted the pliant hickory staff, and brought it down with all his force. Across the bowed back a cut appeared and widened. Blood spurted from it. From Spencer there burst an involuntary, animal-like scream.

With a low moan that was like an echo of that cry, Philippa turned, swaying, to Abel, putting out her hands to seek support. Her strange excitement had reached a pitch which she no longer could endure. She would have fallen had he not seized hold of her. Her flushed face had turned to chalk, her fluttering eyelids had reduced her eyes to sightless slits of white, and she seemed to have ceased to breathe. Abel picked her up and carried her out to the beach. Seating himself on the sand with her head and shoulders cradled in his lap, he reached over her to dabble one hand in the water and began to sprinkle and bathe her brow and face. Jasper came over to look on with sardonic interest.

"She saw him take his first whack," said Abel, "and then she must have fainted. Do something, goddam it. Or tell me what to do."

"You're doing fine," said Jasper. "If her breath gets too short, stick your finger in her mouth to keep her from choking on her tongue."

The intermittent, faint gasps for breath culminated in a long sigh. A tinge of color returned to her lips. Her eyes opened. For a moment she blinked, bewildered, up at Abel. Then, as full comprehension came, she clutched at him, hid her face against his shoulder, and burst into a fit of violent weeping. The shattering sobs which shook her shook him as well. Jasper walked away, flinging up his arms dramatically as though apostrophizing the heavens.

" 'One woe doth tread upon another's heel,' " he declaimed, " 'so fast they follow.' "

Her paroxysm ended as suddenly as it had begun. She withdrew from Abel's arms and sat up with her back to him. The handkerchief with which she attempted to dry her face proved insufficient and she resorted to the hem of her dress. Taking the other handkerchief from his pocket, Abel handed it to her over her shoulder. She took it and dabbed at her nose and eyes. Abel got to his knees and waited. Presently her hands came up to pat and smooth her hair. When she turned to face him she was almost calm again. But the emotional storm through which she had passed had had one aftermath. She was not red-eyed and sniffling. She looked more beautiful than ever.

"You have been so patient, Abel," she said. "And now that I have been as foolish as even a woman possibly can be, will you take me back?"

In the canoe she this time sat facing him and yet seemed not to see him. Her restored outward calm had become a mask behind which her inward state was hidden. Baynton was waiting at the rail to help her over the side.

"To all appearances," he said, "your harebrained expedition was utterly fruitless—as could have been foreseen."

"Not utterly," she replied.

She had reached her cabin door before she turned and came back to the rail to look down at Abel.

"I seem always to be thanking you," she said. "I do again."

"Sure you wouldn't like me to stay somewhere around—for maybe another day or two?"

"Yes, I'm sure. I'm all through, I trust, making a fool of myself."

On the beach Jasper was waiting gloomily to confront Abel.

"That piteous cry for help," he intoned. "That gallant flame of response. Those arms about you. Those tears."

Abel crossed to his blanket and began rolling it up.

"The entire heart-rending scene made incontrovertibly clear the visage of bleak truth. Whatever slight hope there may have been for you before has now forever fled."

"Get your gear in the canoe," said Abel.

Jasper stared. "Do my eyes and ears betray me? Does my reason totter? Or are we after all about to resume our journey?"

"We are if you can stop talking long enough."

Jasper caught up his blanket and sprang to the canoe. They

shot away downriver. But, after passing the third island below, Abel suddenly rounded the point and, screened from the view of the now-distant keelboat, beached the canoe.

"Ah," groaned Jasper. "How premature was all my giddy jubilation. What new misfortune now looms over us?"

"I'll tell you," said Abel. "And pay attention so we won't have to have any long argument. We're coming to the Scioto country where there's more apt to be Indians than anywhere else along the river. That Fortiner's too bullheaded to figure on what anybody's planning but him—and his boatmen are too scared of him to speak up. So we're going to keep a little ways ahead of his boat and keep our eyes open and make sure he don't butt head on into something."

"Our hero always in the offing a-quiver to fly to the rescue," said Jasper. "A picture of devotion to which I can plainly see I may as well become resigned. But do not be deceived that it is the Indian menace which is your haunting concern. The dragon from which our Saint George waits to save the damsel is the bold bad Fortiner himself."

"Nope. I ain't worried about that. Not any more. She's through with him. If she ever had any other idea he stomped it out when she seen him pounding on Spencer. That's for sure."

"H-m-m," said Jasper. "Nevertheless—whatever the occasion—keeping the distance you must, your opportunities to prove of service would still seem somewhat hazy."

"All I got to say is," said Abel, "no matter what comes—if it's something to make her want to holler 'Abel' again—I aim to be where I can hear it."

4

From his lookout Chicatommo could see far and wide out over the two rivers. The Ohio, coursing in majestic curves through the wooded hills, surged around the northern flank of the ridge and rolled on westward over the horizon. The Scioto, a lesser though brighter ribbon, wound down from the north to mark by its junction with the great river the famous wilderness crossroads. The one road was the Ohio itself, a historic waterway that had known the fleets of the mound-builders, the dugouts of the earliest Indians, the bateaux of French explorers and missionaries, the barges of English traders, the armed galleys of Kentucky's revolutionary border defense, as now it knew the lumbering flatboats of the settlers. The other road, crossing the Ohio at the mouth of the Scioto, was the Warriors' Path, that ancient track that stretched along the ridges from the Great Lakes portages to the headwaters of streams flowing into the Gulf. It, too, was a historic way. For a century and a half Northern and Southern Indians had marched over it to make war upon each other, as now they marched to support each other in their common war against the whites.

The old Shawnee chief glanced down at the encampment of his followers in the edge of the woods that fringed the treeless hilltop, and returned his attention to the river. Traffic had been light this morning. Shortly after dawn there had been a bargeload of soldiers. He had gathered his force for the pounce. There would have been little loot but there was an added pleasure in killing soldiers. But the barge had kept cautiously to mid-channel and he had let it pass unchallenged. His eyes gleamed with sudden interest as a new possibility drifted around the bend. This was a prize worth taking. Three flatboats, laden with more than a hundred head of men, women, children, and animals, had been tied together for mutual defense. In response to the low-pitched note from his war whistle his eager followers crouched beside their canoes on the bank. But the great wallowing raft also kept to mid-channel.

Another dot appeared upriver and grew into a small bateau with four occupants. This seemed at first worth little attention, but presently Chicatommo began to watch it. The paddlers' style was Canadian, leading to the conjecture that these travelers might be friendly. This was presently confirmed. The bateau turned sharply from mid-river toward the south shore, the steersman standing to make more obvious his identification signs to the Indian outpost on the bank. Chicatommo clapped his hands. His Mingo wife, Onaya, scurried up the slope from camp carrying his buffalo-horn headdress, his red coat, his bear-claw necklace, his pipe, his tobacco pouch, and a bowl of coals. Onaya was as tough and gnarled as an old root and as able as ever to endure the vicissitudes of march and camp. She decked him in the costume befitting his dignity when receiving visitors, set the bowl, pouch and pipe beside him, and withdrew.

Todd Barklit stepped ashore, greeted several personal acquaintances among the watching Indians, and climbed up to the lookout. Chicatommo's somber, wrinkled face became creased with but the coldest smile of welcome. For, though Barklit was an associate of Alexander McKee, the King's Commissioner to the Indians, and, as a former trader, had for years been recognized as a sympathizer with every Indian interest, he nevertheless was a white man.

"A winter has passed and I have traveled a long, hard way since last I saw my great friend," said Barklit, bending to shake hands. His Shawnee was easy and fluent. "It is a wonderful consolation to find him well—and perched on this height like an eagle waiting to swoop upon his prey."

"I am glad to see my friend who is the friend of the Shawnee," said Chicatommo.

Barklit eased his bulk down against a boulder. Chicatommo picked up the pipe, filled it with tobacco, placed a coal in the bowl, and extended it to his guest. Barklit ceremoniously presented the pipe in turn to the four directions, puffed several times, and handed it back to his host. They smoked by turns, in silence. Chicatommo took care to take no notice of the long, slender package Barklit had tucked under one arm. When at length the pipe was finished, Barklit unwrapped the parcel. The gift turned out to be a brass-bound telescope, an item of military equipment Chicatommo had seen but once before and then in the hands of an English general.

"The famous warrior's eyes have not dimmed," said Barklit, "but with this he will be able to discover his enemies at an even greater distance."

Chicatommo accepted the present, turned it end for end a time or two, and laid it aside as though it were a matter of no great moment. Another pipe was lighted and again they smoked in silence. So considerable a gift indicated that there was an important purpose behind Barklit's visit. Barklit picked up a pebble, tossed it carelessly in his hand, and threw it at an inquisitive chipmunk.

"There was talk in Pittsburgh of a young Shawnee who had come alone to the Monongahela. According to the story I heard, he had come to look for a white girl who had one time been a captive in his town. I asked many questions because it crossed my mind that last summer your grandson, Mauquah, had cut himself with gar's teeth when you sold that girl you took at Hannastown back to her people in Pennsylvania."

No quiver of expression passed over Chicatommo's face. "Mauquah is the son of my son. He would seek a white woman no more than he would a white sow."

"I am happy to hear that it could not have been him," said Barklit. "Because the rest of the story was that the settlers ran him down with a pack of hunting dogs."

The noon sun was warm but Chicatommo drew the red coat closer about him. "The young man forgot his own purity when he forgot the white woman's impurity. It is no wonder he became food for dogs."

"All the same, a poor way to die. And—whoever his family —they should remember the people who brought him to so miserable an end."

Onaya came up with a pot in which bubbled a bear's head that had been boiled in maple-sugar water thickened with the animal's fat and blood. Barklit devoted himself to the repast with all the appreciative gusto demanded by Indian hospitality. It was only when at length he rose to go that he came to the essential point of his visit.

"There is one slight favor you could do me. It would be a favor, as well, to McKee, to the commandant at Detroit, and to the governor general himself. I know nothing that comes downriver can escape your notice. So will you keep an extra eye out for two men in a canoe? One is tall, dark, thin, with one eye a little cocked. When last I saw him he was dressed like a scarecrow in worn out doeskin pants, blue coat, and cocked hat. The other is a young Pennsylvania hunter, red-haired and freckled. What I'm getting around to is this: what you do with the red-haired one is of no moment, but for the tall, dark one they will pay very well in Detroit."

Chicatommo was listening with apparent attention but no

apparent interest. "If we see him he will not get through. But a canoe is not always easy to see. People in a canoe are likely to travel at night when the river is darkened by many shadows."

Barklit again turned to go and again paused for a last elaborately casual word. "I was told that the redheaded one comes from the station where they had the hunting dogs."

Chicatommo sat without moving until his visitor's bateau had put out into the river. He then summoned Oosak, the senior among his Cherokee followers, to man the lookout, and went down to the Indian camp.

"You told me that Mauquah could not come with us because he was sick in bed of a fever," he accused Onaya.

She bowed her head and waited. He struck her to the ground with the flat of his tomahawk and continued to beat her with the handle. The deliberate blows thudded on and on in a measured succession that was brought to an end only by the interruption of Oosak's whistle. Another boat had been sighted. Chicatommo's wrath was turned from his erring mate, who lay as though dead, to the new and less passive victim. He gave her one final kick and returned to his eyrie. After some irritated fumbling he succeeded in getting the telescope adjusted. The discovery of how miraculously his vision was improved by the novel instrument brought from him a grunt of approval.

The new prospect was a big flatboat. Its passengers numbered six men, four women, and ten or a dozen children, ranging from babes in arms to half-grown boys. Of far more interest were the horses. In the stock pen amidships were ten clean-limbed, long-necked, young riding horses, bred to run. Whoever had planned this cargo had known how to pack the greatest value into the least compass. Such horses were beyond price west of the mountains.

Chicatommo watched with sharpening attention as the flatboat approached the moment of decision. A third of a mile upriver a midstream rock ledge broke the surface. There was nothing about the immediate appearance of the river ahead to indicate that the channel on the one side was more favorable than the other. But if they chose to pass on the right, they would be able to remain comfortably in mid-river, while if they veered to the left they would presently be caught in currents which swept them ever nearer the fatal shore at the base of the bald mountain. The people in the flatboat failed to notice the rock until they were almost upon it. They elected to pass on the left.

"Horses," purred Oosak. "Good horses."

He glided down the slope to assemble his companions. Chicatommo laid aside the telescope and followed. It was his custom to remain in his lookout and there to direct an attack by whistles. But his rage yet burned. This time he took his post in the first canoe.

The tall, bearded man in the red shirt and wide-brimmed hat who was working the flatboat's sweep oar presently realized that there were difficulties ahead. He called out and two other men sprang to help him. But their most frantic threshing of the oar was not enough to swerve the heavy craft out of the current that was gradually tightening its grip. The flatboat, wallowing sluggishly, kept drifting nearer that forest-shrouded shore above which loomed the mountain with the sinister bare gray top that was like a skull. The men ran for their rifles. The women and children lay down behind the plank bulwarks.

The critical nature of the threat became each moment more apparent as did the flatboat people's helplessness to counter it. The course taken by their ungainly craft was swinging them toward another partially submerged but more considerable ledge of rock that slanted out from the shore. Off the tip of this miniature headland a whirlpool seized upon the flatboat, spun it twice around, and lodged it solidly upon the mud bank in the lee of the eddy. The bearded man thrust a boat pole over the side. Beneath a foot of water and another foot of mud there was a hard gravel bottom.

The high-pitched, rising and falling, wailing howl of the war whoop burst upon the sunlit river. It seemed to come from nowhere and yet from everywhere, one second to be a shriek of a single evil spirit and the next the baying of a thousand. The flatboat people stared at each other, unwilling to comprehend the enormity of their situation. From the wooded shore two hundred yards away, an Indian canoe put out, its occupants yelling threats, pounding war drums, brandishing rattles. The sight of flesh-and-blood enemies broke the spell. The men on the flatboat lifted their rifles again. All six fired, though the distance was still too great for careful aiming. Thereupon the main attack burst upon them from the other side. Three other canoes rounded the point and were upon the flatboat before the defenders had had time to reload.

Like all Ohio River travelers, the bearded man's company had listened to accounts of the Indian danger that might await them and to every sort of conflicting advice. They had prepared themselves against the threat by earnest consultations among themselves. But nothing could have prepared them for the actual spectacle presented by this pack of naked, painted, screaming savages suddenly springing among them.

Oosak and several of the older warriors stood on the rail calmly shooting down the men who had most nearly completed reloading. The others, howling like lost souls, lunged with tomahawk and war club at their victims, striking down men, women, and children alike. It was not a conflict but a butchery.

When it was over the victors fell to scalping the slain and to tormenting those not yet expired. They continued to howl, to boast wildly of their triumph, to strike their weapons into the bodies of the fallen, to whirl and dance and caper. They stripped the clothing from the women and draped their own paint-bedaubed and blood-smeared torsos in petticoats, sunbonnets, and aprons. They disembowelled the dead and the dying, festooning the flatboat with the entrails. They hacked off heads and arms and legs. Other members they removed intact and tossed from one to another. They had once more overthrown their immeasurably detested enemy and no gesture was too grotesque or too obscene to celebrate the exploit.

Chicatommo, watching from the roof of the shed which housed hay for the horses, observed all this with occasional grunts of satisfaction. A group of his triumphant followers began to call and beckon to him. There remained, it appeared, another survivor. Lying in a sheltered niche among some sacks of corn was a six-weeks-old baby. The gleeful warriors drew back, watching delightedly as he approached. Chicatommo lacked the vigor to mingle freely in the general turmoil of battle, but out of respect for his inclinations an effort was always made to save some personal physical part for him to play.

Gripping the infant's ankles in his rheumatic fingers, Chicatommo swung the small form in a wide arc and splattered the head against a post of the horse pen. The onlookers yelled with laughter. His predilection for dispatching the very young had become a legend. One of the principles he most often impressed upon his disciples was that the advantage in destroying the enemy's young was to be compared with that in stamping out a litter of mice in a granary before they had lived to grow fat on the corn.

A second climactic moment in the victory celebration followed almost immediately. The bearded man had early been recognized to be the enemy leader. Now it was discovered that there remained a spark of life in his mangled body. A pail of water was poured over him and he was carried to the flatboat cooking fire, which rested on a square of sheet iron propped on bricks to protect the deck planking. The undertaking was an initial success, for after being deposited face down on the coals their victim found the strength to lift his head with his beard ablaze and then to raise himself to his knees. But then there came to him the astounding additional strength to emit a bubbling, inhuman roar of rage and to grasp in his hands the iron hearth upon which the fire rested. Chicatommo sprang forward but even as his ax descended, the dying man had cast the bed of coals through the open door of the shed.

Before Chicatommo's whistle blasts of command had regained control of the resulting confusion, the tongues of flame leaping through the hay had become a conflagration. To the victors remained only such spoils as they could snatch from the burning. Most of their efforts were devoted to forcing the horses over the side into the river. However, when they had won leisure to take stock, they were much consoled by the realization that among the various oddments they had managed to carry off were two kegs of whisky. They withdrew with these to their encampment. The flatboat burned to the water's edge. In late afternoon a passing thunderstorm mercifully quenched the charred embers.

Naiad had got under way again toward noon. Abel maintained his self-appointed position several miles ahead. The thunderstorm cut off his view for a while but at dusk he saw the keelboat drop anchor. It was a sensible anchorage, well off from either shore. Abel kept on, studying either bank in the failing light.

"If we don't hit an island round the next bend," he said, "we'll camp on the north bank. I don't want to get too far away from the keelboat."

"Did you say camp?" demanded Jasper. "Can it be true that our knight-errant can stoop to a need for rest?"

"No harm in grabbing us some when we can. Indians mostly like to lay low at night. The first crack of day—that's the bad time. We'll camp early and get up early so's we can take us a good look around just before sunup."

"Admirable program. We devote to sleep the hours when travel is safe in order that we may rouse to search for danger at a period when danger may most certainly be encountered. And did I hear you mention the possibility of camping on the north bank? Is that one not popularly known as the Indian bank?"

"That's right. Only we must be getting close to the Scioto. That's where their main war road crosses and we're as apt to find 'em on one side as the other. So we'll camp where they're the least apt to look for us."

"So. There is a limit—however indistinct—to your imprudence. But there is none to mine. I have only to reflect that originally it was of my own considered volition that I sought this association with a madman."

They rounded the bend. Jasper squirmed about in the bow to peer ahead. The night had become exceptionally dark and there was a mist rising from the water. Both shores had faded from view. They glided on, in silence and in loneliness, their world reduced to a narrow circle of black river and pale fog and yet prodigiously expanded by the loss of any sense that it possessed a boundary. A sturgeon surfaced alongside with a rippling swirl. Jasper started and gripped the gunwales, muttering. Abel swung the canoe on a slanting course toward the invisible north bank. Suddenly he lifted the paddle and sniffed.

"What is it?" whispered Jasper.

"Smoke—don't you smell it?"

Jasper sniffed. "So I do. However, what I smell seems less like smoke than like—like a burned roast."

Abel recharged his rifle and, withdrawing his tomahawk from his belt, laid it beside the rifle in the bottom within reach. Then, taking up the paddle, he turned the canoe toward the south bank in the direction from which the faint odor seemed to come.

"What invariably compels us to fly in the face of all reason?" protested Jasper. "Whatever the nature of the smoke, it almost certainly indicates the proximity of savages. Must we rush into their arms?"

"Be quiet," said Abel, "so I can listen."

The canoe veered in the tug of a new current. Abel was obliged to switch his paddle to the left side since no longer by a mere twist of the wrist at the end of a stroke could he control its course. The persistent tendency to drift to the left became stronger. At the same time the smell grew more noticeable and had become unmistakably the odor of charred wood and scorched flesh. Both the smell and the current were leading them ever nearer the south bank. Presently their nearness to that shore was established by the shadowy reappearance of its range of wooded hills as a formless mass of deeper gloom that seemed to lean outward toward them over the river. At one point only did that mass take discernible shape. One treeless, rocky knob loomed dimly gray against the sky. Jasper had given over endeavoring to look about him. He squatted on the bottom, his head sunk between his upthrust bony knees. From time to time he drew a long, audibly deep breath, as though his ordinary breathing failed to furnish him sufficient air.

The silence of the river's flow was broken by the slap and wash of waves against some obstruction off to the left. A writhing rim of froth where the water was deflected faintly outlined the edges of a low headland. Abel swung wide of its tip. Suddenly the canoe was seized in the grip of a far stronger current with a rotary movement. It required all his strength to fight clear of it. In the calm water below he turned back. The smell, sickeningly heavy now in the damp air, was behind them. Each dip of his paddle churned up mud. He edged slowly through the shoal water and brought up alongside the charred hulk of the flatboat. One or two timbers along the inner base of the bulwarks, not completely extinguished by the rain, still glowed, casting a ghostly gleam over the blackened interior.

"The miserable, maggoty butchers," Abel whispered. "Must be all of twenty—maybe twenty-five—they got at one haul."

Jasper reluctantly raised his head. After one shuddering look he hid his face between his knees again.

"Lord God of Holy Heaven," he murmured. "And all Negroes, too."

"No," said Abel. "Just white folks burned black." He looked off toward the low promontory. "A genuine trap—that's what they drifted into. Once that current took hold of them, they were bound to get sucked into the whirlpool and dumped on this mud bank. Then there they were—stuck fast and goners."

"Irrefutable reasoning," said Jasper. "The natural spawn of a mentality capable of choosing to bring us here into the very shadow of this dark shore. And now—having inspected the charnel house, and numbered the dead, dabbled in the ashes and gore, satiated every whim of morbid curiosity—but one stroke of genius remains. I marvel that you can rest on your laurels until you have landed and taken a census also of the savages."

Abel glanced appraisingly up at the mountaintop, oddly gray against the darker sky. "That's right," he said. "And that's just what I aim to do. No use coming this far without making sure where and how many they are."

"No, oh no," moaned Jasper. "No. My quip was but the condemned man's poor jest." He was overcome by a wave of nausea and leaned over the side.

"Heave good," counseled Abel. "Make you feel a sight better. Only make no more noise than you have to."

Jasper collapsed, face down, in the bottom. Abel cast loose from the hulk and without dipping his paddle to break the water's smooth surface let the canoe drift some hundreds of yards beyond the mud bank. There he angled in toward the shore and in the shadow of the overhanging trees edged back to a point where they were interspersed with great blocks of rock at the foot of the mountain. He thrust his paddle against the bottom to hold the canoe steady and sat without moving for half an hour while he listened. From nearby there came the intermittent rustles and twitterings and splashes of the riverbank forest's normal night life. But from the far distance there occasionally came other faint sounds. He got out and moored the canoe.

"No matter what you hear or think you hear," he whispered, "don't make a sound or a move till I get back."

Jasper raised his head only long enough to take one look at the dark water and the darker overhanging trees.

"Reality can become too unreal to terrify. Have no further concern for me. I shall pass the time dreaming that I am still snug in my tavern room and that I have not yet sent the wench out to hire you."

Abel climbed upward among the rocks until he had reached the edge of the forest skirting the treeless crest, and there bore to the left. By now the occasional distant sounds had become identifiable as human yells and it had also become more apparent that the faint gray cast upon the rocky knob must be the reflection of a number of fires. Working his way ever more cautiously from tree to tree and rock to rock, he came finally to a ravine down which he could see the Indian encampment.

A first glance accounted for the Indian failure to leave pickets on watch at the riverbank. Tonight their preoccupation was not with their next battle but with their last victory. A full half of them were sprawled on the ground wherever they had chanced to fall. The others were fast drinking themselves into the same state. Wood had been heedlessly piled upon the usually discreet cooking fires until the mounting flames illuminated thee whole adjacent forest. To trees in the background were tied a number of horses, while strewn about the camp were boxes, crates, barrels, heaps of white clothing, and several half-butchered carcasses of cows and pigs. One old Indian, still coldly and disgustedly sober, was stalking among the merrymakers with a cudgel in his hand. Whenever one of the revelers raised his voice in too loud a howl, the old man promptly stretched him out with the club.

When Abel stepped back into the canoe Jasper lay so inertly in the bottom that he leaned forward to feel of him.

"I still live," said Jasper, "though without deep interest in the fact."

Abel struck out for mid-river and, having taken careful note of the point at which the south-shore current no longer exerted its pressure, turned upstream. Jasper sat up and began taking long breaths. Abel tossed the pemmican sack to him.

"Eat something," he said. "Help to settle your stomach."

"The pangs that assail me," said Jasper, "do not include hunger. Do my sufferings, however vicarious, entitle me to inquire what you accomplished?"

"I saw their camp. Must be thirty-five or forty in the pack. By the look of the prisoners and horses and stuff they've taken, this flatboat we saw wasn't the first they'd got their hands on."

"Then you think it not a chance roving band but one which from its position here continues to threaten all comers?"

"That's right."

"And so now we rush back with our tale of derring-do to bask in the fair one's admiring gratitude?"

"What we're going back for is to tell Fortiner to get his boat past that mountain before the night's over."

Ben, keeping his first half of the night's watch, sat astride *Naiad's* prow, dangling a fishline in the river. Fortiner came up the ladder and felt his way along the rail to him.

"Dark night," he remarked.

"Darker'n the devil's pocket," agreed Ben. "And quiet, too. Ain't even a fish a-stirrin'."

"I don't seem to be able to sleep," said Fortiner. "So you might as well. I'll take over the rest of your watch."

"You're the boss," said Ben. "There don't seem ever to come no time when me I can't sleep."

He wound in his line and climbed down the hatch. Fortiner stood with his back against the rail and watched the cabin door. It opened and Philippa, her figure a pale blur in the darkness, appeared in it. Neither moved nor spoke while a long minute passed. Then slowly she moved toward him, a step at a time. When she had reached his side she faced not him but the river, her hands gripping the rail.

"Have you done with your thinking?" he inquired.

She shook her head. "I can't think—anymore."

"But you came out."

"I couldn't help that—either."

"Then look at me."

She released her grip on the rail and turned toward him, her arms hanging at her sides. Deliberately he took hold of her and drew her slowly into his embrace. She submitted, her eyes closed, her face upturned. He began kissing her hair, her eyes, her lips, at first lightly and tenderly, then with an increasing urgency.

The canoe, lifting against the current under the impulse of Abel's long, noiseless strokes, swerved past the idly swinging stern and glided alongside. Immediately above, the lovers, locked in their embrace, were outlined against the sky. Fortiner's kisses had become more demanding as they moved from her face down the curve of her neck and shoulder to the neckline of her dress. She gasped and drew back slightly. Her hands came up to tear open the dress, exposing the white gleam of her bosom. Jasper, standing up in the bow of the canoe to grasp the keelboat's rail, rose like a grotesque jack-in-the-box beside them.

"Your pardon, madam—Mr. Fortiner. I appreciate that we come at a most inauspicious moment. But we are here with even more inauspicious news."

Fortiner raised his head and blinked incredulously at the intruder who had so mysteriously materialized at his very elbow. He pushed Philippa aside and seized Jasper by the throat.

"You skulking peeper. I'll teach you to sneak up on people."

Jasper, helpless in the furious grip, began to gag and choke. Abel, rising beside him, swung his paddle against the side of Fortiner's head. Fortiner staggered and sat down on the deck. Shaking his head to clear it, he dragged a pistol from his belt. He was still dazed, but by using both hands he managed to lift the pistol and, waveringly, to aim it.

"Take that away from him, ma'am," said Abel, " 'less you want me to shoot him."

Philippa interrupted the desperate rearranging of her dress long enough to bend and take the pistol from Fortiner's trembling hands.

"Now call up the rest of your people," said Abel. "They got a right to hear what we've come to tell you."

Philippa steadied herself against the chair back, drew a long breath, and rallied the strength to obey.

"Fred—Ben—Rod," she called down the hatchway. "Come up at once."

She went on into her cabin and reappeared in a moment with a flask of brandy, which she held to Fortiner's lips. He swallowed, murmured gratefully, and accepted her aid in getting to his feet. The men from below scrambled up on deck. Jasper, gulping and loosening his collar, and Abel, balancing his rifle across his forearms, were still standing in the canoe, holding to the rail.

"None of us got time for chitchat," said Abel. "So be quiet and just listen. Four miles downriver there's a pack of forty-fifty Indians nested in the rocks on the south shore. This past week they knocked off anyway four-five boats, maybe more.

Yesterday afternoon just before that thunderstorm they got another and butchered more'n twenty men, women and children they caught on her. Jasper and I found what was left of that boat after they'd burned it and counted the bodies ourselves."

"Abel counted more than the victims," said Jasper. "He sallied ashore, crept up on their encampment, and polled the Indians, too."

"You make very plain," said Fortiner, "how deeply you have placed me in your debt. I beg that you will overlook my hastiness just now."

"There's only one thing for you to do," continued Abel, ignoring the overture and addressing the others as much as Fortiner. "That's to get down this stretch of the river and well on past before daylight tomorrow. I got a good look at the river below here by daylight yesterday. I'll go ahead in the canoe and all you'll have to do is watch me and follow along where I go."

"Can you do that, Fred?"

"We can follow where he goes—long's he remembers we draw as many feet as he does inches—and if'n you figger he knows where he's goin'."

"What do you think, Rodney—Philippa? We're all in this together. To my mind our situation sizes up this way: We've no reason to assume these men are merely trying to alarm us. Before we left Pittsburgh we were told the danger from Indians was greatest along this portion of the river. They come and go and evidently we've been unlucky enough to strike a period when they've come. The question then becomes one of deciding whether to make our run past by day or by night. One advantage in waiting for daylight is the chance that meanwhile enough wind may come up to permit us to beat our way back upriver and wait until we can go through in company with other boats. But if there's no wind we are committed to a daytime passage alone at about a quarter the speed they can make in their canoes. The one thing we cannot do is to wait here after daylight because they'll be certain to discover us—if, as is quite possible, they haven't already."

"It strikes me, Heber, you've summed it up rather well," said Baynton. He spoke as collectedly as though he were stating a mathematical problem.

"Get up the anchor, Fred," said Fortiner. "We're in your hands, Traner."

"Don't worry if sometimes I get too far ahead for you to see me," said Abel. "Every now and then I'll be wanting to take an extra look around. But I'll always be back in time to keep you straight where there's need to watch your course."

He let the canoe drift with the current and backed water until the keelboat, too, began to drift. Fred and Ben manned the two sweep oars. Baynton took the tiller, and Fortiner knelt in the prow where he could watch the piloting canoe and call out steering directions to his crew.

In the canoe Jasper felt around for the pemmican sack and tried a mouthful. The experiment was not a success. He laid aside the pemmican and spat out what remained in his mouth. Pretending to search for something amidships, he leaned nearer, striving in the darkness to read Abel's expression.

"Sit still," commanded Abel, suddenly driving the canoe forward with a series of long, hard strokes.

Jasper sank back in the bow.

"It is not for you to judge her," he said. "You are not her keeper."

"And keep still."

"I cannot. My survival may depend on your vigilance this night. Some peace of mind must be restored to you. Can you not comprehend that her behavior is in no sense a reflection on you? You are to her but a passing stranger. Her decisions relate only to herself, her husband, and her suitor, and not in the most distant fashion to you. You have not been insulted."

"I said keep still."

"But can't you realize that it was only in your untutored imagination that she reigned as the golden princess out of a fairy tale? How can you be so astounded when she is revealed as merely a willful, spirited, and very human woman?"

"I was with her when she saw Fortiner laying into his nigger. Whether or not they're brothers, she thinks they are. And she was 'most close enough for the blood to splash on her."

Jasper groaned. "Always you fly off to the most irrational extremes. She was not drawn from her cabin tonight, as you ignorantly surmise, by any perverse echo of his cruelty. Nothing monstrous was involved—nothing to set her apart from other women. All was as simple as the flow of water toward the sea. After Fortiner was revealed to her as a male so ruthlessly determined upon his own way, she could feel as relieved of responsibility as though he were taking her by force. Her surrender was a perfectly normal and predictable feminine response." A gurgle of water caused Jasper to look around. "Look. You're almost upon that rock."

"I've been watching for it," said Abel.

He swung the canoe around and headed back.

The drifting keelboat took shape in the darkness. Abel put about again and led the way downriver. At the rock he kept to the left. The keelboat followed in his wake. Jasper began to fidget and to peer out over the river.

"Indubitably I should hold my peace," he said. "Reasonable discourse but makes you the more obstinate. But shouldn't you take a turn to the starboard before we get into that south-shore current?"

"We're already in it," said Abel.

He angled the canoe off toward mid-river. *Naiad*, however, could not follow. Fortiner raised his voice in reiterated commands. Baynton pushed the tiller over hard. Fred and Ben threw their full weight into the sweep oars. But the keelboat's burden and draft, so much greater than the canoe's, kept her in the grip of the sinister current.

"How much have I underestimated you," said Jasper. "But does not the punishment too greatly exceed the crime? By delivering, in your righteous wrath, the sinners to the Indians you are condemning also the guiltless Fred and Ben —and Buck—and even the much-sinned-against Spencer. Have you thought of that?"

"No use thinking," said Abel. "Too late now for anybody to think."

He paddled back to the keelboat and brought up alongside.

"You're keeping too far to the left," he advised Fortiner. "There's a bad mudbank up ahead. Swing more to the right."

"Goddammit," said Fortiner. "That's what we've been trying to do."

"Follow me out this way," said Abel.

The canoe bounced away again. The keelboat's prow could be turned to follow but the prevailing sidewise drift continued. Fortiner and Buck ran to join Fred and Ben at the oars. The low promontory loomed on the left. The danger ahead became increasingly apparent. But their every exertion was in vain. The keelboat swung helplessly into the whirlpool, spun end for end, and veered off to ground heavily upon the mudbank.

Fred snatched up a pole and began striking it against the bottom. He cursed, jumped over the side, and waded along the hull in the knee-deep water, kicking against the bottom, and at times even bending to feel with his fingers.

"She's grounded for keeps," he reported.

Philippa pulled at Fortiner's sleeve.

"That frightful smell," she said.

He crossed with her to the other rail. Scarcely a dozen feet off was the hulk of the flatboat. The darkness that cloaked the gruesome cargo seemed to accentuate the miasma of death that arose from it. The canoe cut in alongside. Abel and Jasper climbed aboard. Fortiner swung to confront them.

"How near's that Indian camp you were talking about?"

"About halfway round that mountain—back in the woods maybe three-quarters of a mile."

"Puts us right in their front yard. Well, you got us here. Have any more ideas about how to get us out?"

"You got yourselves on the mudbank. But I might have one or two about how to get you out."

"Let's have them."

"They probably won't jump you before daylight. Indians don't much like to work at night. Maybe then you could stand them off, at least for a while. But you'd still be stuck here and with no hope of help. People coming down this river hang to one rule, and that's to stay as far as they can from trouble."

"Your main idea then is that we haven't got a chance."

"No. You've got one pretty fair one. That's this: Right now, while you're still got three or four hours of dark, get your people into your skiff and get as far away as you can. Just before light pick yourself an island and hide on it for the day. Before the next night's over you'd ought to make Limestone."

"How far is Limestone?" Fortiner asked Fred.

"Fifty-sixty mile."

Fortiner shook his head. "They're probably watching us right now. They could run us down in that skiff before we'd got around the next bend."

"Sure they're watching you right now," said Abel. "But they can't see the skiff this far out. When it's this dark they go by listening more than looking. So if Jasper and me stay on the boat for two-three more hours and make some noise like we were throwing off cargo to lighten her, they'd figure you were all still aboard waiting for them to pick you off come daylight. But come daylight you can be ten-fifteen miles downriver."

Fortiner again shook his head. "I can't go this skiff business. I'd feel better staying behind this good planking and taking my chances at fighting 'em off."

"Maybe you haven't taken a good look yet at the last people that tried that here."

Abel walked to the galley, pulled a smoldering stick from the fire, waved it into a blaze, and tossed the brand into the hulk of the flaboat. The flare of light, in the second it lasted, revealed one fearful glimpse of that array of blackened and dismembered corpses.

71

"Ben and me's takin' the skiff," said Fred. "Any the rest of you what wants to come along is welcome."

"We certainly cannot afford to separate," said Fortiner, even in his yielding managing to retain command. "And if we're going, the sooner we start the better."

"Don't forget to slap plenty of grease on your oarlocks," said Abel.

There was a brief scurrying as all hurried to snatch up what they considered they might presume to take with them. Spencer, stretched face down on his pad below, was still stiff from his wounds and weak from loss of blood. Buck carried him up and laid him in the skiff. Philippa paused at the rail to take a tentative step toward Abel, as though moved by an impulse to say something to him, but Fortiner bundled her up bodily and handed her over the side to Baynton.

"When the time comes for you to cut and run, Traner," said Fortiner, "take your pick of whatever you can carry off. I'll look for you in Kentucky and we'll consider then what else I may owe you."

He swung over the rail and the skiff faded into the shadows. Jasper made a clucking sound indicating a high order of approving amazement and clapped Abel on the shoulder.

"Marvelously maneuvered. Machiavelli himself would do well to sit at your feet."

He darted to the hatchway and slid down the ladder. After a time he returned more slowly.

"His money box is empty. I saw that he did not take it with him, but he must have carried off its contents in belts attached to his person. However, much else of value remains. Tell me what you judge the canoe will hold—without too much reducing our running speed. The silver service first, of course. And there are three of his suits as new as when they came from the tailor. And Baynton's microscope. And her amber-backed toilet set. Come, we haven't a moment to lose. We must be far from this macabre spot before besotted Indians and rosy-figured dawn burst upon us in unison."

Abel was leaning over the side thrusting a pole against the bottom. "No sense packing anything into the canoe. Can't you get it through your head that the whole boat's ours now?"

Jasper felt for a chair and dropped into it. "What new and unsurpassable folly is this? Much in your wilderness remains an enigma to me. But one thing I know. I know ships. And this ship is so solidly aground the united efforts of an entire man o' war's company could scarcely drag her off though assisted by a favoring hurricane. Reassemble your fevered fancies and consider the core of our situation. The day will soon be upon us. And so will the Indians—if they wait so long. How do you propose we deal with that fateful moment?"

"We won't have to because we won't be here. If you were half the sailor you keep saying you are, you'd pay more attention to the weather. Don't you remember how hard it rained the first two days after we left Pittsburgh? By the looks of the side creeks, it rained even harder back in the hills. Enough anyway to make up into a middling flood. We came down faster than the high water so it was always behind us, but then we lost that day and a half at the island. Late this afternoon the rise began to catch up with us. I'm surprised an old hand like Fred didn't notice. Anyway, the river's come up a good foot in the last hour, it's rising faster by the minute, and in another half-hour we'll be afloat and on our way."

Jasper started half out of his chair and fell back into it again. "I am struck speechless. I am transfixed by awe—nay, by reverence. I have had some acquaintance with guile and stratagem in my time and I saw each unfolding stage of your design. Yet I lacked the wit to recognize what I saw." He slid from the chair to the deck and into a thrice-repeated Arabic obeisance. *"Allah illah Allah.* Salaam—master. Thy slave salutes thee." His hand clapping against the deck became a caressing pat. "Ours. We set sail in a bark canoe. Already we stride the quarterdeck of a ship. Who can foresee what future beckons?" He sat back on his heels and began to laugh. "The country boy. The backwoods innocent."

"I didn't take all that advantage of him," said Abel. "They've got as good a chance to get to Kentucky as they ever had—and a sight better one than they had this time yesterday. All I did to 'em was to take away the boat. She's too good for the likes of them."

5

No settlement along the river had a long history, but none had one so short as Limestone's. That spring of the Great Migration the town had been in existence something less than a year. Nevertheless, its people were not impelled to regard their locality as without significance. From prehistoric times the mouth of Limestone Creek had been the river gateway to the heart of Kentucky. The mammoth had left acres of bones to prove the antiquity of the ancient path. The buffalo had taken the same road from the bank of the Ohio to the salt licks and bluegrass of the interior, trampling into the earth a trace many feet deep and in places hundreds of yards wide. Indians for generations had made use of the buffaloes' broad avenue through the forest, and it had been natural for the earliest white hunters and landseekers to resort to it.

During the Revolution the landing place at the river end of the memorable road had emerged from the shadows of folklore and legend to take a place in recorded history. The gateway had become alternately the breach and the sally port through which Indian attack and American counterattack ebbed and flowed. After the war, that preposterously utilitarian contrivance, the flatboat, had burst upon the scene. The number of water-borne movers had doubled and redoubled. For them the mouth of Limestone Creek had become more than ever the gateway to Kentucky, for it was the first landing place west of the baleful Warriors' Path. But, upon landing, they had for years continued to scurry from the disaster-haunted bank of the Ohio into the settled interior. Thus Limestone, as a settlement, had come into existence only in time to be deluged by 1788's unprecedented flood of newcomers. This early in the season two and three boats were arriving each day. Each, upon sighting that little cluster of log huts—the first break in the wilderness for hundreds of miles, with, along the shore, the greater cluster of beached flatboats—veered from mid-river with a sudden furious splashing of boat poles and sweep oars. The gaunt and weary voyagers landed with cries of elation and prayers of thanksgiving. That trampled, refuse-heaped, stump-dotted strand, cluttered with the sprawling camps and tethered stock of earlier arrivals who had not yet moved on inland, represented —at least until they had set foot upon it and straightened to face their actual prospects—the threshold of the promised land.

There came a day when not two or three but six boats were approaching. For the hundredth time that afternoon William Neave climbed up on the deckhouse of his, the seventh, to peer off downriver. His hunger for the reassurance that his destination was in sight had become overpowering. Every hour since leaving Pittsburgh he had expected disaster. His had been an unreasoning apprehension, born of a sense of guilt as irrational as the fear itself. He had struggled in vain to persuade himself that there was no foundation for either. He had committed no sin and he had taken every conceivable precaution to guard his venture against every danger any man could foresee.

It was true that he had brought with him his six motherless children, but his had not been another of those witless family enterprises, scrabbled together by adults no better fitted than their youngest to cope with the mischances of river navigation or Indian attack, of which he had en route witnessed so many examples. His flatboat was better built, narrower, stronger, faster, and manned by a crew of professional boatmen reputed to equal any on the Ohio in skill and experience. His entire design had been more astutely planned than any of these others. The management of his boat was not embarrassed by a menagerie of farm animals. It was farthest from his intention to subject his Western expectations to the notorious uncertainties of frontier farming. His cargo, carefully crated and wrapped against the elements, ran to bars of iron, pigs of lead, bolts of muslin and calico, kegs of nails, boxes of knives, axes, and hatchets—all commodities worth many times more in Kentucky than their value on the sea coast. Other men voyaging down this wild river entertained vague hopes of somehow making their fortunes; he was bearing with him the assurance of his.

The flatboat rounded the bend to reveal another stretch of river with the bordering ranks of forested hills as unbroken as before. Neave jumped down and resumed his restless pacing. At each turn he glanced at one or another of his fellow travelers. The feeling had grown on him that all of them were covertly watching him. Jonas Potter, the head boatman, lounged against the rail by the sweep oar, which was being handled by his two hulking sons, Gideon and Zeb. Samuel Hoopes, his storekeeper, as usual was talking to them. Every day Samuel had kept at them, badgering them with questions about the river, the woods, the Indians, the settlements. He could have taken no greater interest had he been considering becoming an Ohio boatman himself. This was unlikely since Samuel was fifty, nearsighted, frail, stooped from spending most of his life on a countinghouse stool, and had one leg two inches shorter than the other.

Neave wheeled forward again and looked toward his children. The baby was asleep in his basket. The three next older were absorbed in a game connected with squares chalked on the deck. Twelve-year-old Edna and her inseparable companion, ten-year-old John, had their heads together in a corner. Neave cleared his throat irritably. There could be no question that they, at any rate, had been watching him.

His pacing took him past Magda Romer, the German bondmaid whose indenture he had purchased the day of his wife's funeral. She was lifting clothes from a tub and hanging them on a line to dry. Her sober demeanor, her intentness upon her task, the neutral gray of her loosely fitting calico wrapper, and the white sunbonnet that covered her hair and all but covered her face, gave her the serene and detached air of a young nun. She bent over the tub and stretched upward to the clothesline. The movement disrupted this impression of tranquility. The calico, tightening, betrayed the roundness of arm and breast and hip.

A burst of laughter came from the group around the sweep oar. Neave wheeled again and strode back to confront Jonas.

"How far from Limestone would you say we are now?"

Jonas pursed his lips with the apparent intention of spitting on the deck beside Neave's feet. He thought better of it, turned, and let fly over the rail.

"Mebbe eight mile beyond thet next bend there."

"Still think we can make it before dark?"

Jonas spat again.

"Oughter—if'n Gid and Zeb there don't snooze off and run us on a snag."

Gideon and Zeb grinned, but their eyes remained as bright and alert as young foxes'.

"I doubt there's much chance of that," said Neave. It was difficult to be at ease with employees in the West. "Then we'll count on getting in tonight."

He moved forward again. Magda had finished hanging the clothes.

"Bring me a basin of hot water," he directed.

He went into his cabin, which had been boarded off from

76

the larger compartment in which Magda and the children slept. Unlocking his trunk, he took out scissors and razor. Magda appeared in the open doorway, holding the basin of water in her two hands. There was barely room for two in the tiny cabin. He let her wait until he had trimmed off as much of his curling blond beard as he could manage with the scissors.

"Hold the basin here by the mirror," he said.

"Yah, Meinheer," murmured Magda, edging forward.

He leaned past her, placing one hand on her shoulder to steady himself, and closed the door. Magda stood, complacent, immobile, waiting, her eyes downcast. He honed the razor and reached for a cake of soap.

"Higher," he directed.

She lifted the basin nearer his chin. She was regarding him now, her brown eyes black in the shadow of the sunbonnet. He soaped his face and shaved, slowly and with immense care. Finishing, he leaned nearer the mirror to study the results. The basin was in his way.

"Put it down," he said.

She set it on the floor and stood beside him once more. He leaned past her, again placing a hand on her shoulder, to peer at his face in the mirror. He was pleased. He looked around at her. His hand was still on her shoulder. "Big difference, eh?"

"Yah, Meinheer." No longer did she murmur. Her voice was low but firm.

"That damn bonnet," he said. "Do you sleep in it? Let's get it off, along with the beard."

She stood, quiescent, as he undid the strings and jerked off the white sunbonnet. Her coppery-red hair was drawn back tightly into a thick, gleaming bun at the nape of her neck. High cheekbones and the slant of her eyebrows gave a faintly oriental cast to her face. Her glance dropped to her hands clasped before her while he studied her as approvingly as but recently he had studied his own image. Continuing to regard her, he began to knead his right shoulder, as though his sudden move in snatching off the sunbonnet might have given him a twinge. Magda's eyes lifted to the bottle on the shelf below the mirror.

"Leenamunt, no?" she inquired.

Neave's outstretched arm pressed against her as he opened the door. The stretch of river ahead was empty and still bordered on both banks by forest. He closed the door and his hand went back to his shoulder.

"It's bad again, for a fact," he said. "Maybe just for a minute or two."

He took off his coat, tossed it on the bunk, sat down on a stool with his back to her and began unbuttoning his shirt. With the calm alacrity of one undertaking a familiar task, Magda peeled back the shirt, wet her hands with liniment from the bottle, and began to massage his shoulder and the back of his neck. Her movements were brisk and business-like. He winced once or twice and then grunted with satisfaction.

Now that her face was hidden from him it was no longer passive. Her red lips were parted in a half-smile that revealed a flash of her even white teeth and, in as clear a flash, her full awareness of all his subterfuges. The brightness in her eyes sprang not from sympathy but from her knowledge that he was being driven to so many transparent devices. The smile broadened. The massage lost its early vigor. The light touch of her fingertips gliding over his skin became less a ministration than a caress. He leaned back, sighing, and for a second she permitted his head to rest against her bosom.

The door was pushed open. Neave spun around on the stool. Edna and John stood in the doorway. They were clinging together but their eyes were big with excitement, with resolution, and with a sense of the importance of the moment. As she entered Edna's mouth had already been opening to speak, but now only a gasp came out. Both she and John stared at Neave's newly shaven face. They nudged each other violently.

"Edna! John!" Neave controlled his anger. "You know better—much better. Now turn right around, go back out, close the door, and knock."

Edna seemed not to hear. Again she opened her mouth and, after one more premonitory gasp, this time a rush of words came out.

"Johnny and me, we've been talking. For days we've been talking. And Johnny thinks—the same as I do, don't you, Johnny?—that it ain't right for us any more—I mean isn't right for us any more—not to tell you."

"Tell me what?"

Edna rushed on breathlessly. "About Magda. You don't have to worry about us. There ain't nothing—excuse me, I mean there isn't anything—that you have to keep from us. That's what we think—don't we, Johnny?—that we couldn't go on any longer without telling you. What I mean is— Johnny and me—we—we like her, too."

Neave leaped up, again controlled his anger, and dropped back upon his seat of judgment upon the stool. "So that's what you've got twisted around in your remarkable little minds. Well, let me tell you something. You couldn't have gotten yourselves more mixed up. At the moment, for instance, Magda was being kind enough—along with all the rest she has to do taking care of the lot of you—to rub liniment into my lame shoulder. You know that it's been lame since I pulled too hard on the sweep oar last week. And let me tell you something else. You will apologize to Magda this minute for entertaining such preposterous ideas."

Magda had put on the sunbonnet, picked up the basin, and stood, waiting. Edna gave her a quick, amicable smile and looked back at her father.

"Is preposterous the same as wicked?"

"Well, in a way, yes."

"And if you did happen to like Magda, would that be preposterous?"

Neave laughed heartily. "Edna, I'm afraid you've gotten in a little over your head. For a while longer you'd better stick to your dolls. And John, I hate to mention it, but something like this could come from playing house with her so much—when any ordinary boy would be fishing over the rail or shooting at river birds or listening to Jonas' Indian stories."

The children's steady, unblinking stare went back and forth between Magda's expressionless face and their father's grinning one.

"Then why," asked Edna, "did we have to leave home and come way out here where nobody knows us?"

"And what for did you shave off all your whiskers?" contributed John.

Neave continued to laugh. "What imagination. What a talent for whimsey. And above all, what concern for my most delicate sensibilities. I am overwhelmed. I am——"

The flatboat thudded against an obstruction with a staggering lurch.

"Look," cried John, in the doorway. "We're right in the woods."

Neave rushed out. The sun had set and shadows were gathering among the hills. One corner of the raft had lodged on the shelving beach of a wooded mid-river island. The boatmen, instead of endeavoring to push the boat off, were laboring with their poles at the opposite corner to hold it steady against the current. Samuel, sweating with an excitement that gave him a strength he did not ordinarily possess, was thrusting a plank over the rail to the beach. Neave ran to him.

"This can't be Limestone. Why are we landing here?"

Samuel clutched Neave's arm. "Come with me and I'll show you."

Teetering on his shorter leg, he ran down the plank and jumped ashore. Angry but still bewildered, Neave followed. Samuel kept on a few yards along the beach before turning to confront Neave. His eyes glittered feverishly.

"No, this ain't Limestone. Limestone's another fifteen miles."

"But not two hours ago Jonas told me only eight. What's going on? What in heaven's name's the reason for stopping here?"

"One you ain't going to like. We came this far and no farther so Jonas can make the run past Limestone in the dark."

Samuel paused to allow the import of this to strike home.

"But that makes no sort of sense," said Neave irritably. "Limestone's where I'm going."

"Maybe you are, but your boat's going on with Jonas."

Neave stared. What Samuel was apparently attempting to convey was an idea too repellent even to consider. "You're going all to pieces, Samuel. I've been noticing it for days. You'd better try to get a grip on yourself."

"Always trying to side-step. That's Mr. William Neave in a nutshell. Well, you're up against something now you can't. No use trying to pretend you don't know what I'm talking about. That won't make it any easier for you."

"I'll ask you to remember who you're talking to and mind your tongue." Neave began to see the malice which Samuel was making so little effort to conceal and began at last to comprehend. "My storekeeper. The trusted custodian of my goods. The leech who for years has lived off me. With what relish he informs me I am about to be robbed. That is what you're trying to tell me? That is it, isn't it?" He seized upon Samuel. "And you—you miserable, deformed little Judas—you yourself planned it."

"Best let go me. What I'm planning is how to save your neck, and your children's necks." Samuel freed himself from Neave's suddenly nerveless grasp. "That's why I brought you ashore. All you got to do now is call them. Tell them you've got something to show them. Tell them anything. Soon's they're off the boat Jonas he'll shove off."

"Without me?"

"Certainly without you. That's what I'm trying to get through your head. He wants your goods, but he'd as soon get out of cutting all your throats."

Neave considered the dismal option that was being offered him. "I won't do it," he decided. "I can't believe you. No white man's monster enough to murder little children—or their father in front of their eyes."

Samuel's first excitement had passed, but his enjoyment of the moment was mounting.

"If you don't care about them, then maybe you don't about Magda either. Gid and Zeb—they're more bent on getting hold of her than they are your other property."

Neave seized upon Samuel again. "You're lying. You're only trying to demoralize me. I'm going back there and have it out with them."

Again Samuel easily shook him off. "Give it a try if you like—you'll never get past the middle of the plank."

Neave wavered. "Your story doesn't hang together. What makes you think they'll let Magda come with the children?"

"His boys may not want to, but Jonas will. That's another thing he'd as soon get out of—seeing them go at each other with knives, over her!"

Neave drew a long and painful breath. "There's one comfort. Whatever happens to us, they're sure to cut your throat before the night's out."

"I don't think so. No one of them can read or write or add two and two. They need me to help them sell off the stuff downriver."

Neave drew another long breath. "Magda," he called. "Bring the children ashore."

"Yah, Meinheer," replied Magda.

She began to herd the children toward the plank.

"The baby, too," called Neave.

She turned to pick up the baby. Samuel scrambled aboard and stood waiting by the rail. The moment the little procession had reached the beach he pulled in the plank. Only then did Gideon and Zeb realize the significance of what was occurring. They dropped their poles and sprang forward. Jonas freed his pole from the bottom and thrust it across the deck, tripping the both of them. Before they could regain their feet the current's pressure upon the no longer restrained flatboat had wrenched it off the beach and sent it careening on downriver.

John was the first to reach his father. "Papa, Papa. Look. The boat's going off without us."

Neave stared after the receding flatboat. Its outlines were already becoming dim in the twilight, the angry curses of the three Potters dying away in the distance.

"You might as well know—all of you. Samuel told me our only chance was to get ashore—as we did."

"So," said Magda. "All that is yours. All is gone."

"Magda," cried Edna. "Why, you speak English most as good as anybody."

Neave looked at Magda for a second, as startled as Edna,

81

and then, when she met his gaze, as quickly away again. "What could I do? They were going to kill us all. I was one against four. They were armed. I was not."

The baby began to fret. Magda rocked him in her arms. She nodded judicially. "You save your children. That is good."

"And you too."

"Yes," she assented. "And me too."

"Papa," demanded John eagerly, "how long do you think before maybe Indians will find us?"

Neave squared his shoulders. "We won't be here long enough for that. Soon's daylight comes the next boat that passes will pick us up."

"Say something else, Magda," said John. "I mean in English."

"Find leaves," said Magda. She swung the baby astride her hip and illustrated by breaking off a cedar bough with her free hand. "Make beds. Soon it is dark."

Inured though they were to novel experiences during their journey, the children were intrigued by the prospect of sleeping in the open on the beach of a desert island. They rushed to obey. Neave edged nearer, striving in the dusk to read Magda's expression.

"Here," she said, handing him the baby. "I help them."

Watching her practical and energetic supervision of the bed making operation, he was somewhat reassured. She returned with an armful of boughs.

"You are a good girl, Magda," he affirmed.

She took the baby from him. "Tomorrow he must eat."

Night fell. The children, curled up about Magda, eventually ceased their excited whispering. The baby cried but Magda managed at length to quiet him again. Neave paced the beach. Toward morning, exhausted, he sat on the sand and he, too, fell asleep, his head on his knees. It was daylight again when he became aware that Magda stood beside him.

"Look," she said. "A boat."

Neave blinked. There were two boats. To the side of a big, drifting flatboat was moored a long, slim packet boat. Aboard the flatboat were many men and horses and among them a veritable apparition—a great red, blue, and gold coach.

Neave leaped to his feet, tore off his shirt, and began to wave it. The children brandished branches and Magda her sunbonnet. But the flatboat, which had been bearing down on the island, veered off into the middle of the channel between the island and the south shore. Its passage brought it near enough for Neave to distinguish the individual figures of men and horses and, in the clear morning light, the scroll work on the coach. Still no notice was taken of the distress signals. Neave shouted and shouted and the children added their shrill voices to the clamor. The flatboat kept on its course. Presently more than half of the men embarked in the packet boat, cast loose, and rowed rapidly on ahead downriver toward Limestone. The flatboat lumbered on. Both craft faded from view.

"How come they didn't see us, Papa?" demanded John. "How come they didn't see us?"

"There'll be another along soon," said Neave. "Keep watching for it."

Aboard *Naiad* a strange peace had descended. The day before had been spent at anchor in mid-channel. Jasper, formerly so impatient to reach his destination, had, now that they were almost in sight of it, insisted upon the halt. He had devoted the day and most of the night to an earnest effort to alter Fortiner's three best suits so as to make them hang less loosely upon his angular frame.

"Tailoring is an art I have never practiced," he had acknowledged, "though once I was apprentice to a sailmaker."

As he had labored with knife, needle, and thread he had whistled and hummed and from time to time even raised his voice in snatches of song. The sudden and totally unexpected prospect of making an entrance upon the scene in Kentucky dressed to conform to his fondest pretensions had sent his spirits soaring.

At dawn Abel had awakened him to view a spectacle that caused his cup of satisfaction to overflow. Not a quarter of a mile away the flatboat bearing Wilkinson's coach was drifting past.

"The high water upriver," observed Abel, "must have given that raft a real good start."

"The tide of fortune," said Jasper, his eyes feverishly bright. "It may be long in turning but when once it turns it sweeps all before it. And look, the cast is complete."

A swift packet boat came frothing downriver, overhauled the flatboat, and tied up alongside.

"General Wilkinson," pronounced Jasper, "marshaling his retinue for his triumphal return. Now all is in train. We will keep a discreet distance but take care to keep him in sight. It will suit my purpose to perfection if, once he sets foot in Kentucky, I make my appearance within the hour."

"You came up with him back at Pittsburgh," said Abel. "What makes you think Limestone will be different?"

"There he was among strangers. Here in Kentucky he will be strutting among his own people. That, I assure you, will make all the difference in the world."

Abel broiled a wood duck for breakfast, but Jasper was too absorbed in his toilet to take an interest. He was trying on each of the three suits to examine the effect in Philippa's mirror in the cabin. Abel pulled up the anchor and slipped on downriver along the south bank.

"Come out here," called Abel.

Jasper emerged from the cabin, resplendent in dark blue broadcloth and snowy ruffles. The beaver hat, though he had padded the band with an entire copy of the Pittsburgh *Gazette,* was much too large, the coat sleeves missed reaching his wrists by inches, and the silver-buckled shoes were so much too small that he walked stiffly, as though on stilts, but, nevertheless, the general impression was a very considerable improvement upon his former rags.

"There's some people over there on that island," said Abel, "making out like they're in trouble."

"Fortiner's party," suggested Jasper.

"Nope," said Abel. "Some mover family. Can't you see how little some of them are?"

Jasper looked out over the river, gleaming in the early-morning sun, at the distant, waving figures. "Whoever they are, we have no leisure to intervene. We must hold to our course. Every minute may count."

"You don't have to argue with me," said Abel. "Could be Indians pushed them out of the brush to yell for help. That's an old trick of theirs. No sense just the two of us sticking our noses within rifle shot to find out."

Jasper nodded with relieved approval. "At intervals you can seem remarkably rational." He looked downriver again. "What happened to the packet?"

"Ran on ahead. Want to keep it in sight? There's wind enough."

"No. The flatboat's the key to the situation. I shall want to be in a position to catch the general's eye just at the moment the inhabitants are agog over the unloading of his coach. But you might pull up a little closer."

Abel half raised the sail. It bellied out in the following wind. *Naiad* picked up momentum. The gesticulating figures on the island behind became smaller and smaller and then were cut off from view by a bend in the river. Abel dropped the sail again and tacked to keep his new and nearer distance from the flatboat. Repeatedly Jasper took up a position in the bow with the folded arms and portentous frown of a man of destiny about to hazard all, and as often he fell to fidgeting and to striding nervously about the deck.

"We must be 'most to Limestone," said Abel. "Them fine clothes you set so much store on—they ain't just what you need to make the last mile or two through the brush."

Jasper snorted. "I have no intention of landing in the brush. The time for stealth has passed."

Abel digested this. "I don't know what you're after and I don't crave to. All I bargained to do was to get you to Limestone. But there's one thing you have to count on. If Fortiner kept a-rowing for two nights—he'll be there when we get there."

"What difference? How often must I remind you that we are not pirates? This ship is ours—yours, to be precise. Aside from the law of the sea, at which you choose to scoff but which will hold in any court, he, in the presence of witnesses, made over to you, in return for distinct and extraordinary services which you were rendering him, all title to the property he was abandoning. Therefore, why should you be alarmed by the prospect of Fortiner in Limestone? Unless it is because of the woman. Could it be seeing her again that you dread?"

"No use your keeping at me about her. No, what I mean is all the fuss Fortiner's going to make when he sees that when we got away we got away with his boat too. He's going to holler and stamp and point and do whatever he can to set folks against us. But if everybody taking that much notice of us doesn't worry you any, it surely doesn't me. I've got the boat, but I don't aim to hide so's I can keep it. I'd figured—after dropping you off—on sailing right on in to Limestone, asking about Fortiner, and telling my side the story to whoever wanted to listen."

"Excellent. Again your native perspicacity comes to the surface. By far the more politic program. But I, for my part, have henceforth no more to hide than you. So—we will hope to find Fortiner there and presume he will still have his money belt. The most likely upshot will be an eventual offer from him for your ship."

"I don't aim to sell."

Jasper ceased his restless prowling. "For one so intelligent in some respects, you are remarkably dense in others. Why this studied scorn of money?"

"I wouldn't object to getting me some. Only I can't work up the worry about it you can. It's all you ever talk about. And always big money—prize money—insurance money—salvage money—a potful at one grab. But I notice that until

85

you put on that coat of Fortiner's you were still out at the elbows."

"It is true that I have been always the gambler. But the gambler for great stakes. The man who seeks little gains little. Such hand-to-mouth plodding is not for me." Jasper resumed his pacing, then came to another stand. "Since you apparently have no design of your own in mind—other than this childish pleasure in this new toy you have acquired—perhaps you would consent to stand by for the moment after our arrival at Limestone. I cannot enlighten you upon the precise nature of my venture. Yours is a face and nature which much too openly advertises your opinions and intentions. So, though you will share in the returns, you must trust me to take sole charge of our expectations."

"Then you've got them by the tail right now. Because here we are."

Jasper turned to discover that *Naiad* had rounded a point and the waterfront of Limestone lay before him. The packet was already at anchor. Wilkinson himself was standing at the rail watching while the flatboat upon which the glittering coach was mounted was being poled toward the beach.

"Anchor a cable's length below the packet," Jasper directed. "Be ready—as soon as he lands—to take me to the beach in the canoe. Then come back aboard and keep a sharp watch. Permit no visitors. Remember that, whatever the law, possession is nine points of it." He looked shoreward again. "But drift in slowly and unobtrusively. We have abundant time. The general, like the experienced pitchman he is, will wait for the novelty of the coach to draw him a crowd."

If so, no long wait was required. In the camps along the shore movers straightened up around their cooking fires, took one look, and began to run to the water's edge. In the town gates were flung open, heads popped out, neighbor called to neighbor, people running toward shore intermittently jumped up on stumps the better to see ahead. The first to reach the river ran waist deep into the water to help pull the flatboat up on the beach. The name of Wilkinson was mentioned, repeated in widening circles, and became a shout as the more observant pointed him out being rowed in from the packet. In five minutes the waterfront was crowded. In ten, movers were streaming in from the most distant camps along the road to Kenton's Station.

Among the last of the residents of Limestone proper to arrive was young Evan Branch, his buckskins dripping from having spent the night spearing sturgeon by rushlight. His uncle, Dorsey Jessop, pushed out of the crowd to confront him disapprovingly.

"Git along to the mill and git on some decent clothes," Jessop commanded. "General Wilkinson's come back and if'n he should happen to shake hands with you there's call for you to look fitten."

Jasper landed on Wilkinson's heels and waited on the outskirts of the milling assembly while the coach was being rolled from the boat to the soil of Kentucky. The inhabitants of Limestone stared, goggle-eyed, at the gilded coach, at the retinue of liveried blacks, at the matched horses, and, most of all, at the commanding and distinguished figure cut by the general. They basked in the warmth of the great man's friendliness. He was not one to be disconcerted by adulation. While Jasper elbowed his way steadily nearer, the general shook every hand he could reach and then climbed to the driver's seat of the coach where he could address and be seen by the entire gathering.

"I have returned from a journey of many months and many thousands of miles," he said. "The knowledge that I spoke not only for myself but for all the people of Kentucky gave me strength to cope with so great a task. I have concluded protracted negotiations in New Orleans and in Havana. I have been closeted with Spanish governors, including the highest representatives of the Spanish King in the New World. And I have brought back with me tremendous news for my fellow Kentuckians—my true friends—as I am yours. No longer is Kentucky doomed inexorably to poverty because she is denied a market for her produce. No longer are we bound hand and foot by the malice of Eastern bankers and politicians. The mountains over which we struggled to enter upon this fair land of ours no longer constitute a barricade against our trade. There at our feet rolls a mighty river. It will henceforth sweep our cargoes effortlessly to the sea. There, at New Orleans, there now waits a market for our corn and tobacco—a Spanish market—a world market."

His listeners yelled, shook hands, pummeled one another. All realized that there could be no greater news than that the Spanish trade barrier at the mouth of the Mississippi had been lifted. It was like a magic wand which by the merest tap had in an instant doubled the value of every acre of land in Kentucky. Jasper worked his way nearer the step of the coach that Wilkinson must use when he descended.

"Yours is a new community," continued Wilkinson, "risen upon ground wet with your blood. Until now it has been but a wilderness haven for the distressed immigrant fleeing from the savages. But those days are ended. The time is upon you, my friends, when Limestone will take its place as a harbor for the world's commerce, a sister port to Philadelphia, Baltimore, New York, or Boston."

Again his listeners yelled. This was the happiest allusion yet. Jasper, wedged in the crowd beside the front wheel of the coach, led the applause. Wilkinson's glance passed over him.

"My task is only begun and I must get on with it," the general concluded. "I will keep you advised—you may rely upon that." He jumped down on the side of the coach opposite Jasper.

Jessop pushed out of the crowd again to inspect the returning Evan. The young man's fresh red cheeks and dancing black eyes were brighter than ever as a consequence of his dash to and from the mill. He was now most presentably clad in yellow breeches, green brass-buttoned coat, wine-colored waistcoat, white neckcloth, and wide-brimmed felt hat. But over his shoulder was still slung the strap supporting powder horn and bullet pouch and he was still carrying his rifle.

"You got some idee this is a militia muster?" protested his uncle.

"I haven't had a chance to tell you yet," explained Evan eagerly. "Corse Price only told me last night. The next time Kenton's boys go out after Indians, Simon's going to let me go along. And it's a rule when you're one of them that you always keep your rifle right by you—no matter where you're at or what you're doing."

Jessop's remonstrances broke off suddenly. Wilkinson was at his elbow.

"Dorsey, I'm delighted to see you," declared the general. "Nothing like meeting old friends to make a man feel he's home again." The miller shot a quick look around to note how many of his fellow citizens were observing the special cordiality with which the hero was greeting him. Wilkinson seized Evan's hand. "I'm happy to meet the son of my dear old friend."

"Not my son," put in Jessop. "My nephew, Evan Branch. You know my brother-in-law, Pete Branch, that keeps the store at Louisville? Evan's his boy. Pete sent him up here to buy movers' flatboats to break up for lumber. They need lumber down in Louisville."

"You cannot get into business too young these days," said Wilkinson. "All undertakings are due to thrive." He shook Evan's hand a second time, even more cordially than the first, turned, beaming graciously, and permitted himself again to be engulfed in the tide of his admirers. Evan started to follow, but his uncle grasped his arm peremptorily.

"Now set your mind on what I'm telling you," he said.

"D'ye see that tall galoot in the blue coat and the beaver hat —over there by the chariot? I want to talk to him, but strictly on the quiet. So you sidle over by him—without nobody taking notice—and tell him to meet you—let's see—tell him to meet you over at the lumberyard. Once you get him out of sight over there, keep him there, if you have to hang on to his coattails, until I can get there."

Evan nodded, intrigued by the note of mystery. But as he circled the crowd, looking for an opening through which to work his way toward Jasper, his roving glance hit upon something that intrigued him more. On the other side of Limestone Creek a file of leather-shirted riflemen was trotting along the trail from Kenton's Station and heading for the canoe landing at the farther end of the beach. Corse Price had left the column and was running toward him across the log that served as a foot bridge. Evan understood and ran to meet him. His first summons to join Kenton's Boys on one of their forays was upon him. Corse swung around and they fell in step, loping along side by side.

"Where at's the Indians?" asked Evan.

"Dunno," said Corse. "Luke Perkins he took off to hunt this morning and from the top o' Cherry Hill he seen some folks waving shirts on the beach the far end of Three Islands."

Evans ran back and seized upon the nearest bystander in the outskirts of the crowd.

"You see that beaver hat sticking up over there?" panted Evan. "Tell the man under it that Dorsey Jessop wants to see him."

Relieved to have discharged his responsibility, Evan settled down to running hard until he had overtaken first Corse and then the company.

Abel, watching from *Naiad's* rail all that transpired ashore, saw the two big canoes filled with riflemen putting off upriver. The crowd around the coach was opening up to make room for the horses that were being hitched to it. It was easy to keep track of Jasper. The beaver hat stuck up out of the crowd like a monument. His movements so far had been few and made without haste. He seemed always to be at the edge of those swirls of special activity which marked the presence of the general. But now he was making a more definite move. He had come out of the crowd, had strode down to the beach, and was beckoning. Abel dropped into the canoe and paddled ashore. As he stepped out he could see that nothing so far had happened to reduce Jasper's glow of satisfaction and importance.

"Seen him already?"

"Not yet. But all goes exactly as I had anticipated. He paled at first sight of me. And already I have had indirect word from a go-between. Control of the situation is now in my hands."

Abel nodded toward the coach, which was starting to move. "Looks to me like he's pulling out."

"Only as far as the mill, so have no concern. The miller is spreading a collation for the general's refreshment—and to offer the principal citizens of the community an opportunity to boast that they have sat at the same table with him. I am about to join that select company, but first I wished to put your mind at rest on two scores. First: Fortiner is not yet here and there has been no report of him from any of the other travelers who arrived yesterday or today. Second: Do not be disturbed if I fail to return immediately. It is more than possible that I shall be invited to accompany the general to Lexington in his coach. So compose yourself aboard *Naiad* until you have further word from me, which I will dispatch to you at the earliest."

The crowd followed the coach to the gate of the stockade that enclosed the mill. The equipage was halted outside while the luncheon party took places about a plank table set up in the mill yard, where Jessop's two blacks rushed back and forth importantly, serving platters of cold ham, corned buffalo hump, pickled trout, cold boiled eggs, and wheat bread, accompanied by tumblers of Kentucky whisky. The uninvited majority of townspeople and movers surged back and forth with unabated interest, preyed upon by an alternating impulse to reinspect the coach and to peer through the open gateway to observe what the thrifty Jessop was offering his guests to eat and drink.

Jasper, moving with unhurried dignity, edged his way through the press until he stood in the front rank of those in the gateway. Here he paused, waiting for the general to catch sight of him. The miller jumped up from his place beside the guest of honor and came forward to receive him.

"My name's Jessop, Dorsey Jessop."

"Jasper Hedges, at your service," said Jasper, bowing.

Jessop took his arm, deferentially but firmly, and led him not toward the table but along the inner wall of the stockade past the corner of the mill.

"I must first have a word with you in private," explained Jessop.

"I can well understand that," murmured Jasper.

Jessop opened a door and politely indicated that Jasper should precede him within.

"I'll be with you in a minute."

"Thank you," said Jasper.

Jessop went out, closing the door behind him. Jasper looked about him with his usual quick curiosity. The room was small, windowless except for loopholes, and appeared to be a combination storeroom and office. There was a home-made desk and stool in one corner. Against the back wall was ranged a pile of sacks filled with some material less angular than corncobs but more knobby than grain. Opposite the desk was a cot and over it several articles of men's clothing on pegs. Above there was a half-loft, which seemed to be unused except as a platform for riflemen when needed to man the upper bank of loopholes. He moved closer to inspect the sacks. One of them was untied. He fingered one of the roots that it contained.

"Ginseng," he marveled. "Nearly a ton of ginseng."

There was a creak in the loft. He turned to become aware of a huge figure dropping catlike to the floor. He sprang back, fell over the outer rank of sacks and backward upon the pile. The shadowy figure was upon him, one outstretched hand closing about his throat. He drew in his breath to scream. A thumb sank deep into his windpipe.

"Best keep real quiet," said Todd Barklit.

Jasper nodded his understanding. Barklit jerked him to his feet.

"You're making a frightful mistake," said Jasper.

"Maybe I'm the best judge of that," said Barklit.

Barklit ripped off Jasper's neckcloth and began to force it into his mouth. This threat that his power of speech was about to be shut off stirred Jasper to a sudden wild resistance. Barklit sank a great fist into his middle.

"Stand still," he ordered.

Jasper was unable to obey. He collapsed, gasping, to the floor. Barklit knelt over him, completed knotting the gag behind his head, drew a pair of rawhide thongs from his pocket, and tied his hands and feet. Rolling Jasper over on his face, he went to the door and beckoned. Jessop returned.

"Just wanted you to see," said Barklit, "that I didn't mess up your place none. Not a scratch on him."

Jessop looked dubiously at Jasper's trussed figure. "You know, Todd, how much I want to help," he said. "All I mean is that I keep thinking I'll be a sight more use to you if my place don't get a bad name."

"Don't fret about that another minute," said Barklit. "Come night, I'll bring my boys in by the back way over your flume. After we've lugged him down to the beach and across the river, nobody'll ever know what happened to him or that he ever was in your place." He opened the door and paused to

91

glance back at Jasper. "Make sure the weasel don't wiggle loose or spit out that gag. While I'm gone you better look in at him every now and then."

Barklit went out. Jessop came over and made a painstaking examination of Jasper's bonds. His state of mind was obvious. He felt no compunction over Jasper's fate but a very great concern lest his fellow Kentuckians learn of the use a notorious English agent was making of his premises. He straightened, listened for a moment to the sounds from the table in the yard and the crowd at the gate, and braced himself. Taking a wrought-iron key from a peg beside the door, he went out and turned the key in the lock.

From the mill yard came the continued murmur of speeches, punctuated by bursts of applause. Jasper at length ceased his frantic attempts to loosen either the gag or the rawhide thongs. After rubbing his chin, his ankles, and his wrists raw, he had been forced to the conclusion that Barklit's knots were hopelessly effective. Now he embarked upon a new and extravagantly complex project. The one movement, with his ankles bound and his wrists tied together behind him, that was simple for him to make was to roll over on the floor. He rolled over to the desk. By leaning against the wall he got to his knees and then with a final lurch to his feet. Able now to lean over the desk he nosed the ink horn over the edge. It fell to the floor where it became the center of a spreading pool of ink. He dropped back to his knees beside the pool. One starched fold of the neckcloth Barklit had forced into his mouth stuck outward like an artificial projection of his nose. He bent over the pool and dipped this in the ink. Hitching over to an unstained portion of the puncheon floor, he lowered his head and began with this make-do brush to draw a design upon the planking. Pivoting on his knees to replenish his ink supply, he persisted laboriously in the slow extention of the design. Gradually a series of numerals and letters, each nearly a foot high, took shape. The design became a legend, which read:

7.00 @ #

While working on the "#" he had heard the sounds of Wilkinson's leave-taking and had made excessive haste with the last cross line, expecting the miller's momentary return.

The key rattled in the lock and Jessop came in. No longer was he ill at ease. His nervousness had been largely relieved by the departure of Wilkinson, the other guests, and the crowd about his gate. He swore with normal ill temper when he saw the spilled ink and jerked Jasper about while inspecting his bonds. Jasper endeavored by way of nodding his head and contorting his features to direct Jessop's attention to the message on the floor.

"What ails you?" said Jessop. "Couldn't be having a fit, could you?"

Jasper sat up, inclined his head violently toward his message, and then, leaning the other way, bounced his head against the sacks. All was in vain. Jessop was momentarily puzzled but his curiosity was brief. Once his impatient glance returned for a second to the arrangement of ink daubs, but though at this instant Jasper began making eager moans behind his gag, Jessop failed to attribute significance either to Jasper's works, his gestures, or his groans. He swore again over the spilled ink, gave his prisoner a parting kick, and withdrew. Jasper groaned in earnest, struggled to his knees, and resumed his laborious writing. To the array of earlier characters he began adding the letters to compose the word "ginseng."

Jessop locked the door and started for the kitchen, bent on locking up the remnants of food from the recent repast before his Negroes had hidden too large a portion for their own later use. He stopped in mid-stride at sight of the strange procession coming through his gate. Evan was at its head, carrying a baby, and trailing after him were six children, ranging from a grown girl to a four-year-old boy.

At sight of his uncle, Evan ran forward, became conscious of the baby in his arms, and turned back to the girl. She took the baby from him. During the exchange their attention was so much more upon each other that they all but dropped it. Jessop's sharp glance took in the girl. Her sunbonnet dangled by its strings from one elbow instead of resting decently on her head and her long reddish hair, very bright in the sun, flowed down her back. The top of her dress had been turned under, exposing a considerable expanse of her bosom and shoulders. By the way the two of them were looking at each other, it was clear that she was as taken by Evan's fine clothes as he by her red hair and white skin. Evan turned to his uncle.

"This," he said, "is Magda."

Jessop grunted. From Evan there burst more explanation. "They're the Neave family. That is—all but Neave himself. He's still back at Jim Mackay's store telling people what happened. We found them on the beach up at Three Islands. First we thought it was Indians but it was the boatmen they'd hired at Pittsburgh. They dumped them on the island and made off with everything they owned."

Evan was flushed and breathless. Jessop looked stonily at

the brood of children and at the girl and back at his nephew.

" 'Pears like just once you might by accident show just one sign of ordinary common sense," he said.

"I'm sorry I didn't have time to take the man in the beaver hat over to the lumberyard," said Evan. "But the boys came along and I had to take off with them right then or they might never have taken me again. I hope it didn't upset you too much. I did send word to the man you wanted to see him." He returned to his principal and more congenial theme. "These people have lost everything but what they've got on their backs. They know nobody here and got no idea which way to turn. So I figured we might take 'em in 'til they had a chance to look around."

The children had swarmed about Evan and Jessop, peering up into the faces of the two men with the observant and penetrating curiosity of childhood.

Jessop surveyed the group, blinking as though he still could not believe his own eyesight. "If you wasn't my own sister's son I'd say it was born in you to be the town natural." He choked back his exasperation and resorted to a simple, flat statement. "We ain't got room for 'em."

"Sure we have," protested Evan. "To begin with, there's the storeroom where I sleep. Plenty of room for Magda and the children in there. Neave and I can bunk in the granary. Look, I'll show you." He pushed past Jessop and grasped the iron latch bar. "Magda, here's the place I was telling you about. . . . Why, it's locked." He looked at Jessop.

"And it's going to stay that way."

"Why? It's never been locked before."

"Get away from that door."

"What for? What's in there?" He laid his ear against the door. "Sounds like something thumping around."

Jessop seized Evan's arm and pulled him away, though his manner had suddenly become much less intransigent. "If I have to account for everything I do around my own place, then I have to," he said, managing a chuckle. "I'll tell you why I had to lock it. General Wilkinson left a part of his luggage in there."

"Oh," said Evan. He grinned reassuringly at the children and a trifle less confidently at Magda. "But never mind. There's a slather of other room."

The children's earlier interest in Evan had been entirely transferred to Jessop.

"Is he really your uncle?" asked Edna. "He don't look— I mean, he doesn't look—much like you, does he, Johnny?"

John had his own question. "Why don't he want us to stay here?"

Evan forced a cheerful laugh. "Uncle Dorsey's a great one to bark, but he won't bite you. He likes to make out he's real mean, but after he's done with his growling he'll make you welcome. Won't you, Uncle Dorsey?"

Evan having been maneuvered away from the storeroom door, Jessop's face was once more like granite. "I will not. Eight mouths to feed. No telling when we'd get them off our hands. Makes no kind of sense."

Evan forced one more laugh. "See. That's what I meant. But it's too late to back out now, Uncle Dorsey—after all the big talk I've fetched them. And I've given this more thought than you guess. I've worked it all out. For example, Edna and John there are big enough to help. And Magda can cook for us, can't you, Magda? Lord knows we need a cook. Your niggers are the worst in Kentucky."

"Take 'em away," said Jessop.

Evan ceased to smile and his attitude became suddenly as hard as his uncle's. "I'll pay their board, if that's the way you want it."

Neave had come through the gateway unnoticed. He spoke up coldly.

"We have no need for charity—least of all when it is grudging." He bowed with formal politeness to Evan. "I appreciate your good intentions, Mr. Branch, but please give the matter no further thought." He gathered the children about him, though he watched Magda as he addressed them. "You remember the Stalniker and Pendergast families who camped next to us in Pittsburgh? They're here and on their way to Lexington. They've asked us to join their party."

Evan gave a start. "When will you be leaving?"

"In the morning. Come, children, they've a place for us in their camp."

Magda and Evan exchanged a sudden searching look.

"For how much longer is Magda bound to you?" Evan demanded of Neave.

"I fail to see how that might concern you. Come, children. Come, Magda."

Edna, however, fascinated by the situation, was loath to see the mounting drama come to a premature end. "Until May third of next year," she informed Evan. "Papa gave Magda's stepfather a hundred and fifty dollars—didn't he, Johnny?—last May third—that was the day of Mama's funeral—remember, Johnny? to pay for Magda's working for us for two years."

"Edna, will you please be silent," said Neave.

"No use, Papa. Didn't you notice? He and Magda had their heads together in the canoe, and back at that blacksmith's shop—and then when you were in that store, they walked clear over to that lumberyard."

"Magda, have you been talking this over with him?" Neave asked accusingly.

"Makes no difference what Magda and I have been saying to each other," said Evan. "What you'd better be listening to is what I'm saying to you now. You're in a fix. If you don't get hold of some money real quick, the question won't be how long you're going to be able to hang on to Magda but how soon you're going to have to bond out Edna and Johnny there."

"Magda," said Neave. "Look at me. You've known perfectly well what I've had in mind. And I tell you nothing that's happened can change my plans."

"But, Papa," said Edna, "if you're not rich any longer, doesn't that change anything?"

Magda and Evan exchanged another look.

"Mr. Neave," said Evan. "I'll give you a hundred dollars for her papers."

"As young and as ignorant and as uncouth as you are," said Neave, "does it not still occur to you that a proposal to purchase another man's betrothed is something of an insult?" He drew himself up with the air of a Roman senator gathering his toga about him. The gesture was robbed of full effect, however, by one of Magda's. At that moment she placed the baby in his arms. His voice rose sharply. "I tell you I will not sell. Not at any figure. Not now. Not ever."

"No call to fly off the handle, mister," said Jessop. He looked at Evan. "Along with all this tall talk about buying you strange gals—you got some idea what you're going to use for money?"

"Yes. My own. It may be in your strongbox, but it belongs to me. My father sent it for me to use."

"He sent it for you to use to buy lumber for him. You keep forgetting the business he sent you here to mind. And these folks might as well know now you'll get never a penny of it to use for anything else."

"It's mine, I tell you. It's not for you to decide what I do with it."

"But I am deciding. And your father will thank me for it."

"Spare your family squabbling," said Neave. "You're beating empty air. I have already informed you that I will not sell—under any circumstances."

Evan, wheeling back to confront Neave, discovered Magda's contemplative gaze fixed upon him.

"You have no money," she said.

"But I have," he insisted. "Or will have soon as I can get word to my father in Louisville."

Magda shook her head regretfully. "You have try very hard."

She gave Evan a parting smile and took the baby from Neave.

"Come, children," said Neave, fastening a spasmodic grasp on Magda's arm.

The procession moved out the gate, Edna and John hanging back and looking over their shoulders at Evan in the lingering hope that there might even yet be some additional development. Evan kept wheeling toward Jessop and then back to look after Magda. Finally he ran several steps toward the gate, came to a stop, and ran back to confront his uncle.

"You made me look mighty bad," he said and began to wag a most disrespectful finger an inch from the end of Jessop's nose. "Now I'll give you something to think about. When you write to my father to try to explain to him why you took my money—and why you can't pay back that other five hundred dollars he loaned you last fall—and why you're obliged to ask him for more—you can tell him in the same letter how you the same as ran me off your place."

Jessop endured his nephew's fury with righteous calm. "I ain't done nothing that ain't for your own good, as your father'll be the first to agree."

Evan gave the finger one more emphatic wag. "I'll be doing you the same kind of good the first chance that comes along."

He stalked out the gate. From the storeroom came the sound of muffled thumping. Jasper, having worked himself upright against the door, was thudding upon it with his knees. Jessop unlocked the door, gave Jasper a shove that toppled him to the floor, and fell to kicking him. Jasper, rolling away from the kicks, contrived to lure his oppressor to a point directly over the design on the floor. The word "ginseng" caught Jessop's eye. He stared at the black scrawl of letters and numerals, at the pile of sacks against the back wall, and at Jasper. Jasper began vigorously to nod his head.

"Sure you mean seven a pound," scoffed Jessop, "not seven hundred?"

Jasper continued to nod more violently than ever.

"Wherever'd you git the idea I might be any such fool?" Jessop demanded, extending a toe toward the inscription and then driving it once more into Jasper's ribs.

Jasper could only continue to nod in the hope of thus sufficiently indicating his earnestness.

"Been nobody in Kentucky last year nor this able to get more'n a shilling a pound for it," said Jessop, "and costs half that to pack it out."

Jasper began as violently to shake his head to establish his complete disagreement with this view. Jessop grunted in new scorn, turned to go, and paused with his hand on the latch. His eyes went back to the diagram on the floor.

"Made yourself a sight of trouble getting that set down. Whatever for?"

Jasper's disgusted shrug conveyed the unmistakable impression that by now he realized that it had been a hopeless effort in the face of a stupidity so monumental.

"You meant seven dollars? And meant me to take stock in the figure?"

Jasper not only nodded but beat his heels on the floor. Jessop took a scowling turn about the room. He looked again at the seven, at the sacks, and at Jasper. Jasper began to moan eagerly behind his gag. Jessop swore and bent over him.

"Better for you if you got something real plain to say," he warned.

He untied the gag. But Jasper's lips and tongue were so numbed that he could not speak.

"Water," he whispered.

When Jessop returned with water he also carried a club, which he waggled threateningly. He trickled water from the mug into Jasper's mouth.

"Now," he said, "best come right to the point."

"I'm a merchant," croaked Jasper. "I am but recently returned from a trading venture upon the China coast. There, as you know, is the only market in the world for ginseng. And there I learned that they value the root only when it has been treated, shortly after digging, according to a special secret process. So treated, it is to them worth its weight in gold. Otherwise it has no value—not even the shilling our ignorant traders pay for it."

Jessop considered this statement. "I have heard tell before there's some such trick to it," he admitted. His eyes were beginning to gleam. "But I never come across nobody that had ever heard of nobody that knew what the trick was. So you claim you know?"

"I do know."

"Then the one chance you got is to tell me quick—between now and dark."

"Mr. Jessop. You surprise me. Obviously my one chance is lost if I tell you between now and Mr. Barklit's return."

"For you there ain't going to be no other time."

"In that case the secret dies with me."

"That'll be too bad—and worst of all for you." Jessop rose to his feet.

"Pause to reflect, Mr. Jessop. In your unschooled hands the material in those sacks has a value not greatly in excess of so much of your flour—while in association with me, it can represent a fortune. Have you no need for money, Mr. Jessop?"

Jessop swore and began once more to pace about the room. Jasper's eyes followed him.

"There is an element of chance involved—that I must admit. On the one hand, I may be an imposter spinning a far-fetched tale to save his neck. But on the other there towers a potential profit of five or six thousand—not five or six hundred—but five or six thousand dollars."

Jessop sank down on the stool, rubbed his sweating palms upon his knees, and glowered at Jasper.

"We're in a real bind," he said. "You don't dast tell 'til I let you go and I don't dast let you go."

"That phase of our problem is easily solved, Mr. Jessop. I have a keelboat lying off the waterfront. We need only to load the ginseng aboard and sail together to Louisville. There, where I will be safe and you will have the cargo still in your personal custody, we can make such further arrangements as seem of mutual benefit."

Jessop started up from his stool and sank back with a groan. "That ain't a way out. Somehow I got to make Todd believe you got away, and I got to stay here to do that."

"You can scarcely fear Barklit's following you to Louisville. Even in Limestone he must skulk in the shadows."

"He don't have to follow me anywhere to make me all the trouble there is."

Jasper squirmed.

"Surely you must have friends or associates you could trust to accompany the shipment and guard your interests in Louisville?"

Again Jessop started up. This time he ran to the door and began bellowing to his Negroes.

"Shem, you get yourself down to the movers' camps. Find Mr. Evan and get him back here right now. If he don't want to come, tell him I've changed my mind about what he wanted to buy. Dan, hitch the oxen to the stone boat and get it over here."

By the time Evan arrived, most of the sacks were already loaded on the sledge. Jasper was limping about, rubbing his wrists and ankles and stretching his mouth into odd shapes, as he sought to ease muscles cramped during the hours he had been bound and gagged. Jessop, at his desk, was folding and sealing a letter. Evan paused in the doorway.

"It's too late now for anybody to change his mind," he said.

Jessop swung around.

"Forget all that. This is something a sight more important. Meet Jasper Hedges. I have commissioned him to sell my ginseng for me. This letter to your father will tell him all about it. You will go along with the cargo to make sure it reaches him safely, and the letter will tell him how to handle the business after that. You're starting the minute the stuff is loaded in the keelboat that is waiting now to take it."

Across Evan's somber face crept a slow smile. "Could this be a favor you're asking me? If it is—the answer's easy. I won't do it."

"It's no more favor to me than to your father and you."

"Keep on asking. It pleasures me every time I say no to you."

Jessop clawed the air to gain enough to give voice to his fury. "Goddamme if you don't want the wit to carry guts to a bear. Here's a chance to pay off your father and make him some more besides. There's a wad of money for all of us and even some for you. And all you can think of is nosing around after that little mover slut you never had sight of before this morning."

"And I don't aim to lose sight of her ever again," said Evan.

Jessop tore open the waistband of his trousers and began digging at his money belt. "Then here—take your money and go buy her and get that off your mind."

"It's no use. He won't sell. He wants to marry her. The best that's left for me is to follow along and to try to keep her from it as long as I can." Evan spoke so quietly that his words carried conviction.

"If her master don't shoot you—and the girl give you pox and your father disown you and God forget you—then I myself will . . ." Jessop again ran apoplectically out of breath.

"Pardon me, gentlemen," said Jasper. "May I offer a small suggestion? We might get both birds with our one stone. I gather, young man, that the damsel looks upon you with some favor. Could you not persuade her to stand ready at nightfall to accompany you aboard the keelboat? Then when we sail for Louisville the cargo would include items of great value to all of us. Even in the eyes of the law it need not be regarded as the theft of an indentured servant. Your uncle, remaining here, will be offering to pay over the purchase price, and the obdurate owner, knowing he has already lost the girl, can only accept it. What say you?"

"I say yes," cried Evan.

Jasper scribbled a note and handed it to Evan.

"This will make you known to my associate, Abel Traner, master of *Naiad*. You will take his place as watch on board while he comes here to consult with me. Meanwhile, your Negroes, Mr. Jessop, will be transporting the ginseng to the waterfront."

Evan set off at a run and the Negroes with the ox-drawn sledge at their slower pace. Jessop, whose humor had improved as the actual shipment got under way, now began to scowl and rub the back of his neck.

"Notice how smoothly all proceeds," Jasper encouraged him.

"Your part maybe," objected Jessop. "But here I've gone off half-cocked without making even a start at figuring out how my part's going to go. Everybody and his brother can see my niggers making off down to your boat to load it with my ginseng, which Todd knows was stored in here where he left you. What kind of a story does that leave me to tell him about how you got away?"

"A perfectly reasonable one. Observe how precisely it hangs together. Your nephew some days ago bought your ginseng on his father's account. Today on his own initiative he hired Mr. Traner's recently arrived keelboat to transport his purchase to his father's depot in Louisville. Naturally he knew nothing of my connection with the ship or about my presence here. You, for your part, had no excuse to deny him entrance here to remove his cargo. To refuse would have made your situation only the more difficult. You therefore hauled me out of sight to the loft above while the removal was in progress. Is that not a trapdoor I see in the roof above the loft—no doubt to permit men to crawl out to extinguish Indian fire arrows? While in the loft I in some fashion freed my hands, untied my feet, and made off through said trapdoor and into the woods. You, of course, could not rally your neighbors to organize a pursuit without betraying your secret association with Barklit. Now—does not your story account for everything?"

"It does, for a fact," admitted Jessop. "Todd, he won't believe all of it, but he can't pick any wide-open holes in it either."

Abel appeared. Jasper explained to him the significance of his cargo and took his leave of the miller.

"I shall go out by the trapdoor," he proposed. "It is on the slope of the roof toward the town so that my curious egress will undoubtedly be noted by a number of people. Their comment will further support your story. But after dropping

101

from the eaves I will disappear into the woods and remain invisible until *Naiad* sails at twilight."

"You're a real sly one," said Jessop, beginning once more ruefully to rub the back of his neck. "From here on all I can do is shut my eyes tight and pray to God. Sending that nephew of mine along to keep track of you and my ginseng is like picking a mole to catch a rabbit."

Abel came upon Jasper in the agreed-upon thicket across the Kenton's Station road. Jasper had removed his shoes and was solicitously caressing his feet.

"You never told me you'd been to China," said Abel. "Where'd you learn about how to fix ginseng?"

"The future will undoubtedly afford us many long and leisurely evenings in which to spin out the story of my life. At the moment we have many more pressing concerns."

"That's a fact. The sooner we get shut of Limestone the better. When we're ready to take off, whereat along the beach do you want me to pick you up?"

"Nowhere," said Jasper, beginning to draw on his shoes. "I shall still be on the heels of General Wilkinson. At Kenton's Station I shall hire a horse and be at Lexington before midnight."

"Twice already nothing but luck saved you. That kind of luck can't last forever."

"This time all will be different."

"That's what you said about Limestone."

"But this time it will be true. My one error has been my failure to enlist a trustworthy confederate. That failure I am now about to remedy. Pay the closest heed, for I shall now be taking you into my innermost confidence and making you my full partner. These are my instructions: When you reach Louisville, you will keep in touch with the storekeeper father of the miller's nephew—your supercargo. If I have not joined you by the fifth day from tomorrow, you will then go to General George Rogers Clark. You will tell him in detail all you know of me of your own knowledge. You will tell him, next, that I was in New Orleans last summer all the time that Wilkinson was negotiating with the Spanish governor. You will then tell Clark that Wilkinson's great design goes far beyond a mere arrangement to permit Kentucky to trade at New Orleans. It envisages the secession of the entire West from the United States and its delivery to the Spanish Empire. You will tell him that on August twenty-second Wilkinson took an oath of allegiance to the King of Spain and that his every energy here in Kentucky henceforward is devoted to the service of his royal master. This you must believe and tell with the earnestness of belief."

"I might believe it, but is it a story you can prove?"

"Unhappily, no—though every word of it is true. But it is a story that so well fits such facts as are known that .Clark will believe it. Many will believe it and everybody will repeat it. It will spread through Kentucky like wildfire. It will utterly ruin General Wilkinson and his entire design. This represents an elementary precaution I should have taken in the first instance. Can you not grasp General Wilkinson's dilemma? To eliminate me will merely be to bring George Rogers Clark into the lists in my stead. Clark—the great Western hero, the darling of the frontier, the towering patriot—and an honorable man who has ample reason to hate Wilkinson. Clark will destroy him forthwith."

"'He would, at that. One thing, though, I don't see. Todd Barklit's been the one most on your neck. You said he was working for the English. Where's he fit in?"

"That is a separate affair—which will no longer concern us once I have confronted Wilkinson in Lexington."

Abel plucked a blade of grass and chewed on it thoughtfully. "So you're counting on General Wilkinson's paying you off real big?"

"What else can he do? He has all the treasure of the Indies at his fingertips, and we will plunge our hands into that coffer—and our arms, too, up to the shoulder."

"And along with that we'll be throwing in with him."

"Does that so much distress you?"

"Not too much."

"Patriots on the seaboard will raise a fearful cry."

"People back East ain't sweat much so far over how we made out this side of the mountains."

"Your breadth of vision reassures me."

"Still, that Wilkinson's a real low reptile, ain't he? I don't want nothing to happen to you, but if the time comes I'll surely enjoy watching the look on Clark's face when I tell him how low."

"That happy moment, however," said Jasper, "will not be a moment of your choosing. For five days you will constantly remember that I have placed my life in your hands." His fingers closed on Abel's arm. "One other item may help you keep that in mind. No matter what else ensues, my safe return will mean that we share a modest fortune in ginseng."

"So we will," said Abel. "Big money."

"Don't scoff. Money has values you have never even considered. Allow me to leave with you one parting thought. Mull it over. The Mrs. Bayntons of this world are never so far out of the reach of men of Fortiner's wealth."

Jasper hobbled rapidly off down the Kenton's Station road.

Abel returned to *Naiad* to find Evan waiting impatiently.

"Your niggers got the sledge down to the beach," said Abel. "Thought you'd be half loaded by now."

"Won't take us long once we start in," said Evan. "But first unlock the cabin. I want a look at it."

"What for?"

"I want to see what kind of place you've got for Magda."

"Better find out first if she's coming."

"I've already found out. She'll be waiting at the lumberyard soon's it's dark."

"I hadn't stopped to think on where she'd sleep," admitted Abel. "Jasper and me been sleeping in the hold. But we can put a mattress for her most anywhere here on deck—maybe stretch a tarpaulin, if she wants it."

Evan flushed. "What's wrong with the cabin? She's not a dog or an Indian."

Abel also reddened. "Nothing's wrong with the cabin. But it's not fixed—not for anybody to use."

Evan's temper slipped another notch. "I've had to stand for a good bit today and I'm not standing for much more. When she sees she's the only woman aboard and still she's expected to sleep out on deck, when there's a perfectly good cabin, she's likely not to go—and I wouldn't blame her. And if she don't go, I don't go."

"That's your business—or maybe your uncle's."

"And some yours, too. If I don't go—the ginseng don't either."

Abel turned his back and stood gripping the rail. But when he faced around again he was calm. "You're shooting a little nearer the mark than I can."

He unlocked the cabin, went in, and locked the door behind him again. Within he stood, staring about him. The cabin was exactly as Philippa had left it—the bed rumpled and with the impress of her body still upon it, her blue dress hanging on a peg, her toilet articles strewn across the washstand, even her nightgown flung over the lid of the open chest. Slowly and methodically he began collecting her things, smoothing them, folding them, and stowing them away in the chest.

Evan, his irritation succeeded by curiosity, tried the door and attempted to peer in the portholes, but drew no reply and could see nothing on account of the drawn curtains.

Abel took one last look around. Everything that was Philippa's had been forced into the chest and the chest locked. The bed had been remade. The cabin was as bare and empty and waiting as when he first had slept in it and Esther had come down the ladder wrapped in her buffalo robe.

6

Jabez Lamb lowered himself on the stump, laid his rifle and crutch on the ground beside him, and stretched out his leg. The river had the gleam of silver in the early light, making the contrasting dark green of the shores and islands seem nearly black. A big sturgeon, coming up the rapids, broke water, his snout in the air as though he too were bent upon seeing how the wide valley looked at dawn. A spike buck, bedded down for the day in the clump of willows sprouting from the new mud flat below Bird Rock, belatedly changed his mind and swam wildly to the north shore. A flock of geese rose from the lagoons back of Louisville, wheeled into formation, and resumed their northward flight. Smoke from morning fires curled from the stick and clay chimneys of the town. A drum tapped at Fort Steuben. Jabez twisted around to look down and across the rapids toward the north bank. There was no smoke from the George Rogers Clark cabin. The general could not yet have returned from Kaskaskia. The drummer at the fort ceased his dispirited tapping. The sentry on night watch crawled wearily down from his post on the gun platform.

The rocky islet at the head of the falls was as much the center of Jabez' inner life as of his outer world. In his estimation his life had only really begun the day, ten years before, that he had come out of the woods with a pack of otterskins on his back to catch sight of Clark's campfires on the island. That same memorable day he had met Clark, had joined his army, and as one of that famous few had run the rapids in the livid light of the sun's eclipse. There had been dispute at the time whether the eclipse was a good or a bad omen, though not for long. Victories that decided the war in the West had been just ahead. Those great days with Clark's little band of conquerors had not been many, ending for Jabez in the ditch before the English fort at Vincennes; but even the days since had been better than any he had known before. A half-acre of corn and an occasional hour's fishing off the rocks sufficed for his needs, leaving him peace to sit and remember and watch the river and speculate upon the doings of the more ordinary people of these more ordinary times.

The first craft of the new day to appear out on the river showed up from below. The army barge that twice a month made the run with dispatches and supplies from Fort Steuben here to Fort Knox at Vincennes crept around the point below Clark's landing. The oars were splashing raggedly, with scarcely enough drive to make headway against the current. The chances were that the barge had again been jumped by Indians and that the oarsmen had worn themselves out rowing hard ever since. Jabez watched as the barge docked at the fort and a blanketed figure was lifted out. There had been a brush with Indians all right. Before long he would know all about it, for Isaac Mealy had changed from the barge to a canoe and was headed for the island. This past year Isaac had been a sutler with the army, but in the old days with Clark he had been a good enough man. Jabez picked up his rifle and crutch and swung down to the riverbank. Isaac beached his canoe and straightened, stretching his back.

"So they tuk 'nother whack at yuh," said Jabez.

Isaac nodded disgustedly. "Mebbe a dozen shots—from thet bunch o' alders just below Big Salt Lick. Nobody was hit 'cept Jacques Papin."

Jabez spat and wiped his mouth judicially. "Thet Jacques Papin he's changed sides so many time he was bound to git hisself shot by somebody."

"Had a mind oncet to shoot him myself," said Isaac. He took a flap of folded, sewn buckskin from his pouch. "Reason I come over was to give yuh a letter Jacques was fetchin' to Louisville. He said 'twas fer Colonel Hawley, but I ain't got time to make it over to Louisville, so I brung it to you."

Isaac was being studiedly offhand with his explanations.

"Where'd Jacques git it?"

"Injun brung it to Vincennes from Detroit."

Jabez took the leather packet. It was easy to see what was in Isaac's mind. Jabez agreed with him and agreed also that it was better for him to handle this than Isaac. Isaac returned to his duties at the fort. Jabez got in his canoe and paddled on across to Louisville.

Aaron Creamer, the young schoolmaster, was in the yard back of his cabin washing his white shirt. He dried his hands, sat down on the doorstep, and drew from the packet the folded paper sealed with blobs of wax.

"I want you should read me what it says," repeated Jabez.

The schoolmaster went right on pretending to be slow of wit.

"But if it's for Colonel Hawley, why should I read it for you? It could be a perfectly legitimate business letter."

"If'n thet's what it was, they'd of put Hawley's name on the outside, like folks always do with letters, and sent it down by anybody in the army barge 'stead o' makin' Jacques come all this way."

"You do make something of a case. Your suspicion then is that in this letter there may be evidence of some kind of dealings with the English?"

"I don't suspicion nothin'. I only want to know what it says—and only reason I come to you is I can't read."

The schoolmaster laid down the letter, got up, and began thoughtfully to wring out his shirt.

Peter Branch drove the last nail into the board over the door to his store, dropped down off the bench, and backed off to regard the sign with satisfaction.

PETER BRANCH
Keeper and Dealer
in
Guns, Tea, Coffee, Salt, Nails, Hats,
Thimbles, Pins, Buckles,
Boards, Planks, Timbers

"Maw," yelled Branch.

His wife, Alvina, and his three daughters had been expecting his summons. They came running from the family living quarters alongside the store.

"How d'ye like it?" he asked.

All craned upward admiringly at the sign.

"It's real neat, Paw," said Alvina.

The attention of the girls, however, already had wandered.

"Look, here comes Aaron," whispered Charity.

Purity reddened. Charity and Equity giggled. The absence of their respective husbands—the one surveying on the Muskingum for the New Ohio Company and the other serving with the Kentucky delegation to the Virginia Constitutional Convention at Richmond—gave the two older sisters leisure to take an undistracted interest in the schoolmaster's halting courtship of Purity.

"Hush," scolded Alvina. "He mayn't have a seat to his pants, but he's an eddicated man and that's somethin' not to be laughed at."

Aaron came up, bowing to the ladies and trying not to look directly at Purity.

107

"Good morning, Mr. Branch. I know that you're a busy man, but could you come with me for a moment? There is a problem upon which I need your opinion."

"I reckon I could," said Branch reluctantly.

He shot a glance beseeching guidance in this crisis, first at Purity's flushed face and then at his wife's placid one. But Purity only looked away, and Alvina's affable smile completely disguised her attitude.

"You go right along, Paw," said Alvina unhelpfully, "I'll mind the store."

"Your pardon, Mrs. Branch," murmured Aaron, bowing again. "Your pardon, ladies."

He and Branch started off. Equity and Charity tittered. Purity darted into the house.

Keeping up with Aaron's long strides down the sandy street, Branch stole rueful looks at his companion's grave face while he attempted to formulate the phrasing of his reply to the forthcoming declaration. Thus he was altogether unprepared, as they entered the one room cabin, for the spectacle of Jabez Lamb hoisting himself up off the cot. Jabez took the letter from his pocket and tossed it out on the table.

"Thet," he said, "is a letter brung from Detroit by an Injun and from Vincennes here by a Frenchie who's in the pay o' the English. It's fer Colonel Hawley, though it don't say so on it. I say we should take us a look at what's in it. But Aaron, he figgers he's a mite too nice to peek at other folks' mail."

"Jabez' singleness of purpose does him credit," said Aaron. "The fact remains that that letter is to a man who fought mightily for our cause all through the war."

Branch had been relieved to discover that the schoolmaster's problem, while serious, was not the complete poser that he had anticipated.

"I can name more Kentuckians than I got fingers and toes," he said, "who were as hell-bent as Marsh Hawley during the war who don't see much differences now between our side and most anybody's side. I'm not saying Marsh Hawley is one of 'em, mind you. I'm only saying Kentucky is full of such."

"These are restless times," acknowledged Aaron.

In the street outside a horseman plodded past.

"There's Ed Mercer," said Branch quickly. "He's a lawyer and they say back East he used to be a county judge. Might be he could tell us if there's some more legal way to handle this."

Aaron looked at Jabez. Jabez' fingers closed on his crutch and his rifle.

"Call in anybody yuh want. All I got to say is: this letter don't git out'n this room 'til somebody's read it to me."

Edmund Mercer slid down off his horse and came in. His garb was very nearly as threadbare as the schoolmaster's, but he carried himself with that air of complete confidence in his own opinions peculiar to lawyers.

"We have a letter which we have reason to believe may connect one of our principal fellow citizens with an English plot," explained Aaron. "Can you advise us to what duly designated official of the government it would be the most appropriate to refer the matter?"

The inquiry seemed to release the springs of a catapult of indignation already wound tight in the lawyer's bosom.

"Official of what government?" he roared. "That of the Confederation? Its Congress has abdicated. That of the new union under the Constitution? It does not yet exist, and if the present insane resistance to ratification persists, it will never exist. That of Virginia? It ceased to be our government when Virginia gave her consent to our becoming a state. That of Kentucky? We have none. We are neither republic, state, county, nor province—neither fish, flesh, nor fowl. You ask what government? We have but one. The government of chaos."

Mercer's explosion ignited in the schoolmaster a rival detonation.

"You speak the jargon of all Federalists. You are all monarchists at heart. I tell you, Edmund, we did not strike off a foreign tyranny in order to embrace tyranny at home. This Constitution would rivet upon us the chains of a rigid central government."

Mercer, in his best courtroom manner, dropped his voice from ferocity to sorrow. "You profess to be alarmed by the threat of English intrigue. I do assure you, sir, that your prejudiced notions threaten to rend our country more fearfully than ever could any foreign plot."

"But surely you must be able to see, Edmund," begged Aaron, grieved in his turn, "what it is you threaten. We have made ourselves free men and we cannot live unless we remain free. Once we allow ourselves to be subjected to this Constitution devised by Eastern merchants and bankers we are forever lost."

Each, mortified by the other's incomprehension, looked to Branch for support.

"To listen to you two talk," he said, "and nobody in Kentucky's talking any different—we're bound to be wrong whichever way we jump. But what you both been saying makes one thing clear as window glass. We've got ourselves so mixed up we ain't got room to side-step. One stumble and we could pitch right into England's lap—or maybe even Spain's. So we can't afford to worry about hurting Marsh Hawley's feelings. Jabez is right. We have to look."

"If'n everybody's done makin' speeches," said Jabez, "let's hear the letter."

The schoolmaster picked it up, held it out for Mercer to break the seals, and handed it on to Branch. Branch opened it and after a brief glance at the contents began to speak in a harsh, dry voice.

"There's nothing to show who it was sent to or who sent it. But this is what it says:

"I am sorry to hear that there seems so little hope of justice being done me with regard to my property there. But I do not give up hope for the future since nothing could be more plain than that in this immense Western country the genuine interests of your people there and of our people here totally coincide. On the Atlantic seaboard there may be room for commercial rivalry, but in the West whatever is good for you is good also for us. Your primary need must be to drive the Spanish from the Mississippi, because unless that is soon done you cannot even survive. I have talked to Lord D. upon this subject. He warmly sympathizes with your aspirations. Were you to determine to take your destiny into your own hands—as sooner or later you must—you may be assured of the assistance of ten thousand British troops from Canada, of which two regiments are already in Detroit, together with supplies and armaments to equip your own forces, and, at the mouth of the river, the cooperation of an English fleet. This is a prospect which you are at liberty to reveal to any of your fellow countrymen whom you judge worthy of your confidence. I cannot close without reminding you once again that our two peoples, of the same race, the same speech, the same character, should never have been separated."

"Goddamme," said Jabez, as elated as though he had heard the summons of a trumpet, "the Injun-lovin', Tory bastard."

"There can't be much doubt who wrote it," said Mercer. "There's but one Tory who once claimed land at Louisville and who still has the standing to gain the ear of Lord Dorchester. Dr. John Connolly."

"And less doubt that it was intended for Colonel Hawley," said Aaron. "He thinks all problems are to be settled by military force. How often have we heard him declaim that Kentucky's sole hope is to seize New Orleans, but that the achievement must be accompanied by the support of a fleet to keep the port open to our commerce?"

There was a timid knock at the door. Aaron flung it open and started back. Purity, blushing and panting, stood on the step.

"Paw," she said. "Evan's home."

"Whatever's he doing here?" demanded Branch. "What's the matter with him? Is he all right?"

But Purity already had fled. Branch turned to face his fellow judges.

"I got to get me over there to see what sort of mess that boy's got himself into. So I better shoot my say straight off. I don't hold with Marsh Hawley's English scheme. The way I figure, the less truck we have with the English the better for us. Same time I'm as sure as I was yesterday that Marsh is just as bent on what he thinks is good for Kentucky as any of us think we are. And he's got one argument there's no answer to. Unless somehow we can get the Mississippi open, we might's well all go back where we came from. We got to grow or die and we got no more chance to grow than a calf in a box. The rest I got to say is this: No use our throwing this letter in Marsh Hawley's face. Only make him more bullheaded than he is, and turn him to worse mischief. Best for us just to hang on to it. May slow up Connolly some when he gets no answer. And while he's waiting, we can watch Marsh to see what's his next move."

To this anticlimactic advice none of the others had a ready answer.

"Perhaps now you're beginning to see, Aaron," said Mercer, "what measureless confusion can spring from the want of a responsible central government?"

"On the contrary," said Aaron. "It but proves how mortally we have weakened our republic by attempting to divest ourselves of our right to govern ourselves."

"Never lissened to sech a goddamme pile o' talk," said Jabez. He slung his rifle strap over his shoulder, grasped his crutch, and got to his feet. "But they's still a dribble of us left"—he ran his hand over the stock of his rifle—"who'll know when to leave off talkin'."

Magda sat on the stool in the Branch chimney corner, her hands folded in her lap, her eyes cast down.

"You just set there," said Alvina for the tenth time, "and make yourself at home."

Whenever directly addressed, Magda raised her eyes long enough to smile shyly and to take another quick look at Evan's home. It consisted of a single large room, with a side door to the adjoining store, a big fireplace in one end, an outer door in the other, and a table and benches down the middle. Aside from glass instead of oiled paper in the two windows, a fireplace of stone rather than stick and clay, a plank floor, and one piece of Eastern furniture, a big mahogany sideboard, it appeared superior only in size to the simplest frontier cabin.

Evan came running back and poked his head in the door. His mother and sisters turned to beam at him, but he had eyes only for Magda.

"Like I said," he reassured her, as though she were an exceptionally timid child among strange adults, "I'll be back 'fore you can tell I'm gone."

"If she fixes to run off," said Charity, "we'll catch right on to her."

Evan laughed. "If she has to be chased some more, I aim to do the catching myself."

Still laughing, he started out again.

"He's only gone to borry us a Dutch oven," said Alvina. "We had us a real good one—only Paw he sold it yesterday. That's one big trouble with running a store. Paw he's apt to sell most anything we own."

"Like as not to anybody just out from Pennsylvany," said Equity, "it don't look like we own much."

Magda gave them a deprecatory smile and took advantage of the upward glance to make another quick survey of the present members of Evan's family. None of them had any of his color, his red cheeks, or dancing eyes. His genial, fat, and perspiring mother, flushed with excitement over his unexpected homecoming, was kneading dough at the end of the table. His grandmother, addressed always as Granny, sitting against the wall, her chin resting on her gnarled hands clasped about the head of her cane, was keeping a fierce, unwinking gaze fixed upon Magda's face. The two sallow, sharp-featured sisters, whispering continually and making only a show of attending to what they were doing, were removing innumerable squabs that had been imbedded in goose fat in a large crock, wiping the surplus grease from them with their hands, and tossing the little carcasses into an iron pot by the fire.

"Them's three-week-old pigeons Evan himself helped gather last summer," explained Alvina. "When they're young as that pigeons can be real tasty. And they keep real good, too, when you put 'em down just right in deep fat. Ain't nothing Evan's so partial to as a pigeon pie the way I make it. That's why the minute we seen him coming up from the landing we knowed right off what it was we had to have to eat this first day he was back home."

Alvina chattered on. Magda resumed her fugitive inspection of the Branch establishment. In Limestone people had spoken of Peter Branch as a well-to-do man and Louisville's leading storekeeper. But there was little enough in evidence here that suggested the household of a prosperous merchant. The sideboard, though now so scratched and battered, might once have been a good piece. But everything else, the table and benches, the loom, the spinning wheel, and the plank beds, was homemade. The beds—frameworks of poles with the mattresses resting on lacings of rawhide—particularly engaged her attention. One was in a curtained recess beside the fireplace, but the other two were out in the open in the corners on either side of the front door. She had already gathered that Evan's father and mother occupied the first, Charity and Equity the second, and Purity and Granny the third, and that the necessary rearrangement in prospect for the coming night included Evan's taking to a cot in the store, the three sisters sleeping together, and her turning in with Granny.

Magda's wandering glance again encountered Granny's basilisk stare, and this time she tried a half-smile in the place of hastily looking away. Granny's expression did not warm. Her eyelids slowly closed and she fell immediately into a doze, accompanied by a faint, hissing snore.

"Here comes Purity," said Alvina, stretching to peer from the window. "She must of found Paw. She did. There he is right behind her."

Purity appeared in the doorway.

"Paw's 'most here," she announced. "Where's Evan?"

"He's 'most here too," said Evan, rounding the corner from the other direction. "Here, take this." He was pretending to stagger under the weight of the iron pot on his shoulder, and then made the gesture of handing it to Purity before lowering it to the doorstep.

Everybody but Magda and Granny shrieked with laughter over this display of humor. Alvina, Charity, and Equity began frantically wiping their hands, and then all three rushed out to preside over the meeting of father and son. Granny dozed on.

Through the open doorway Magda could see Evan and his father shaking hands, Evan pulling a letter from his pocket, Branch taking it, all four women clinging to Evan, and, tied up to the landing at the riverbank beyond, the keelboat that had brought her. She rose and moved about the room, making a closer examination of utensils, furniture, and garments hanging along the wall. Suddenly she was aware that Granny's unwinking gaze was again fixed upon her.

"Parcel o' women in this house already," said Granny. "When Charity's and Equity's men come back 'twill be most as bad. They live right next door."

"You think too many?"

"Evan takes to women. Too quick sometimes. Like that grass widow last fall over at Elm Springs and next that yellow girl at Nat Ewing's." The stare became even more searching. "You ain't strictly what his folks been counting on, but the main chance was he'd do worse."

"That is what his mother thinks?"

"She wouldn't think the Queen of England good enough for him, but you don't have to fret none about what she thinks. Nor them sisters o' his neither. They might pester you some, but being as he's the only boy, and the youngest, too, he's been used to his own way since he was a babe in his crib. All you got to fret about is what his father thinks. His father thinks the sun rises and sets in the seat o' that boy's pants."

Abel quit his restless pacing of the landing float alongside *Naiad*, climbed the bank, and circled the family reunion, endeavoring to catch Evan's eye. Evan pulled free from the women and steered his father toward him.

"Meet Abel Traner, Paw."

Branch, engrossed in the letters in his hand, nodded and went on studying them.

"Jasper not here yet?" Abel demanded of Evan.

"Paw says no."

"And no word from him?"

"That's what Paw says."

Branch looked up, blinking and wagging his head. "This letter from Wilkinson's the damnedest thing I ever heard of."

Abel was scowling off among the houses of Louisville as though hoping even at this last moment to catch some sight of Jasper. "What letter from Wilkinson?"

"The one my brother-in-law sent along with his. So he didn't tell you about that part? He's real closemouthed, Dorsey is. But long's he's taken you in on the deal, no sense in keeping it from you."

Abel gave a passing glance at the Wilkinson letter. On a page torn from a notebook was scrawled:

> Pass bearer and cargo through all customs.
> James Wilkinson

"What good's Wilkinson's name on a thing like that?" asked Branch.

"I've been trying to tell Paw how Wilkinson fixed himself up a big deal with the Spaniards," said Evan.

"It's good enough to give us all the leeway there is," said Abel, suddenly angry. "No telling how long it will stay good, but if we got going fast it ought to pass us straight through."

For the first time Branch looked up from the letters long enough to give Abel an appraising look. "So it's your idea we ship right off slap-bang now?"

"It surely would be if my partner was here."

Branch's attention returned to Jessop's letter.

"Dorsey he claims you got some way to fix ginseng so's it's worth more'n the going market—he says maybe twenty times more."

"It's my partner who knows how to do that." Abel was as impatient as though it were Branch's fault Jasper was not here. "He was to meet me here yesterday. I'm a day late myself because I tried to travel at night and got hung up two days on a sand bar."

"Seven dollars a pound." Branch continued to blink. "That Dorsey. He gets his thumb into more different pies. He's a real caution, he is."

Abel shook Branch's arm to regain his attention. "How long ought it to take a man to get from Limestone to Lexington and on here?"

"Afoot or horseback?"

"Horseback."

"Well, it's an easy two days Limestone to Lexington and a mite stiffer two days on here. But if a man was pressed for time, he could make it to Lexington in one day, lay over a day, and get clean here before night the third."

Abel's lips tightened to a thin, hard line as he considered this estimate. "Where's General Clark live?"

"Sometimes with his folks out at Mulberry Hill and sometimes in that cabin of his over at Clarksville. Only he went off to Kaskaskia last week and I ain't heard of his getting back yet."

"Who might be the most likely to know when to expect him back?"

"Jabez Lamb's the most likely to know about everybody's comings and goings. Now Dorsey he talks like he expected me—or maybe Evan—to go with you and the ginseng to New Orleans. And he talks about allowing him a shilling a pound and splitting what we make over and above that ten per cent to me, thirty to you, and the rest to him. Is that the way you understand it?"

115

"There's nothing to understand until I get hold of my partner again. Whereat might I find this Jabez Lamb?"

"He's got a cabin over there on Corn Island."

Abel slid his canoe over *Naiad's* rail and paddled to the island. Jabez was squatted at the river's edge, gutting and cleaning a still-wriggling bass. Abel came about in the lee of a rock and thrust his paddle against the bottom to hold the canoe against the current.

"People tell me you know all about General Clark."

"Nobody does," said Jabez. "He don't hisself."

"Any idea when he might be expected back?"

"He's back already. His boy Mose was just over to git me to ketch him a fish fer the general's supper."

"Is his cabin the one there on the point at the foot of the rapids?"

"Thet's right. Save me a trip if yuh was to take this bass with yuh. They's no hurry. He won't see yuh afore dark. He traveled all night and he's gone to bed with a bottle."

"Does he drink as much as people say?"

Jabez spat irritably. "How would I know how much folks say? Oncet in a while when he gits another turndown from them yellow-bellied pinch-pennies back in Virginny—or somethin' else riles him more'n ordinary—well, he do take to the jug fer a spell."

Abel paddled on down the rapids, noting in passing the depth of the channel and the location of the rocks and ledges. With the water rising, passage in *Naiad,* presuming the time were to come to make the passage, would present few difficulties. He landed on the rocky strand before the Clark cabin. Mose, his wrinkled face as black as his wool was white, came out, closing the door behind him. After a long look at Abel he smiled with a trace of friendliness.

"No use tuh wake him up," he said. "Mebbe by dark he'll talk to yuh."

Mose took the bass and went back in. Abel prowled restlessly along the beach, made the more restless by the passing of each hour. If Jasper had already come to some disaster, to call down the Clark thunder and lightning would not save him. Shadows crept over the river. Twilight came. And then night. Lights twinkled in Louisville. Finally the cabin's oiled-paper windows began to glow. Mose came to the door.

"Be a while yet," he whispered.

Two more hours passed. Sparks and smoke poured from the chimney, but there was no smell of cooking fish. Evidently Clark was taking a while to get up. Mose came to the door again. This time he beckoned.

Abel went in. The interior of the plain log cabin was brightly lighted by a dozen candles. Clark was pacing around and around an object on a stool with the fierce, energetic stride of a man who all his life had been accustomed to violent physical activity. The silence of his moccasined feet added a lithe grace and power to his tread. He looked younger, not older, than his thirty-five years. His black eyes glowed like coals in the candlelight. The room smelled of whisky, but there was nothing else to suggest that he might have been drinking. His red hair was smoothly combed, his clothing neat, his frown merely thoughtful.

"Come in," he said without looking around.

As Abel came forward he saw that the object on the stool was a small model of a river barge. There were dummy figures to represent oarsmen, but instead of manning oars they had hold of cranks which operated banks of paddles on the order of small mill wheels.

"One more proof of the unlimited stupidity of the people of this Western country," said Clark. "We are condemned to perpetual poverty until we manage some practical means to haul a cargo against the current. I have invented a device far more effective than oars. But do you imagine I can prevail upon a soul either here or in Congress to give me so much as a moment of their attention? Stupidity, sir, is far too kind a word for it."

"Surely would be a big help," agreed Abel, "to get up river half as easy as you can get down."

"It would be like loosening the rope from about our necks," said Clark.

He picked up the model and thrust it into a cupboard. Wheeling, he gave his visitor a sudden, sharp look, followed the look with a brief welcoming smile, and resumed his pacing.

"Sorry to keep you waiting. But there was something on my mind I had to get settled. What's on yours?"

"Wilkinson."

"What about him?"

"He's back."

"He is, is he? Last time I heard of him he'd left New Orleans for Havana. Where'd you see him?"

"Limestone. He was headed for Lexington."

Clark came to a stop and kicked a couple of stools alongside the table.

"Abel—did Mose get your name right?—sit down, Abel. Now tell me about Wilkinson."

Abel told in detail so much of the story of his association

117

with Jasper as reflected on Wilkinson's activities. It was a complicated story, but it was a comfort to have so shrewd a listener.

"To prove how far he was ready to go," finished Abel, "last summer in New Orleans he took an oath of allegiance to the King of Spain."

"The hypocritical, slimy, conniving trade-rat," said Clark. "The mealy-mouthed, poison-pen-scratching, sanctimonious son of a bitch. How he's feathering his nest."

"The main part of his scheme," added Abel, "is to turn over Kentucky—and maybe Cumberland and the Holston too —to the Spaniards."

Clark sprang up and paced again. When he wheeled back he was in a blazing passion.

"You have brought your story to me because you imagine I will rise in the stirrups, rally honorable men, and utterly destroy Wilkinson and all his works. That I would do were I still myself an honorable man. But I am not. Honor no longer exists. Honor is dead in our country. Be silent. I have listened to your story. Now listen to mine. Ten years ago I took this country from the English and the Indians. Unaided, except for a handful of men ready to go where I went. I took it for Virginia and for our new nation. And what has been my reward? Every year since I have been discounted and derided and despised. I am bankrupt because my expenditures for the common cause have been repudiated. Meaner men—even such vermin as this Wilkinson—have been preferred over me. All this I could endure, and without a whimper, were there any aim apparent—any greater good in view. But there is none. Virginia has disowned us. She claims title to our land but withholds so much as a farthing to help defend it. The Congress of the United States makes no pretense of representing us, and is filled with men who hold us in contempt and gloat over our every affliction. Five years after we won the war the English are still on the Lakes, the Spanish on the Mississippi, the Indians in our dooryards and no Eastern finger is lifted to ease our miseries. You ask me to fly to the defense of our country. What country? We have no country."

Abel shoved his stool back and stood up.

"Good many folks talking the same way," he said, "and without the reason you have."

"But you don't hold with us?"

"Only thing I hold with is that everybody's got his own row to hoe."

Abel was edging toward the door. Clark leaned across the table, appearing suddenly reluctant to be left alone.

118

"Stay and sup with me."

"It would pleasure me to do that," said Abel. "Only I got to get me to Lexington as fast as I can get there."

He opened the door.

"Wait," commanded Clark.

For a moment his brow was ridged with thought. Then he brought his fist down upon the table so hard that it caused a small camp chest resting on it to bounce. He whipped out a key, unlocked the chest, and took from it a letter, already folded and heavily sealed.

"On your way through Louisville," he directed, "hand this to John Rogers. His is the house with the whitewashed fence—the third this side of Pete Branch's place."

Abel worked his way up the rapids and along the dark Louisville waterfront until the outline of *Naiad* loomed before him. He landed and found the white fence without much difficulty but had more kicking off a large dog and getting Rogers to come to his door.

"A letter from General Clark," Abel announced, handing it over.

Rogers seized it and held it to the light of the candle he was holding in his other hand to examine the minute inscription between the seals, which, as Abel had noted when Clark had handed it to him, consisted of the laconic notation: *"for 33 from 10 per 27."* Rogers gave a start, not so much of surprise as of awed excitement.

"So he's finally made up his mind," he exclaimed. He raised the candle to get a better look at Abel.

"Name's Abel Traner," said Abel. "I just happened to be coming past and he gave me the letter to bring to you. He said you'd know what to do with it."

"I do, I do, indeed," said Rogers hastily and as hastily closed the door.

It was well past midnight by the time Abel reached the Branch house, but he could hear mother and daughters still talking animatedly from one bed to the other. Branch, a quilt wrapped around him, came to the door.

"I need a horse," said Abel. "I have to get to Lexington."

"Bad news about your partner?"

"The same as bad. I got to find out what kind of a fix he's got himself into."

"You'd best wait for daylight. Every couple of nights there's Indians creeping around the edges of the woods looking for a chance to steal a stray horse or ax a stray drunk and, anyway, the trail's a hard one to keep to in the dark."

"If Evan shows me where it takes off from town, I can follow it."

119

"I'll get you a horse and show you myself. Evan's sleeping on the ginseng down on your boat."

Branch got him started on the trail out of town, but Abel had not gone far before he discovered that the counsel against night travel had been justified. There were so many new stations along the Beargrass and so many crossing and connecting side trails that the main track was impossible to distinguish. He was forced to sit by the wayside and wait for dawn.

At daybreak he started on and had not been traveling an hour when his quest came to an end as ridiculous as it was unforeseen. Plodding down the trail toward him was Jasper, leading his saddled horse. The silver-buckled shoes were slung to the pommel and he was hobbling along in his stocking feet. Abel pulled in his horse and waited.

"Few men have traveled more extensively than I," began Jasper while still some distance away. "However, I have been more accustomed to ships and stagecoaches than to saddles and shoes. To be specific—what detained me was a most desolating array of blisters, including a number in quite unmentionable places."

"Blisters your only trouble?"

"I regret to confess that that is so. Wilkinson, who laughed at me in Pittsburgh and ignored me in Limestone, welcomed me in Lexington. I represented no threat to him whatever. To the majority of his fellow Kentuckians any charge that he was wedded to the Spanish interest could but add to his popularity."

"So it turned out you had nothing to sell him?"

"His best offer was to pay my tavern bill if I'd stay in Lexington and whisper my story to whoever might listen."

"It's just as well you didn't get yourself into another fix because you missed on your other proposition just as far. Clark would have been no help. He figures that long's the country's going to the devil it don't matter much which road it takes."

Jasper nodded sadly. "I began to guess that my first hour in Lexington. According to the talk there General Clark's even giving the devil a hand."

"He got me to take a letter to a man in Louisville who handled it like it smelled of tail and hoofs both."

"The story going around is that Clark is organizing a company of friends and associates to found a colony of Kentuckians in Spanish territory and to be offering to become a Spanish subject in return for Spanish approval of his project." Jasper sighed as though such callous disregard for his country's interests were something he could not understand. "So

120

even the supreme patriot has feet of clay. If there were a band anywhere among these benighted settlements, it should be playing 'The World Turned Upside Down.'"

Abel shrugged. "It's not our place to turn it one way or the other. If you'll make out to sit sideways in the saddle, I'll lead your horse and we'll get us back to Louisville."

After a succession of groans and experiments Jasper found a position that he was able to tolerate. For some time they traveled in silence. Then Jasper produced another groan.

"When the jug's busted, no use kicking the pieces," said Abel.

"You have been too kind. You have not once reproached me."

"You made your try."

"And it could scarcely have been a more ignominious fiasco. All my pains resolved into an ultimate one in my backside. I had planned so long and, as I conceived, so astutely, only to have it turn out—as you so well said—that I had nothing to sell."

"We've still got the ginseng to sell."

Jasper laughed wryly. "My long-suffering friend, you but embrace another and lesser illusion. That ginseng is not worth so much as the miller's interest in it."

"A thirty per cent share at seven dollars a pound ought to be worth something."

"It ought, indeed. The difficulty is that our windfall must remain in the shilling-a-pound category. For the truth is that I have never been nearer China than the Barbary States, and I've no clearer idea of the secret refining process than you have."

For another half-hour they went on in silence. The outlying houses of Louisville appeared ahead.

"I never did take much stock in easy money rolling in," said Abel. "I've never been around like you have, but I never heard of money falling in anybody's lap. But the way I figure, we still got more left than just a hole to crawl into. We got the boat and that customs pass of Wilkinson's."

A flicker of interest crossed Japser's dejected face. "Customs pass?"

"The one he gave Jessop. And whatever the ginseng's worth, we got a thirty per cent interest in what anybody wants to think it is. Here's what I'm coming to. Branch has twenty-five or thirty tons of tobacco he's had to take in at his store because so few folks have money to pay for what they want—just like Jessop had to take in the ginseng at his mill."

Jasper slid from his horse and ran up to catch at the bridle of Abel's.

"Can it be true?"

"Can what be true?"

"That you are beginning to allow your mind to unfold. When last the crass subject came up, you professed yourself superior to all concern for money."

"I'm not talking now about potsful under boards."

"Money, my friend, whether by the hogshead or the thimbleful, is useful—invariably and under every circumstance."

Jasper ran back to retrieve his shoes, drew them on, washed his face and hands in an adjacent brook, combed his hair, and beat the dust from his clothes. He then bravely mounted, and when he rode up to the Branch door, he presented the confident and spirited figure of a man for whom all had been going particularly well. At dinner with the family he was gracious and urbane, as befitted a distinguished guest accustomed to more elaborate boards.

After the noonday dinner the four men withdrew to the deck of the keelboat. Jasper passed Fortiner's cigars and Abel served a round of his brandy and then Jasper tipped Branch off balance with his opening announcement.

"Due to a turn of affairs that came unexpectedly to a head in Lexington," he said, "I find that I must be in New Orleans at the earliest possible moment. I know of no other immediately available vessel and therefore have prevailed upon my good friend Mr. Traner to take me in his. We must leave by dawn tomorrow at the latest."

"That's bad," said Branch. "My brother-in-law expects either me or Evan to go along with the ginseng and I don't know that either of us can get away that quick."

"I know for sure that I can't," said Evan with decision.

"It happens that the ginseng doesn't enter into our immediate situation," said Jasper. "The refining process upon which its chief value depends is one that requires time—a matter of a month or six weeks. It involves a series of alternate boilings and dryings—which could not be conducted on shipboard and could not be delayed until the end of the voyage, since the roots tend to lose their efficacy if kept too long untreated after digging. Therefore I will leave written instructions with you so that you can have the process completed before we return. The ginseng shipment then must fall on some later date—perhaps Mr. Traner's next voyage. Abel, I seem as usual to be doing all the talking. You look as though you might have some remark to make."

"I have," said Abel. "Shame to run all the way down to

New Orleans with an empty boat." He looked at Branch. "Maybe you know where we might pick up fifteen or twenty tons of corn or tobacco?"

"I might," said Branch, his tradesman's instincts instantly alert. "I might have that much tobacco myself."

"What's wrong with that?" continued Abel. "If it's yours we could use the Wilkinson pass. With that we wouldn't have to worry about paying off Spanish guards or dealing with smugglers, and it could be worth seven or eight dollars a hundred more down there than it is to you here."

Branch was clearly caught and ready to bargain. "Long's the tobacco is mine—and the use of the pass too—appears to me I ought to have a piece of the New Orleans price."

"That's reasonable," said Abel. "What I had in mind was something along the lines of the ginseng deal."

"You mean the first money we get goes to me for what the tobacco is worth here and we split whatever there is over that seventy-thirty?"

"What do you think, Jasper?" asked Abel.

"It's only a matter of a few hundred dollars either way," said Jasper, flicking the ashes from his cigar. "Still, I agree that it's a shame to go down the river empty."

"I'm not going," declared Evan, looking at his father.

"No need either you going," said Abel. "You'll have the ginseng here as security—in case something happened to your tobacco—like a wreck or the Spaniards grabbing it in spite of the pass."

Branch squirmed in his chair. "Let me think this over for a minute. Mostly I'm right quick to size up the way I feel about something—now and then too quick."

Magda came out and sat down on the Branch doorstep. Her hair glowed in the sun against the dark doorway behind her. Evan started up.

"Paw, you don't need me any more."

"You sit down," said Branch. "You're getting old enough to act like a grown man part of the time." The sudden vigor with which he had addressed his son carried over to his business problem. "There's something about this I don't like. I ain't got any real good reason I can put my finger right on. In most ways it looks like a fair enough proposition. Maybe it's that Wilkinson pass I stick at. That kind of smells to me like throwing in some with the Spaniards."

"Downriver's the only way you can trade," said Abel. "And you got to deal somehow with the Spaniards to do it. More people in Kentucky beginning to figger that out every day."

"But me—I don't like it. I don't like sidling up to Spaniards

any better than I would to the English or the Indians.'
Branch got to his feet. "No. I reckon I better wait a while
and see how some of the dust settles. Maybe when you get
back from New Orleans things will look different."

Jasper rose beside him. "We must respect so discriminating
a conscience. It is a rarity these days. Though in this instance I think you may be exercising it unduly." He took
Branch's arm. "Would you step this way for a moment?"

The cabin door closed behind them. When they came out
Branch's expression was at once decided and serene.

"Evan, you run over to George Bent's and see can he hire
me out his three niggers for the rest of the day. We got to
get this ginseng lugged up to the warehouse and as much tobacco loaded as the boat will hold."

Father and son hurried away.

"What was it you told him that brought him around so
fast?" asked Abel.

"That you had already examined the rapids and that with
this high water you thought it perfectly feasible to leave during the night."

"Why should that make any difference to him?"

"Because it gives the German girl a chance to steal out
and go with us."

"Is he that anxious to be rid of her?"

"There seems to be a certain doubt that she will fit
smoothly into the Branch family—that is, on the part of
everybody but Evan."

"So we're to carry her off? Not me. Stealing women's not
my business."

"You persist in missing the essential point. We will not be
abducting her. If she goes, it will be entirely of her own
volition. This Branch is a most forthright fellow. If she
seizes the opportunity to run off with us, that to him will be
in itself the necessary demonstration that she is not the girl
for his boy."

"She's worked herself into a comfortable nest here. Why
should she want to leave it?"

"You could be right. But she is not a timid damsel, and
something tells me the prospect of New Orleans' wider hori-
zons may appeal to her."

Branch returned with the Negroes and the labor of removing the ginseng and stowing the tobacco got under way. A
number of townspeople gathered to watch. This latest attempt to ship a cargo to New Orleans, where in recent years
confiscation by delighted Spanish officials had been the invariable result, was a sufficient novelty to arouse much comment. It was generally agreed that Branch had lost his mind.

Then, later in the afternoon, the blacksmith, Marvin Cooper, got back from attending the funeral of his father in Lexington. He brought with him added trimmings to the story of Wilkinson's return to Kentucky. According to Cooper, Wilkinson was passing out to a number of people whom he considered worthy of the favor passes through the Spanish customs. The popular estimate of Branch's sagacity was swiftly revised upward.

The loading was completed by dark. Abel and Jasper supped pleasantly with the buoyant Branch family. After supper Branch got out his fiddle. Jasper, gallantly ignoring the delicate state of his feet, danced in succession with each of the ladies, his whirl with Alvina proving especially notable. Despite the gaiety, Abel and Jasper withdrew in good time, professing the need of rest in view of the ardors of the coming day. In the place of farewells there was much light talk of all rising in time to see them off in the morning.

The Fortiner baggage, having been removed from the hold to make room for cargo, was stowed on deck in the bow, along with Abel's and Jasper's beds, under a canvas fly.

"Hope there's no wind tonight," said Abel, jerking at the canvas. "Tomorrow I'll nail this down right. I'd do it tonight only I don't know whether or not to leave room for our beds. If she don't come, no reason we shouldn't move into the cabin." He looked at Jasper challengingly. "You talked to her. You still sure she'll come?"

Jasper was not. "She took a somewhat more cautious view than I had anticipated," he admitted. "But she sleeps with the old woman beside the door. As soon as the household falls asleep she will slip out for a further talk with us. I gather all will depend upon her appraisal of the accommodations she may expect en route."

"She already knows about the cabin. She spent nearly a week in it."

"You force me to come into the open. I am thinking not of her ease but of yours. You go about with a perpetual scowl —you groan in your sleep—you have the soured temper of a dyspeptic old man. There is no solace so eligible, if I may say so, as the companionship of an enterprising and quite personable young woman."

"I'll pick my own women—when I want one."

Jasper laid an exaggeratedly sympathetic hand on Abel's shoulder. "Can it truly be that you are so haunted by the memory of Fortiner's fair one that you cannot imagine ever resorting to any other woman?"

Abel shook off the hand and was about to lay his own hands on Jasper.

"S-s-sh," said Jasper. "Here she comes."

He leaned over the rail and helped Magda aboard. Abel snatched up the lantern and stepped forward to confront her. His eyes glittered and he was still panting.

"Come here," he said.

He flung open the cabin door and went in. Magda followed only as far as the doorway. The hoarse invitation had been more startling than persuasive. Suddenly her eyes widened with amazement. Jasper, peering over her shoulder, began to nod and then to chuckle with amused relief.

Abel had unlocked Philippa's chest and was strewing the contents about on the bunk, the washstand, and the chair— gowns, petticoats, slippers, corsets, gilt buckles, perfume bottles. Some of the latter items he merely dumped on the floor. One nightgown he hurled into a corner. When the chest was empty he stepped free of the heap of feminine finery and made a curt gesture embracing the entire array.

"There," he said.

Magda moved slowly forward. "You give—to me?"

"Why not?"

Abel stalked out. Magda stood still, looking about her, attempting breathlessly to estimate the amount of her price. She picked up at random a pair of stockings and ran them through her fingers. Then, as though the feel of the soft fabric had convinced her of the moment's reality, she darted to close the door. Stripping off the drab gray dress, she began feverishly trying on first one and then another garment that chanced to catch her eye. Each successive metamorphosis, from blue to yellow to pink, she examined in the mirror, holding up the lantern to cast a brighter light over the already bright reflection. Several times she shook down her hair for the pleasure of rearranging it with the help of the ivory comb and the silver-backed brush. The air in the cabin became heavy with the mingled scents shaken from the perfume and toilet water bottles.

She was unaware that the keelboat had cast off and paid little heed to the ship's veering and tossing in the rapids. It was the calm of the smooth river below that recalled her to the second reality of the moment. Her attention centered on the door through which her benefactor must presently come to claim his reward. She ran to it, took the key from the peg, and locked it, as she had against Evan's importunities during the voyage from Limestone to Louisville. Glowing with a new excitement, she drew on her favorite among the gowns, a wine-colored satin, thrust a jeweled comb in her hair, and ran back to take her station at the door. Gently removing the key from the lock, she tossed it in her hand, smiling as she contemplated the negotiation of terms that must precede the eventual opening.

But no summons to open came to relieve her vigil. Tiring, she pulled the chair over and sat in it, leaning her head against the door. Still there was no low-voiced appeal, no knock, no tentative rattling of the latch. Waiting, no longer smiling but with patience, for the inevitable, she drowsed and, at length, fell asleep, to awaken at dawn, still in the chair, the key cold in her hand.

7

The whippoorwill, swooping low over the Salt River meadows, trailed behind him his mournful yet urgent cry. Tim Crohon stood up in his blankets and pulled the block away from the loophole. It was still too dark on this west side toward the woods to see much, but he could listen. There was the dawn twitter of small birds, the thump of a rabbit's foot, the gnawing of a porcupine at the elm stump by the woodpile.

Across the cabin his half-sister, Hagar, stood to the loophole on the side toward the river. There was enough light from the eastern sky coming through the opening to gleam faintly on her face, to pick up the blue of the cloth she kept wrapped tightly about her head even at night when she was in bed, and to pick out the white tracery of the scar that ran from her temple down across her cheek and past the corner of her mouth to her chin. Above the scar her dark eyes were as big and soft and beautiful as a cow's and yet, as nearly always, hot with resentment, as when a cow has found out she cannot pull free from a quicksand.

Tim slid over to the loophole by the door. It was getting lighter fast. Three buffalo were grazing under the big elm in the nearest meadow. A feeding catfish was rooting in the mud near the river's edge. A bear sat on the bank, with one paw poised, waiting for the catfish to come within reach. A coon was washing something in the spring. In the girdled sycamore a flock of roosting parakeets preened themselves sleepily.

"Real quiet for sure," he said.

"Nothin's sure," said Hagar, " 'cept some mornin' they'll be there."

Tim sighed, pulled on his moccasins, picked up his rifle, looked to the priming, and opened the door a crack. Nobody could blame Hagar much for having Indians always on her mind. She had been born under a woodpile during one Indian attack, at six had witnessed the tomahawking of her mother during another, and at fourteen had herself been scalped and left for dead during a third. What made things so much worse for her was that she was almost as worried about other people seeing how she looked as she was about herself seeing Indians coming at her again. Yet living far enough away from the nearest settlement to keep out of the sight of neighbors laid them that much more open to more Indian trouble. If it was a pack of twenty or thirty that happened to stumble on the cabin, there would be no use fretting because there would be nothing anybody could do to hold them off. The best they could do was to keep themselves on the lookout against the more likely risk of three or four creeping up during the night either to get set to make a rush for the door when it was first opened, or to hide and wait for a chance to shoot somebody on the way to the spring or the privy.

Ordinarily, Tom, Tim's twin brother, took his turn going out at daylight to make sure something like this had not happened the night before. But while Tom was away in Louisville Tim had the job to do every morning. He opened the door another inch, sniffed the air, listened, and opened it wider, watching which way the wild animals moved off. All edged away in different directions, the buffalo straight upwind against the faint puffs of a southwest breeze. There could be no strange scents drifting around. He closed the door behind him and set out upon the accustomed round, keeping far enough back in the woods to come up on every fallen log, thicket, or hollow from the side away from the cabin and paying particular attention to the edge of the nearer canebrake and the fringe of weeds along the high-water mark on the riverbank. The way the blue jays and chipmunks and catbirds were going about their ordinary business made it certain that there was nothing new around to be worth their watching. But he kept at it until he had examined every patch of cover within long rifle shot of the cabin. There was no getting out of doing that if he was to face that quick, questioning look Hagar would give him when he got back.

Tim was a good two inches over six feet and still growing. The size of his hands and feet indicated that he would be a really big man when his growth was complete. He still walked with the shambling gait of a boy, but the first fuzz of manhood was thickening along his jawline. Already immensely strong, he was beginning to become aware of it. Were he actually to stumble upon an Indian, his immediate instinct would be not to shoot him but to try to get his hands on him.

The sun pushed up out of the greater canebrake across the river. There had been but three or four sunny days this whole wet spring, but this promised to be a warmer one. He started back, pausing only to shoot a brace of wood ducks swimming so exactly abreast that he was able to take off both heads with the one shot. It was a great waste of powder for so little meat, and they always had more game than they could eat, but he was tired of the spring leanness of venison and elk and buffalo. He waved to Hagar peering from the doorway to let her know there had been nothing alarming about the shot, reloaded, retrieved and cleaned the ducks, and kept on to the cabin.

Hagar had already eaten, but there was a dish of deer tripe boiled with swamp lettuce waiting for him. She had a hoe in her hand and had tied her dress up above her knees to keep it out of the burdocks and blackberry vines. The sudden warmth of the morning had decided her to begin planting corn. Having had the sole care of the twins since they were five, she had become so accustomed to doing all the heavy work that it seemed never to have occurred to her that now at sixteen they were more than able to do their share. She began chopping with the hoe, grubbing out roots and old weeds and sod, as she dug hills for her corn. The harder the work the more fiercely she went at it. She was as strong as most men and seemed never to tire, though she always tried to tire herself out by night.

Tim finished eating and stood back in the cabin in line with the doorway watching her. The hoe rose and fell, each descent as quick and hard as though she were taking a cut at a copperhead. Yet, no matter how hard she worked, she put so much into it that she made it look as smooth and easy as a deer jumping over a log.

She was sweating already and her thin cotton dress was beginning to stick to her bent back. She was big of shoulder and bosom, narrow at the waist, and big again across the hips. Below her tucked-up dress her thighs were round and white. When the scarred side of her face was turned away, and if he had been able to forget that under that cloth wrapped around her head she was bald, he would have counted her as fine a looking woman as any he had seen when he had taken his furs to Louisville last spring, which was the first time that he had ever taken any notice of how women looked.

His breath went short and his glance went to the kettle of water Hagar had left beside the fire to warm. Shivering, he came to a decision. With the point of his knife he removed a tiny bit of clay from the chinking between the logs of the wall. Stepping out on the doorstep, he stopped to stretch, yawn, and look down at the river.

"If yuh had some fish," he called to Hagar, "yuh could plant 'em in yer corn hills."

"If'n yer fixin' to go fishin'," she replied, looking up not at him but around at the woods, "fetch me my rifle."

He took her rifle to her. She drew the charge, reloaded, and leaned the piece against the girdled sycamore.

"I'll be right there in sight on the bank," he told her, "makin' me a fish trap."

He went down to the river and began cutting and peeling willow withes. He was shivering again and twice he dropped his knife in the water. The day was beginning to get almost hot. He gave up all pretense of working on the trap and squatted against the bank watching Hagar and the sun. The sun crept upward, until finally it was overhead.

Hagar straightened, glanced at the sky, did three more hills, exchanged the hoe for the rifle at the sycamore, and went to the cabin. Picking up the ducks beside the doorstep, she plastered them with wet clay at the spring and went in. She thrust the ducks into the ashes in the fireplace and raked a heap of the warmer embers over them. Then, with sudden swift, impatient movements, she barred the door, stripped off her sodden clothing, and began to scrub herself with warm water from the kettle by the fire. She was brisk and vigorous until she had removed all obvious traces of dirt and grime and then began to take more care. Her face was tanned and still streaked with dust, but from the neck down her skin glistened. Her body was as smooth and firm and white as ivory. As she continued bathing herself she twisted and turned to examine every part that she could see, bestowing upon her figure the detailed, lingering, critically affectionate inspection which a lady of fashion might give her face. When she was dry she continued to stroke her thighs and flanks, to cup her breasts in her hands, to touch a fingertip to the glowing nipples. She could not have endured one glimpse of her face in a mirror, but she could find some appeasement in the contemplation of her body. Its beauty was her one consolation.

Tim backed away from his peephole in the cabin wall. His face was as pale and drawn as though he had been tied to a post and watching the approach of Indian tormentors with outthrust firebrands. He turned and ran, stumbling.

From across the river came the whistle of an elk, thrice repeated. Tim pulled the canoe out of its hiding place in the nettle patch and paddled across to meet Tom. Tom came along the buffalo trace out of the big canebrake. He tossed his pack into the canoe and got in facing Tim. Except that one held a paddle and the other did not the twins looked as much alike as the two ends of the canoe.

"Pete Branch he wouldn't take some of the muskrat," Tom said. "But he give a right good trade fer the marten and otter. Twan't argufyin' with him, though, thet made me a day late gittin' back."

There was something out of the ordinary about the nature of the occasion for this delay, and Tom paused to give Tim a chance to ask about it. Only then did he notice that Tim was possessed by an excitement of his own. Tim's pallid, damp face indicated a possible disaster.

"Whut's happened?" Tom demanded.

Tim went on paddling until the canoe grounded on the west shore. He laid the paddle across his knees and forced himself to meet Tom's eyes.

"You know how she's always washin' herself," he said. "This noon I watched. Recollect how many times we've wondered whut else she might have wrong with her—such as mebbe the Injuns sculpin' her in both places like they sometimes do? Well, there ain't nothin' else wrong with her. I looked and I could see plain. They ain't a mark on her from the chin down."

Tim spoke defiantly and braced himself for an outburst of disapproval or ridicule. But Tom gave sober consideration to the revelation. At length he nodded judiciously. There was apparent in Tom a more worldly poise than when he had left for Louisville four days before.

"Then there ain't no real good reason why she shouldn't have her a man," he pronounced.

"They's one real good one. How's she goin' to get one way off here in the brush? There ain't one nearer'n old Sol Trexler over on Flint Creek."

Tom shook his head sagely. "Old Sol won't do. He's too old and he wan't but half a man when he was young. She's got to git her a fit one."

"Was any kind of a man to show up, she'd only run and lock herself in the cabin like she does when old Sol comes past. She don't even like you or me to look at her."

The smile Tom gave Tim was tolerantly superior. "You don't know no more about it than I might of last week. But I ain't fooled no longer. She wants a man all right. Thet's why she can't sleep nights. She's ten years older'n us—and most o' thet time she's bin a-wantin' one. I know. I found out."

"Whut did you find out?" inquired Tim, at last cooperative.

Tom launched happily upon the accounting that he had been eager to make from the first. "Yuh know thet widder thet keeps the pigs in thet cabin the tother end o' the first pond this side o' Louisville? Well, as I come past, one of her pigs got away and I helped her ketch it. We got to talkin' about this'n thet—and she tuk me in and give me some supper—and then she tuk me to bed with her."

Tim's eyes grew round. This, the first consummated experience either twin had had, was an important milestone in their secluded lives. He gulped and reddened but finally got out the question.

"How was it?"

Tom drew a long breath and made a helplessly expansive gesture that embraced river, forest, and sky. "There ain't no way to tell yuh, Tim. All I got to say is thet it's one o' them things yuh got to find out fer yerself. I told her you'd be comin' past in a coupla days with yer half the furs and she'll be watchin' fer yuh."

When Tim returned from his journey to Louisville, he brought news even more momentous than had been Tom's.

"Yuh know who I seen at Pete Branch's store?" he announced. "Peleg Dobson."

"No!" exclaimed Tom.

"He was there tradin' in furs fer fixin's—same as I was. He said him and Gareb and Boaz wintered in a cave down the Ohio below the Wabash. He said they bin trappin' mink and huntin' buffler. He said they aim to stay there—leastwise 'til their corn's ripe."

"Didn't yuh stop to see the widder neither comin' or goin'?"

"Both times. So I know whut you mean when yuh say we got to do somethin' about Hagar findin' her a man."

The twins stared at each other. There was no need for an exchange of further words on the subject. They thought as much alike as they looked alike, and their recognition of the miraculous opportunity was simultaneous. Each was recalling with the dreadful clarity of childhood memory that day at Heron Creek eleven years ago when last they had seen the Dobsons. Their father had been breaking the colt, their mother making soft soap in a keg by the doorstep, their sister Melissa teaching a calf to drink from a bucket, their brother Bert splitting rails, and Hagar pounding corn in the hominy stump. So complete had been the surprise that a moment which had begun with the loudest sound their father's chuckle when he got the halter over the colt's nose ended in an eruption of gunshots, war whoops, and screams.

Only they, then five years old, had escaped. They had crawled off behind the pigpen into a pile of uprooted stumps that had been stacked for later burning, and there had lain, faces pressed against the ground, eyes screwed shut, until the second din of gunshots had commenced. They had looked out then to see their nearest neighbors, the three young Dobsons, working forward along the edge of the woods. Peleg, Gareb, and Boaz had come on, darting from tree to tree, only one of them ever shooting at a time so that always there were two rifles loaded and ready to fire. The dozen Indians capering about the burning cabin had taken off over the hill toward the Ohio. The Dobsons, after one glance at the mutilated bodies in the dooryard, had kept on after the Indians.

Tim and Tom had crouched, overwhelmed by terror and grief, in their hiding place until they had seen Hager rise to her feet and stagger off through the knee-high corn. She had been blinded by the blood pouring down over her face. When she had heard them running after her she had herself tried to run. At the ford she had pitched in among the horses of the militia platoon on its way over from the Fish Creek stockade. Somebody had guessed there might still be hope for Hagar and a horse litter had been contrived to carry her to Fort Henry, where there was an army surgeon. When she had lived and her strength had been restored, she had refused to return to the neighborhood where she was known. The three survivors of the Crohon family had thereupon embarked upon their wandering existence along the wildest fringes of the settlements.

To the twins the most vivid memory of that terrible day had been the deadly and business-like competence with which the young Dobsons had driven off the Indians, and behind that picture there was the other memory that for the month preceding the attack the three brothers had been coming over nearly every evening to sit by the Crohon fire and make sheep's eyes at Hagar.

"Did yuh tell Peleg Hagar was here?" asked Tom.

"I didn't tell him nothin'."

"Yuh was right. We can't afford to skeer him off. And we don't dast tell her about him yet neither."

"I figgered thet out, too, on my way back. But she's always ready to move on—no matter where—just so long's it's someplace else."

"Yuh'd have to put her in a sack to git her to a place where there's as many folks as at Louisville."

"Whut I figgered was a sight better'n gittin' her to Louisville. Was we'uns to show up down the Ohio at thet big cave —accidental like—it'd be too late fer her to back off. And all three Dobsons would be there, not jest Peleg. There ain't nothin' soft-nosed about any o' them and they bin spendin' their time off in the woods near as much as we have. Mebbe the first couple o' looks at her will put 'em off some, but like as not they'll come around to recollectin' the way she looked when she was fourteen and take to elbowin' one another off as hard as they uster then. Leastwise, thet's the way I figgered it out."

"I couldn't o' figgered it out no better myself," marveled Tom.

They had made so many other moves that a new one was not a matter of much moment. Loading their few belongings in the canoe, they set out. Their precipitate departure did not, however, pass unobserved. From his perch in the huge sycamore that stood on the bank immediately across the river from the cabin, old Sol Trexler watched disconsolately. During the months the Crohons had spent here he had many times crept to this hidden lookout. At first he had been moved by the natural curiosity of a lonely old recluse. The most ordinary activities of his new and only neighbors engrossed him. Later he had taken a special and growing interest in observing Hagar. Three notable times his hours in the tree had coincided with occasions when she had come right down to the riverbank to wash clothes, and there had been one unforgettable spring afternoon when, with the boys away, she had bathed in the stream. His neighbors' sudden departure was to him a stunning deprivation. He could only hope that sooner or later they might come back, at least long enough to harvest their corn when it ripened.

The Crohons kept on down the Salt and then on down the greater river. They were now in country lonelier even than the meadows. From the mouth of the Salt the next white settlement downriver was the Spanish town of New Madrid five hundred miles away on the farther bank of the Mississippi. But the wilderness gave them no qualms. Since their recent trading in Louisville they were well provided with powder and salt. All else they could take from the country through which they traveled and they were free to travel on as far as they chose. Hagar was comforted, as always, by movement and solitude. Her brothers controlled their impatience and paused often to hunt or to fish or to investigate an island. They had proposed to Hagar that when they found an island properly situated they would settle on it at least long enough to raise a corn crop. Any island, they argued, would prove a safer site than their former exposed location on the Salt River meadows. But with each island that they examined they found some unsatisfactory feature. Hager was content to keep on going.

When they had passed the mouth of the Wabash the twins yielded to the temptation to make a longer day's run of forty miles and began eagerly to scan the north bank. They found the cave just where they had been led to expect it—but along with it a crushing double disappointment. It was not a third as big as the cavern Peleg had described, and there were no signs that it had ever been occupied by anybody.

"Thet Peleg," muttered Tom. "He surely aimed to put you on a cold track."

Tim was bewildered. "It don't make no sense," he said. "He tuk on like he was real glad to see me. And this here cave's got a spring in it just like the one he said they wintered in. Only trouble it's so much littler'n he made out."

"And thet nothin' but a litter o' wood rats ever wintered in it," added Tom.

Hagar backed out after an inspection of the cave's inner recesses.

"Be a real good place to camp," she said, "if'n it only was on an island." She looked across at the rocky island in mid-channel opposite the mouth of the cave.

" 'Fore we push off," said Tim, "I'm goin' to take me a look around."

He began climbing the limestone escarpment above the cave, but before he had reached the top he slid hurriedly down again.

"Flatboat," he said.

They pulled their canoe farther out of sight into the brush on the bank and crouched beside it, watching. The flatboat that Tim had sighted from above swung around a bend. Traveling so much faster in their canoe, they must have overtaken it within the past hour and have missed it behind one of the many islands in this stretch of the Ohio. Flatboats were uncommon this far down the river, but this one was being handled by men who seemed to know what they were about. There were no farm animals aboard, indicating the owner was more likely to be a trader headed for Kaskaskia or Saint Louis than a settler bound for New Madrid or Natchez. It swung away to pass on the far side of the rocky island. Then one of the four-man crew pointed and yelled and with much vigorous splashing of sweep oar and poles the flatboat swung back into the north channel and directly toward the cave.

The three Crohons reacted as instinctively as so many wild animals. Tim and Tom picked up the canoe and, keeping behind the fringe of willow and aspen at the water's edge, moved it to a new hiding place two hundred yards downstream. Hagar caught up a branch and smoothed the tracks left about the cave and during their retreat. Tim and Tom looked to their rifles and crept back partway to watch the disembarkation and judge the character of the men who were making it.

The flatboat grounded. While Gideon and Zeb held it steady old Jonas landed and peered into the cave.

"Dry," he said and glanced at the sky. "She's fixin' to rain 'fore mornin'."

Gideon and Zeb snubbed the mooring lines to trees and joined him. Instead of following, Samuel Hoopes crept along the rail under the overhanging branch of an oak leaning out over the boat from the bank. Each day since they had passed Louisville without stopping the words of Neave's prophecy—"they're sure to cut your throat"—had rung the more fearfully in his ears. But he was unable to swim and never until now had they camped except on an island.

"Whereat's Sam?" asked Jonas.

Samuel shivered and looked longingly at the mainland bank but an arm's length away. Overcome by the panic that had been growing on him for days in the confinement of existence aboard the flatboat, he scrambled over the rail, jumped awkwardly ashore, and burrowed frantically into the brush at the river's edge.

"Come back here, yuh one-legged pack rat," roared Jonas.

Gideon and Zeb sprang into the undergrowth. Samuel reappeared, crawling desperately up the cliff. Jonas raised his rifle deliberately and fired. Samuel pitched backward. Gideon and Zeb came back out of the thicket.

"Daid?" inquired Jonas.

"Right back o' the ear," said Zeb.

"Whereat's thet catfish yuh ketched this mornin'?" asked Jonas, beginning to kick together sticks for a fire.

Tim and Tom exchanged glances, pursed their lips, and began backing noiselessly away on hands and knees. Regaining their canoe, they slipped it into the water and started on downriver, hugging the cover of the overhanging trees along the north bank. A half-mile farther on, Tim, in the bow, suddenly dug his paddle into the bottom.

Just above them and not five feet above the level of the river was the yawning mouth of an immense cavern, many times larger than the disappointing first one. Tim gestured. Tom leaned forward to peer up through the overhanging branches of a clump of cedar that partially masked the caverns mouth. On the crest of the cliff above the entrance stood two bearded men, rifles ready, staring off upriver in the direction of the recent shot. The twins looked at each other. They could not be sure.

"Git on past," whispered Hagar fiercely. "Git on past 'fore they come down."

Her brothers, usually so quick to consider her slightest frown, only signified to her to be quiet. She attempted to wrest the paddle from Tim, but in the silent test of strength he was as determined and much stronger. One of the bearded men had disappeared from the crest above. There was another entrance somewhere back in the hill, for presently he reappeared in the mouth of the cave. Again the twins exchanged glances. Now they were sure. Hagar turned to clutch at Tom but he pushed her away.

"Gareb," called out Tim. "Gareb Dobson."

Gareb was as startled by the sound of his name coming suddenly up at him as he might have been by a thrown tomahawk whizzing past his head. He sprang back, lifting his rifle.

"Yuh tol' me yerself," whispered Tom, "they wasn't goin' by the name Dobson no more."

"Thet's why I put it to him," said Tim. "To show him right off somebody's come thet knowed him way back."

Gareb had been startled but far from intimidated. He crouched, darted out from the cave to the edge of the bank, and squatted by a stone, attempting to see down through the cedar branches.

"Speak up," he demanded. " 'Less yuh want a bullet to loose yer tongue. Who be yuh?"

"Tim Crohon," called Tim. "Me and my brother Tom."

"Come out where I kin see yuh."

The twins got out of the canoe and beached it, taking care to retain possession of the paddles but laying aside their rifles. Then, together, they stepped out into the open. Hagar, with a low moan, tore open her pack, snatched out a shawl, and wound it about her head and face. Tim and Tom pushed out of the cedar and grinned up at Gareb. He stood erect but still stared suspiciously, his rifle halfway to his shoulder, his finger on the trigger. On the cliff above his brother, Boaz, was watching with his rifle all the way up and aimed.

"You remember the Crohons," said Tim, "back at Heron Creek—thet spring you was clearin' a place up by the forks— and the Injuns jumped up. We was the twins thet got away."

Gareb continued to stare coldly and suspiciously. "They was only a pair of knee-high snotnoses when last I seen 'em." He relaxed slightly. "Yuh do put me some in mind of yer paw, if'n Andy Crohon was yer paw."

Tim and Tom climbed up on the rock ledge that formed a kind of forecourt to the mouth of the great cave. Gareb stepped past them and peered again down through the cedars.

"Who's thet still down there in yer canoe?"

"My sister Hagar," said Tom. "You remember Hagar?"

Gareb's attitude changed materially. He slapped first Tim and then Tom on the shoulder.

"Whyn't she come along up here with you?"

"She's powerful bashful around strangers," explained Tim.

The slithering of Boaz' moccasins far back in the recesses of the cave decided Gareb.

"Mebbe I better mosey down and tell her we ain't eggsactly strangers."

He laid aside his rifle and plunged down through the cedars. Boaz came running out of the cave and scowled at Tim and Tom. He was even more stand-offish than Gareb had been at first.

"So you call yerself the Crohon boys?" he said coldly. "Whereat's Gareb?"

"Down there talkin' to Hagar," said Tim. "You remember my sister Hagar?"

The disclosure that Hagar was one of the visitors made as instant an impression on Boaz as it had on Gareb. He turned to jump down into the cedars, but Gareb was climbing back up. He was nursing the side of his jaw and fuming with indignation.

"She could o' pushed me off if'n she wanted, but she had no call to clout me with the butt of her rifle," he said. "All I done was give a little pull at her shawl."

"Like we told yuh," said Tom, "she's powerful bashful."

Boaz laughed loudly at Gareb's discomfiture.

"Gareb he's got mighty low manners. Mebbe I better go down and tell her she don't have to pay him no mind."

But Hagar herself was coming up. She stood beside them, her eyes burning in the shadow of the shawl as she glared at the Dobsons and then at her brothers.

"You knowed all along who was here," she accused them.

"That's right," said Tim. "I seen Peleg in Louisville. Tom and me we figgered we better stop past and say howdy to Gareb and Boaz—bein' as they useter be neighbors."

"Long's yuh crave to have folks look at me," said Hagar, "let's let 'em look."

She whipped off the shawl and turned the scarred side of her face to Gareb and Boaz. Gareb took a step back, but Boaz spat nonchalantly and grinned at her.

"I've seen plenty o' folks thet bin left by Injuns lookin' a sight worse'n thet," he said.

Hagar's knees buckled and she sagged to a seat on a stone. The shawl slipped from her fingers. She recovered it and began, desolately, to wrap it again about her head. Gareb caught Boaz' arm and drew him aside. Their whispered conference was marked by a sharp difference of opinion. The twins had been standing, rigid, silent, breathless, but now they shifted uneasily.

"We got us a brace o' turkeys down in the canoe," remarked Tim.

Hagar rose. "We done all we come to do here," she said bitterly. "Time fer us to git movin' on."

Boaz pulled away from Gareb. "No," he said. "Too nigh dark to find yuh a fit place to camp. Bring up yer turkeys—and yer blankets too."

Hagar faced him, her eyes steady and no longer fierce. "Yuh don't fer sure want us to stay," she challenged him.

"Why not?" His tone became more hearty. "We was neighbors oncet, wasn't we?"

The cooking fire was well back in the cave where no glint of its light might reach the open river. Before it was full dark Hagar had one of the turkeys plucked and the halves split, spitted, and grilling over the coals. Gareb and Boaz lounged by the fire, pulling at a jug of whisky which presently, as their mood became more jovial, they offered also to their guests. The twins, unaccustomed to the fiery liquor, choked and blinked and thereafter only pretended to drink when the jug was passed. But Hagar poured out a cupful and sipped it at intervals during her attention to cooking the turkey. Each time that she stepped back and lifted the cup, her eyes, big and bright over the rim, passed speculatively over the Dobsons, sprawled beyond the fire beside their jug. The twins, watching, took heart. Hagar, inspecting Gareb and Boaz, must perceive their essential qualities, just as they, given time, must perceive hers. Not even along this border, where it was common to find men big and hardy and handy, was she likely often to come across their equal. For all their long beards their laughter had the readiness and their glances the quickness of young men. Neither could be much over thirty. Either was as right for Hagar as when he had come courting her back at Heron Creek.

After the turkey was eaten, the Dobsons refilled the jug. Tim and Tom stirred about restlessly, increasingly curious about the Dobson way of living and yet careful not to seem to pry. People who dwelled in a cave must handle a good many things a little differently, but for all their laughing and talking the Dobsons had volunteered no remarks throwing any light on what these differences might be.

The floor of the cavern sloped up gradually toward the back which, judging by the echo, extended more than a hundred feet deeper into the hill. Trickling down the center and on past the fire was a tiny stream of clear, sweet water. Along either wall was a wide rock shelf, five feet high near the entrance but becoming lower and eventually merging with the inclined floor farther back. These shelves provided platforms, which had been converted to storage space for the Dobson possessions and to a raised location for their beds. Nothing about the cave was more interesting than the amount and the variety of the effects stowed along the two shelves. The accumulation oddly exceeded the ordinary needs of three men living in the wilds. Within the range of gleams from the fire were eight barrels, nine kegs, four bales of blankets, seven extra rifles, half a dozen iron or brass kettles, and even one rocking chair.

Hagar banked the fire, picked up her blanket roll, and withdrew toward the back of the cave. Gareb and Boaz watched her until she had disappeared into the darkness. Boaz handed the jug to Gareb and grinned.

"Still skeered?"

Gareb swore and started to rise. Boaz pulled him back down.

"You've done had one try," he pointed out. "Next go is mine."

But instead of embarking immediately upon it, he reached again for the jug. Tim and Tom, spreading their blankets on the shelf across the way, pretended to be taking no notice. Boaz took a long drink, rested one big hand playfully upon the top of Gareb's head, and pushed himself to his feet. He was none too steady but after a couple of long breaths regained his balance. The twins rolled over to watch as he sauntered slowly back into the darkness. When he had faded from view they stared at each other, and held their breaths and listened.

The silence was broken by a laugh from Boaz, followed by an oath and then a howl of pain. He came stumbling back into the firelight. There was a dribble of blood from a bruise on his temple, but he was more awed than angered.

"She surely is meaner'n three catamounts," he acknowledged. "I put a foot on her rifle and got hold of her knife hand, but she swung around with the other and hit me with a rock bigger'n yer two fists."

Gareb laughed immoderately. Hagar came into the circle of light. Her eyes were burning again but her voice was cold and measured.

"Whoever happens on the idee he wants to come sidlin' over by me," she said, "let him pick his time when it's light —fer if'n he comes creepin' up in the dark it'll never be no use."

Having published her decree, she strode back to her couch. Gareb looked at the bruise on Boaz' head, fingered the lump on his own jaw, and began again to laugh. This seemed, belatedly, to arouse Boaz' anger. He prodded Gareb with a moccasined toe and motioned to him to get up. The two went to the mouth of the cave, but there, instead of fighting, they became involved in a muttered consultation.

"You two sprouts in there," said Boaz. "Come out here."

The twins slid off the rock shelf and joined the conference in the cavern's mouth.

"All we got to say is this," said Gareb. "First crack come mornin' you uns figger on pushin' off. We got no room fer yuh here."

The ruling was handed down with a finality to match the one Hagar had pronounced. Gareb and Boaz went into the cave and rolled into their blankets. The twins slid down the rocky bank, squatted at the water's edge, and squinted out over the gleaming black river.

"All them extry fixin's they got stacked back there in the cave," said Tom. "Yuh know whut they spell out, don't yuh?"

"Whut?" asked Tim absently.

"They's off other folks' boats. The Dobsons they ain't bin trappin' nor huntin'. No—nor plantin' corn neither. They've turned river pirate. And you've heard how river pirates work, ain't yuh? They send off a man to some place like Louisville where he kin look around and size up whut boat is most worth takin' and then mebbe git him a job on thet boat hisself. Thet makes everything easy when the time comes to go fer it. Thet's what Peleg was doin' when you seen him in Louisville. All of it goes to show why the Dobsons can't afford to have us hangin' around here."

Tim voiced neither assent nor dissent to this hypothesis. He merely continued to stare out at the river. Tom stirred impatiently.

"If'n you'd oncet stop to think," he said, "you'd git it thunk out just as plain as I done."

"Whut I was gittin' thunk out," said Tim, "was how much better fixed we'd be if'n we stayed on here 'til Peleg shows up. Peleg he's younger'n Gareb and Boaz and not so sot in his ways. And I keep recollectin' how real glad he was to see me back there in Louisville. We might make out real good was we to stay on here."

Tom grunted scornfully. "How long's it goin' to take yuh to ketch on why they ain't a-goin' to let us stay? They don't want us around when they knock down the next river boat. They take us fer just a couple of boys who'd git in the way."

Tim was still mildly thoughtful. "But if'n they aim to keep on jumpin' boats, they'd be better off if'n they was more

142

than three o' them. And you and me—we're some better than boys. Whut we got to do is make 'em see thet."

"How? Pound on 'em like Hagar done? Mebbe we could, but oncet we started in, we'd have to keep at it 'til it was either them or us—and whut good would thet be to any-body?"

Tim turned slightly to look off upriver. "No, it wasn't the Dobsons I was thinkin' about poundin' on."

Tom gave a long, low whistle. "Yuh got it," he exclaimed. "Yuh got it." He sank a congratulatory fist into Tim's middle. "I couldn't o' figgered thet no quicker myself."

They returned to the cave for their rifles. Gareb and Boaz were already snoring in their beds on the shelf. One of the more useful features of dwelling in the great cave was relief from any need to post a night guard. Potential attackers were not likely to venture into that mysterious expanse of darkness, unable to know from what direction the invisible defenders might not spring out upon them.

The twins crept down to their canoe. The lower point of the rocky island was just opposite the cave. From the south bank beyond jutted out a towering cliff that narrowed the river and speeded its normally sluggish current. In this swifter water they rounded the point and drove upstream on the farther side of the island.

There were one or two distant rumbles of thunder but, to their relief, no revealing glows of lightning. It began to rain. They drew on the deer-bladder shields over the locks of their rifles to keep the priming dry, and resumed paddling. The rain was a mixed blessing. It provided welcome cover to their approach to their quarry, but it also meant that if some un-foreseen emergency developed they could not rely certainly upon their rifles.

They rounded the upper end of the island, crossed to the deeper shadows of the north bank, and drifted with the cur-rent down toward the lesser cave and the flatboat that was moored before it. The rain grew heavier, with some signs that it was a spring shower that might soon pass. When they were within what they estimated was something like a hun-dred yards of their destination, they beached the canoe, picked up their rifles, and waded in the shallows under the overhanging trees.

At length the dim shadow of the flatboat took shape before them. The downpour was driving so hard on trees and river as to drown out any sound they might have made as they waded on, but from here on Tim, in the lead, took hardly more than a step a minute. The project upon which they were embarked was too important to be handicapped by the slight-

143

est want of care. They were not troubled by scruples, but they were gripped by an intense excitement of the sort that might have possessed them had they been moving in on a wounded bear in a canebrake or crawling up on an Indian hunting camp. They had had opportunity to witness how venomous was the prey they were stalking.

Tim ducked under the upstream mooring line and presently was able to reach out and touch the side of the flatboat. He crouched and hitched forward between the boat and the bank under the overhanging tree into which they had seen the lame man plunge when he had tried to escape from his companions. Parting the drooping branches an inch at a time, he looked out and then reached back to draw Tom on alongside him.

The rain was slackening and through it what awaited them was suddenly identified by two dim glows of light. The one was the heap of coals of the cooking fire in the cave mouth. Beyond it, sprawled in sleep in the cave's shelter, were the two younger boatmen. Their rifles were leaning against the wall of the cave by their heads. The other and much fainter glow fell upon the old man's beard from the pipe held upsidedown in his mouth. He was seated on a stool in the open door of the cabin of the flatboat, and his rifle was across his knees. These were not senseless movers, seldom able to tell the difference between night and day. They were seasoned rivermen who were never for a moment off guard.

Tim's grip on Tom's wrist tightened. His gesture encompassed the two principal tasks confronting them. The two rifles leaning against the wall of the cave must be snatched before the owners awakened, and at the same instant the other rifle in the old man's lap must be taken away from him. Tom nodded. Tim made another gesture allotting responsibility for the two undertakings. Tom nodded again.

Tim retreated beyond the tree to the corner of the flatboat and crawled over the rail. He was the dimmest shadow in the wet darkness, but in any event the old man, sitting in the cabin doorway out of the rain, could only see toward the cave and downriver. The flatboat's cargo was stacked between the stern and the cabin, lashed to the deck, and covered by a tarpaulin. Tim edged along beside its bulk and then, crouching, alongside the cabin until he was in a position to throw himself upon the old man the second that he jumped up out of the doorway.

Tom crawled ashore and up the brushy slope toward the mouth of the cave. The rain had almost stopped, but there was still a loud drip from the trees. The clouds were parting

144

in the east and the first gray light of dawn was beginning to filter through. Tom worked nearer the cliff to place a serviceberry bush between him and the old man on watch down on the flatboat. He was now within ten feet of the cave's mouth and could hear the heavy breathing of the two sleepers. Lying on the ground before him was a peeled fifteen-foot length of hickory sapling which one of the boatmen had begun shaping into an extra boat pole. Tom was just gathering his feet under him to make his spring into the cave when the old man stood up in the cabin doorway and let out his yell.

"Gid—Zeb," he bellowed. "Daylight."

With the automatic precision of men accustomed to awaken instantly at any hour, the two sleepers rose in one continuous movement from their blankets, grasped their rifles, and stepped out into the open. Tom, crouched to one side almost at their feet and looking up at the huge figures looming over him, was suddenly confronted by a situation in which they were two to his one and armed with dry loaded rifles, while the lock of his was still covered by the dripping deer bladder. His hands closed on the end of the peeled hickory pole. There was not time to lift it. He could only swing it in a quick horizontal arc to bring it crashing into Gideon and Zeb at the level of their elbows and the hands clasping their rifles. The spasm of fear that he was about to fail lent an explosive strength to his powerful shoulders. The impact of the ghostly pole materializing suddenly out of the shadows knocked both men to the ground. Cursing, clutching at one another, they lurched up to their knees. By then Tom had whirled the pole high in the air and was bringing it down like a gigantic flail upon their heads. Again and again he struck, panting and grunting, until his sprawled victims had ceased to squirm.

When the old man had yelled, Tim had looked down for a second while stripping the cover from the lock of his rifle. His immediate thought had been that there might after all be need for shooting. It was still too dark to see what was happening up at the mouth of the cave, but the confused sounds of struggle there brought the old man out of the cabin doorway with such surprising agility that he was halfway over the rail before Tim had sprung upon him. The two fell from the rail into the shallow water between the flatboat and the bank. Here, threshing about, locked in one another's embrace, it became a question of which could go the longer without breathing. The old man's strength proved as surprising as his agility, and Tim was twice on the verge of letting go before he managed to wedge him under the edge of the flatboat and to hold him there with his feet while he got his own head above water.

The two victors met on the bank. Each was pale, gasping for breath, vacant-eyed.

"Whut call yuh got to shiver thet way?" said Tim. "Yuh seen plenty dead folks 'fore this."

"I ain't a-shiverin' no more 'n you," said Tom. "The water I was a-wallerin' around in was colder'n ice. Thet's the only reason I'm a-shiverin'."

Tim wrung out his old felt hat and, to still the chattering of his teeth, mopped his face with it. The old man's body bobbed to the surface and was rolled against the bank by the current. Tim looked away quickly and contemplated instead the crumpled forms behind Tom.

"Yuh surely smacked 'em good," he said.

"After the old geezer yelled," said Tom, "there wasn't much time to set and think."

The sun broke through, low and angry in the east, to cast a scarlet glow upon the river and to make the drip from the trees as red as blood. The usual morning bird chorus was still. The whole forest was silent, seemed to harbor nothing that breathed. The one sound was the implacable drip from the trees. Tim clapped his hat on his head.

"We better be gettin' back 'fore Gareb and Boaz git to wonderin' where we're at. I'll go fetch the canoe."

"I'll go with you," said Tom hastily. "Might be you'd miss seein' which bush back there I left my paddle under."

They returned with the canoe, lifted it aboard, and began to loosen the mooring lines. The sun was losing its earlier redness. Woods and river were taking on a more normal daytime hue. There came the first rustlings and twitterings of the lesser creatures of the wild resuming their ordinary activities. The two boys still moved stiffly, as though dragging weights, still kept their eyes averted from the dead, but were beginning to breathe with less effort. Tim climbed over the rail and picked up a boat pole. Tom let the upstream mooring line begin to slip around its tree to allow the flatboat to swing out into the current. Tim threw down the pole again.

"Hold on," he said. He paused to clear his throat. "Long's we done it, no sense in our not gettin' all the good there is out'n it."

Tom straightened, choked back a gasp of protest, and nodded. There could be no denying the wisdom of their being able to show Gareb and Boaz not only the captured flatboat but the full fruits of their achievement. They dragged the bodies over the rail and dumped them against the cabin on the side toward the river. The locks of the two younger boatmen's rifles had been smashed by the terrible pole, but the old man's had only fallen into the water and was a fine, nearly new Deckhard. They drew in the lines, poled off shore, and began drifting with their prize down to the big cave.

Boaz awoke slowly, grunting and coughing discontentedly, sniffed, opened his eyes, and raised himself wonderingly on one elbow. Hagar had rekindled the fire and had a batch of corn cakes already browning. He prodded Gareb awake so that he, too, could contemplate the novelty. The two eyed one another guardedly. There might be something to be said, after all, for the privilege of awakening of a morning to the smell of fresh hot corn bread and the knowledge that breakfast was ready and waiting. Gareb looked away uneasily and his attention fell upon the twins' empty blankets. The Dobsons scrambled from their shelf and went to the cave's mouth to look out. Instantly they sprang back, lifting their rifles.

A flatboat was being poled in against the bank before the cave. Its two-man crew jumped ashore with the mooring lines. A briefest second look identified the two. Gareb and Boaz, irritated but interested, slid down the bank.

"Yuh never told us nothin' last night about yer havin' yuh a flatboat," said Gareb.

"We didn't last night," said Tim.

The twins continued to appear preoccupied with tying the lines.

"Then whereat yuh come acrost this un?" asked Boaz.

"Up the river by thet little cave," said Tom.

"We seen it last night on our way here," added Tim, "and sort o' figgered we might's well slide back this mornin' and git it."

Gareb swung over the rail, cut one of the lashings and threw back a fold of the tarpaulin.

"Trade goods," he cried. "A real slather o' trade goods."

Boaz' interest rocketed and burst likewise into the open. He sprang up beside Gareb and peeled back more of the tarpaulin. Then, as suddenly, he jerked it over the cargo again and swung around, scowling.

"Whereat's the traders?" he demanded. "Couldn't be no bigger mistake than havin' folks runnin' up to Louisville blattin' about all they lost along this here reach o' the river where we'uns hang out."

A direct reply was made unnecessary by Gareb's having

147

caught sight of the display on the deck behind the cabin. The twins sat on the rail and waited. The Dobsons stared and blinked at the bodies and then at their young guests.

"They look like a tree fell on 'em," said Boaz.

"Or," amended Gareb, "like Dode Tucker thet time he got run through his mill wheel."

"The two with the cracked heads," said Tim, "Tom tapped with a boat pole."

"And the old one," said Tom, "Tim stuffed down under the flatboat."

"Ain't no manner o' question," admitted Boaz handsomely, "they sure ain't a-goin' to do much talkin'."

"The way we looked at it," said Tim, making at last his move to clinch the matter, "was long's we was visitin' here we might's well see if'n we couldn't be some help around the place."

Boaz and Gareb turned aside to mutter for a moment and then turned back to announce the verdict.

"Git yuh some stones to tie to 'em," said Boaz, "and take yer canoe and take 'em out and sink 'em in the river."

"And when yuh git back," said Gareb, "there'll be breakfast a-waitin' fer yuh."

"There's breakfast a-waitin' fer 'em now," said Hagar.

The twins whirled to see Hagar standing on the bank above them. They edged aside, avoiding her eyes. Hagar climbed over the rail and walked steadily to the corner of the cabin. She looked at the bodies, at the Dobsons, and at her brothers. Her face set cold and hard and the thin, white scar became a thread of fire.

"Everybody's got to belong with some kind of folks," she said. "Looks like we've done found the only kind we belong with."

The twins returned from their funereal task to find that the morning repast had taken on some of the aspects of a ceremony. Hagar had ransacked the stores on the rock shelves, and there was even the unprecedented smell of coffee in the air. She did not lend her presence, however, to the atmosphere of celebration. When they came in she passed them in silence and went outside to sit in the sun with her head bowed on her knees. They did not themselves get so far as a sampling of the principal delicacies—the panful of fried ham, the bowl of plum jelly, the tray of corn fritters, and the crock of maple syrup. Gareb and Boaz had first got out the jug. The twins recognized in their acceptance as comrades-in-arms an occasion demanding something more significant than merely pretending to drink. For them, all soon began to swim in a pleasant mist and, overcome by fatigue

148

along with the whisky, they fell into a sleep from which they were only awakened by the sudden new commotion of late afternoon. The day that had begun with one sensation was now to culminate in a greater. Peleg had returned.

He landed his canoe against the bank beside the flatboat. Gareb and Boaz slid down to greet him, smugly prepared to answer his eager inquiries concerning the captured craft and the value of its cargo. But Peleg's entire interest was centered upon his own news. With the flourish of a magician flicking a handkerchief from the rabbit in his hat, he whipped from his pocket a sheaf of banknotes and fanned them out like a hand of cards.

"Fifty pounds in English money," he announced. "More real money'n either you mossbacks ever seen before. And fifty more like 'em a-comin' to us 'fore the deal's over."

Gareb and Boaz stared, fascinated, at the notes, fingered them, and stared, equally fascinated, at Peleg.

Off the big island at the mouth of the Wabash, *Naiad* shot out of the rain squall and came about with a sharp crack of her sail. This was but the last of a succession of squalls that had enlivened existence for those aboard since passing the falls. Wind on the river, here funneled by islands and banks, there deflected by promontories and bends, and next released by wide stretches of open water, could play strange tricks. After only the faintest warning a dead calm could be displaced by the flukiest of gusts. None of these had been sufficient to threaten a keelboat with the sail furled. But with the big sail spread and a lee shore never more than a few boat's lengths away, there had been perpetual hazard. Jasper, his judgment fortified by his years at sea, again and again had prophesied disaster. But Abel, gripping the tiller, leaning with the keelboat's heeling as he might to keep his balance in a canoe, eying the bending trees ashore to estimate the oncoming wind, grinning at Jasper's concern, had persisted in keeping the sail set during the sharpest blows. Twice *Naiad* had all but capsized and had three times run aground. But still he had persisted.

"Long's I got me a sailboat," he had declared, "time I learned how to sail her."

Magda had, of necessity, spent most of her time in the cabin. Whenever, in an interval of calm, she had ventured on deck, there had seemed always to be another riffle of white water sweeping up the river toward them. Abel had been too intent upon his navigation to notice her. It had been nearly as useless to attempt to engage Jasper's attention, for they had seldom exchanged more than a glance before he had looked anxiously away at the sky, the river, or the swinging boom.

Coming out of the squall off Wabash Island with *Naiad* heeling over until one rail was in the water, Abel threw his weight against the tiller and yelled in elation as once more she righted herself.

The wind eased and turned fair. *Naiad* glided swiftly on downriver, swerving gracefully in and out among the islands. Magda came out, climbed up on the cabin, and stood by the mast. She was again wearing the old gray dress, but her hair was bright in the sun, her lips were parted in a half-smile, and glints off the water danced in her eyes. Abel's every necessary glance at Jasper in the bow watching the river ahead, at the drifting clouds, and at the slant of the sail, returned to her. When he was obliged to change course slightly to avoid a sandbar, the taut edge of the sail crept over to cut off his view of her. He shifted his position so that again he could see her.

There was enough wind to ruffle her gleaming hair. She closed her eyes and lifted her face to the sun. As she swayed with the slow roll of the ship she seemed as natural a feature of the scene as were the sunlight, the wind, and the water.

Jasper, as so often, seemed almost as aware as Abel of what was passing through Abel's mind. He came strolling aft, craning over his shoulder at the river ahead.

"Straight reach and a wide channel," he said. "No hurricanes or monsters of the deep in prospect. Could you bring yourself to trust me to take over for a while?"

Their eyes met. Abel grinned.

"I can't think of any real good reason why not," he said.

He relinquished the tiller and walked forward. But instead of keeping on to the bow he paused to lean against the rail just below Magda's station on the cabin roof. After a casual glance toward the bow he looked up at her.

"Nicer day for a change," he remarked.

"Yes," she said. "I notice, too."

She moved from the mast to the head of the ladder nailed to the side of the cabin. He stepped forward. Instead of taking his upstretched hand, she bent, placed one hand on his shoulder, and sprang down to the deck. The brief, firm clasp of her hand upon him was withdrawn. She went into the cabin. He followed and leaned in the open doorway. She paused before the mirror to smooth her wind-tossed hair. Raising her arms lifted her breasts against the thin gray gown.

"At New Orleans what will you do?" she asked.

He took a quick glance at the river ahead and looked back at her. "Sell off the tobacco. Then figger out what I feel like doing."

"You always do what you feel like?"

150

"No. But I like to try."

"And that is what you try now?"

"Depends some on what you feel like."

She lowered her arms and turned slightly, one way and then the other, thoughtfully examining her image in the mirror. Then, continuing to turn, inspected him as thoughtfully.

"How can I know—until——?"

"Until what?"

"How long to New Orleans?"

"Maybe a month."

"In New Orleans you marry me?"

"Like you say, how can we know—until——"

The first step he took toward her ended in their staggering into each other's arms. *Naiad's* headway had come to a sudden, thudding stop. The ship tilted violently, slid, groaning, over some obstruction, righted herself, and swung sidewise. Abel pushed Magda away and ran to the rail. The jagged upper end of the submerged log that he might have failed to perceive in time even from the usual lookout's station in the bow was pounding against the side. The keelboat, shuddering, bumped on past.

He thew back the hatch cover and peered into the hold. He could see nothing but the closely packed rows of tobacco barrels, but he could already hear the faint swish of water and gurgle of water washing back and forth among them. He sprang up on the cabin and climbed the mast to survey the nearer islands and the flat north shore along which they had been coasting. Less than a mile ahead there was a little lagoon, parallel to the river and shut off from it by a brush-covered sandspit except for one sluggish estuary. He slid down the mast, ran to the stern, and seized the tiller from Jasper.

"Get up in the bow," he directed. "I'm going to pull off the river into that pond."

He stood on the rail and, peering ahead, steered with one foot on the tiller.

"Mud bottom," called Jasper from the bow, "but a steady three feet of water in the inlet."

Abel dropped the sail and picked up a pole. Jasper, with his pole in the bow, kept the prow in the middle of the narrow channel. They poled the keelboat into the lagoon, along its south shore and drove the stem up on the beach under an oak, the one big tree along that bank. Clouds of waterfowl rose to circle and scream and then to settle, squawking irritably, upon the farther reaches of the lagoon. The sandspit separating the lagoon from the river was clothed in brush high enough to conceal the hulk of the keelboat from anyone passing on the river and the oak masked the most of the mast. Abel grunted his relief. This was a better spot than he had expected.

"We'll pull out all the barrels in the hold forward of the hatch," he said, "and stack 'em on deck in the stern. That'll weigh down the stern so's with a line over that big oak branch we can hoist the bow up off the beach and give me a chance to get at wherever the leak is."

"Our own dockyard, with one wave of a hand," assented Jasper, sighing, however, at the labor in prospect.

Tim, paddling upriver along the north shore, cut across to the upstream tip of the fourth island above the bend marked by the leaning cottonwood. Here he pulled his canoe out of sight and sat down to wait for Tom who, with Peleg's canoe, had been engaged in a similar sweep of the south channel. They were working according to a set and thoroughly developed plan. At dark they would drop downriver ten or fifteen miles and tomorrow repeat the patrols. They were in separate canoes so that they could at the same time inspect both shores of the river and of every island and so that, when they did sight the keelboat, one could remain to keep her in sight while the other raced down to the cave to inform the Dobsons.

Surveying the shores upriver from his post, Tim had immediately noted the glint in the sky and the parades of ascending and descending waterfowl advertising the existence of a lagoon behind the north bank. He had taken special note of the brush-covered sandspit and of the big oak in the middle of it. He had seen the tip of *Naiad's* mast sticking up above the green circumference of the oak but had decided it was a dead branch. Then, the third time his roving glance returned to the oak, he saw that the angle of the dead branch had changed. Tom arrived and two pairs of keen eyes were devoted to a study of the evidence.

"Them birds they're comin' and goin' like usual," said Tom.

"Soon's yuh bin in a place an hour they start fergettin' yer there," said Tim.

A closer inspection was clearly indicated. Tom waited on the island until Tim had made his dash across to the brushy sandspit. With Tim's hidden rifle now covering his move as his had covered Tim's, Tom made his run. Then together they crept through the brush toward the oak.

The spit was narrow and soon they could make out through the screen of foliage the shape of a keelboat in a most unlikely position with barrels stacked in her stern and her prow pulled up into the lower branches of the oak. They crept forward another ten feet and their eyes glistened. It was not only a keelboat but *the* keelboat. Of the two men busy with a pot of pitch over a little fire, one was red-headed and the other exceptionally tall and thin, exactly according to the description given Peleg by the man in Louisville. Tim twitched Tom's sleeve and jerked his thumb. This was an undertaking of such importance that they must follow instructions to the letter. He would settle down here to watch while Tom hurried to the Dobsons with the good news.

But Tom had scarcely started to hitch his way backward when Tim stuck out his foot and prodded him violently. Tom hitched foward again. They stared, aghast, both paling with an instant realization of how far their situation had turned toward absolute disaster. A young woman had stepped out from behind the oak. They saw in a flash the lovely, unblemished oval of her face and the bright luxuriance of her long, flowing hair. They turned to stare, appalled, at each other. Were such a girl as this one to become a captive of the Dobsons, it must indisputably mean the end of their every hope for Hagar. Slowly a full appreciation of their dilemma sank into them. Merely to withdraw and to affirm that they had never sighted the keelboat was no answer. The boat was bound downriver and the Dobsons, watching at the narrows, were too likely still to gain possession of her and along with her of the girl.

Abel and Jasper crouched under the uplifted bow. Abel was tapping the hull with a mallet.

"See," he said. "Planking's still sound. What happened was that a splinter gouged out the caulking between these two planks right here at the water line. I'll get up inside. You tap here to show me the place—because I've already crawled all around in there and there was no daylight showing through."

Abel climbed aboard and disappeared down the hatch. Jasper picked up a stone and began tapping the hull. Magda had sat down to watch. He heard a sudden gasp from her, but even as he was looking around hands closed on his throat, he was yanked from his squatting position to his back on the sand, and a pair of knees dropped down on him, driving the last vestige of breath out of him. Past the buckskin legs he caught one glimpse of a second pair of buckskin legs swinging over the rail to the deck of the keelboat. Thereafter the point of a knife pressed gently just under his chin held his entire attention.

"Yuh just lay right quiet," advised Tom cheerfully. He spoke to Magda with equal magnanimity. "If'n yuh feel like hollerin', Miss, go right ahead and holler."

"Abel," screamed Magda. "Watch out."

As Abel came scrambling up the ladder out of the hold, a loop of grapevine was slipped from behind around his neck. He got the tips of his fingers under the loop as he was being jerked backward from the ladder to the deck but the vine continued to tighten remorselessly.

The next he knew he was lying on the beach beside Jasper. There was a sapling running up the back of each from heels to head to which they were efficiently tied at neck, elbows, waist, knees, and ankles.

"Can you breathe again?" inquired Jasper. "There was a time I feared you might not."

"Yes," wheezed Abel. "Just."

"That is an immense relief. Our one other comfort is that they have no immediate intention of dispatching us. When the desperadoes saw you were getting black in the face, they made haste to loose the cord around your neck."

Abel started to turn his head to look about him and gave up the effort with a grunt of pain. "How many of them are there?"

"Two. And beardless youths, at that. But of the stature of giants. Giants who look so much alike as to make all seem more than ever a bad dream. Why must it be my fortune always to be set upon by villains of enormous strength?"

"Where's Magda?"

"Escorted in the direction of the river by one of them."

"Didn't she try to put up a fight first?"

"No. The maneuver was explained not only to her but to me in the most careful detail. It seems that her fresh young charms stirred in their rude bosoms a spark of chivalry. They are members of a band of ruffians inhabiting a cave on the riverbank. After gazing at Magda they became reluctant to see her subjected to the starved attentions of their even more uncouth companions. The upshot was that they decided to deny to their associates the pleasure of her company, and they threaten us with unspeakable consequences if we ever mention to any of the others that she was with us when we were taken."

"She won't be much better off left here in the woods."

"They even considered that. From the supply of food they assembled for her and from some mention of canoes, I gathered that their scheme involves escorting her nearer the Wabash, as well as farther from the cave, and setting her free in one of their canoes to make her own way to Vincennes. Have no further concern for Magda. She has all so well in hand that she was able to insist the chest accompany her."

There came a great splash in the lagoon. Abel painfully

twisted his head to look. Tim was casting barrels of tobacco over the rail into the water.

"Note the ease with which he tosses those barrels about," complained Jasper. "The infantile blackguards are possessed of the devil's own strength."

"Strong, all right—except in the head. You'd think he'd have some idea what that tobacco's worth."

"I brought up that point. He replied, I suspect with more point, that the bottoms of the barrels had become water-soaked due to the leak and the tobacco was certain to spoil within the month."

"Could be. I never had much truck with tobacco. Anyway, it's gone now. But before we're through we'll have the boat back."

Jasper's voice rang hollowly. "Before conjuring up hopes for your ship, take thought to what hopes we have for ourselves."

"Don't give in so easy. Just wait a bit. They'll get careless. Something'll go wrong for them. For one thing, before they can shove off they'll have to let us loose long enough to help them roll the boat over on the beach to spill the water out of her. And one of them's only got to look away just once for me to make him wish he'd twisted that vine around somebody else's neck."

"Your perpetual optimism is commendable but this time, I fear, wholly unfounded."

Abel twisted to regard Jasper inquisitively. "What's got you so down? Nobody's dead yet and you said yourself that ain't what they've got in mind."

Jasper groaned. "I am indeed depressed—and with ample reason. You are noticing but the frame of the picture. Consider how much more sinister the entire canvas. Do you not remember that these demoniac children are but members of a band having a settled habitation in a cave?"

"Could be the same big cave Pete Branch told me to look for, down where the river narrows."

"Quite so. The ideal place to lie in wait for a designated victim. For remember also that these fuzzy-cheeked buccaneers were watching the river not just for any victim but for victims of whom they had had a precise description—ours— and you cannot escape the conclusion that Todd Barklit has employed these cave-infesting bandits to assist in our capture."

"Somebody in Louisville could have got word about us downriver all right. That's the way river pirates work. You're just guessing about the rest because you're so scared of Todd."

"Speak with more force, my friend. I yearn to be persuaded. But the truth is inescapable. It came out when our loutish captors referred to our being worth nothing dead. What would ignorant river pirates want with us alive? Who would ransom us?"

"Well, what would Todd Barklit want with you alive?"

"Dead men cannot speak."

"So you know something he doesn't, eh? Every time we get in another fix you come out with something new."

"I have not wanted to burden you with the sum total of my anxieties. But now I shall withhold nothing."

"It's about time."

"Spare me your reproaches since now you must share my fears. I will unveil the principal one. Last summer in New Orleans I offered to sell what I had learned about Wilkinson to the English consul there. He was willing to pay my price, but only if I revealed the source of my information. He had no great interest in Wilkinson but a very great interest in the nature of my access to Spanish councils, which seemed so much superior to his. You must know that all over the world the English are constantly prying at Spanish official secrets. And English agents are everywhere. By the time I reached Pittsburgh, Todd Barklit had been sent from Detroit to intercept me."

"But you've already found out there's no money in Wilkinson. If Todd catches up to you, what's wrong with making the best deal with him you can?"

"Now you have come to the heart of my difficulty. There is no use endeavoring to tell him the truth because he will not believe it were I to tell him. The truth is that it was through the keyhole of the governor's water closet that I witnessed Wilkinson taking the oath. I had crawled there through a window from the garden that night to escape the husband of one of the governor's kitchen maids. That is a full, unvarnished account of my masterpiece of espionage. But who—least of all an English agent—would credit it? Do you, for example? Also, if I may say so, this is distinctly not a seasonable moment to laugh."

"I was only thinking of the trouble the English government has been taking to have you chased all over North America. That and at how serious that busy bastard Barklit has been taking it."

"Nevertheless, it is serious also for me. And, I might remind you, for you as well."

"That I can see. Todd has hung out with Indians enough to have picked up some fancy ways of persuading you to talk.

156

It surely looks like we better get loose before he shows up at that cave."

"How true. But how? This past hour while you lay comfortably oblivious to our situation I have had my wits stretched on the rack—to no purpose. Now you can bestir yours."

The delivery into their hands of the keelboat and the two valuable captives, coming so soon after the acquisition of the fifty pounds and the trade goods, all but overwhelmed the Dobsons' capacity to appreciate their fortune. These were riches far in excess of even the glib Peleg's most farfetched schemes. Possession of the keelboat particularly struck their fancy. Cruising in that swift craft, they could foresee their piratical sorties establishing an absolute dominion over the lower river.

For the Dobsons so great an elation could seek but one sufficient expression. Before the twilight through which *Naiad* had turned the corner around the island had darkened into night, all three were lolling by the fire, each with a pan of whisky at his elbow. This, they assured one another, was an occasion that called for some really important drinking.

The twins moored the keelboat alongside the flatboat. They tossed their captives on the ground far back in the cave. The Dobsons were roaring jubilantly over their recent luck, their present good cheer, and their future prospects. Peleg was taking entire and personal credit for every step in the sudden phenomenal rise in their fortunes.

"The minute I seen Tim back there in Louisville, I seen how handy them two lads would work out fer us. Didn't take me no longer to see thet than it did to sidle up to thet Detroit bugger and git his fifty pounds."

Boaz nudged Gareb. "Like as not next he's goin' to start in tellin' us how the minute he took him a look at Hagar he seen how handy it was goin' to work out to have her always around in easy reach."

"What's wrong with Hagar?" declared Peleg. "Have yerselves another couple o' drinks and mebbe it'll give yuh spunk enough so's yuh don't have to look so close."

"On account o' Peleg's bin doin' so much fer us," said Gareb. "Whut d'ye say, Bo, we let him have his turn first?"

"No call to talk about turns," said Peleg. "Yuh know how it allus is with us. Whutever we git we whack up even."

Gareb and Boaz, lifting their pans of whisky, bellowed with laughter. "That Peleg he's jest as slick as grease," said Boaz. "Whack everythin' up even, he says. Whut he's workin' around to is fixin' so's we'll have to hold her fer him."

157

The twins had walked out on the ledge before the cave to look down at the shadowed outlines of their moored prizes and to settle who would stand first night watch. The Dobsons might scorn all simple precautions, but the trade goods and the keelboat were too valuable to be left unguarded at night. Hagar came out and stood beside them. She spoke with grim calm.

"When they get a mite drunker yuh better watch yer chance to git their guns and knives away from 'em. Then if'n somethin' comes up where yuh'll have to cross 'em, nobody'll have to git hurt bad. If'n yuh leave 'em to me to handle somebody's apt to git his brains knocked out."

In the black darkness of the cave's depths Abel and Jasper, stretched in rigid discomfort side by side, stared toward the distant glow of the fire, and listened to the echoing shouts of drunken laughter.

"How soon would you guess Barklit might arrive?" asked Jasper.

"Depends mostly on how soon he left Louisville and some on how much he fooled around looking behind islands. But I'd guess he might show up 'most any time after daylight tomorrow."

"Daylight tomorrow," complained Jasper. "Since you were but making a guess—why not say noon—or mid-morning—or some time tomorrow? Why select the dawn, that hour so usually allotted to the condemned?"

"He ain't here yet," said Abel. "And we got one piece of a chance in the morning. Back there at the lagoon I made the boys see that the leak was so near the water line that with any kind of a load or rough water she'd go to leaking again. So in the morning they're going to take me down to work on it. The other three are getting so drunk they'll be sleeping it off and I'll have only the two to handle. Maybe I can do something."

Jasper was not in the slightest cheered. "You are a stout fellow, Abel. But you are no match for that pair. Not only are they giants but they are as wary as cats."

"Well, we'll see. What we have to do is try and keep track of what each one of the six of them is up to. Did you get any kind of a look at the girl?"

"A fleeting one in the twilight. She looked a fine stalwart backwoods wench, though sadly disfigured by a scar across her face. I gathered from a remark by one of the bearded ones that the cloth she wore around her head might cover some additional blemish. He referred to her, if I caught the term aright, as 'baldy.' "

"Could be," said Abel. "Every now and then somebody gets scalped and doesn't die after all."

"Ah," exclaimed Jasper. "At last a ray of hope."

In the darkness Abel could not see the play of expression over Jasper's face and thus gain any clue to his sudden excitement. He could hear him smacking his lips, clicking his tongue, giving a succession of low whistles.

"What's come over you?" said Abel.

"More than a ray," said Jasper. "A very substantial straw. Now pay heed, my friend, while I tell you how we clutch it."

The twins had found the task of keeping the Dobsons within bounds a lesser problem than Hagar had forecast. Tim had discovered a keg of cider among the miscellany on the shelf. Filling a jug of their own with this so much milder brew, they joined in the drinking. Stirred to new enthusiasm by this enlargement of their convivial circle, the Dobsons heroically emptied their pans of whisky. Hagar herself refilled them and downed one cupful of her own. After this round the Dobsons continued to debate various interesting projects, but lacked the enterprise to get them under way. Boaz kept mumbling his determination to "ketch her fer Peleg," but each time he struggled to rise, it needed no more than a gentle push to topple him again beside his pan. Hagar, sipping a second cup of whisky sat in the rocking chair beyond the fire in full view. Finally Peleg, stung by his brothers' maudlin taunts, set out to crawl on all fours around the fire. Hagar reached for the ax handle on the ground beside her. But midway in his course Peleg's forearms weakened and he sank slowly flat, his nose doubled against a pebble. Gareb and Boaz made a staggering and gallant effort to retrieve him but, soon exhausted by their exertions, they collapsed sprawling beside him. Without more ado the twins bundled all three into their beds.

Tim went down to the riverbank to stand the first watch. Tom turned into his blankets on the shelf across from the snoring Dobsons. Hagar, forced to realize that there was to be, after all, no emergency, rose from her chair and moved, a trifle unsteadily, toward her own bed back in the cave. Abel, seeing her shadow between him and the distant fire, called out to her.

"My friend's sick. Come look at him."

Hagar went back to the fire, lighted a lantern, and returned, holding it out suspiciously in front of her. In the other hand she gripped the ax handle. She set the lantern down and rolled Abel over to inspect his bonds before turning to look

159

at Jasper. He was panting hoarsely and his eyes were rolled back.

"Whut 'pears to ail him?" she asked Abel.

"I couldn't say. It came on him all of a sudden. He looks like he's got a fever. He's been talking like he's out of his head."

"Water," gasped Jasper. He ceased weaving his head from side to side and his attention became fixed on the lantern. "The water in that pitcher. Let me have it. Pour it over me. I am on fire."

"Thet ain't no pitcher," said Hagar. "Thet's a lantern."

She squatted down, holding it out to get a clearer view of him. His wildly rolling eyes focused on her face.

"Molly," he exclaimed. "Molly, my darling—my beautiful. I knew you would come."

"I ain't yer Molly," said Hagar, turning her face abruptly away.

"Stay with me, Molly," whispered Jasper. "I can soon be well if you will only stay with me."

"I keep tellin' yuh I ain't yer Molly," said Hagar, getting up. "But I'll git yuh some water."

She returned with a cup of water and, lifting his head as far as the thong about his neck would permit, placed the cup to his lips. He strained toward it so frantically that he choked and strangled against the thong.

"Molly. How can you be so cruel, Molly? I am dying. How can you begrudge me even a sip of water?"

Hagar drew the knife from her belt. "No sense a man as sick as you bein' tied up so tight he can't breathe."

She cut the strip of rawhide about his throat. He raised his head and stared up at her ecstatically.

"Bend closer, Molly. Never have I see you so lovely. You are radiant as an angel."

Hagar swung around with the lantern to look at Abel. "Who's this Molly he keeps mewin' about?"

"I couldn't say. Sick people get funny ideas. Sounds like somebody he knew once."

"Molly," implored Jasper. "Don't go. Don't leave me. Come back where I can see you."

"She ain't here," said Hagar. "And lookin' at me ain't goin' to do you no good."

She picked up the lantern and started away.

"Molly," cried Jasper despairingly.

He struggled weakly against his bonds, breathing loudly. Hagar turned to look. His gasping for breath was harsh as a death rattle. She walked slowly back to him and stood looking down at him. His eyes were closed.

"Only wait until I die," he murmured. "It will not be long. Then you can forget I ever lived."

"This Molly must o' treated you right bad."

Jasper eyes suddenly opened and caught her.

"I have never stopped loving you, Molly. And I never can."

Hagar put down the lantern.

"Crazy as yuh are, yuh might's well die comfortable."

She rolled him over roughly, cut the thongs tying him to the pole, pulled it away, and rolled him back again. He was so cramped that he was actually as unable to move as an invalid, but he managed to grasp one of her hands. She tugged to pull it away, but he clung to it.

"Only let me touch your hand, Molly," he whispered. "Have you quite forgotten how much more kind than than this you once were?"

Hagar stopped trying to pull her hand from his feverish grasp. He took her hand in both of his and began to pet and fondle it. She glanced defensively toward Abel.

"He's real bughouse, ain't he?"

Jasper pressed her hand against his cheek and then against his lips. She jerked it away and stood up.

"Whut yuh need more'n foolin' with the hand o' somebody that ain't here," she said severely, "is a blanket to get yuh warm."

She left the lantern on the ground and strode away into the darkness. Returning with a blanket, she spread it over him and with brusque solicitude tucked it under him. His eyes were closed and he seemed scarcely to breathe. He worked one hand out, but it was only to pluck at the blanket while he whimpered feebly. She sat down, watching him.

"Here," she said, putting her hand in his, "if'n it really makes yuh feel any better—grab a-holt."

Jasper's fingers closed over hers. She sat, patient, motionless, her eyes fixed on his face. His breathing became more even. He seemed to have fallen asleep.

"I do believe he's some better," she said.

"Looks like it," agreed Abel. "Cutting him loose was what helped most. A sick man can't stand being cramped that way. Getting warm helped, too."

Jasper's eyes opened. They seemed suddenly lucid.

"Abel," he said. "Where are we?" He looked up at Hagar. "Who are you?"

She snatched her hand away. "I ain't Molly."

Jasper raised his head and stared at her. "Molly," he exclaimed. "Did you say Molly?"

"That's what you kept calling her," said Abel, "while you were out of your head."

Jasper sank back. "So I have been delirious." He raised himself again to peer more closely at Hagar. "And then in my feverish fancy mistook you for her."

Hagar drew away. "Who was this Molly?"

"Someone I knew a long time ago." His head dropped back and he became lost in a mournful reverie.

"He never talks about her," said Abel in a low voice. "But I recollect now his once telling about when he was a young sprout there was a girl he was going to marry when he got back from his first voyage. But she died before he ever got back."

"Thet was right sad," said Hagar. She turned back to Jasper. "Yuh kept chompin' on about how she looked."

"I did?" He sighed. "No wonder. That is something I can never forget. She was very lovely."

Hagar's snort of laughter was like a bark. "Yuh surely was out o' yer head—to keep mixin' me up with her."

Jasper raised himself again to look at her. "Neither is that so strange. You are very much like her—the same eyes, the same coloring, the same expression."

A harsh cry burst from Hagar. "Yer a goddamned liar." She leaned forward, turning the scarred side of her face to the light. "Look again. Did she have something like thet too?"

Jasper's gaunt, saturnine face softened. "No. But that does not change the fact. You are still so much like her you might be sisters."

"Then look some more." In her fury she unwound the blue cloth and bent her head. Extending from her forehead to the nape of her neck was a fringe of silky black hair which she kept cropped short, but the whole top of her head was naked and crisscrossed by a network of thin red seams.

"A truly grievous affliction," admitted Jasper.

She began readjusting the cloth with the same fierce jerks with which she had removed it. "Better if I was as dead as yer Molly."

Jasper shook his head, smiling gently. "That would be a great pity, when you have so much to live for. Yours is a frightful misfortune, but you take it so much harder than necessary because it had been your lot to inhabit this wilderness. Now if you lived in a city—London, for instance—it would make no difference whatever."

"Yuh must think it's me thet's sick in the head, I s'pose in London folks don't care whut wimmin look like?"

"They care very much. So much so that most women spend many anxious hours every day laboring over their appearance. But you"—he sat up and studied her as impersonally as a doctor might a patient, gravely inspecting each feature

162

in turn—"would need have no such anxieties. A touch of rouge and powder and that scar would disappear. Hair could be even less a concern. All great ladies wear wigs. I know more than one lady of fashion who keeps her head shaved so that her wigs will fit more comfortably. No, my dear. You are listening to one who knows. It is a manifest fact that in a city such as Philadelphia, which is my home, you could go about confident that you were looking as much like a queen as nature intended you to look."

Hagar slapped him across the face. "Will yuh shet yer lyin' mouth? Yer crazier'n when yuh was gabblin' about yer Molly." Shaking with a fresh paroxysm of rage, she rolled him over and tied him again to the pole. Then snatching up and blowing out the lantern, she strode away toward the cave's mouth. Not until she had reached the open air did she begin to sob.

With the first streak of dawn Tom came up from his second night watch to awaken Tim. Hagar had a breakfast of bacon and grilled perch ready. The Dobsons remained sunk in sodden slumber. Tim and Tom moved out on the ledge where while eating they could contemplate their prize flotilla. The rising sun began to warm the chill air. Hagar came out of the cave carrying Jasper wrapped in a blanket.

"He was sick all night," she said. "We don't want him a-dyin' on us."

She sat him against the rock wall in the sun. He whispered his gratitude but seemed too weak to lift a hand. She brought out a pan of the perch and bacon and fed him with her fingers. The twins watched this process with sudden interest. Hagar gave them a scornful glance and went back into the cave.

"We better fetch out the other one too," said Tim. "We got to git thet leak fixed. No tellin' when we might want to use the boat."

Abel was so cramped from his night-long immobility that they had to carry him out too. Even after the time it took him to eat he appeared scarcely able to hobble, and required assistance to get down to the river's edge.

"What you got to do," he explained, "is weigh down the stern so's you can get the bow up on the beach where I can get at it. Pile a few hundredweight of rocks there to the back. Wait a minute. What's that stuff under the tarpaulin over there on the flatboat?"

"Trade goods," said Tim. "Bales and boxes and kegs and such."

"That'll do fine. Pile about half on deck and the rest down in the hold—well to the back."

Tim and Tom went to work with a will. Tossing and catching kegs of nails and bales of calico was like play to them. Slowly the stern began to settle deeper in the water and the bow to rise. Abel sat on a rock to watch. Whenever one of the twins glanced toward him he was bending or stretching painfully or tenderly massaging his arms and legs. Hagar came down with an armful of clothes and squatted a few feet away to wash them in the river. For many minutes she seemed intent only on her scrubbing.

"Was he turrible mad at me fer tyin' him up agin?" she finally inquired.

"No," said Abel. "Getting mad at you would be too much like getting mad at his Molly."

"Is thet whut he said?"

"All he talked about after you left him there in the dark was how much you put him in mind of her."

Hagar rose and stared fiercely at Abel. "He kin lie easy. He'd tell a body most anything jest to make her feel good. But you look some different. So you tell me straight. Do I fer sure put him in mind of this Molly?"

"No question about it. He knows he's going to die, and yet all he thinks about is how glad he is he got a look at you first."

Hagar whirled and looked up toward Jasper sitting by the cave's mouth. "Whut makes him think he's goin' to die? He can't be thet sick."

Abel lowered his voice. "Ain't nobody told you? That's why the man back in Lousville hired 'em to catch us. The minute he gets here—that will be Jasper's last."

Hagar returned to her clothes washing. After thoughtfully wringing out several garments, she looked around again. "Is a hundred English pounds a real heap o' money?"

"It's quite a bit. But this parcel of trade goods I've been watching the boys move off the flatboat—it's worth ten, maybe twenty, times that much."

This was a startling thought to Hagar, but she held her interest in check. "Trade goods ain't worth nothin' 'cept yuh sell 'em. And we'uns can't take 'em back to Louisville."

"Louisville's not the place to sell them. The farther you get into the back country the more trade goods are worth. I know a man in Saint Louis who'd trade you furs for 'em— furs which you could sell in Philadelphia for enough to make you well off for the rest of your life."

Hagar bent over her washing again. Abel resumed his gingerly massaging of his arms and legs. Tim came to the bow of the keelboat.

"Got all the stuff moved," he said. "What next?"

"You and Tom come down here," said Hagar.

They sprang ashore. She rose and faced them.

"You got us into this. Now I'm a-goin' to git us out. This ain't no place fer us. It's worse fer you than it is fer me. So we're takin' the keelboat and yer trade goods and pushin' on."

Tom was dumbfounded but Tim began to blink thoughtfully.

"Soon's they git a little more used to yuh, they won't bother yuh so much," said Tom. "Leastwise, no more'n yuh want to be."

"I don't never want to be," said Hagar. "Not by them whisky-swillin' no-goods. Now don't give me no back talk. We got to be gone whilst they're still sleepin' it off."

"But ain't yuh bin seein' how good we bin makin' out here?" protested Tom. "All this." He gestured toward the two boats. "And all the English money Peleg got."

"You'll never see a penny o' thet," said Hagar. "And all this is yers already. No sense whackin' it up with them. We'll take it with us."

"The big trouble with you is," said Tom, beginning to becomes genuinely concerned by her insistence, "yuh ain't stopped to figger nothin' out. Tim and me did. Thet's why it all worked out so good. And thet's why we're a-goin' to go right on havin' all the say."

"Hold on, Tom," said Tim. He nodded toward Jasper, sitting against the rock wall above, his chin sunk on his chest, and eyed Hagar. "Yuh git sweet on him this quick?"

"No use studyin' to be simple," said Hagar angrily.

"But yer figgerin' on takin' him with us—if'n we go."

"He ain't a well man. I'd do as much fer a sick dog. And another thing," she indicated Abel. "We're takin' him too. He knows somebody in Saint Louis who'll give yuh a proper price fer yer trade goods."

"Tim, you tell her whut's whut," implored Tom. "Mebbe she'll listen to you. Tell her we ain't boys no more."

"Thet's so," said Tim slowly. "We ain't boys no more. Thet's whut Hagar's tryin' to say. Thet the Dobsons might need us, but we don't need them. Or do you reckon we do?"

"We don't need nobody," said Tom. "We already proved thet."

"Then Hagar's right. We better take whut's ourn and go our own way." Tom looked at Abel. "How long'll it take yuh to fix the leak?"

"You find me about a pound of balsam pitch and cut me a twenty-foot-by-eight-inch pole to pry up her bow and I'll have her patched in half an hour."

The twins sprang aboard the flatboat and picked up axes. Abel turned painfully on his rock to look up at Hagar.

"Maybe you better keep an eye on the Dobsons. If they start in getting up too soon, you might have to have the boys tie 'em up."

The twins plunged through the cedar clump into the strip of forest that stretched along the riverbank at the base of the cliff. Hagar disappeared into the cave. Abel, who had appeared so stiff that the slightest move had caused him the greatest difficulty, jumped up on the rock, waving his hat at Jasper, and vaulted from there to the deck of the keelboat. Jasper sprang from his invalid's blanket and in three flying leaps had reached the water's edge.

"Hand me up them canoes," said Abel. "If they're bound to chase us, let 'em take to the flatboat."

The canoes were heaved aboard. While Jasper was loosing the mooring lines, Abel was raising the sail. The keelboat swung out into the current, the sail filled, and they were under way. *Naiad* was somewhat down by the stern but not too much so to respond to the helm.

"What could you have told them to cause them so suddenly to run off in all directions?" asked Jasper.

"Mainly I talked about how much the fur would be worth. I mean the fur they could trade this stuff for in Saint Louis. That's what we're going to do with it—only in Kaskaskia."

"Astounding," exulted Jasper. "Like the phoenix we again arise from the ashes. We lose the tobacco and gain a cargo worth much more."

"Maybe twenty times more," said Abel, "if we work at the deal."

Hagar, back in the cave, caught a flash of the white sail blossoming in the sun. She snatched up her rifle and ran out.

"Down," warned Jasper, grasping Abel's arm.

They were still within range. But Hagar after lifting her rifle let it slowly sink again. She stood stock-still in the cave's mouth, looking after them.

8

In New Orleans history was on every hand, in the very air, flaunted upon the persons of the first dozen figures chancing at any given moment to be passing along the street—who were as likely as not to be a beruffled French planter, his satin coat threadbare and patched; a naked Choctaw, a feather in his hair, red stripes across his face and belly; a barefooted Cajun girl with a basket of shrimp from the bayous; a ragged Spanish soldier, still an alien in this Louisiana over which his king had had dominion for a quarter of a century; a general's mulatto mistress swishing her silken gown; a stone-faced German farmer on his way to the slave market; a pigtailed English seaman on shore leave from a Bristol trading bark anchored discreetly off Fort Plaquemine; a stalwart Santo Domingo Negro eying with disdain the shuffling, submissive gait of his mainland fellows; a scarlet-sashed Vincennes *voyageur* happily drinking away in a day the wages of a wilderness winter; a leather-shirted American backwoodsman grinning contemptuously to conceal his secret fascination with this first city he has ever seen; a black-robed abbess leaning forward in the seat of her carriage to prod at her drowsy coachman with a silver mounted cane; a straw-hatted Boston merchant stepping disapprovingly through the mud toward the customs office to pay his weekly tribute to the harbor master.

The Boston merchant, Manasseh Pomeroy, left the customs office, climbed the levee, and turned to face the town, fixing his attention, as though he felt a need again to be reminded of them, upon its deplorable imperfections. These he found innumerable. During the eight interminable years that he had spent here, his daily indignation had represented a nearly intolerable price to pay for the fortune that he had accumulated.

His glance came to his own house fronting the river, and, his frown lightening somewhat, lingered over the iron grillwork of the balconies, the slate roof, the warehouse, the high-walled courtyard. The great March fire that had consumed his neighbor's rickety tenements had recoiled from his limestone walls. The courtyard gate opened and Philippe, his fat black coachman, drove out, as always grazing a gatepost in making the turn into the street. Before the gate swung shut again Pomeroy caught a glimpse of Andrew Swaine in the warehouse doorway. In spite of the mid-afternoon heat he still wore hat and coat as he stood at his desk. Since he had begun to suspect the possibility of mounting from the status of factor to that of partner, Andrew's sense of self-importance had taken on new proportions.

Philippe drew up beside Pomeroy and heaved his bulk around on the box to indicate his eventual intention of getting down to stand by the step of the caleche. His master's habitual impatience could usually be counted upon to save him the trouble of completing the gesture. But this time not until Philippe had let himself, wheezing and grunting, all the way to the ground did he turn abruptly and get in. Sighing, Philippe climbed up again over the wheel and spoke to the horses.

Pomeroy sat back in the seat with his eyes closed. As the caleche rocked and jolted on, he could tell by the smells, by the sound of the wheels, by the greater and lesser lurches of the carriage, by the varying humidity of the waves of heat, when they had passed the Bastion of Saint Francis, when they were passing through the suburb of Saint Marie, and when they had reached the plantation country north of the city. Not until the wheels crunched on the crushed oyster shell of a suddenly smooth driveway did he open his eyes. Here was one plantation where the hedges were trimmed, the trees pruned, the gardens tended, the crops cultivated, the slave quarters whitewashed. The carriage drew up before the house. He got down and stood for a moment looking up at the satisfyingly balanced proportions of the red brick and the green shutters and the white pillars.

Madame Roxanne Marillac was awaiting him in the shadowed recesses of the veranda. As he advanced upon her he found the same pleasure in surveying her that he had had in surveying her property. The fine luster of her pale skin, her black eyes, her blue-black hair, also seemed ordered, planned. She was as well kept as her gardens.

"Monsieur Pomeroy, welcome to Marquay," said Madame Marillac.

Pomeroy bowed over her hand.

"It is an inestimable privilege to be here," he said.

For many years he had called at Marquay twice a week,

but always he was received with this same unvarying formality.

"It is so very hot, Monsieur Pomeroy. Would you not sit out here for a moment?"

Madame Marillac spoke nearly faultless English, though with a faint New England accent.

"You are too kind, Madame Marillac. But, with your permission, first I will change."

In the hall beyond a white-coated house boy waited. Pomeroy bowed again to his hostess and followed the boy up the stairs. In the chamber above he embarked upon that enjoyment of Marquay's hospitality which had varied so little through the years that it had become a kind of ritual. Throwing aside the damp clothing in which he had arrived, he sponged off, with cold water from a marble basin, the last taint of the city's heat. Laid out for him were crisp, newly laundered linens and a combed, freshly powdered wig. With leisurely anticipation he shaved and dressed and, feeling a new man inwardly as well as outwardly, descended the stairs to join Madame Marillac waiting at the foot.

Outside the cooler shadow of evening had replaced the blazing heat of the day. Her fingertips barely touching his sleeve, they sauntered about the gardens. Their talk was of plantation affairs. As a seasoned man of business he was perpetually able to give her sage advice on how most sensibly to take advantage of the going market and, upon occasion, to suggest when it might be wise to commission him to take personal charge of a transaction. Decisions reached by such consultations had through the years restored the house at Marquay, filled the barns with oxen and the barracoons with slaves, added new acres. In these discussions they maintained the same polite formality that had marked their greeting. He was Monsieur, she was Madame. This was an essential part of the ritual.

They came abreast of a great oak, its branches, festooned with Spanish moss, drooping to the ground. A narrower path led off from the main one and was lost in the gloom under the immense tree. Here the ritual approached its culmination. This narrower path traversed the darkness under the oak and came out upon a little summerhouse, shrouded in vines and encompassed by a jungle of azalea. Moving ever more slowly, they kept on and entered this waiting, shadowed, utterly secluded haven. Here, so many years ago, the first such moment had taken him unawares, as it had seemed also to have taken her. Since then the re-enactment of that unpremeditated surrender had become for him the essence of the ritual. In this place only did they ever for an instant lift the mask of urbane formality that clothed every other phase of their relationship. Here, also, more than in any other place, all was supremely well ordered.

Strolling back through the darkening garden toward the now lighted house, they resumed their bland conversation.

"I have a surprise for you tonight, Monsieur Pomeroy. Félicie is home."

Pomeroy's pace slowed a half-step. "A most delightful surprise. And you have also asked Swaine—according to that overjoyed young man's report this morning."

"You men of affairs, Monsieur Pomeroy—how terribly quick you are to suspect in the most simple action the most intricate motive."

"Not at all. Not at all. Certainly never where you are concerned, Madame Marillac. I was only about to observe that you have never before asked him."

They paused at the lighted doorway. Félicie was starting to descend the stairs. In a gold-dotted white muslin gown, her arms and shoulders bare, her hair piled high but with loose curls escaping, she was a vision to startle Pomeroy. Madame Marillac smiled.

"Are you then so astonished, Monsieur Pomeroy, that my daughter should have grown so beautiful?"

"On the contrary, Madame Marillac," said Pomeroy, recovering and bowing to her, "I should be astonished if she had not."

Andrew Swaine had started to his feet. Pomeroy crossed in front of Andrew and made straight for Félicie, scrutinizing her as he approached the meeting at the foot of the stairs with an interest that he, as an old friend of the family, had no need to disguise. There was about the daughter none of that striking contrast of black hair and black eyes against a very white skin which distinguished her mother. The younger woman was of a warmer tone. Her skin had a golden tint and her eyes were almost the color of amber. In place of her mother's regal carriage, her movements were quick, graceful, unstudied.

"Eet ees my great plasir to see you again, Monsieur Pomeroy," said Félicie, her convent English made to seem graceful by her voice and her smile.

There came upon Pomeroy a sharp awareness, accompanied by a mingling of sadness and relief, that he had reached a time of life when meeting a girl so delightful as this one committed him to no response, no anxiety, not even to a whiff of idle speculation. The challenge that she represented pertained to another generation than his. Nevertheless he was irritated by the sight of Andrew edging forward, red-faced in

170

his thick broadcloth and tight stock, gawky, eager, beaming —and young enough to be his son.

"May I present Mr. Andrew Swaine," said Madame Marillac. "My daughter, Mr. Swaine."

"I am so pleezed to make your acquaintance, Meester Swaine," said Félicie.

"The pleasure is mine, I assure you," said Andrew.

Félicie gave him a second polite smile and looked at her mother. "Ees somebody else come?" she asked, sticking bravely to her English out of regard for her guests. Seeing her mother's puzzlement, she added: "The boat—from my window I see eet."

At her gesture toward the open door at the end of the hall, all turned to look. A tree-lined avenue led toward the river with at its end a patch of still-gray western sky. Across this pale backdrop glided the black silhouette of a sail. The ship, its hulk invisible in the darkness below, came about toward the plantation landing. The sail dropped.

"Louis," said Madame Marillac sharply to a servant, "tell Raoul to see who it is."

Pomeroy felt Andrew's clutch on his arm.

"If you will excuse us, Madame Marillac," stammered Andrew. "I must consult with Mr. Pomeroy—a matter of business which cannot wait."

Pomeroy, scowling, accompanied Andrew to the veranda.

"You are a guest here," said Pomeroy. "And for the first time. You are indeed distinguishing yourself, Andrew."

"I can't help it," said Andrew. "Something's come up you'll have to know about."

"The boat out there. So it does have something to do with you?"

"To a certain extent, yes."

"Then why were you so unpleasantly surprised when you saw it?"

"You'll have to listen, Mr. Pomeroy, or how can I tell you?"

"I'm listening."

"Today—just after you left—an American backwoodsman showed up in a canoe. He said he'd left his keelboat hidden in one of the bayous. Judging by the samples he showed me, he's got a cargo of furs worth ten, twelve, maybe fifteen thousand."

"Which you naturally yearned to get a look at before anybody else in New Orleans got wind of the prize. What, you decided, could be more convenient than to meet him tonight at the home of your hostess?"

"No. That wasn't the way I looked at it at all, Mr. Pomeroy. He wouldn't meet me anywhere. You were the one he wanted to see, and somebody had told enough about New Orleans to give him the idea you were often here."

"Why don't you come out with the truth without all this hemming and hawing? Must you be devious even with me? So you felt easy about making the disgraceful appointment since you thought you could in the meantime arrange with that scoundrel Pierre Sarpy to intercept him before he could get here."

"Yes, I did. And what would have been so wrong with that, Mr. Pomeroy? Pierre couldn't have come to town to sell the furs. He knows the governor will hang him the day he catches him. He'd have had to keep in touch with me and let us have them for whatever we felt like offering."

"Andrew. I've no objection to irregular devices. It's impossible in New Orleans to transact business in a straightforward manner. But I prefer devices that work. You thought of Pierre Sarpy—no doubt on the spur of the moment. You can now take a second thought—also on the spur of the moment—on what you will say to the backwoodsman. Because—if I mistake not—there he is."

Raoul Peyroux, Madame Marillac's overseer, stood aside in the doorway. Abel walked forward into the hall, his rifle held loosely in the crook of his arm. From a slight cut on his cheek blood dripped, a slow drop at a time, down on his buckskin shirt. His glance shot swiftly to the stairs, the open windows, the doorways, passed over Félicie, Madame Marillac, returned for an instant to Félicie, and held on Pomeroy and Andrew coming in from the veranda.

"Our most abject apologies, Madame, Mademoiselle," said Pomeroy. "Due to an unfortunate misunderstanding, a most inappropriate item of personal business has intruded. It will take, I trust, but a moment."

He looked at Andrew. Andrew ran a finger around inside his stock.

"Have much trouble finding the place?" he asked Abel.

"Not much," said Abel. "Some people tried to head us off, but they didn't try too hard."

Pomeroy was not content to see Andrew get off too easily. "Would you say it was a matter for the police?"

"No, I wouldn't," said Abel. "We didn't hurt 'em much. We just dumped them back in their bateau and kept their oars. They'll drift ashore somewhere by morning."

"Sensible solution to a dilemma so minor," said Pomeroy. "Andrew, since you have brought this off so well so far, you might as well excuse yourself to take your look at his cargo."

Andrew started forward. Abel ignored him.

"You're Manasseh Pomeroy?"

Pomeroy nodded.

"My name's Abel Traner. No use his looking. If there's to be any deal, it'll have to be with you."

"I quite agree, Mr. Traner. But Mr. Swaine is my factor. After he has had time to come to some conclusion about the quality of your merchandise, I will come aboard and determine the offer I can afford to make."

Abel wiped his cheek on his sleeve, gave Félicie another passing glance, and went out. Andrew followed.

Pomeroy composed himself to conversation with the ladies. No company could have seemed to him more delightful. But for him there could be no pleasure sufficient entirely to withdraw his attention from the prospect of an as-yet-unexplored business opportunity. Upon Raoul's reappearance in the doorway he started up, then resolutely lingered to reiterate his apologies. Quickening his step only after he was out of sight, he set off down the driveway to the landing.

There was a lantern in the keelboat's cabin and he could hear Andrew's voice. It was once more ringing with his usual smug assurance. As Pomeroy went up the gangplank he caught a glimpse of a shadowy, long-legged figure seated against the rail beyond the range of light from the cabin and, as well, of the glint on the barrels of two cocked pistols lying at hand on the deck beside the figure's knobby knees. Andrew was at a table in the cabin, busily writing. Abel, leaning on his rifle in the doorway, stood aside for Pomeroy to enter.

"I found all in order, Mr. Pomeroy," said Andrew briskly. "I opened enough bales at random to indicate the pelts are of a remarkably even quality. I am prepared, therefore, to recommend that you pay five piasters a pound for the prine beaver. Mr. Traner understands, of course, that, when all the bales are unpacked for counting, any skins that prove to be poorer than strictly prime will be set aside for separate negotiation."

"Five piasters," said Pomeroy. "That's a strong price."

"It is. We have never paid higher. Two circumstances, however, lead me to recommend it to you. The first is that Mr. Traner states positively he will accept no less." Andrew chuckled at his little joke. "The second is of rather more weight. Up to this moment Mr. Traner has not been obliged to declare his cargo to the Spanish customs. He passed Natchez in the night. It hence has occurred to me that he may dispense with the customs charges altogether. If you will permit me to remind you—the brig *Penguin* lies at anchor forty miles downriver. What I propose then is that after dinner I return aboard here and accompany Mr. Traner. We'll pass New Orleans before daylight, slip past Fort Plaquemine, and deliver the furs direct to Captain Bartlett. Mr. Traner can be paid as his skins are weighed in over the side, and both you and he will be saved the tariff charges, making it a distinctly profitable transaction for all parties concerned."

"The payment to be in what kind of currency?" asked Pomeroy.

"I've stipulated here," said Andrew, indicating the paper on the table, "that the first three thousand piasters' worth is to be paid for in Spanish silver dollars, the next five thousand in English banknotes, and the remainder, whatever it totals, to be covered by a negotiable draft on Baring Brothers of London."

"That suit you?" Pomeroy asked Abel.

Abel picked up the paper, read it, and laid it back on the table.

"Yes," he said, "once you've signed."

Pomeroy took the pen from Andrew and scratched his signature on the bill of sale. Abel folded the document and stuck it in his pocket. Andrew shook hands with him.

"I'll be with you within a couple of hours," he said.

Pomeroy and Andrew walked up the drive toward the house.

"A somewhat sounder scheme than your first," said Pomeroy.

"I'm desperately sorry about the Sarpy fiasco, Mr. Pomeroy. It was a case of snap judgment and, I must confess, most ill-advised. I had no idea this Traner would be so much on his guard."

"What makes you so certain that he no longer is?"

"How can he be? This time we're foolproof. If I may have the use of your coach for an hour, I can make sure there will be no delivery. Lieutenant Godoy will have his customs galley waiting at English Bend when the keelboat reaches there in the morning. Since Traner did not declare his goods either at Natchez or New Orleans, it will be a clear case of attempted smuggling. He will still be in possession and therefore all responsibility will be his, not ours. By the time we succeed in getting him and his cargo out of the clutches of Spanish authority, he must feel grateful for whatever is left over for him. Godoy will want a thousand piasters. What should we allow Traner? Would you say a piaster a pound was too much?"

"We can decide upon that, Andrew, when the time comes."

The time to decide came within an hour after dawn the

next morning. Pomeroy was awakened, with scant ceremony, by a furiously agitated Andrew.

"The goddamned half-wit," said Andrew. "I beg your pardon, Mr. Pomeroy. But make no mistake. We're dealing with an ignorant, pigheaded imbecile. He fooled around for so long it was sunrise by the time we got off New Orleans. Then he swung about all of a sudden and came straight in. There wasn't a thing I could do to stop him. He's down there now—tied up to our landing."

Pomeroy slid out of bed and, the morning breeze off the river plucking disconcertingly at his nightshirt, went to the open window to look down. There, as Andrew had said, was the keelboat tied up to the landing. Half a dozen Spanish soldiers were standing about on deck.

"The customs people seem already to have taken over," remarked Pomeroy.

"Certainly," said Andrew. "First thing I did was notify them. We couldn't have Traner rushing in here waving his bill of sale and demanding his five piasters a pound. So far as he goes, it'll work out the same as though he hadn't got so obstinate. Trouble is, it'll cost us more. These are Colonel Barela's men and Barela will be harder to handle than Godoy. He'll want three—maybe four thousand."

Pomeroy dressed, somewhat more hastily than was his custom, and, the fuming Andrew at his elbow, descended to the waterfront. The chattering Spanish soldiers came to respectful attention and stood aside. In New Orleans a prominent foreign merchant was a figure outranked only by a general or a governor. In the cabin Abel had just finished shaving and was shrugging into a dark blue coat. His breeches, equally new, were of a fashionably lighter shade; he wore polished leather boots; and there was a cravat at the throat of his white linen shirt. It was not a perfectly tailored outfit, but the general effect was more than respectable. There was little resemblance to the moccasined and leather-shirted backwoodsman who had stood in the hall at Marquay with a long rifle in the crook of his arm. Pomeroy leaned closer and fingered the fabric of the coat.

"Good English woolen," he said. "Are they getting goods like this in Kentucky now?"

"Kaskaskia," said Abel. "Where I got the furs. There's a store there that once in a while gets stuff by way of Montreal and Detroit."

He picked up the leather shirt and transferred the bill of sale to the inner pocket of the blue coat.

"I have endeavored to explain to Mr. Traner," said Andrew, "that a bill of sale is without effect until the seller can deliver the goods without encumbrances."

"If you mean I have to hand over the skins before you have to pay," said Abel, "I know that."

Andrew, in the doorway, gave a sudden start.

"The governor," he exclaimed.

The governor's carriage, attended by two mounted officers of his guard, was coming along the levee road. Pomeroy and Andrew climbed from the landing to the roadside. Abel followed at a more deliberate pace. The carriage halted abreast of Pomeroy. The door opened, Jasper's long legs swung out, and he stood, hat in hand, at the step, glittering in all of his Fortiner finery, from the silver-buckled shoes to the ruffled shirt. Governor Miro shoved over to the side of the seat Jasper had vacated, leaned out, and greeted Pomeroy affably.

"Good morning, Mr. Pomeroy I note that you are more than ever the early bird this fine morning."

"Good morning, Governor Miro. I am more than rewarded by so early a glimpse of Your Excellency."

The governor laughed. He seemed in exceptionally good humor. "Unlike you heathen, I have the righteous excuse of early mass to bestir me. So good an errand made it seem the more appropriate to turn aside for a moment to bring you good news. May I congratulate you on receiving so profitable a consignment?"

"At the moment the cargo appears to be in the custody of your soldiers, Your Excellency."

"That is my good news this so bright and early morning." The governor raised his voice, addressing one of his mounted aides. "Captain, order the soldiers back to barracks." His benign attention returned to Pomeroy. "Your so valuable cargo is free and clear, Mr. Pomeroy."

Andrew gasped, but Pomeroy's fixed smile did not waver. "Your many kindnesses far surpass my poor power to reciprocate, Your Excellency."

"Governor Miro," said Jasper, "may I present Mr. Abel Traner?"

The governor leaned farther forward, extended his hand to Abel, and spoke warmly to him.

"He says that he hopes you soon may find time to pay him a call," interpreted Jasper.

"Tell him I surely will," said Abel.

"Good morning, Mr. Pomeroy. Good morning, gentlemen." The governor beamed once more on one and all and drove on.

Pomeroy surveyed Jasper. "Are you Mr. Traner's partner?"

"Scarcely his partner," said Jasper. "Let us say—his disciple I am Jasper Hedges, at your service, Mr. Pomeroy. I take it I escaped your attention when last I was in New Orleans."

"Not entirely. We did not meet, but I believe that when you departed—rather hurriedly, I seem to recall—it was aboard one of my vessels that you stowed away."

"Your recollection is correct. And I may say that the vessel had a master who saw to it that I most thoroughly worked my passage."

"I am relieved to hear that. Andrew, will you see to weighing in Mr. Traner's furs? Mr. Traner, you will no doubt wish Mr. Hedges to represent you during the tally. Meanwhile, will you do me the honor of breakfasting with me? Unless, of course, you feel inclined personally to check Mr. Swaine's count?"

"No need for that. Only counting I'll want to see is when it comes to counting the ones he claims are not prime."

To Abel it was a breakfast almost as novel as the sights and sounds and smells of New Orleans beyond the open windows. They were served beans cooked black in pork and molasses, extremely salty codfish fried in balls, slabs of apple pie, and tea in pewter mugs that stayed too hot to touch.

"This pass of Wilkinson's," said Pomeroy, returning to the subject. "How could you be so certain the governor would honor it?"

"I wasn't real sure. But it looked to me like a good gamble. Mine was the first boat to show up from Kentucky since Wilkinson got back there, and no matter what the Spaniards figgered on doing about him in the long run, it didn't look like they'd want word to get back right off that his passes were no good. Anyway, that was my guess."

"A fairly close guess, it would appear. Now if you will overlook the discourtesy, Mr. Traner, I will take a minute to glance through some of this. There may be something requiring early attention."

During breakfast a sack of American mail, sent overland from a Baltimore schooner that had put in at Mobile, has been brought in.

"Go right ahead," said Abel.

Pomeroy began breaking the seals of letters and unfolding newspapers. Abel looked about him. Everything that he saw this morning he saw with a peculiar vividness, and yet all remained as unsubstantial as if no more than part of a remarkably detailed and complicated dream.

At this time yesterday he had been anchored in the reeds under a cypress at the end of a bayou where everything in sight had been as wild as any of the shores and woods with which he had been familiar since childhood; and now so soon afterward here he was in this house, which was like nothing he had ever seen. He gave up trying to take in everything at once and let his mind wander idly about the fringes of the problem. He had never been in New England, but once in a while a mover from there had come past the station with a table or chair among the stuff he was trying to take all the way west with him. But here was a whole house filled with such walnut chairs and mahogany tables—and braided rugs and brass-handled chests of drawers and silver candlesticks and bookcases lined with books and framed pictures on every wall and any number of other possessions any one of which is most any house along the Monongahela or the Ohio would have been the talk of the neighborhood. And then there had been that other house last night which had been even less like anything he had ever seen before. There he had not taken so much notice of the furniture—except for the golden harp in the room beyond the archway. He had been too busy sizing up the people. The tall, black-haired woman had made him think of the picture of a queen in that book that the schoolmaster had used while teaching him to read, and her smile had been just as pleasant and meaningless as the one in the picture. The girl had not seemed at first so unlike people he had seen before. She had made him think of Magda until he had looked at her a second time. Nobody could just walk toward her or lean in her doorway, even if her mother were to take him there by the hand. She might be only a few miles away, but she was farther out of reach than Magda was, wherever Magda was by now.

Pomeroy looked up from his mail.

"Maryland has ratified," he said. "She's the seventh state. It's beginning to appear that the Constitution might be adopted after all."

Abel recalled his attention with an effort and made another effort to seem polite. "Make much difference here?"

"That depends largely on how much difference it makes in Kentucky."

"Only one thing makes any difference in Kentucky. That's for anybody to try to tell 'em what to do."

"Isn't Wilkinson trying to do that?"

"What he's trying to tell them is what they already want to do. They'd dicker with Spanish or English—or anybody except Indians—if they thought they could get more for their corn and tobacco."

"Doesn't he run the risk of being accused of Spanish sympathies?"

"They don't know for sure yet that he's turned Spaniard, but if they did they wouldn't care. Even Clark would take a Spanish oath if he could get what he wanted for one."

"Ah," said Pomeroy. "You seem remarkably well informed, Mr. Traner."

"Anybody that spent three days in Kentucky could find out all I did. There's no secret about any of it."

Abel had less interest in the conversation than in what he could see from the window. Some time since the file of sweating Negroes had carried the last bale of furs into the warehouse, and Andrew Swaine, tally sheet in hand, was headed for the stairway that ran up the outside of the house to the balcony. Andrew appeared on it and came in. He was still unhappy but seemed resigned to the principle that under whatever circumstances business was business.

"The lot weighed out at three thousand four hundred and seventy-eight pounds," he said. "Three skins were of questionable quality, but since there were only three I took the liberty of lumping them with the rest. Therefore seventeen thousand three hundred and ninety piasters are due Mr. Traner."

"Very good, Andrew," said Pomeroy with no more apparent concern than though the total had been seventeen. "As soon as you have had something to eat, will you attend to having the shipment repacked for sea transport, have it loaded in the sloop, and see that it is stowed aboard *Penguin*. Consign it to Abraham Littauer in London."

"Yes, sir. Anything else, sir?"

"Nothing more for the moment, Andrew."

Andrew scowled at Abel and went back down the stairs.

"If you will come with me, Mr. Traner," said Pomeroy.

Abel followed him into another room with windows overlooking the harbor. This one had been fitted out as an office, with furnishings that included a wide desk with many pigeonholes, a breast-high bookkeeper's desk, shelves lined with ledgers, a table, and a huge iron safe. Pomeroy took out a key and unlocked the safe.

"You might as well sit down," he said. "This may take a little time."

Abel sat down and watched. Nothing either last night or this morning had seemed half so unreal as this moment. Pomeroy pulled out a large drawer in the safe and began removing from it paper-wrapped cylinders. These he lined up on the tabletop after breaking open the first to allow the coins to spill out.

"Fifty Spanish silver dollars in each roll," he said. "Everyone newly minted—every one full weight."

When there were sixty of the cylinders ranged in meticulously even rows on the tabletop he closed the drawer and opened another. From this he removed a packet of banknotes, wet his thumb, and began peeling them off into a pile beside the rows of dollars.

"May I make a suggestion, Mr. Traner? The bill of sale calls next for the payment of five thousand piasters' worth of English pounds. However, the foreign exchange rate in New Orleans is most irregular and always weeks out of touch with the going European market. Suppose I pay you an even thousand pounds to fulfill this clause in the contract? Then in the Baring Brothers draft to cover the remainder due we can make allowance for the payments made here in dollars and pounds, and thus the final amount established to your credit in London will be governed by the exchange rate current in London on that date. This may prove to your advantage or to mine, but in either event will be fair to both of us."

"Sounds reasonable to me," said Abel.

"Good." Pomeroy smoothed the pile of banknotes on the tabletop. "Then here are eighteen fifty-pound notes and ten ten-pound notes. Now if you will sign the bill of sale while I am preparing the draft."

He moved an inkhorn and a vase of pens from his desk and sat down opposite Abel to write the draft. Abel took out the bill of sale, selected a pen, signed the bill, and leaned back, contemplating the array of money. Pomeroy finished writing and handed Abel the draft.

"There, Mr. Traner, I believe all is in order."

Abel looked not at the draft but at Pomeroy.

"Your man Swaine acted real sour toward the last, but you don't look like you think you made such a bad bargain."

"There are no bad bargains, Mr. Traner. Once they are made, all are good."

Abel picked up the ten-pound notes and two of the paper-wrapped stacks of dollars.

"Got any objection to keeping the rest of this for me in your safe—that is, until I need it?"

"None whatever. A very sensible arrangement, if I may say so." Pomeroy drew another sheet of paper toward him. "I will draw you a demand note covering the amount. I take it, then, Mr. Traner, you plan to remain in New Orleans possibly some time."

"Only plan I have is to look around some."

Pomeroy pulled a bell cord. "You will not want to delay paying the call on the governor that he himself so kindly suggested. A good time to see him is around noon. He is usually finished with his routine official business by then and in a good humor because his dinner hour is approaching." A house boy appeared in the doorway. "Have the coach brought around for Mr. Traner."

"His place is only around the corner," said Abel. "I can surely walk that far."

"One does not walk to pay a call on the governor—if one has a carriage. In that connection, may I make another suggestion?"

"You don't have to suggest, Mr. Pomeroy. You better just tell me."

"Whatever your eventual plans, you will scarcely be able to make them except upon the basis of some acquaintance with the way people manage their affairs in New Orleans. This is not a simple matter for a stranger to grasp. No business is ever transacted in a direct and orderly manner. Moreover, certain people will be wary of you on account of the apparent favor of the governor has shown you. Which brings me to my suggestion. Your associate, Hedges, speaks Spanish and has had certain earlier contacts here. If you were to seem to divorce yourself from him—instead of relying upon him as companion and interpreter—he would be able to circulate more freely and pick up more information of possible value to you than he otherwise might."

"We'd already figgered that out. I'm going to stay on my boat and he's going to live at a boardinghouse in town he knows about."

"No doubt the one kept by the Irishwoman, Katie Donovan. A good selection. It is a place frequented by sea captains and the local agents of foreign trading firms. It is also convenient to many cafés, billiard parlors, ballrooms, and gambling houses. This is a community of as many eddies and shoals as the river. He will be in a position to gain experience in navigating some, you others."

"Jasper's a boy able to get around."

"I'd gathered as much. You encourage me to make one final suggestion. You may feel inclined to pay your respects to Madame Marillac and to thank her for the rather impromptu use we made of her premises last night. I am paying a visit to Marquay this afternoon. Would you like to accompany me?"

"Yes, I would," said Abel.

The late afternoon turned cooler. There was a tumble of clouds along the horizon and freshening puffs of wind off the lake. Abel sat beside Pomeroy in the carriage, looking out with mild curiosity at whatever came into view from the road atop the levee. He was no longer disturbed by the sense of unreality. Getting used to the idea of that money, his money, in Pomeroy's safe had made all the difference. That was no dream. That was a fact as solid as one ever could be. It was a lot of money, enough to make a lot of difference. It was enough, for instance, to buy out Job Moyer with a good bit left over. Fortiner, himself, had probably never had that much cash at one time right where he could put his hands on it. Pomeroy, rich as he undoubtedly was, regarded it as a very substantial sum. Most encouraging of all, it was enough even to make it seem natural to be paying a social call at the house of the golden harp.

The carriage turned into Marquay's oyster-shell drive.

"Right nice place," said Abel conversationally.

"There's not its equal along this river," said Pomeroy. "A perfect example of how well good management pays even in this misgoverned province. Madame Marillac is a remarkably capable and intelligent woman."

"Think she's going to be surprised to see me showing up?"

"Madame Marillac is never surprised. She may be mildly astonished not by your appearance but by mine. I call quite frequently, but always it has been by appointment."

"Anyway, she's right there on the porch and all dressed up like she was expecting company."

Not one but both ladies were waiting. As Madame Marillac advanced toward the head of the steps Félicie came into sight behind her.

"Monsieur Pomeroy—this is an exceptional pleasure."

"I pray not one that was too unexpected, Madame Marillac. Allow me to present Mr. Abel Traner. Madame Marillac. Mademoiselle Marillac. Mr. Traner was in a natural hurry to pay his respects after his somewhat informal appearance here last night."

"We are flattered, Monsieur Pomeroy, that you found the time to escort him here. And delighted, Mr. Traner, to welcome you to Marquay."

"A great plasir, Meester Traner," murmured Félicie, her smile, as always, giving to each word of her halting speech its own pleasing significance.

"I'm real glad to meet you," said Abel, emulating Pomeroy's bow to each lady in turn. "Hope my shoving in here with a gun last night didn't upset you."

"Not at all, Mr. Traner. We understood you had been set upon by ruffians out on the river and that you had been too much for them. We congratulate you. But—please, gentlemen—will you not sit down?"

"We can stay only a moment," said Pomeroy.

"Monsieur Pomeroy," exclaimed Madame Marillac. "Say no

182

more, Monsieur Pomeroy, about dashing straight away again. You have but just arrived. Give us time to contemplate our good fortune. Félicie, do you not think Mr. Traner might like to see the garden? Would you, Mr. Traner?"

"Yes, I would," said Abel.

"Be sure to show him the lily pool and the orangery," said Madame Marillac.

"Oui, maman," said Félicie.

She walked beside Abel down the steps. They turned from the drive into a garden path.

"Surely is a fine place you have," said Abel.

"Thank you. Ees that what I should say? I mean—what is correct? My Eengleesh—eet ees not—easy."

"You speak it fine. Anyway, I aim to learn Spanish."

"My Spaneesh ees a leetle bettair."

"That's right—you're French, aren't you? I'm going to learn that too."

"Until then, my Eengleesh, when I speak eet wrong, you will tell me?"

"You don't say anything wrong."

"You Americans, you are not suppose to be gallant. You are suppose to tell always the truth."

"I always do."

Abel cast about hastily for something else to say inasmuch as talking to her gave him an excuse to keep on looking at her. Her hair was unbelievably soft and fine; her eyelashes were curved in a way to add meaning to her most innocent glance; her lips seemed always about to part in that pleasant readiness to smile that was so nearly the shape they might assume in a readiness to kiss; even the faint golden down on her bare forearms had the happy perfection of the bloom on a peach.

"Are those little green things there oranges?" he said.

"Yes. And the next, eet ees a feeg tree. And that one, pomegranate."

"Imagine being in a country where oranges and figs and pomegrantes grow all around just like they might be crab apples."

They had come to a farther border of the garden. Beyond a low wall of cypress logs stretched a wide expanse of brilliant green.

"What crop is that?"

"Sugar."

"Sugar," marveled Abel. "Must be three hundred acres of it. Do you know that I was twelve years old before I ever tasted sugar?"

"You had nothing sweet—nevair?"

"Oh, yes. We had maple sugar."

Standing face to face with her beside the wall of cypress logs, he embarked upon a detailed account of the mechanics of sugar-making in the Northern forest, tapping the trees, gathering the sap, rendering the syrup. With her listening so attentively, everything he said seemed remarkably interesting and important. The puffy wind had ceased. Upon the canefield the sun still shone. The oak under which they stood cut them off from the darkening western sky. Neither noticed the new chill in the air or the distant mutter of thunder. His discourse was suddenly interrupted by a great clap of thunder directly overhead. Following the flash, drops of rain the size of thimbles began to splash, hissing, upon them.

He seized her hand and they ran back through the garden. Already the wind was whipping the trees, the flashes of lightning and peals of thunder coming in rapid succession, the rain becoming a drenching torrent. He saw that she was laughing, that she was no more frightened than he.

"My shoe," she gasped. "Eet ees gone."

Emboldened by her continued laughter, he swept her up in his arms and ran on down the drive and up the steps. He set her down on the veranda, relieved to see that Pomeroy and Madame Marillac had withdrawn into the house. Félicie stood before him on one leg, her stockinged foot lifted. She was still laughing. Her hair had tumbled down and was plastered about her shoulders. Water trickled from her chin down into the crease between her breasts. Her rain-soaked dress was clinging not only to them but to every other curve of her body. His arms still had in them the feel of her. The sense of reality that had sprung from the drawer in Pomeroy's safe had extended suddenly to this veranda. This girl was as real as she was wet. She was as real as Magda, as much a flesh-and-blood woman as Magda could ever have seemed. It was an idea to sober him, even for a moment to arouse in him a flash of panic.

During half the drive back to the city after the storm Pomeroy sat in musing silence and then began to speak as though continuing a conversation that had been but momentarily interrupted.

"Seventeen thousand dollars is a sufficient sum to constitute a considerable responsibility. Does it represent your entire capital?"

"Except for the boat and this suit of clothes."

"There are two sensible ways to treat money. One is to attempt to hang on to it. The other is to attempt to put it to work to make you more. There are risks in both undertakings —a rather greater risk, of course, in the second."

"Especially in New Orleans would be my guess."

"True. But it is a law of business that the greater the risks, the greater the possible gain. And the possible gains here are about to multiply. So far there has been but a dribble of trade from the interior. These antics of Wilkinson will add a few drops. But presently there will be the deluge. The Spaniards will be no more able to stop it than they could the flow of that river. For one of two things is bound to happen. Either a new government of the United States under the Constitution will insist upon a trade outlet here, or the growing population of Kentucky will turn away from that government and take it upon themselves to insist. In either event the result will be the same. The trade of a continent will find here its outlet to the sea."

"What you're getting at then—is that I'd be smart to settle down here?"

"You may eventually so decide. But what I am getting at is something rather more immediately practical. It is that you wait a little before making up your mind to anything. For the moment undertake to hang on to your money, even though some quite attractive opportunity to risk it may seem to turn up. Wait. Larger opportunities are certain to come. And while you are waiting you will have the advantage of becoming better acquainted with the peculiar conditions with which business here is obliged to deal."

"A man couldn't very well quarrel with advice like that."

"I have yet to come to my principal point. About as quick a way as any to gain an insight into what a New Orleans merchant has to put up with would be for the next few weeks to spend several hours every day in the office of one of them. I do not mean as an employee. I mean merely to look on and take note of the business that he accepts and declines and his apparent reasoning in either case. Since you have already made my acquaintance and it may take you some little time to make a similar acquaintance with some of the others, I suggest that you try my office first."

"No harm in starting at the top," said Abel. "Only thing that bothers me is—and I have to come right out with it— why are you putting yourself to so much trouble for a man you've known but overnight?"

"Not, alas, because I am a philanthropist. I have my own interests in mind. The return from your furs represents an item not to be sneezed at. I am foreseeing the possibility that the time may come when you can see your way clear to invest it in some enterprise from which we both may profit."

"My guess right now is that it surely might," said Abel.

The new regime proposed by Pomeroy was marked by an

initial flurry of minor practical arrangements. Abel bought two more suits of clothes. He hired a carriage. He employed Hubert, a free Negro, to cook, clean, care for his wardrobe, and drive the carriage. Thereafter, his days fell into a regular pattern. After the months of hourly uncertainties and surprises of river travel, now once more his expectations upon awakening each morning were as ordered as when he had worked in Job's shipyard. Forenoons he spent in Pomeroy's office. The merchant had taken personal charge even of the details of his business, for Andrew, upon his return from *Penguin,* had been sent off again, to his great irritation, to Pensacola to buy cattle from the Creek Nation for the Santo Domingo trade. At two Abel dined with Pomeroy while they discussed the pros and cons of the decisions Pomeroy had taken during the morning. After dinner Pomeroy took a nap while Abel struggled by earnest practice to make his handwriting more legible. In late afternoon they walked on the levee, however hot the weather, for Pomeroy believed exercise a protection against malaria and yellow fever. Evenings Abel pored over ledgers and letter books of earlier years in which he was able to trace the devious course of eventual profit or loss on cargoes purchased in New Orleans and sold, months later, in London or Antwerp or Genoa. Late at night, often after he had been hours asleep, Jasper usually came aboard, always filled with stories of his adventures, always smelling of wine or perfume or both, and always in need of money. Though it was drawn from Jasper's not yet defined share of their capital, Abel doled out a grudging allowance, five or ten dollars at a time, for Jasper, in spite of reiterated and penitent resolutions, invariably spent whatever was at any given moment in his pockets.

"You understand that I must maintain a certain position," explained Jasper. "The English consul here is still most curious about my activities and it is necessary that I keep him puzzled."

"Does your losing so much gambling puzzle him?"

"I confess my luck has been bad," said Jasper. "But I must indignantly deny your unspoken implication. It has always been a principle with me never to pay a penny for feminine favors."

Pomeroy made no further reference to the possible investment of Abel's money. The second week he took Abel with him to dine at Marquay, the third week he included Abel when the ladies dined at his house in town, and the fourth he brought them to pay a call aboard *Naiad;* but not again, as in the garden, was Abel ever alone with Félicie. Abel waited, comfortably. He no longer regarded his wealth as an astonishing and revolutionary change in his circumstances. The acquisition of a fortune had already begun to seem quite a simple matter. Further advantages seemed not only possible but likely.

This new assurance was with him that morning, at breakfast under the awning on *Naiad's* foredeck, when he first noticed the keelboat tacking shoreward from mid-river. He paid little attention after idly noting that the newly arrived craft was old and dirty, that the sail was patched, and that, except for two of them who looked like they might be Americans, the crew was French. But when next he looked up from his Jambalaya he could have been no more startled had the stranger opened fire on him with the rusty swivel gun in her bow. One of the two Americans was leaping and gesticulating and pointing in a frantic endeavor to attract the attention of the other. Whoever he might be, it was clear that even at that distance he had recognized *Naiad*.

Abel controlled the impulse to spring into the cabin to reach for his rifle. Instead, he sat sipping his coffee while he ran over in his mind the range of possibilities. The excitement the American had manifested inidicated a sharper, more personal interest than any that could have moved an ordinary resident of Limestone or Louisville who might chance to recall having noticed *Naiad* at anchor off either place. The list of men whom he had left behind him on his way downriver with special reason to remember *Naiad* was not a short one. There was Fortiner, who could claim the boat and who had money enough possibly to make the claim stick in one of these Spanish courts; Todd Barklit, who had already chased him two-thirds the length of the Ohio; William Neave, who had owned Magda; Evan Branch, who had wanted to marry Magda; Dorsey Jessop, who had consigned to him the cargo of ginseng; and Peter Branch, who had trusted him with the cargo of tobacco; not to speak of that whole parcel of rascals at the cave. Any one of them had plenty of reason to remember *Naiad*.

The French boat drifted sidewise with the current to a landing out of sight beyond the moored Spanish customs galley. But a moment later the two Americans appeared on top of the levee running toward Pomeroy's landing. Both of them were bigger than Fortiner, Neave, Jessop, or either Branch, and neither was as big as Barklit or the twins. Before they were near enough to distinguish their faces, his view of them was cut off by a corner of the cabin. He held out his cup for Hubert to pour him some more coffee. He could hear their pounding feet on the gangplank. Then, panting for breath, they came around the corner of the cabin.

187

Abel gave a grunt of disgust at his own slowness of wit. They were two that he had not thought of and yet, because of their profession, were the most likely of any to have traveled so far downriver and to have recognized *Naiad* from a distance. They were Fred Burd and Ben Taafe, Fortiner's boatmen. And they did not represent trouble, for they were beaming at him as though he were their long-lost brother.

"It's him all right," cried Fred. "It's Abel himself."

"It is fer a fact," said Ben. "Trap me fer a squaw if it ain't."

Fred looked about him and ran his hand along the rail. "And the boat, too." His marveling glance came back to Abel. "The last time we saw her she was stuck fast on that mudbank. How'd yuh git her off?"

"I didn't have to," said Abel. "The river rose and floated her off."

"Noticed myself it was startin' to come up. But me I'd never of had the gimp to squat there and wait to see did she come up fast enough—not with them woods so full of Injuns you could smell 'em. I been skeered time and again—but never that skeered. But here all three of us be, way off down here in New Orleans. What d'ye think o' that? You must o' made a real fast trip."

"I picked up a cargo the day I hit Limestone and kept right on coming. You didn't make such a slow trip yourself."

"Nope. We didn't lose much time neither. Them Shawnee had no sooner got us home and got through poundin' on us than this Frenchie from Vincennes showed up and bought us off old Chic. The Frenchie had a cargo to send down here and needed a couple of good hands for his boat."

"Shawnee," said Abel, setting his coffee cup down slowly and still spilling some of it.

"Don't tell me," said Ben, "thet they ain't heered in Kentucky even yet about the Injuns ketchin' us?"

"They hadn't when I came through," said Abel. He wet his lips. "Where'd they take you?"

"In the brush just west the mouth of the Scioto."

Abel shook with sudden anger. "But I told you to keep going—to get as far as you could in the skiff while it was dark. Who was fool enough to want to stop that near?"

"Nobody was fool enough." Fred was aggrieved by Abel's injustice. "It was that goddammed nigger. He was layin' in the bottom where we dumped him. He'd been so used up by the beatin' he'd had that nobody had any reason to watch him. Down there on the bottom in the dark he got hold of the hatchet and worked the blade into a seam between the planks.

188

First thing we knew, the whole goddammed river was in the skiff along with us. Only thing that saved any of us was we was so near the north bank by that time. Ben and me we got Mrs. Baynton to shore. Baynton and Buck made it too. We didn't think about Fortiner because we knew he could swim."

"Nobody kin swim," said Ben, "not when he's got three money belts strapped around his middle."

"That's what Ben thinks," said Fred. "Me, I think Spence grabbed hold of him and wouldn't let go."

"Then why didn't Spence drown too?" argued Ben. " 'Stead o' thet, he washed up on a sand bar and there he was—still life in him next mornin'."

"But you knew the Indians were right across the river," said Abel. "Didn't you even try to hide?"

"We surely did. We hid like rabbits. But that next mornin' there was a helluva hullabaloo when the Injuns went to swimmin' all the horses they'd taken over to the north bank. They seen Spence there on the sand bar. Injuns like niggers and when they seen all the hide off his back they liked him that much better. All o' them shook hands with him, and when he told them about us bein' right there in the brush, they all shook hands with him again. They kept after us until they took us. That is all except Baynton and Buck. Spence he just pointed at Baynton and then at Buck and the Shawnee they axed 'em both."

"This Frenchman that bought you—why didn't he buy Mrs. Baynton off them while he was at it?"

"He tried to. He offered a hundert dollars—twicet what he paid for Ben and me both. But Spence he wouldn't let her go."

"Spence wouldn't?"

"Old Chic—that's the hundert-and-eight-year-old catamount that bossed the pack that got us—he took a big shine to Spence. Give him a couple of horses and a house of his own and set around all the time listenin' to Spence tell him about white folks. Spence has Mrs. Baynton keepin' his house for him."

Abel's throat had become so dry that he continued speaking with difficulty. "This Frenchman come downriver with you?"

"No. He stopped off at New Madrid to set him up a new post there."

"What's his name?"

"Anthony Gamelin."

Fred and Ben were beginning to eye Abel curiously. He got up suddenly.

"Hubert, get these men some breakfast. And then get into town and find Mr. Hedges. Tell him I want to see him right away here on the boat."

Abel climbed the stairway to Pomeroy's office.

"I've got to ask for my money, Mr. Pomeroy. Something's come up that makes me have to go back to Kentucky."

Pomeroy rested his weight on his knuckles on the table. He looked old, tired, almost as though he might have been taken by a touch of malaria.

"You are leaving immediately?"

"Right now."

"You will require all of your money?"

"I don't know how much I'll need. So I'd better take it all."

"And you are absolutely certain this trip is necessary?"

"No question about it."

Pomeroy took out the key, turned toward the safe, turned back, and sat down heavily.

"You are evidently determined. And yet I cannot forbear inquiring if you have thoroughly canvassed your situation. You are in a unique position, Mr. Traner. You are young. You are a born and bred Westerner, familiar with the special character of the people who inhabit the West. You already know the great rivers, from here to Pittsburgh. Only a Westerner of your experience can hope to take full advantage of the years now immediately ahead. But what makes your position unique is the additional advantage that you have some capital with which to operate, and the other advantage of your connection with Hedges and his talent for getting to back doors, which here are often more important than front doors, and the final advantage of your association with me and through me with my acquaintance with foreign trade. Have you thought of all this?"

"Yes, I have. But there's something else I have to think about. I just this morning heard about something I owe—back where I came from. I got to go back and pay it."

This explanation appeared to clinch the matter for Pomeroy. He rose, took out the key, put it back again, and lifted down from a shelf a small iron-bound strongbox and placed it on the floor before the safe.

"Too much money just to carry off in a sack," he said with a testiness unusual in him.

He unlocked the safe and began counting and transferring to the strongbox first the paper cylinders of dollars and then the banknotes. When he had finished, Abel lifted the box to the table. He was surprised by the effort required. There was enough silver to make the chest weigh nearly three hundred pounds. Pomeroy sat down at the table and began sharpening a pen. Abel took out the demand note and laid it down.

"With regard to this Baring Brothers draft," said Pomeroy. "My signature is known in Louisville and Pittsburgh—and, of course, in Philadelphia. But this is rather a large lump sum. May I suggest my replacing it with a number of smaller drafts that you might find more readily negotiable?"

"I don't like putting you to the trouble," said Abel. "But it would probably save me some."

"Since you are in such haste," said Pomeroy as he wrote, "I take it you are traveling overland by the Natchez trace?"

"No. I want to hang on to my boat."

"Have you a crew?"

"Got my eye on a couple of good hands who just got in from Viccennes."

"You will need extra oarsmen to make any sort of time against the current. It occurs to me that yesterday Colonel Barela managed to capture a smuggler's galley. Four of the Negro oarsmen were uninjured and are now in his jail. They are big strapping fellows who must have been accustomed to hard rowing. I have an idea Barela might release them to you on very reasonable terms."

"Thank you," said Abel. "I'll see him."

Pomeroy rose, placed the drafts in the strongbox, locked it, and handed the key to Abel.

"There, Mr. Traner. I believe all is in order."

"I aim to come back," said Abel desperately. "I can't say how soon—but I'll be back."

Pomeroy slowly shook his head. "When you're as old as I am, you will begin to realize how time passes. No longer may plans admit of indefinite delay—or even of any delay. No, Mr. Traner, I fear we must recognize the fact that this has not been the kind of opportunity that will ever come to either of us again."

"I hate to keep on saying the same thing. I still have to go."

Pomeroy again sat heavily in his chair.

"That is evident. Good-by, Mr. Traner."

On board *Naiad* Hubert was serving a third breakfast. At the table with Jasper sat a buxom young woman whose creamy complexion more than faintly reflected the bright yellow of her gown. Jasper sprang up, smiling, as Abel mounted the gangplank, followed by two of Pomeroy's warehousemen carrying the box.

"Your summons found us already at breakfast—hence we took the liberty of finishing the repast here. Mr. Abel Traner —Mademoiselle Duchouquette."

"How do you do," said Abel. "Hubert, will you get the

carriage and take mademoiselle wherever she wants to go."

He opened the cabin door and gestured to the Negroes to place the box on the table within. When they had come out he bowed civilly to Mademoiselle Duchouquette and went in. Jasper followed.

"Jeanine will be rendered insufferable by the distinction of riding through town in the Traner equipage. Meanwhile there is no need to withhold your news. She knows no word of English."

"So you didn't see Fred and Ben?"

"No, nor Dick or Harry neither."

"Fred and Ben were Fortiner's boatmen."

"Oh-ho." Jasper sat down and stretched his long legs. He attempted a sigh but his eyes sparkled. "Some break in our blissful calm was overdue. So the estimable Fortiner is here."

"Fortiner is dead. So is Baynton."

Jasper slowly drew in his legs and slowly rose, his spindly mustaches quivering as though in their own independent response to the sudden alarm that gripped him. He scanned Abel's set face.

"That is bad. Very bad. But I can plainly see there is worse to come. And Mrs. Baynton?"

"The Shawnee have her."

"Dreadful. Dreadful beyond comprehension. An unspeakable outrage. But not so dreadful as what I can already see you have in mind."

"I sent them off in that skiff. I even started it all by catching Spence and bringing him back."

"Cast dust on your head. Rend your garments. You have reason to lament. But do not give way to lunacy."

"You can talk. You didn't take their boat."

"I exulted when you did. But neither am I a monster. Of course, Mrs. Baynton must be saved—if she be still within the reach of human salvation. No one could deny you that. But ransoming a captive from the Indians is a transaction to be handled by expert negotiation. People of sense deal through the English authorities in Canada. And a moment's reflection would remind you that funds dispatched from here can reach Quebec by a sea much faster than you can make your way through the wilderness."

"I know of a Frenchman at New Madrid who knows right where she is. He saw her. I can make New Madrid fast enough."

"Excellent. Send trusted emissaries to both places. Let them compete to see who will first make contact with her captors and who first will ransom her."

"I'm not sending anybody anywhere. You don't seem able

to figure out that both men she had a right to count on are dead. That was my doing. That leaves me right in line."

"Where it so far has left you is out of your mind. In all this babbling about your obligations, have you given no thought to some you have here that are far more defined? You may not know it but the whole town does. Pomeroy is about to take you into partnership with him, which is to say that wealth is at your fingertips. And does it cast no haze of disillusion over your mawkish dreams of Mrs. Baynton to know that Madame Marillac is holding her beauteous daughter in store for that partner? Surely before taking so disastrous a decision you will talk with Mr. Pomeroy?"

"I already have."

Jasper stared. "And so in that sinister box rests all your money—about to be scattered to the winds of this demented mission."

"That's right."

Jasper beat upon his head with his fists. "You are truly a fool. You are worse. You are a maniac. I disown you. I totally disown you."

Abel unlocked the box.

"We've never talked real plain about your share of this. The boat that hauled the cargo was mine. And I handled most of the business. But you took all the chances I did. The way I figure, a third for you might be about fair."

"Then give it to me. I'll waste it, too, but I'll get something in return. Give it to me."

Abel began making piles of money on the table but soon paused and instead took up a pen.

"You'll be here in New Orleans where it'll be easier for you than for me to cash these drafts. So I'll pay you mostly with them."

Jasper paid no attention. Abel signed several of the drafts and made notations of the amount. Jasper paced the cabin, waving his arms. Then, glaring at the money, he seized upon it and began stuffing handfuls into his pockets.

"Hey," protested Abel. "Give me a chance to finish counting it."

"Count it at your leisure. Count what you have left. If more is due me throw it in the river. I can endure no more."

Jasper ran from the cabin. On the levee Hubert was helping Mademoiselle Duchouquette into the carriage.

"Wait," Jasper called. "Wait."

As he ran up the slope of the levee the lining of one of his pockets broke and he left behind him a trail of silver dollars. He climbed into the carriage without looking back.

"Drive on," he commanded. "Drive on."

193

A covey of Negro urchins, playing at the water's edge, scrambled, with shrill birdlike cries, to pick up the scattered coins.

Abel estimated the supplies he would need for the voyage and, upon Hubert's return, sent him off to the market with the list. He himself called upon Colonel Barela. At sight of the crisp, new English banknotes the colonel's eyes brightened and he released the galley slaves for five hundred dollars each, which was a full third less than he might have demanded in silver. The four Negroes, as Pomeroy had said, were young, healthy, and muscular. The smuggler, their former master, being an ex-Moravian missionary, had named them Dan, Shad, Shach, and Nego. They were delighted to be released so soon from their damp Spanish dungeon and fascinated by the prospect of the North-bound voyage. Among the Negroes of New Orleans the virtues of any move upriver were held in legendary regard, since in the North there beckoned the reputed ease and freedom of life in the little French towns in the forest and, beyond, the ultimate ease and freedom of life among the Indians.

Abel presently realized that it was as well that he had enlisted this black crew, for as the afternoon waned it became apparent that Fred and Ben were already beyond his reach. After breakfasting aboard *Naiad* they had embarked upon an enthusiastic sampling of the delights of New Orleans. Their trail led through various bars and brothels and, before night fell, ended in the municipal hospital, Fred with a broken arm and Ben with a broken jaw.

Last of all, Abel called on the governor, whose interest in him became even warmer than before when he learned that Abel was returning forthwith to Kentucky, where he might be expected to spread the news of his favorable reception in New Orleans. The governor himself signed his passport, adding a personal footnote recommending him to the favorable attentions of all Spanish authorities whom he might encounter en route, and entrusted him with a letter to be delivered discreetly to General Wilkinson.

Early next morning Abel set sail, with no one but the disconsolate Hubert at the landing to bid him godspeed. There was no breath of wind to make the sail an aid in stemming the current but there was some satisfaction in observing with what cheerful gusto Dan, Shach, Shad, and Nego settled down to hard rowing. Some miles past Marquay he turned back and put in at the landing there.

Before he was halfway up the drive he saw Madame Marillac, a parasol over her shoulder, languidly emerging from the doorway on the river side of the house. She stood, awaiting his approach, and, as he came up to her, received him with a smile as gracious as when last he had seen her.

"I am happy, Mr. Traner," she said, "that for all your haste you yet came to bid us farewell."

"I came to tell you I'll be back."

"I do hope so. We shall look forward to seeing you again."

"I'd like to say good-by to Félicie too."

"Unfortunately Félicie is not here. The poor girl has been trying to do too much. She has gone to the convent to rest for a few days."

Madame Marillac's smile spoke as plainly as had Pomeroy's words of opportunities that were never to return.

"Well, good-by then."

"Good-by, Mr. Traner."

Walking back down the drive, Abel saw a Cajun pirogue coming upriver, the paddlers laboring very hard, but at the same time he noticed a faint stir of wind beginning to riffle the water. He ran to the landing, vaulted the rail, and began raising the sail. The blacks backed water vigorously. *Naiad* slid stern foremost out into the stream. They reversed their beat and pulled hard, bringing her bow around. They were working with a will but covertly watching Abel set the sail. With no more than a whisper of wind, the measure of his success in catching it might well also measure how hard they would have to work for the weeks to come. The sail flapped, steadied, slowly filled. Abel reached back to ease the tiller ever so little. The sail tightened. From Shad burst a low, wild cry that trailed off into the opening bars of some tribal chant. The voices of the other three picked up the beat. Under sail and oars, *Naiad* shot ahead. Abel sat back, well satisfied, and again saw the pirogue, now much nearer. There could be no doubt that the Cajun family, two men, three women, and a boy, were trying to come up with him.

"Hold it," he said.

The blacks lifted their oars and the keelboat drifted. The pirogue came alongside. Abel leaned over the rail. In the hot sun the dugout stank of fish and decayed vegetables and the reek of rum. Jasper lay sprawled in the bottom, pallid, sweating, dead drunk. Abel's first thought was to look sharply for any sign that he had been hurt, for in all of his experience with Jasper's many weaknesses he had never known him to drink too much. But the Cajuns shrugged, grinned, heaved Jasper over the rail to the deck, and tossed a small sea chest after him. Abel drew a pail of river water and dumped it over him. Jasper sat up and held a weakly protesting hand to ward off another pailful.

"Want you sober enough," said Abel, "to know for sure where you are."

"I am fully aware of where I am," said Jasper. "I am here as a result of a difficult but final choice. In my cups all became clear to me. I am no less fool than you and manifestly the company of two such fools should be primarily inflicted upon each other."

9

The people who lived there regarded the name New Madrid which had been so recently bestowed upon their town as a distinctly poor joke. Most of the inhabitants were French, for whom neither the English word "New" nor the Spanish word "Madrid" had much meaning, and the eminence of the Spanish governor and American land speculator who had between them invented the name somewhat less. As long as anyone could remember, the bend of the great river at the mouth of the Chepoosa had been known as L'Anse à la Graise. This had been born of an equivalent Indian name and it was only when there had been an attempt to translate the term into English that it came out so badly as Greasy Bend. At any rate, people here had always lived plentifully on the fat of the land because buffalo and bear, fish and wildfowl were to be had in such numbers that it was as though every man possessed a flourishing estate of well-stocked pastures, chicken runs, and fish ponds. It must always have been so, for the shore was dotted with the mounds left by the ancient, long-forgotten people who had been here even before the Indians.

Hagar sat on the doorstep of the cabin, her hands folded in her lap, her gaze fixed resolutely upon the little settlement stretching between the yellow bayou and the bright blue lake. She had struggled hard to accustom herself to living so near so many people. It was not an effort that had yet begun to seem easier. Each day she doggedly set herself some special task which obliged her to confront strangers. Today, soon after the sun had cleared the top branch of the oak and surely before it sank quite to the top of the ridge, she was to make her weekly call upon old Therese Cruzat who lived in the last house at the far end of town. Therese was bedridden and eager to talk to anyone who would take the time to visit her. Hagar felt no sympathy for the whining old hag and could understand practically none of her French, but to

197

reach her house she was required to pass the full length of the street, to speak to anyone who chose to speak to her, and to pretend to take no notice of stares and whispers.

She turned from the town to the pleasanter prospect of the cornfield. In the half-moon of open meadow between the clump of butternut trees and the great oak that overhung one end of the cabin were nearly ten acres of corn. It was a fine stand, already ten feet tall and beginning to ear. Tom and Tim were hoeing weeds somewhere among those ranks of towering green stalks. They were working hard, as was evidenced by the sound when a hoe blade struck a stone, but, big as they were, as hidden from view as though deep in a forest.

Another sound came from the path curving around the corner of the corn patch. Someone was approaching from the direction of the town. Hagar sprang up and back toward the interior of the cabin and reached for the latchstring to close the door behind her. But almost as part of the same movement she let herself down again on the doorstep. She even took care to turn her head slightly so that, whoever it might be who was coming, the first glimpse of her would be of the scarred side of her face. Then she saw it was Todd Barklit and sprang up again, hiding her dismay under a cloak of astonishment.

"I never seen yer canoe come in off'n the river."

"We got in during the night and been sleeping all morning," said Barklit, amiably talkative. "Before we shoved off again thought I'd look in and see if you were still as sick as when we left."

"Some days I'm some better—some days no."

"It was your back, wasn't it, that got so bad you couldn't set in a canoe any longer?"

"I couldn't stand the canoe no longer—fer a fact."

"The boys somewhere around?"

"I ain't never real sure where they are. Though they've been around enough to make us a corn crop. They figgered they had to stay here to look after me—else they'd been chasin' thet keelboat yet. How far'd you chase it?"

"Far's Natchez. The commandant said they hadn't come through there, and anyhow the people I work with wouldn't stand for me running any farther into Spanish country. I waited at Natchez a spell to see could I maybe have run past them somehow. Then I heard they'd got on all the way to New Orleans and there was nought left for me but to come back. They cost me a whole spring and the most of a summer." He looked at Hagar. "But they cost you more than that."

"A sight more," said Hagar.

"They got enough for them furs to buy out this whole settlement twice over. And they'd no right to a penny of it."

"Mebbe not. But we uns had no better."

"They got the furs with your trade goods."

"The way we got them trade goods never made 'em our'n."

"All the same, they stole them from you," argued Barklit. He came at last to the point of his visit. "They've made me so much trouble that I'd surely like to make them even a little. I couldn't follow them to New Orleans. But you could. If your brothers showed up down there they could make enough fuss so that they'd have to pay 'em something to keep 'em quiet."

"I'll talk to Tom and Tim about thet when they git back. But I don't know what them no-goods in New Orleans could pay worth one row o' thet corn crop. When we shuck thet corn we'll have us something thet belongs to us."

"Well," said Barklit, his pretense of friendly interest passing, "think it over. Me, I'm a month late getting back where I belong and I have to get going."

Hagar watched Barklit stride away until he was lost to view where the path entered the clump of butternuts. She leaped up then and ran after him to see if he had chanced to hear Tom and Tim in the cornfield. When she saw that he was keeping on toward the town she ran back, again like a deer, to the cabin and once more composed herself in her invalid's pose on the door step. In the restored silence she could hear the distant clop-clop of the twins' steady hoeing. Her strong hands opened and closed, as though yearning for the smooth, solid feel of a hoe handle, but she determinedly folded them in her lap.

Naiad wallowed sluggishly through the shallows along the bank below the last of the Chickasaw Bluffs. Jasper threw his weight against the stern oar, threshing it back and forth to add this impulse to the boat's grudging progress. In the bow Abel shifted his setting pole first to one side and then to the other and strained against it. The blacks were forced to devote to the oars the last ounce of their strength in fierce, spasmodic jerks in order to make any headway at all against the oily, swirling clasp of the river. Sweat spouted from their naked bodies. They breathed in long, shuddering gasps. Not for days had they raised their voices in one of their cheerful chants. The river widened and spread out across flats.

"Yah," yelled Abel.

The panting blacks drew in their oars and seized poles. They went to the bow, set the tip of the twenty-foot pole against the bottom, settled the padded butt of the pole against a shoulder, and crawled, pushing, straining, scrambling, toward the stern, reaching which they wheeled and ran back to the bow to repeat the performance. No labor could be more laborious or more discouraging. The boat seemed merely to inch ahead.

Everything about this journey northward had been as different from the southbound voyage as though made on a different river and in a different world. Then the river had nobly filled its bed; now it had fallen to expose noisome expanses of stinking mud flats. Then the air had been cool and crisp and bracing; now the heat of summer lay like a miasma over the steaming water. Then the majestic sweep of the current had been their friend; now it was their inplacable enemy. Then frequent winds had often caused them to seem to fly; now days of suffocating calm left the sail, their only ally, hanging lifelessly.

"Yah," yelled Abel.

The blacks laid aside the poles and groped wearily for the oars.

Hagar, forcing herself to walk at that slow and circumspect pace which still seemed so unnatural to her, came to a stop under the butternut trees. The visit to Therese this week had seemed even more of a task than usual. After the strain of her passage the length of the street through town, it was a comfort to stand here and look at the corn. It stood twelve feet high and had escaped any of the blights that seemed so often to attack corn when it grew so well. For three weeks they had had roasting ears to eat. In another two weeks it would be ready to harvest and there would be an almost unheard-of yield of up to a hundred bushels to the acre. She was glad that the twins' first crop had turned out so favorably, and she had encouraged them to take it for granted that it was not so much the soil or the weather as it was because they were men that their crop had been so much better than any of hers had ever been. It was another comfort to look toward the cabin. They were at work on a corn crib. Next they planned to build a pigpen. There would be corn in plenty to eat through the winter, to trade for salt and gunpowder, and enough left over to raise a litter of pigs.

The corn rustled in a stronger gust of the fitful south wind that had been stirring for the last hour. There would likely be rain by dark. She had started on when, out of the corner of her eye, she caught the same flash of white sail as when she had last seen it from the mouth of the cave. A keelboat had turned off the river into the mouth of the bayou and was gliding close along the nearer bank toward the town. There could be no mistaking it. It was passing not a quarter of a mile away. It was the same one. And the same people. She could see Jasper's lanky figure standing lookout in the bow and Abel's red hair as he leaned to the stern oar. A low moan burst through her clenched teeth.

Then she saw that Tom and Tim, intent on their pole-splitting, were still hard at work. From now on until it reached the landing their view of the keelboat would be cut off by the big oak, the cabin, and the butternut trees. She began to run. Darting into the cabin, she snatched down their rifles, powder horns, and bullet pouches and ran out to them. They straightened to stare, astonished by her sudden activity after the summer-long complaints about her back when she had so much as tried to gather a basket of chips.

"I ran all the way from town," she gasped, pretending to be out of breath to allow herself one more moment to think. "They—they's on their way back up from New Orleans—and they's stuck high and dry on thet sand bar off the mouth o' Little River."

There was no need to explain to Tom and Tim whom she meant by "they." "They" represented a bitterness that had inflamed every hour of their lives since the day all three of them had been hoodwinked at the cave.

"How come yuh heard thet?" demanded Tim.

"Anatole Tabeau," said Hagar. "He's jest got back from Little Prairie. They can't git their boat off 'til the water comes up—but thet could be by daylight tomorrow if'n it rains to-night."

Both reached for their rifles.

"We paddle hard and we kin make it plenty 'fore then," said Tom.

Hagar hung on to the rifles' straps.

"Not by canoe you can't, no matter how hard yuh paddle. Not with all them bends in the river. Only way yuh can make it is cross-country. Pick up thet Injun trail t'other side the lake. Thet's the way to make it so's yuh kin bust in on 'em 'fore they're up in the mornin'."

The twins looked at each other.

"She's right," said Tim.

Hagar released the straps. They bent to pick up their toma-hawks, with which they had been splitting corn-crib poles, thrust them in their belts, and set off at a trot. They disap-peared into the corn and, minutes later, reappeared running up the slope on the far side of the lake. Hagar sat down on the doorstep. She had a little more time to think. They could not very well get back until at least this time tomorrow.

After a while she rose and, appearing to make as great an

201

effort as though she were pushing an oxcart before her, walked down the path toward the town. When she was near the landing she paused behind a dogwood bush to study what awaited her.

The loungers along the waterfront were wandering off, having already lost interest in the new arrival. Abel had already been in the town and was coming back to the landing with a keg of brandy on his shoulder. A step behind him was one of his Negroes with a squealing pig clasped to him. The other three had got a fire started on the beach. They were beginning to laugh and chatter like children. Abel tossed the keg of brandy into the arms of one and a knife to butcher the pig to another. He was rich, all right. Rich enough to own four slaves, to feed them on pork and brandy, and to hire Etienne Chamard's horse, so that even on land he did not have to walk. He mounted the horse and rode off through the town, taking the trail that led over the ridge toward Honore Lalande's place. Jasper, idly watching from the rail of the keelboat, waved to Abel, stretched, yawned, and went into the cabin.

Hagar was seized by a fit of shivering and waited behind the dogwood until it had passed. Then she walked steadily down to the beach, past the singing Negroes, and up the gangplank to the deck of the keelboat. Through the open doorway of the cabin she could see Jasper lying on the bunk, his arms and legs flung wide, his long mustaches quivering as he snored. Once more she waited until she had stopped shivering. Entering the cabin, she staggered as though from a blow. On the wall there was a mirror and in it she had been suddenly confronted by the image of her strained, scarred face, made to seem the more stark and repellent by the tightly fitting turban of faded and ragged blue cloth. For a moment she clung to the door frame, staring beseechingly up toward the one glimpse visible past the butternuts of the twins' patch of yellowing corn. Turning, she kept her back carefully to the mirror and prodded the sleeping Jasper.

His eyes opened, staring vaguely at first and then widening as he recognized her.

"Reckon yuh didn't count on seein' me ever agin," she taunted him.

His mouth began to open and close at the same rate his eyes were blinking, but he was a moment assembling the wit to bring an intelligible sound out of it.

"Strictly speaking, I did not. Though I confess I have many times too often dreamed that I was again in your cave."

Slowly, reluctantly, he turned his head enough to look past her toward the portholes and the doorway.

202

"No call to be so skeered," said Hagar. "My brothers ain't here. They left off chasin' yuh."

"And their three unspeakable companions?"

"If'n yuh mean the Dobsons—I got no idee where they be. We ain't seen 'em since we left. And you don't have to be skeered o' Todd Barklit neither. He was here three weeks ago but he's left off chasin' yuh too."

Jasper sat up, swung his legs over the side of the bunk, and transferred his attention from the portholes and doorway to Hagar.

"A tangled web, indeed. So you also became involved with the redoubtable Barklit?"

"He showed up at the cave thet same mornin' yuh stole us blind. The Dobsons they woke up and blamed us for lettin' yuh git away, and Tom and Tim they had to pound on 'em to shut 'em up. Then we uns and Todd Barklit and his Frenchies tuk off cross-country to beat yuh to Saint Louis. When yuh didn't show up there and we found out you'd been and gone to Kaskaskia, we tuk off after yuh downriver. Now I've told yuh how we got here. What brung yuh here?"

Jasper, his poise completely restored, sprang up and drew forward a chair. "Since your visit promises not an imminent assault but a sociable chat, pray be seated and I will tell you. We came here to consult a certain Mr. Anthony Gamelin."

Hagar ignored the chair. "Tony Gamelin left for Vincennes last week."

"Alas, you seem not as fully posted on all local affairs as on the wider aspects of our situation. He merely planned to leave. Fortunately for us, his departure was at the last moment delayed by an illness of his sister, Madame Lalande."

"Makes no difference who's here—just so you ain't. That's whut I come to tell you. Don't stop here. Git goin' to wherever yer headed fer. 'Cause my brothers'll git back by this time tomorrow and if'n yer here they'll kill yuh quicker'n yuh could squash a bug."

Jasper winced. "A somewhat too apt simile—when one visualizes those sturdy feet. But a mystery arises. Are you endeavoring to imply that you do not wish us dead?"

"I ain't never wished nothin' else—not fer one minute—since the last I seen o' yuh. I hope to God somebody kills yuh, and somebody's bound to 'fore too much longer. Only I don't crave fer Tom and Tim to be the ones to do it."

"The mystery deepens. What can have moved you to deny your pets their just revenge?"

"I kin tell yuh thet too. I got so nothin' shames me no more. They settled down here and raised 'em a crop 'cause they thought I was sick and had to be looked after. The way things

203

been goin' they got some chance to be like other folks. But if'n they kill you they'll have to take to the woods agin and be right back like they was with the Dobsons."

Jasper walked to the door, looked out, pulled thoughtfully at his mustaches, and came back to her, wagging his head.

"Your case might well touch the most calloused heart— even one so hardened as mine. You persuade me to offer you terms."

"Only one thing I want from you—thet you be gone from here by this time tomorrow."

"First hear my offer. It envisages one of two alternatives for you. On the one hand you must realize that Mr. Traner while in New Orleans became a great friend of the Spanish governor. He has a letter from His Excellency which has already been much remarked on by all three of the yokels here who are able to read. Furthermore, following us upriver is a galleyload of Spanish soldiers. The governor has decided to establish an army post here. By this time tomorrow there will be a garrison in residence, and it will require but a word from Mr. Traner to the commandant to have your brothers clapped into whatever passes for the local calaboose. You do not believe me?"

"Was you to say thet's the sun shinin' in thet doorway I'd know it was black night." Hagar's bitterness sharpened. "Only one thing I know better. We'uns can always count on the worst of it. We'll have to take to the woods agin."

"You have not yet heard your other alternative. I can assure you that we will be gone from here with the first streak of daylight and as a consequence that your brothers' bucolic peace will remain undisturbed. On but one condition, a rather easy condition. This is that before you go ashore you permit me to offer you a present I purchased for you in New Orleans."

Hagar laughed harshly. "Yuh kin lie faster'n fleas kin jump off'n a dead deer. So yuh expect me to think yuh went to the trouble to buy a present fer me?"

"Most especially for you."

"Even if'n I didn't know yuh like I do, thet wouldn't make no sense. To start off with, yuh never counted on ever seein' me ever agin."

"People embarking upon hazardous voyages frequently take insurance against unforeseeable disaster. My present was in the nature of a propitiatory offering—provided against the event that by some ghastly misadventure we were again detained at the cave during our return journey. Perhaps you will be convinced if I produce it."

204

Jasper picked up his sea chest, set it on the bunk, and lifted the lid. Hagar backed away.

"I don't want nothin' from you."

"Come, come. At least you will want to see what it is." Jasper lifted a fold of scarlet silk and let it drop back into the chest. "My offering is a garment of sorts—but you must let me arrange it on you. Just sit in this chair."

"You must think I'm crazier'n when you made out you was sick."

"Sit down here, please," persisted Jasper mildly, moving the chair toward her. "You may keep your back to me, if you like—so that you will not even be obliged to look at me."

Hagar's basic resentment became tinged with the dawning suspicion that she might be dealing with a madman.

"Let me out o' here."

She shoved the chair aside and started for the door. Jasper made no move to detain her. He turned to close the chest. Hagar swung around in the doorway.

"Yuh keep thinkin' yuh kin make a fool o' me agin, 'cause yuh think yuh got me where I got no choice."

Jasper shrugged. "If, as you say, your brothers will not be back until this time tomorrow, you have until then to consider your choice."

"I got me one right now. I kin kill yuh myself."

"Ah," said Jasper. "A happy thought. Wait."

He delved deeper into the chest, brought out a pistol, charged it, and extended it toward her. She moved back into the cabin, took it from him, and regarded it scornfully.

"I never shot one o' these here things."

"Then—to make doubly certain—here."

He drew the hunting knife from the sheath at his belt. She snatched at this.

"Now that we have established a basis of complete mutual trust, will you be pleased to sit down."

Hagar stared at him, torn by anger, by continued suspicion of all his designs, and by a growing desperate curiosity.

"This here toy gun could misfire," she warned, "but this knife's got blade enough to rip you wide open."

"Keeping so dismal a forfeit in mind, shall we proceed?"

Gripping her two weapons in either hand, Hagar sank into the chair. Jasper lifted the folds of scarlet silk from the chest and shook them out. They became a scarf. He moved behind Hagar and draped the scarf over her shoulders, crossing it in front so that it quite covered the upper part of her patched and threadbare linsey-woolsey gown. She continued to stare

205

straight before her at the cabin wall. Jasper reached again into the chest.

"What I am about to undertake involves certain liberties with your person. I beg that you will for the moment regard me as impersonally as—shall we say—your attending physician?"

"Whatever yer up to," said Hagar grimly, "git on with it."

Jasper opened the two small boxes in his hand. Into one he thrust a forefinger and with it lightly touched her scar from end to end with rouge. From the other he took a puff and swiftly and delicately dusted her face with powder.

"Whatever the hell's takin' yuh so much time," said Hagar, "it smells real good."

"Patience," begged Jasper. "Patience, for just another moment or two."

From a little silk bag he drew a pair of earrings of Aztec gold filigree and fitted the clasps over the lobes of her ears, watching warily, meanwhile, for some sign of rebellion against the slight discomfort. She did not stir.

"Earrings," she remarked, more coldly than she had upon the smell of the face powder. "Like Injuns wear—and oncet in a while a nigger gal."

"Now," said Jasper, bracing himself for the moment of crisis, "we come to the final step. Will you permit me to remove this cloth around your head?"

Hagar leaped up and whirled to face him, the gold earrings spinning and flashing.

"Yuh'll never git out o' here alive."

Jasper met the new threat with his blandest smile. He indicated a large satinwood box in the top of the sea chest.

"Equally—how can you, my bellicose Pandora, until you have first learned what is in that box?"

Against her will, she glanced down at the box. She flushed, swiftly transferred the pistol to her left hand and the knife to her right, and glared again at Jasper. He continued to smile. With a grunt of final warning, she turned and planted herself once more in the chair.

From the satinwood box Jasper lifted a black, glossy, curling woman's wig. Holding it ready in one hand, he unwound the blue cloth with the other and slipped the wig into place. Whipping around in front of the chair, he bent to study the effect, to smooth and tuck and arrange and to draw one pendant curl forward over a shoulder. Hagar had closed her eyes. She seemed to have stopped breathing. The knife and pistol slipped from her hands to the floor. He ran behind her again and, taking her by the shoulders, raised her gently to her feet.

"Now open your eyes," he commanded.

Hagar began to tremble but at last obeyed. Once more she was confronted by the mirror. But the image in it was of a woman she could not recognize, a woman she could never have imagined, of whom she could never have dreamed. It was an image made dazzlingly vivid by the flame of the scarlet scarf, the gleam of the gold earrings, the crowning dark cloud of hair. The harsh, strong molding of this strange woman's face had been smoothed and softened by the glow of color and by the pleasingly irregular frame of curls and ringlets. No frown split the delicate arch of the brows, no bitterness smoldered in the wide eyes, no tightness compressed the full lips, the scar was all but imperceptible. It was a beautiful face and, more amazing still, an utterly feminine face.

"Behold," murmured Jasper with a master craftsman's pride in his handiwork, "conceivably not the queen—but inevitably the sultan's favorite."

"This Molly o' your'n," said Hagar, "did she fer sure look like thet?"

"She did not," said Jasper. "There never was a Molly. No one else looks like that. No one in the world but you."

Hagar sank slowly to the floor, bowed her head, and began to weep, at first softly and then with convulsive, tearing sobs. Jasper went out, closed the door, and leaned at the rail. Clouds were scudding across the sun, now almost down to the ridge over which Abel had long since disappeared. In the town someone was tuning a fiddle and people were already drifting toward the arbor where so many of their summer nights were devoted to dancing. The Negroes on the beach had become so engrossed in the brandy keg that they had not noticed their pig had fallen from the spit into the fire.

In the cabin Hagar's sobs became less strident, subsided into child-like moans, and faded into the silence of exhaustion. The wind freshened and an occasional drop of rain spattered upon the deck. The dancers, laughing and shouting, ran for cover. The twilight darkened swiftly. Hagar came out. She was wearing neither scarf nor earrings and the old blue cloth was back in place around her head.

"I never figgered nothin' like thet was ever a-goin' to happen to me," she said.

"But those things," protested Jasper. "They were for you. What did you do with them?"

"They're back there in yer box."

"But they belong to you. They're yours."

"I can't take 'em. Tom and Tim they'd figger right off I got 'em from you, and even if'n they didn't take to chasin' off after yuh agin, they'd have no more truck with me. The only

207

chance them boys has got is to figger they have to look after me. I ain't never been able to give them much chance. I got to work at givin' 'em so good a one as I kin."

Jasper groaned. "You have an amazing faculty for making the most complex problems appear simple. You come to conclusions that are—humanly speaking—quite indisputable. But let me do this. Let me make up a package. I'll wrap it in waxed cloth—safe from the weather. You can take it with you and hide it in your cabin—or, if you like, somewhere near in the woods. Then you'll at least have the comfort of knowing that—were time and circumstances to change—you had still always within your reach what you saw in that mirror."

"No," said Hagar. "I could stand to set there in thet chair and wonder what was a-comin' at me. But I never could stand to have them things close by. I couldn't stand thet. I couldn't leave 'em alone. Better fer me to make up my mind now."

She ran down the gangplank and disappeared in the darkness. Jasper looked after her, gripping the rail, unaware of the rain that was beginning to fall steadily.

Abel rode into the Lalande farmyard along with the first spats of rain. After the tedious labors and delays and forebodings of the long pull upriver, it had been reassuring to learn, upon arriving, that Anthony Gamelin was still here. His meeting with him now was even more reassuring. Gamelin was a substantial, middle-aged Frenchman who had spent his life trading with Indians. He was first of all a businessman. He had often, in his long experience among the Indians, negotiated the ransom of captives; this was an undertaking in which he always took a deep interest; and he comprehended Abel's problem at once. Even his English was business-like.

"Chicatommo he have learn to like money," said Gamelin. "Not because he like money but because he want the good rifles for his young bucks. For that he always need money. He would not sell her to me for one hundred dollar. But if I go back and offer him more he will listen. How much can you pay?"

"As much as it takes."

"No. That would be bad. If he see we are too anxious it will take a long time for him to make sure how anxious. Three hundred dollar—that would be about right. Many rifles for Chicatommo, but not so many he think you are rich."

"Anyway, I'll be there with as much more as you find out you need."

"No. That would be very bad. If you are there, he will not talk with me. He will talk with you. No. I will tell you how we will do. I go soon to Vincennes and from there I will go to Chicatommo's town. I will tell him that I have three hundred dollar, and he will take it because he will believe me when I say that is all I have, and because he is always in a big hurry to get more rifles. You will go to Limestone and wait."

"Why Limestone?"

"I will tell you why. The Kentuckians they have made the agreement with the Shawnee to make the exchange of captives. Next month there will be the council on the Indian side of the Ohio at Limestone. For some of the Kentucky captives their relatives will pay. For some the Kentuckians will trade Shawnee captives they have taken. Chicatommo know about this and it will make it the more easy for me to talk with him. I will bring Madame Baynton to you at Limestone."

"Sounds reasonable to me," said Abel. He drew a leather pouch from his pocket. "I'll give you six hundred dollars. What's left after you pay the ransom is yours for your trouble. If the business costs you more, we'll settle that when I see you at Limestone."

"My sister she is better," said Gamelin. "It is time for me to go and I will start in the morning."

Hagar sat for hours by the cold hearth in her cabin. The slow patter of rain on the roof made so mournful a sound that to her intense annoyance she was weeping again. A branch of the oak, swaying in the wind, swished gently against the log wall. A cricket in the chimney corner set up a brisk clatter. Suddenly these natural sounds were overlaid by others most aggressively unnatural—pounding footsteps, muffled shouts, hoarse whispers. Hagar snatched down her rifle and sprang to the loophole beside the door. Her first thought was of an Indian attack, though she knew that this dozing little French trading settlement had not been troubled by Indian hostility in a generation. Then she recognized the voice of Etienne Chamard. He was excitedly calling her name. She threw open the door. Several men pushed into the doorway, but the first one through was Abel. He had his rifle and he held it ready as he looked toward the corners of the dimly lit cabin.

"We're looking for your brothers," he said.

"They ain't here. They's down at Little Prairie."

"Not unless they can fly they ain't. This man"—Abel indicated Etienne—"when he was bringing in his cow just before dark, saw them crawling into that patch of willows between the lake and the town."

Hagar looked around at the dozen Frenchmen who had

pushed into the cabin in Abel's train. They were armed with rifles and axes and boat hooks. One had a broadsword. They were as excited as only Frenchmen could get, but they were in earnest too. Law had not yet come to New Madrid. People took affairs into their own hands.

"Whut do you claim they done?"

"While I was away they busted into the cabin on my boat and killed Jasper—or come so close to killing him you couldn't tell the difference."

Hagar clutched her rifle by the barrel and swung it with an intent so threatening that the men fell back away from her. She plunged through their circle and out the door. Once in the open she began to run, casting aside the riffe lest it impede her. She slipped on the muddy, rain-soaked path and fell, rose and ran on, collided with the butternuts in the darkness, recoiled, and raced on.

On the beach Abel's Negroes were sprawled in drunken sleep about their quenched fire. There was a lighted lantern hanging by the door of the keelboat's cabin and other lights within. Hagar ran up the gangplank. Seven or eight Frenchwomen were jammed in the cabin, chattering, clucking, and fussing over Jasper who was stretched out on the bunk, covered with blood. Hagar burst in among them like a fury, drove them from the cabin, closed the door, and ran to Jasper.

He was breathing, but there was a froth of blood on his lips. His face and head had been so battered that he was unrecognizable. Hagar dropped to her knees beside the bunk and for a moment her head sank down against his shoulder in a gesture of utter despair. Then she straightened and, outwardly, became cold and calm. Swiftly she ran her fingers over Jasper's head, feeling for spots where his skull could have been broken, and as swiftly stripped his clothing from him in her continued search for major wounds. His whole body was as covered with bruises and contusions as his head and his face. He had been beaten, apparently by gun butts and tomahawk handles, and the beating had continued long after he had become insensible. His attackers had been obsessed with a frenzied desire to hurt him. But there were no gashes from the blades of knife or tomahawk, no gunshot wounds.

One of the Frenchwomen had left a pail of river water beside the bunk. Hagar tore off a piece of her dress and began to wash the drying blood from him. Occasionally he roused slightly from his stupor to squirm or wince. Once he moaned.

"Better git this part over 'fore yuh come to," muttered Hagar almost cheerfully.

She heard Abel's voice outside and hastily drew the blanket up over Jasper. When Abel came in she faced him defiantly.

"They never aimed to kill him," she declared. "Was they a mind to, they could o' twisted his head off like thet." She illustrated with thumb and forefinger. "But all they aimed at was to pound on him good and plenty."

"Makes no difference what they aimed at if they killed him."

"Makes some to me. Means thet whilst they ain't learnt much, they's learnt something. Anyhow, they never killed him. He ain't a-goin' to die."

Abel pushed past her to look down at Jasper.

"He is breathing some easier."

"He's a-goin' to feel real bad fer quite a spell, but he'll make out." Hagar was still contemplating her own inner thanksgiving. "They was a sight smarter'n me. They seen you come in soon's I did. All the time they seen through me—like I was window glass."

Jasper's swollen lips moved.

"Is that you, Hagar?" he whispered.

"Don't try to talk," she directed.

He turned his head toward her, but his eyes were too blackened to permit his opening them.

"Retribution," muttered Jasper. "Once I shammed sickness for you."

"Like she says," said Abel, "better for you to stay quiet and rest."

"Abel?" Jasper's whisper was barely audible. "They took your strongbox."

Abel whirled and wrenched open the door of the wardrobe. The ironbound box was no longer on the shelf. A bitter groan burst from Hagar. Her moment of thanksgiving had so soon passed. She seized hold of Abel and pulled him with her from the cabin. At the door she glanced back once at Jasper, closed it, and clutched Abel by the shoulders.

"How much was in it?"

"All the silver and English money I had."

"How much?"

"Close to forty-five hundred dollars."

"Gawd-a-mighty," moaned Hagar.

"If they'd have come to me peaceable, I'd have dickered with 'em. They had maybe some right to reckon something was due 'em."

Hagar was not listening. She was pursuing her own unhappy train of thought.

"More money'n they ever heard of. More'n enough to ruin them fer good."

"We'll run 'em down come morning."

"No, you won't. They's tuk off by canoe and got the whole Mississippi to hide along. You'd never come up with 'em was yuh to git every bushwhacker in Kentucky and Tennessee helpin' yuh look—and all the Injuns in North Ameriky to boot." She released her grip on Abel and stared off into the rain-wet darkness. "They know I got the corn crop to keep me. They won't be back 'til they've spent it and by then nothin'll make no difference." Her despair-haunted eyes came back to Abel. "Would you like to know where to look fer 'em?"

"Yes, I would."

"Then listen to me. Every time they ever got a chanct to set down and chew the rag, there was just one thing they talked about. They talked it so much thet they never tuk even one look at none o' the French gals here—and some o' them ain't so bad-lookin' neither. When they got to talkin', first they'd talk about a bitch widder back in Louisville both o' them had bedded with once, and then they'd git around to thet wench you had on yer boat and the way they remembered she looked and talkin' about thet would git 'em so worked up they couldn't talk no more."

"The widow could be still at Louisville, but no telling where Magda is now."

"They think they know. Right after Tom turned her loose in his canoe she run across Todd Barklit camped on Wabash Island. He put her on an army barge that was comin' past on its way to Louisville." Hagar's voice trailed off into weary bitterness. "So they'll lay low in the woods back o' Louisville and sneak in nights to see the widder, and next they'll take to figgering if'n with thet much money there ain't some way to git at the redhead. Thet's whereat they'll be, fer sure, 'less they hit trouble 'fore they git thet far."

"Anyhow, Louisville is right on my way."

Hagar clutched him again. "Yer takin' me with you."

"What for?"

" 'Cause if'n yuh do come up with them, and I'm along, there might be some less trouble fer yuh and them both. And 'cause fer the next couple o' weeks Jasper's a-goin' to need lookin' after."

Across Abel's face of cast iron crept the faintest sugggestion of a grin. "Either reason is good enough for me."

Hagar went back into the cabin. Jasper was rolling and tossing and muttering but again asleep. When she bent over him and laid a hand on his forehead his sleep became quieter. As she knelt beside the bunk her knee struck his sea chest under it. Edging the chest out with the greatest care to make no sound, she opened it. Her fingers wandered over the folds of the scarlet scarf, touched the bag containing the earrings, and came to the satinwood box. She removed the lid and lifted out the wig. For moments she held it in her hand, contemplating it, smoothing the curls. Then, her breath catching, she began to unwind the blue cloth.

10

October 25, 1788, was a critical day for the people of Louisville, as, for that matter, had been every other day of that whole summer and fall. In common with all Kentucky they were in the throes of reaching a decision as historic as could be taken by Americans. Kentuckians had been long unanimous in demanding independence from Virginia, but the nature of the next step had divided them more violently than they were again to be divided until 1861. The larger party to this dispute, rallying around Wilkinson, was openly recommending union with Spain; a smaller party, led by men like Colonel Hawley, was proposing an arrangement with England; while the disorganized general public milled about, listening uneasily to the exhortations of such articulate lesser advocates as Aaron Creamer and Edmund Mercer. The sudden and unexpected news that the Constitution had been ratified had magnified the controversy. There was henceforth not only Virginia to consider. There was also this strange new federal government of the United States.

On this October 25 Abel, Jasper, and Hagar, Tom and Tim Crohon, Evan Branch, and Todd Barklit, all pursuing their several personal designs, were converging upon Louisville from as many different directions. The latter two, the first to arrive, all but collided in the street before Colonel Hawley's house. Barklit, after leaving New Madrid, had raced up the Ohio and then on up the Miami to meet and escort Dr. John Connolly to Kentucky. Evan was galloping into Louisville along the Lexington road. The week of Magda's flight his father had packed him off to Pittsburgh to buy ironware in the hope that the change of scene might hasten a rational recovery from the blow. In the course of his return journey he had heard from Dorsey Jessop at Limestone of Magda's astonishing reappearance in Louisville and, unable to endure the slow pace of his flatboat, had rushed the rest of the way overland. He gave an incurious glance at the

214

two strangers turning into Hawley's gate, and a second, not much more interested, at Hawley's new house, the first brick house in Louisville, which had been completed during his absence. Then he saw Magda. She was sitting on a bench in the back yard between the brick house and the earlier clapboard cabin that it had supplanted, surrounded by the brood of young children the hardy veteran had fathered since his belated second marriage.

Evan leaped from his horse and vaulted the fence. A young colored girl darted from the cabin to shepherd the children to one side. Magda looked up, biting a thread. Her eyes widened in well-simulated surprise.

"Are you staying here at Hawley's?" he stammered.

"Yes. I take care of his children."

"Well, it's no fit place for you. Everybody knows about his wife. She's sick—she's not been outside her room this past year. The old goat's the same as a widower."

His outburst seemed to lend her added calm.

"He took me in. When nobody else would."

"Only because he thought it might devil my folks—'less he had a worse reason."

"Your people did not like it," assented Magda with a faint smile. "That is so. Your sisters. They run to every house in town. They tell everybody I am a bad woman."

Magda resumed sewing. Evan tried vainly to draw a long breath to ease the tightness in his throat. He was saying none of the things that during the ride from Limestone he had rehearsed, that he had intended to say as recently as when he had jumped the fence.

"Why?" he implored. "Why did you run off with them, Magda? Why?"

She gathered up her sewing. "What is the use? You will not believe."

"Try me. Try me and see."

She rose and turned toward the cabin. "I believe Jasper when he tell me you go with them. That is why I get up in the night and go down to the boat. I think it is with you I am going to New Orleans."

She opened her door and went in.

"So that's how it happened." He rushed into the cabin after her. "Of course I believe you. Whatever made you think I wouldn't? There couldn't be a more reasonable story. It explains everything. Why didn't you tell it to my folks when you came back?"

"I try. They would not listen."

"Come with me now. I'll make 'em listen."

Magda looked at him doubtfully.

"We come first. You and me, Magda. If they don't like it, then in a place of our own."

Her candid eyes caught and held his.

"Where?" she asked. "What place?"

It was then that Evan chanced to catch sight of the brass-bound chest. He had good reason to remember it in the cabin of the keelboat. During the trip downriver from Limestone Magda had been perpetually fascinated by it.

"Where'd you get that?" he demanded.

For the first time since he had confronted her she showed a trace of confusion. He brushed past her and threw open the lid. An array of neatly folded woman's garments, the uppermost a blue silk nightgown, came into view. He plunged his hands into the chest and lifted a reckless handful of its contents. The faint scent of lilac rose in the air. A pair of lace-trimmed drawers dangled from the bundle in his hands. Lifting the layer of clothing had uncovered a second layer of perfume bottles, toilet articles, ornaments, a leather jewel case. Magda snatched the things out of his hands.

"Mine," she said with terrible distinctness. "All mine. Abel give it to me."

She knelt beside the chest and began swiftly restoring order among her possessions. Evan backed slowly out the door.

In that same twilight *Naiad* was scraping and bumping over the rocks in the course of her laborious ascent of the rapids. For the harassed upriver voyager, after sails and oars and poles in turn had failed, there was, as a last desperate resort, the *cordelle*. Clinging to a long line attached to the top of the mast, the crewmen scrambled along the brush-entangled shore, floundered over mud flats, waded waist deep in the river itself, dragging the craft against the current by main brute strength.

Abel, as nearly prostrated by fatigue as his staggering blacks, kept them going with threats and abuse, against which they were too exhausted to rebel. No longer could there be permitted the briefest pauses for rest while there yet remained a glimmer of daylight. For this struggle with the rapids was but the last of many delays since leaving New Madrid. The most serious had occurred at the cave. This had not been by reason of any sortie by its inmates, for it had proved to be uninhabited and, according to every sign, to have been abandoned by the Dobsons months before. But that stretch of the river had nevertheless remained a passage of ill omen. A sawyer—a submerged tree embedded in the river bottom, rising and falling under the impulse of the current intermittently to break the surface—had torn half a dozen planks out of the *Naiad's* bottom. It had taken more than a week to beach and careen the ship, to fashion new planks to replace those damaged, and to get under way again.

Anchoring in the darkness off the Louisville waterfront, Abel leaned wearily against the cabin and endeavored to canvass his situation. Since the morning he had left New Madrid he had contemplated pausing at Louisville long enough to gather up those loose ends which he had resolved not to leave dangling as he kept on upriver. There was obvious need to settle in some fashion the matter of the tobacco cargo with the storekeeper and to pay some heed to the problem of Hagar and her brothers. But with Gamelin already in the Shawnee country, there was no longer time for these detours. They must await some later day. Another far more pressing anxiety had arisen, however, which could not be postponed. Jasper had not improved as might have been expected. His bumps and bruises had healed but, in spite of Hagar's indefatigable nursing, his general condition had seemed steadily to deteriorate, and in the last two days he had taken a decided turn for the worse.

Hagar came to the cabin door and he turned to look at her inquiringly. He was still startled every time he was reminded of the difference that had been made by her having taken to wearing that wig.

"He's worse," she said. "He's a-burnin' up with fever."

"I'll find out if there's a doctor in Louisville," said Abel.

The Negroes were sprawled asleep on deck where they had dropped the moment the anchor had caught hold. It would be trouble enough awakening them when the time came to get them up at daylight. He found it an effort to lift his canoe over the side and another effort to paddle it ashore. Stumbling up the bank, he came upon the white picket fence of the John Rogers house where he had delivered Clark's letter the last time he had landed at night on the Louisville waterfront. Most of the windows of the town were already dark, but there was still one lighted one here. He was just lifting his fist to knock on the door when it opened a foot and caught on a length of chain. Rogers peered out. He had a pistol in his hand.

"Who's there?" he demanded belligerently.

"You don't know me," said Abel. "I'm the man that stopped past last spring to give you a letter from General Clark."

Rogers looked past him into the darkness to make sure that he was alone, loosened the chain, pulled him inside, closed the door, and put his back against it. He was not pointing the pistol, but he was holding it ready.

"That's all over," he said. "Clark changed his mind and so did the rest of us."

"I knew nothing about it then," said Abel, "and I know less now. Only reason I stopped then was because Clark asked me to give you the letter. Only reason I'm stopping now is your house was the first I came to and I have to find out if there's a doctor in town."

Rogers emitted a grunt of digusted understanding. "So you're looking for John Connolly. He's in town, but you've come to the wrong place to look for him."

"Damn Connolly," said Abel. "I've got a sick man out on my keelboat."

Rogers seemed partially convinced by the urgency in Abel's voice. "If that's the case," he said grudgingly, "you'll need a real doctor. There's a new young one from Virginia been here about a month. I don't know much about him."

"Where can I find him?"

"He bought him John Dobcrick's house. That's the second one the other side of Sam Stubb's stable. You can tell it in the dark by the smell, but if you miss it the Dobcrick house is the third this side of Joe Borke's tavern. You can smell that too."

"Much obliged," said Abel, turning to go.

His relief upon hearing about the doctor reminded him of a lesser relief that he might as well also have. He turned back.

"I have to push off before daylight. I've got a letter for Wilkinson. Would you turn it over to some friend of his for me?"

All of Rogers' initial suspicion was revived. "I don't know you. I don't know what you're driving at. I'm through with messing with things I don't know about."

Abel took out the governor's passport. "This will account for how I happened to have the letter." He tossed the two on the table. "You and Clark used to be friendly with the Spaniards. If you're not any more, you surely will know somebody who is. Or you can throw Wilkinson's letter in the fire if you feel like it. I've done my part."

He walked out, leaving one of his problems, at least, behind him.

Dr. Nathaniel Callender was sitting on his doorstep, smoking a bedtime pipe. He was young enough and new enough to take an immediate interest in Abel's summons and the expedition to which it led. He was intrigued by Abel's swift, sure handling of the canoe, by a great garfish surfacing so near that water was splashed in his face from the creature's swirling turn, by the mysterious shadow of the keelboat looming up in the black river ahead, by the recumbent Negroes he

218

stumbled over on deck, and, most of all, by his first glimpse of Hagar stationed like a dark, brooding guardian angel by the sick man's bed.

Abel's uneasiness, aroused by the doctor's youth and levity, was quieted by the professional manner with which he at once embarked upon his examination. He took Jasper's pulse, rolled back his eyelids to peer into his eyes, estimated his fever by thrusting his fingertips into his armpits, ranged back and forth across his bared chest with a tapping forefinger, and crouched for minutes with an ear pressed against him to listen to Jasper's breathing, before he straightened to announce his diagnosis. Jasper's fever-bright eyes opened and he, too, hung on the verdict.

"He has two broken ribs. The breaks have not knitted—possibly due to the constant movement inescapable on shipboard. The jagged ends have rubbed until they have set up a pleurisy in the lungs. Pneumonia is threatened but not yet inevitable. Tossing about on this boat—any movement whatever—is injurious—might prove fatal. You must get him ashore."

"Impossible," said Jasper.

"Pay no attention to him," said the doctor, continuing to address Abel. "He is not responsible. You are."

"How about putting him up in your house?" proposed Abel. He saw the doctor's hesitation and added: "We can pay—whatever it's worth."

"I wasn't thinking of pay so much as care. I'm apt to be called away from time to time and for a while, at least, he'll require constant watching—day and night."

"I'll be there," said Hagar. "I'll be watchin' him every minute."

Her eyes were fierce. There seemed in her such a glow of strength and vitality that it must surely shed its warmth upon any weakness that might be brought near her.

"This is a great mistake," objected Jasper.

"Shut up," said Abel. "I'll be back in a week—two weeks at the most."

While the doctor bound Jasper's chest with bandages, Abel sawed a boat pole in half and, with a blanket, contrived a litter. The still-feebly protesting invalid was lowered into the canoe. Abel made a bundle of his three suits and other effects. Hagar sat in the bow clutching her rifle and Jasper's sea chest. For all their care in handling him, he complained bitterly during the earlier stages of the passage, but by the time the canoe was beached he had apparently lapsed into unconsciousness. At last he was tucked into bed along with several heated bricks.

"I shouldn't hesitate about going if I were in your place," said the doctor, appreciating Abel's dilemma. "There's nothing you could do for him by staying. And nine chances out of ten, by the time you get back he'll be up and around."

Hagar added her reassurance. "Me and the doc kin look after Jasper. And if'n Tom and Tim happen to show up 'fore yuh git back—I kin slap 'em down faster without yuh here."

"How about Jasper?"

Her eyes flashed. "Nobody—not Todd Barklit if'n he showed up—not Tom nor Tim nor nobody—will touch him."

"If Branch, the storekeeper, noses around, you can tell him I'll talk to him when I get back." Abel turned to the doctor. "How much money will you need?"

Jasper's eyes opened again. "I am not a charity case. Sewn in the waistband of my maroon trousers you will find a draft for fifty pounds. That should be ample."

"Fifty pounds," said Abel indignantly. "No wonder you've kept so quiet about what happened to your money. So that's all you got left?"

"The sum total," said Jasper. "When faced with the prospect of so abruptly abandoning the opportunities of New Orleans I determined to leave rich or a pauper. Both cards and dice were unkind that memorable night. I left a pauper."

"If you cash this draft of his before I get back," Abel advised the doctor, "give the money to Hagar to handle. And both of you keep a close watch on him. He ain't got the sense he was born with." He turned to go and paused to look back at Jasper. "Be sure you are up and around by the time I get back. Just keep your mind on all the advice you'll be craving to give me—and maybe I'll be needing."

Having situated Jasper as well as possible under the circumstances and, at any rate, in such good hands, Abel sagged with fatigue the moment that he was out of the house. He was asleep on his feet most of the way back to the waterfront. As he approached his canoe he saw that it had been dragged higher up on the beach and that there were three shadowy figures sitting on it.

"Here he be," said Jabez.

Aaron and Mercer rose to stand on either side of Abel. Jabez confronted him, propped on his crutch, holding his rifle ready to strike either with the barrel or the butt. Abel's rifle was on the keelboat. He fought off his weariness as a man in deep water might struggle up for air.

"What's on your mind?" he demanded.

"Isn't it rather a matter of what's on your mind?" said Mercer softly. "Surely while in Louisville you propose to call on the man who befriended you when last you were here."

"If you mean Branch, I was aiming to talk to him when I get back next week."

"But how much better to settle with him now," said Aaron.

"I haven't the time now. Not an extra minute."

Jabez lifted the butt of his rifle. "Git goin'," he directed. "Whatever yuh got to say, save it for Pete to listen to."

Abel's captors closed in around him. Branch was waiting with a lantern in front of his store and led the way into his warehouse.

"Where's Evan?" asked Aaron.

"In there," said Branch, jerking his thumb toward the store.

"But I should think he might want to be in on this—even more than you," said Mercer.

"Let him sleep," said Branch shortly.

He set the lantern on a pine desk in a corner and turned to face them. He looked nearly as tired as Abel.

"Well," he demanded, "what's all the roar about?"

"That's whut we aim to find out," said Jabez. "I kin tell yuh right quick what we know so far. Just 'fore dark I seen his keelboat a-workin' up the falls. From then on I kept track o' him. He come ashore and left two letters with John Rogers. Then he fetched young Doc Callender and after a while they brung his pardner to the doc's house. Way they was handlin' him he'd been hurt bad. 'Fore thet I routed out Aaron and Ed here and we had us a talk with John. John he was burnt so bad in his own half-cocked Spanish deal thet he wasn't too hard to talk to. He give us the two letters."

Jabez dropped the letters on the desk and looked at Aaron.

"One appears to be a Spanish passport and the other's a letter to Wilkinson," said Aaron. "Both are signed by Governor Miro. To get at their full significance we'll have to wait until we find someone who can read Spanish—and it may take quite a while to find anyone who can who we can also trust."

Branch poked at the letters with a stubby forefinger. "But why dump this on me?"

"We wanted fer yuh to hear whut the polecat had to say fer hisself," said Jabez.

"What have you got to say?" Branch asked Abel.

Abel's voice was hoarse with justified anger. "The passport is good only for travel up river through Spanish country—where everybody has to have one. As for the Wilkinson letter, everybody that travels anywhere—in this country or Spanish country—is handed letters to take along. I know no more about what's in it than you do. I got my own business to look after and that takes all my time. I never mess with politics."

"He is convicted out of his own mouth," declared Aaron.

"The most innocent role to which he aspires is errand boy for the Spanish governor. While his sole defense is to accuse himself of complete disregard for his country's good."

"You keep talking about holding him," said Branch. "How? The Spaniards ain't here yet. This is still a free country."

Mercer cleared his throat. "I by no means hold with Aaron's assumption that we may forthwith set ourselves up as a kind of impromptu committee of public safety. But as an attorney I can give you a very simple answer to your question. You entrusted him with a cargo of tobacco. You can hold him legally by having him arrested for debt. That will give us ample time to sort out his Spanish activities."

"From what I hear, river pirates took the tobacco away from him," Branch temporized.

"If that is his defense, then it can develop in due course. Our present legal position is that we now make a citizens' arrest, wake up Judge Stebbins, and have Traner remanded in my custody as your attorney. Our practical position then will be that we can question him at our leisure until he decides to talk."

Branch began suddenly to nod agreement. "No matter what happened to the tobacco, he trimmed me good and plenty on the ginseng." He directed a severe and reproachful look at Abel. "All that boiling made a mush of it. Dorsey he hollered so loud I had to buy it off him."

"Best git us on over to the squire's," said Jabez, " 'fore he gits him so sound asleep God couldn't wake him."

Abel gathered himself. "You'll only be making fools of yourselves and a fool of the judge. Trouble is, I haven't got time to hang around and prove that to you. I don't admit, Mr. Branch, that I owe you a penny, but I don't want to leave you with it sticking in your craw that maybe I do. So to give us all a chance to get on with what we might better be doing. I'll make you a proposition. You give me here and now a quitclaim acknowledging a final settlement of our accounts. I'll buy from you here and now your tobacco cargo for what you'd have got for it in New Orleans, and I'll buy the ginseng for whatever you had any right to pay Jessop for it."

Without waiting for Branch to accept, Abel walked around the desk. Digging under his shirt, he unstrapped his money belt and from one of the pouches extracted an oilskin packet.

"I'm assigning you four Manasseh Pomeroy drafts for fifty pounds each." Abel sat down at the desk and reached for goose quill and inkhorn. "Your seventy per cent interest in twenty tons of tobacco at the June price in New Orleans of nine-fifty a hundredweight and two thousand pounds of gin-seng at what it was worth here when I left it with you adds up to around nineteen hundred dollars. When you've discounted the drafts you'll have a surplus of some ninety or a hundred dollars for which I'll take your note now along with the quitclaim."

His antagonists stared, speechless with astonishment. Aaron was the first to recover his voice.

"We're the same as selling out," he declared. "That's what we're doing. And so is he."

"Will you kindly inform me, Aaron," said Mercer, "upon what grounds I can now, as an attorney, take this man before Judge Stebbins?"

"He's sure'n Christ wet our powder," said Jabez. "Folks git so mixed up nowadays nobody kin tell north from south, but yuh still have to count it in a man's favor when he pays what he owes."

Branch sat down heavily and took up the pen. "I don't know but what it's more'n what he owes. But I have to take it because I need it so bad. The big trouble with my boy Evan's been that I've kept him so close under my thumb. What might straighten him out is the chance to feel he's his own man, only I've never got the money ahead to turn him loose. Now I can."

That same day Tom and Tim Crohon were paddling up Salt River, edging watchfully along close to the wooded bank. So long as they had been on the Mississippi or the Ohio they had traveled only at night and during the full of the moon not even then. They had been wildly impatient to reach their destination but determined to run no single unnecessary risk that might threaten the full and perfect flowering of the reward awaiting them. During every one of their many long days of hiding ashore they had awakened periodically to discuss in infinite detail the surest measures to avoid every faintest shadow of risk. Gradually, all facets of the problem had come into view along with the indicated solutions.

Their overriding preoccupation was with the security of their treasure. Unlike other forms of wealth—land, horses, cattle, crops—money represented so great a value in so small a compass that it could easily be stolen or lost. The paper money especially aroused their apprehensions. It was so fragile. It could not withstand wetting or tearing. A chance spark and it might char to nothingness. All this they discussed, weighed, pondered. Among their earliest decisions was the agreement that only the smallest amounts of money would ever be carried about upon their persons and that the strongbox itself, the mother lode of their fortune, must be

223

deposited · in an unquestionably secret and unmistakably secure hiding place. From this, as from a citadel, they could then make such excursions as they chose, and to it they could resort when in need of a new allowance. In their estimation there was money enough in their hoard to last them a lifetime—if they lived. This chance that one or the other might not live was one that they faced cold-bloodedly. Were either to encounter fatal misadventure, the principal store must be so situated as to remain available to the other. And in the not too unlikely event—for according to their frontier experience few men ever lived to die naturally in their beds—that both were cut off, it was imperative that the secret location be one that would permit Hagar to inherit the benefit. This was for long their greatest problem. But for this one, too, eventually they hit upon a solution. They reasoned that she would wait at New Madrid for them to return to her. This, of course, they would do—in time and if their luck held. But it was against the chance that neither might ever be able to return to her that they were endeavoring to provide. Attempting to foresee the chain of circumstances that would then ensue, they further reasoned that in this event she would wait a year or so and then, in search of some trace of them, would begin to visit places where formerly they had lived. This would bring her first to the cabin at Salt River meadows. Clearly, somewhere near that cabin was the hiding place that would answer all purposes.

Concealing their canoe in the willows, they crept to the edge of the clearing. They could see at a glance that no one had been near the cabin since they left. A sumac creeper had grown up and over the door. There had been a fair corn crop. Much of it had been trampled and browsed by buffalo and elk, but there were some hundreds of ears waiting to be picked. They decided, however, to stay out of the clearing no matter how acceptable a little pounded corn would seem after their weeks of living on fish and game.

A few yards deeper in the woods stood a tall elm. With his knife Tim cut three small notches in the bark on the side toward the cabin. Fifty yards away was another elm, which had fallen. Under the dislodged roots they dug a hole, carefully piling the earth that they removed on a blanket. In the hole they placed the strongbox, wrapped in elkskin, and replaced the earth, taking the greatest pains to cast every grain of the surplus into the river and to replace every leaf, every twig, every tuft of grass and vine. Stepping back, they studied their handiwork. No roaming hunter or Indian who might chance to pass the spot, however sharp his eye, would ever be able to detect the fact that the ground had been disturbed.

But Hagar would know immediately and exactly where to look. If it did turn out that there was occasion for her to return to the cabin, she would first examine the edges of the clearing to look for sign that they had or had not been here, and, when she saw the three notches on the standing elm, would make her way directly to the nearest fallen elm. It had been an old family trick when one or the other of them had left a cache of game or tools or whatever thus to call attention to its location.

Returning to their canoe, they dropped downriver two miles, buried it with as much care as they had their treasure, and happily set out for Louisville. They were agreed that they had every reason now to dwell comfortably on their prospects for they had taken every conceivable precaution to protect their interests.

They had not, however, passed the second bend downstream before old Sol Trexler slid down out of the huge sycamore across the river from the cabin. During the summer he had several times a week made the ten-mile trip from his camp to see if the Crohons might not have come back. After the corn had ripened, increasing the chance that they might return at least long enough to harvest their crop, he had taken to coming every day. When his long vigil had been climaxed by the sudden sight of the twins' canoe, he had been gripped by excitement but with nothing like the excitement that grew on him as he continued to watch.

He ran the mile upstream to his canoe and paddled back down through the fading twilight. He was woodsman enough to be able to go directly to the spot where he had glimpsed their digging. Until he had uncovered the iron box he was moved merely by a frenzy of curiosity to learn what they had been up to, but when he saw the key left hanging on its string beside the lock and had raised the lid, he was carried away on the tide of a different kind of frenzy. Staggering under the weight which was a great strain upon his ancient sinews, he got the box into his canoe and pushed off. The strain had been too great. In mid-river his overexertion exacted its price and one of his brittle arteries gave way. Paralyzed by the stroke, unable to move though still able to see, he could only watch the shore move past as the canoe drifted on downriver.

Rounding the second bend, it struck upon a snag and overturned. Old Sol, with air still in his lungs, floated for a time in the deepening shadows, as did the water-logged canoe. The iron box sank into the mud of the river bottom.

11

For the past week Limestone had been absorbed by a sufficient sensation to distract attention from every local controversy over secession, the Spanish conspiracy, or the Constitution. On the frontier there could be no interest to begin to rival the spectacle connected with an exchange of captives with the Indians. A whole pack of Shawnee and Wyandot, the most belligerent of all the tribes, was encamped on the north bank within sight of the town. Scores of savages, ordinarily to be glimpsed only through the smoke of burning cabins amid the din of gunshots and war whoops, were this week to be observed closely, safely, and at the cost of no greater effort than paddling across the river. To signalize the event, oxen had been slaughtered and barrels of whisky broached. White hospitality had spared no pains to make the Indian visit agreeable. A weird aura of celebration, almost of good fellowship, enveloped the occasion. Inveterate enemies—divided by race, by generations of inherited hatred, by every aversion that can divide men—greeted one another, shook hands, traded jokes, and exchanged reminiscences of battle. Many of Kentucky's most distinguished militia commanders—Kenton, Boone, Logan, Todd, Patterson—were present to make sure that the brief truce remained unbroken by the imprudence of any white man. A dozen of the most renowned barbarian chieftains were taking the same care with their followers.

Of the bereaved families who had assembled, some had come confidently in the happy assurance that their missing kin were about to be restored to them. Others had crept here in the last desperate hope that their lost ones might, after all, be still alive and might, by some miracle, still be delivered up by their capricious captors. The attention of the staring onlookers was as often engrossed by some of the scenes of reunion as by the renewed despair of those who had been disappointed. One family, here to welcome the promised

226

return of a son, was presented in his stead his black servant who had been his companion in captivity. An eight-year-old girl, a captive since infancy, was staring without recognition into the faces of her distraught parents while her weeping mother frantically crooned a lullaby in the hope of stirring some spark of recollection. A young wife, her breasts swollen with the milk of which her Indian-fathered baby had been but that morning deprived, was walking with trembling and uncertain step toward the waiting white husband who had ransomed her. A fifteen-year-old boy was stoically submitting to the embraces of his brothers while already scheming an escape back to the wild freedom he had learned to prefer.

Abel, skirting the north shore, came about off the site of the treaty encampment and drifted shoreward. The cooking fires were still smoldering, the hovering buzzards had not yet dropped to the litter of beef bones, the empty barrels still reeked of whisky, but the place had the night before been abandoned by white and red men alike. A bullet whee-ed from a buckeye copse on the farther side of the camp grounds. The Indians, finished with feasting and frivolity, had reverted to their normal hostility. Abel came about again and tacked across the river toward Limestone.

For the last three days there had been a gusty west wind. He had been able to set his sail and, with his partially rested Negroes once more fit to take turns at the oars, had made excellent time. But Todd Barklit in his four-man canoe had been able to make better. Having passed the keelboat just before dawn that morning, he was already in Limestone and already hurrying to the mill. Dorsey Jessop jumped up in immediate alarm when he turned from his breakfast table to see who stood in his doorway.

"Sit you down, Dorsey," said Barklit, shaking the miller's limp hand and clapping him on the shoulder. "Last time I was here I'd have cut your gizzard out if I'd had time to stay around long enough to find you. But I've had too many other buckets kicked over since for me to keep on howling about the one you upset. So spear you another sausage, Dorsey, and eat it with good appetite. I didn't come back to make you trouble. I come back to make you a wad of money."

"Nothing could set better with me than a wad of money," said Jessop, making only a token attempt to match Barklit's heartiness. "What bear trap do I have to stick my foot to this time?"

"No trap. No risk. No tricks for the English. I've quit them myself. We'll be working for nobody but you and me, and anything you have to do you could do in the middle of the parade ground at noon on muster day. Your part will be to stand up in court and yell for your rights. That's the part I can't do—not in your courts—'cause I ain't a citizen."

"Some folks ain't so sure they want to count me still one," said Jessop. "And I ain't been hollering much about it myself."

"Then you might be glad of a chance to. And try to catch on quick, 'cause we ain't got much time. You remember a man named Neave—six young uns—who showed up here last spring after his boatmen had robbed him of his cargo?" Barklit took a sheet of paper out of his pocket. "The same goods was sold to a Kaskaskia trader not more than a month later, and here's a copy I made me of the bill of sale that proves it. The man that sold them went on to New Orleans, where he threw in with the Spaniards and made a real big profit with the furs he got for the goods. Now he's had no better sense than to come back to Kentucky where we can get at him. And you've got reason to want to. He's the same Traner that made off with your ginseng."

"The one I'd like most to get at is that gabby chum of his."

"You'll have to wait a bit for that. He's sick in Louisville. But Traner's the one that's got the money. And he'll be here in Limestone some time this morning. The minute he sets foot on shore, have the sheriff grab him for selling your stolen cargo in Kaskaskia."

"My cargo?"

"It'll be yours by the time you have to show cause in court. I'll find Neave—he's working for a soap-maker in Lexington, according to what I heard in Louisville—and buy his title to the cargo. He thinks it's a dead loss and he's so hard up he'll be glad to sell for whatever I offer. You'll have Traner right by the neck. He's got the money to pay and he'll have to pay to shake you off. You and me—we'll have us maybe a couple of thousand to whack up. Along with me getting back at him for some of the dirt he's done me. Don't stand there blinking like a sick owl. You got nothing to worry about. Like I said, he's got the money. And he's already scared. Back in Louisville they only had to look sour at him and he shelled out nineteen hundred to your brother-in-law."

"Pete he always has all the luck," said Jessop. "But me— 'most always I don't. How we aim to prove it's the same cargo?"

"Easy. Even if Neave tries to back out of his deal with us, we've got a sure witness. His bond girl, Magda. She knows the cargo that was stolen and can testify that it stacks up item for item with the one Traner sold in Kaskaskia. He's got away from me more times than I can count. But he can't get away this time. She come with me to Limestone. She's waiting down at Froom's tavern right now where I left her not fifteen minutes ago."

Jessop gave a disgusted grunt. "I knew there'd be a catch to it. I could smell one. What makes you so sure you can count on this Magda?"

"That's one of the parts you don't have to worry about. She likes me—or would if I was to come into a little more money."

Jessop sat down and reached for his fork. "You'd best start in to worrying some your own self about how much you can count on her. Neave ain't in Lexington. He come back here last month to hire out to run Arnold Froom's tavern for him, so's Arnold could spend more time on his fishing and drinking. If you left the gal at the inn she and Neave have had time to put their heads together by now."

Abel dropped anchor fifty yards off the Limestone waterfront. Almost the first figure he saw ashore was Gamelin. With Gallic thriftiness the trader had, while waiting, arranged board and lodging with a family of movers encamped on the beach. Abel stepped from the canoe. Gamelin, advancing to meet him, was alone, Abel's uneasy glance caught no glimpse of Philippa among the shawled and sunbonneted women about the campfire.

"My news," said Gamelin, "is not all good and not all bad. Madame Baynton is alive. Chicatommo will sell her to you for five hundred dollar—which I have still here in my belt. But he will not sell her except if you will come to his town to talk to him."

"Did you see her?"

"No. She never come out where anybody can see her. She never come even to the door. And they would not let me go near the house."

"Then how do you know she's alive?"

"I know."

"She still in the—the same house?"

"You mean the black man's house? Yes. She belong to him. She is his captive. He have been adopted into the tribe. He is almost like a chief. He have married to a Shawnee woman who is niece to Chicatommo. But Madame Baynton, she is in his house too."

"So he's getting even with white folks by having himself a white slave. Is that it?"

"Yes. And maybe he will not want to let her go. But Chicatommo will make him. Chicatommo very much want the five hundred dollar for the rifles."

"Then what's he want me up there for?"

"I do not know—not for sure. I cannot sit by the

Shawnee fire until I am sure. I have not so much time for gossip. I must come here to you."

"Won't they just grab me when I show up?"

"No. Chicatommo have give his word. He always keep his word."

"When do we start?"

"The more soon the more better. The black man—he could think of something maybe to make all more hard for us."

"I'm ready right now. That is—soon's I've hired me somebody to watch my boat and left a letter at the tavern for somebody going in a downriver boat to take to Jasper, so's he'll know what's holding me up."

Edna, watching at the door of the tavern, went flying to the kitchen where Neave was talking to Magda.

"The red-haired man from the keelboat, he's coming," she announced.

As Abel approached the tavern, the group of idlers lounging about the hitching rack made way for him grudgingly. He was briefly puzzled by their hostile stares but too preoccupied to give the circumstance a second thought. Neave met him in the empty barroom with a smiling welcome.

"How do you do, Mr. Traner."

"I don't reckon I just remember you," said Abel.

"Think nothing of it. It's an innkeeper's business to know his guests. What can I do for you?"

"I'm looking for a man I can hire to watch my boat for a spell. And I want to write a letter."

"I'm confident I can oblige you in both respects. Will you kindly step in here please?"

Neave led the way to the dining room between the bar and the kitchen. It also was empty. From a cupboard he took inkpot, pen, and paper and placed them on the table before Abel. While Abel was writing his letter, Neave went out and whispered to the group around the hitching rack. There were more of them now. Four of them, after a consultation with Neave, nodded importantly and set off for the waterfront. Neave rejoined Abel in the dining room, bringing with him a candle to melt the sealing wax. Abel ran his eye over what he had written:

Dear Jasper: The Indians will sell Mrs. Baynton but I have to go to their country to finish the deal. So it may be a while longer before I get back to Louisville. Make sure you stay real quiet until you get your strength back.

Abel.

230

He folded and sealed the letter. Neave sat down across the table from him and withdrew a paper from his pocket.

"Would it surprise you, Mr. Traner, to know that my name is William Neave?"

"Why should that surprise me?"

"Having never heard the name before, I take it you are suggesting. Since nothing surprises you, perhaps you would not mind looking at this."

Abel glanced at the paper and then gave it a longer look. It was an itemized list of articles that corresponded almost exactly with the cargo of trade goods that he had sold at Kaskaskia.

"That," said Neave, "is the original bill of lading for a flatboat load of goods I was shipping to Kentucky last spring. The entire lot was stolen from me. Does the list not appear familiar to you, Mr. Traner?"

"You don't look like a fool," said Abel. "You know you can't claim I stole your goods. The best you can do is try to make out that after you lost some calico and iron I sold some calico and iron a thousand miles off from where you lost it. Maybe you think I might pay you something to keep you quiet. Is that what you're getting at?"

"No, Mr. Traner," said Neave gently. "I am not thinking of hush money. I am thinking of a settlement in full."

"Then you're crazy."

"No. Merely resolved. Please try to understand my position, sir. I came to Kentucky with the intention of setting myself up in business. I had great need to succeed for I had a large family. The loss of my goods swept away my every prospect. I have had to hire myself out to other men—at whatever work I could find—to get bread for my six children. I do not relish working for other men. You must guess how determined I am to get back into a business of my own. You are about to make this possible."

"How wild a mark are you shooting at?"

"Compensation in full for my goods—at frontier prices. The manifest in your hand adds up to four thousand seven hundred and eighty-nine dollars and two cents."

"Then sue and be damned. You can't prove a thing."

"Again you mistake what I am thinking. I am not thinking of a civil action. That could involve me in months of delay and afford you many opportunities to conceal your assets. Happily I have a more serviceable alternative." He raised his voice. "Magda."

Magda opened the door from the kitchen.

"Have you ever seen this man before, Magda?"

"Yes."

"Look closely. You are absolutely certain?"

"Yes. More than two weeks I am on his boat, before I get away."

"Thank you, Magda."

Magda closed the door.

"She was my bondservant," said Neave. "She was one portion of my property that there can be no question you did steal."

"Young Evan Branch left money with the miller to pay you for her," said Abel.

"Money I never received and would not have accepted had it been offered. She belonged to me, she wanted to belong to me, and she was taken away from me."

"Not by me."

"Mr. Traner, you grew up on this frontier. You know the kind of people who inhabit it. Many sorts of crime are ignored—even condoned. But one crime never. The abduction of a woman is the one unforgivable sin. Women are few and highly regarded. To take one against her will is considered far worse than murder. You know that better than I. You must also be able to guess the temper of those men now gathering outside the door."

"She's a lying bitch."

"No use being stupid as well as unchivalrous. Who do you think they will believe? You—a stranger? Or the beautiful and distressed young woman who accuses you?" Neave rose. "Perhaps you would like five minutes to reflect, Mr. Traner?"

Neave went out. From the window Abel saw him walk out into the street to meet two men coming up from the waterfront. Also, he could see that the group of men standing about the tavern had increased to thirty or more. To attempt to take flight was useless. Before he had taken three jumps, he would be caught or shot. Edna came in with a glass of whisky on a tray.

"Father said you might want a drink."

"I would," said Abel, sitting down and taking the glass.

Edna, her eyes big with excited interest, lingered by his chair.

"Are you rich, Mr. Traner?" she asked.

"No."

"That's too bad. Then it's not much use your talking to Magda."

"Why should I talk to Magda?"

"Because if you were rich she might tell the story you want her to tell instead of the one Father wants her to."

"What makes you think that?"

"Oh, I'm very sure of it. You see, while I've been watching you and Father, Johnny—he's my brother—he's been watching Magda. She's been trying to make up her mind who to listen to. First there was the big man with the scar on his chin talking to her at the back door. He kept saying that it was on account of her that he had quit the people he had been working for the last ten years and that she couldn't throw him over now. And then Evan—he's the young man who took us off the island—he was at the kitchen window. He was so tired from riding all the way from Louisville that he could hardly stand up, but he kept taking money out of his pocket and showing it to her. Only she couldn't talk very long to either of them because Father kept coming back to the kitchen and she had to talk to him."

"What is your father offering her?"

"The same as the others. He wants to marry her."

"And you don't want that?"

"Oh, yes. We like Magda. Only this time we'd like it to be for keeps. It makes Father so unhappy when she goes away. He can't sleep and he won't eat and he's so cross. Johnny and me, we don't want to go through all that again. That's why we thought maybe she better talk to you too. So that this time she would know for certain what she wanted to do. If you married her, nobody could say you had stolen her, and it just might be that you are the one she really wants to marry. Though if you're not rich, maybe not."

"I doubt much would come of my talking to her," said Abel. "Call your father. He's the one I'm ready to talk to."

Edna sighed and reluctantly withdrew. Neave came in smiling.

"You've got your thumb right in my eye," said Abel. "If I say uncle how do I know you'll take it out."

"I can make you quite certain of that." Neave took several papers from his pocket and laid them before Abel. "Here are two bills of sale involving Magda. One, dated the day you left Limestone, records my sale of her contract to you, and the other, dated today, your sale of it back to me for the expiration of her term which has still some months to run. This third instrument is a receipt acknowledging your payment in full for my cargo which you sold for me in Kaskaskia. When these are signed—and there's a notary waiting outside to witness the signatures, if you so wish—any abduction charge will have become obviously frivolous and my every claim against you obliterated."

"It could be something is due you," said Abel. "But I can't pay anything like what you're asking. I haven't got the money."

"What sort of a figure are you suggesting?"

"To be surely shut of all this foolishness," said Abel, pushing the papers away from him, "I might go twenty-four hundred dollars."

"Cash?"

"No. Drafts. Manasseh Pomeroy drafts."

"May I see them?"

Abel unstrapped his belt, opened the oilskin packet, and produced his remaining drafts.

" 'Course they're no good 'til I sign them."

"Another mistake, Mr. Traner. A court order can make them payable to me." Neave scrutinized each in turn and leaned back, smoothing the sheaf thoughtfully. "I accept. Even after the probable discounting expenses are deducted the return—in conjunction with the value of your Negroes and keelboat—should come sufficiently close to the amount of my claim to save us further haggling."

"Hold on. I said nothing about my niggers nor my boat. I'm not letting go of them."

"You astonish me, Mr. Traner. For a man of your experience you seem remarkably slow to grasp your situation. You have already let go of your Negroes and your boat. You let go the moment you stepped on shore. Your property is, in effect, no longer your property. It is mine. You must realize that while you are awaiting your trial for abduction —presuming those men out there permit you to await trial —I shall have attached whatever you own in this county. Therefore, the one choice that remains to you is do you prefer to have this handled the easy way—or the hard way?"

Abel rose and stood at the window. He could see *Naiad* riding peacefully at anchor. Two men from a skiff were climbing over the rail. It was giving her up that griped him the most. The Negroes had worked hard and well for him, but in turning them over to Neave he was the same as doing them a favor. After all of their experience with smuggling in the bayous and with the long wilderness voyage upriver, they would know how to look after themselves. They had none of the ordinary slave's awe of white men. Before they had been with Neave a week all four would have run off to the woods. He turned back to the table.

"The easiest way for me," he said, "would be first off to stuff your teeth and both your elbows down your throat. Trouble is I'm in a fix where I can't afford even so small a comfort as that."

Gamelin was waiting at the canoe. Abel got in and set off for the north bank with long, driving strokes. At any rate, he reflected grimly, he still had as much as when he had started out on his travels. He still had his rifle and Ish's canoe.

12

Amaquah was the least considerable of the four principal
Shawnee towns but could assert the unhappy claim to by far
the most lurid history. Its inhabitants were able to feel that,
like salamanders, they had lived in the midst of flames. Three
times in seven years the town had been destroyed by fire.
The original Amaquah on the shore of the long beaver pond
between the great buffalo trace and the Miami had been a
fortunate location, where the cornfields were deep and wide
and fish and waterfowl were to be had in abundance. But
the townspeople had accepted Abner Colby's famous exploit
of blowing up the beaver dam in full view of two thousand
stunned warriors as an ill omen of intolerable dimensions.
That time they had themselves burned the town and moved
to another site a dozen miles further upriver. The next year
Clark, invading the Shawnee country with an army of Kentuckians bent upon avenging the terrible disaster of Blue
Licks, had burned this second Amaquah. Four years later
the third Amaquah, another dozen miles upriver, had been
burned by Logan. It was not an uncommon thing for an
Indian town to choose to move to a new site for the sake
of new corn land and fresh hunting grounds. To erect a new
set of pole and bark dwellings and to girdle forest trees to let
sunlight into a new garden patch was not a great labor. But
in Amaquah's case so many successive moves had exacted a
price. Regard for many long-established customs had faded
and public opinion, the paramount authority in any Indian
community, had become uncertain of its judgments in cases
about which formerly there could have been no doubt. Even
the town's leading citizen, Chicatommo, was a newcomer
who had taken up his abode in it since its last removal, and
its oldest resident was a white man, Pierre Ariome, a French
trader who had clung unenterprisingly to his customers' failing fortunes while his own had likewise dwindled.

In one of its bark huts, Philippa sat before the crude

frame of an Indian loom. To be constantly and laboriously occupied during her every waking hour was her one refuge. A sudden outburst of calls, whoops, and shouts of laughter rose from the farther edge of the town. She pulled aside a shred of bark in the wall beside her and peered out through the slit. Spencer was returning after his weeklong hunt. She had guessed that he had been about to reappear when his wife, Nacawah, had left at dawn leading both of his horses. Now she was leading them back, each laden with the butchered quarters of a buffalo.

Among the lesser aggravations of Philippa's captive life was her inability ever to gain any advance hint of other people's intentions, even with regard to the simplest and most routine projects. She could only watch the household's ordinary activities, which she so much despised, and endeavor to guess whether she was about to be left alone with Nacawah, as she had been this past week, or whether she was to be left entirely alone as she had been the week before, when both of them had paid a visit to Nacawah's relatives in the next town.

She looked again through the slit. They were much nearer now. Nacawah's arms were red with blood to the elbows and there were smears on her face and in her hair. It was an Indian woman's duty to butcher the game brought down by her husband. She would likely not wash for a week, taking pride in these badges of her husband's success as might a wife in the world beyond the forest flaunt a new silk dress. Spencer, gaunt and drawn from having fasted during his hunt, was walking at the head of the little cavalcade, grinning, acknowledging the teasing yet friendly congratulations of his fellow townsmen, brandishing the bow from which he had launched the arrow that had struck down the buffalo. It had been his first such kill. Hunting success with a rifle had not been enough for him. He had not been content until he had proved himself also with the more primitive weapon. Always he was striving to make himself more of an Indian.

"Tawik, Tawik," even the children were shouting.

Tawik was his Shawnee name. There was no quicker way to infuriate him than to address him as Spencer. Tawik—her lord and master. She ran to the bark barrel in the corner in which was stored the household supply of pounded corn. Her thrusting fingers encountered the jug buried deep in the grain. She hesitated, shuddered, and drew it forth. The fiery trade brandy scorched her throat but she gulped it down in long, choking swallows. The jug she broke on the flat cooking stone beside the fire. Blue flames shot up from the spilled liquor hissing among the coals. Catching up a stick of firewood, she demolished the loom and from the gourd dangling from a ceiling pole poured bear oil over the rumpled tangle of buffalo-hair cloth. Scooping up handfuls of ashes, she smudged her hair and face, her arms and legs, every part of her that was not covered by the short doeskin dress that was her single garment. Fighting off the waves of drunken nausea breaking over her, she sat on her rawhide bed and waited.

Before the house Spencer was directing Nacawah in the division of the meat. With scrupulously reckless Indian generosity he was dividing it into thirds—one to be set aside as a donation to his grinning neighbors, one to be devoted to a feast for his many bosom friends, and only the remainder to be smoked to provide for the future needs of his own household. In all of his behavior he strove to be more Indian than any Indian.

He shouldered aside the elkskin flap hanging in the doorway and stalked into his house. In spite of his racial susceptibility to cold he had spent the chill November week stripped to the traditional hunter's costume of breechclout and leggings. With his head shaved to a topknot in which hung a single heron feather, the bar of red paint across his face, the circlet of bear claws about his neck, the tattooed clan marks on his chest, his oiled, coffee-colored skin stretched over his lean, muscular frame, he had even the complete look of an Indian. Before so much as a glance at her or at anything else in the room he advanced to the fire and deposited in it a piece of the choicest and fattest meat, making the returned Indian hunter's prescribed sacrifice to assure equal fortune upon his next hunt, his lips murmuring the supplication to the spirit of the buffalo that he had killed that he might be forgiven on account of his need for food. Opening his eyes, he looked deliberately at the broken jug and at his disheveled slave.

"Nacawah," he called.

His wife came in. She saw the jug, shot an angry look at Philippa, and bowed her head. Spencer picked up one of the fragments of the jug and thrust it at her accusingly.

"Is this what you bring into my house when your husband is not here to watch you?" he demanded.

He was already fluent in Shawnee and Philippa had been unable to avoid learning to catch most of the meaning when it was spoken.

"I was sick," said Nacawah sullenly. "It was for my stomach."

Spencer gestured curtly. Nacawah took from a peg on the wall a peeled hickory wand the thickness of a finger and handed it to her husband. Whipping her dress off over her

238

head, she stood before him. With righteous calm he laid five stripes across her shoulders and handed the wand back to her. She turned and looked balefully at the despised captive woman whose folly had been the cause of her humiliation. Philippa peered up through the tangle of hair fallen over her eyes and grinned mockingly at Spencer.

"Get up," Spencer commanded in Shawnee.

Philippa made no move, gave no sign that she had heard.

"Do you hope to drive me to kill you?" he asked, still in Shawnee but spacing his words carefully so that there might be no doubt of her understanding him. "Is that why you so continually provoke me?"

"You have taken your pleasure with her," said Philippa in English. "You can now have the greater pleasure of beating me."

"It must rather be you who takes pleasure in my beating you," he said. "Else you would not take so much care to invite it."

"Once I saw you beaten. You can never forget that."

"I can very well forget it, for the man who did it did not live to remember it. And I shall teach you to forget it too." There was no anger in his voice. He went on speaking as calmly as any judge reproving a prisoner in the dock. "I intend also to teach you what is required of you. That loom represented your sole usefulness. You refuse to go out to bring wood or draw water. You hide from one day to the next here in the shadows like a bug under a board. You will not so much as look from the doorway at my friends and neighbors. You shame me by acting as though you considered them lepers. Since you have made weaving your only service to this house and this community, I shall not permit you also to refuse that. The affair of the brandy is worse. You well know how much worse. You know how I feel. Alcohol is the great Indian curse. You know that I will not have it in my house. Still less will I permit the disgrace of drunkenness in my house."

"So long and eloquent a speech," mocked Philippa. "What a shame it should be wasted. Never mind. Nacawah is listening. She will applaud."

"It is a speech that is not finished. And I assure you it will not be wasted. You scoff at Indian ways and at me because I have adopted them. They are good ways—honest ways—better ways than you or I have ever known. You would do well to open your mind to that. Whether you do or not, I cannot permit you to pull me down again—not by so much as an inch. I cannot have it come to the notice of these people who have become my friends that I am unable even to manage the captive who is my servant. Most certainly I shall beat you and I shall go on beating you until I bring you to accept what is your due and what is mine."

Spencer reached for the hickory wand. Nacawah handed it to him. With a grunt of satisfaction she jerked Philippa to her feet and began peeling off her dress. Philippa pushed her away and herself removed the garment. Turning, she leaned over and grasped one of the poles to which the bark of the wall was lashed, her begrimed and disordered hair hanging down over her face. In the dusky light of the hut her white skin gleamed palely, almost phosphorescently, in contrast to that of the two darker figures who stood over her. Spencer lifted the wand and brought it down sharply. A long red welt appeared across the bent white back. He repeated the measured, swishing blow and continued until a ladder of red welts extended from the back of her neck to the back of her knees. Handing the wand to Nacawah, he crossed to his bed beyond the fire and sat on it.

"Come here," he commanded.

Philippa's impulse to rebel had run its course. Sickened by pain and by the brandy, she crept wretchedly across the hut to his feet. Pushing herself up to her knees, she began to untie and remove his soaked and muddied moccasins and leggings, fulfilling the traditional duty of the Indian woman when the man of the house has returned from a successful hunt. When she had finished he shoved her away with one bare foot.

"Now clean yourself," he directed.

Nacawah brought in the meat and began preparing it for the feast that Spencer was to spread for his friends. Philippa, after the long and painful ordeal of washing her hair and scrubbing off the ash stains, reached for her doeskin dress. Nacawah snatched it from her and presented her instead with a leather apron such as she wore, consisting of no more than a flap of deerskin hanging from a belt at the waist. This was the usual costume of an Indian woman when busy with domestic tasks, but until now Spencer had condoned Philippa's never laying aside the knee-length dress. It marked another step in the discipline calculated to lead to her complete subjection that even this poor privilege should now be denied her.

The guests arrived, shouting and laughing, and, between eager glances at the amount of meat broiling over the coals, dwelling enthusiastically upon Spencer's prowess as a hunter and his bounty as a host. His eyes glistened. The esteem of his peers was a sensation of which he could never get enough. The guests settled down in a circle about the fire. Decorum ruled briefly while the ceremonial pipe was lighted and passed. Then with many grunts and belches of anticipation all leaned forward and began to gorge themselves. Philippa assisted Nacawah in passing the bark trays of meat and keeping them replenished. Spencer's friends were urbane as well as merry. If any took notice of the nudity of his captive white woman none was so impolite as to give it more than a passing glance.

Only a like number of Indians could have made away with the amount of meat that they consumed. Even after they had sprawled, sluggishly replete, full length on the earthen floor of the hut, as intoxicated from overeating as they might have been from overdrinking, each from time to time reached out to select another morsel. Relieved of the need to attend further to their appetite, Philippa staggered to her bed and collapsed face down upon it. Despite her churning stomach, her aching head, and her burning back, she was so utterly exhausted that she dozed.

She was intermittently aware of bursts of laughter and song from the guests. Nacawah got into her own bed and settled herself comfortably, Philippa was chilled on one side by the cold night air seeping through the cracks in the bark wall and feverishly hot on the other side toward the fire, but lacked the spirit to reach for her blanket. Spencer spoke to Nacawah, who got up reluctantly. Philippa was aroused by Nacawah rubbing oil into her back. The ministration was accompanied by a continuous disgusted muttering, and the oil was applied most ungently by Nacawah's work-calloused fingers, but the effect was soothing. Nacawah turned away, saw that Spencer was watching her coldly, and came back to cover the white woman with a rabbitskin robe. Relieved by the oil and comforted by the robe, Philippa drifted into a deeper sleep.

When next she awoke the guests had departed and the hut was quiet. She could hear the creak of the rawhide straps as Spencer got into his bed and then the murmur of his summons as he called Nacawah from her bed to his. His long hunter's fast had been broken when he had feasted with his friends. The continence that he had likewise observed was now also to end as he resumed the exercise of his conjugal rights. Listening to the suddenly accelerated creaking of rawhide, Philippa was engulfed in new waves of impotent fury.

The next morning Abel and Gamelin stood on the riverbank across from the town. Since leaving their last camp where they had hidden the canoe and their rifles, their approach along the hunting trail had been observed, as they

241

were well aware, but for a time no notice was taken of their presence. In the town people continued to go about their ordinary concerns. Then Gamelin nudged Abel.

"Pierre Ariome will come over to get us," he said. "That is good. Pierre was in Detroit when last I am here. He know as much as any Shawnee. There may be something he can tell us."

Old Pierre, his dirty white beard blowing in the cold November wind, stepped rheumatically from his canoe to embrace Gamelin. He shook hands with Abel, eying him with some curiosity, and then became involved with Gamelin in a conversation in which each spoke so rapidly that Abel could detect not even one of the French words that he had picked up in New Orleans. This conversation continued without pause, like the constant rushing of a mountain stream, while they paddled across the river and walked through the town to Pierre's one-room log trading post. A tattered Union Jack fluttered from a staff over the door as a continual reminder to the Shawnee that it was the English who were their indispensable friends and that even this trickle of such items as gunpowder which were so necessary to their survival was dependent upon England's favor.

Instead of going within, the three white men sat circumspectly on a bench beside the door in plain view of the townspeople. During their deliberate progress from the canoe to the post they had attracted, apparently, no slightest attention, but Abel had the feeling that every Indian eye in the town had been and still was upon them. The two Frenchmen ceased talking but continued to regard one another reflectively. Abel looked at Pierre and then at Gamelin.

"Well," he said, "what does he know?"

"Nothing," said Gamelin.

"Take all that talk to say that?"

"He have not even know that you will come to buy Madame Baynton. Chicatommo have told nobody here that he will sell. He maybe have not even told Tawik. That is the black man's Shawnee name. One thing Pierre have say. Maybe it is good for us. Maybe it is why Chicatommo talk about selling her. Maybe it make Tawik also ready to sell her. Pierre say that Madame Baynton—how you say in English—that she is strange, that she no more is just so in the head. That is what everybody here think."

"What makes them think that?"

"She never come out of the house. She want nobody to look at her. She all the time make trouble so that Tawik must all the time beat her."

"That doesn't make her crazy."

"Maybe no. But it is maybe possible. She have had much most bad happen to her. I have not tell you before because it is so bad. But now I must tell you. You have many times hear much how Indians try to make the captive unhappy. They try most hard when the captive is first taken. The first night when Madame Baynton have been taken they have her beside the trail, fast to stakes on the ground. Because she is a white woman she is most bad luck for any Indian. So they themselves amuse by putting the black man with her. Nobody care about his luck. They dance and laugh and keep him at it so many times as he is able."

"You didn't have to worry about telling me," said Abel. "It's not much worse than what I've been thinking all along. I've had two months now to think about it." In his lap his folded hands tightened until the knuckles whitened. "Once I've got her out of this country, I'll have to make me another little visit and take me some real care with his luck."

"You will never rest until you have kill him, eh? I cannot wonder. Still it is so that the blame is not all his. Since he have been here he have turn Indian. So since he have been here he have never take her again." Gamlin was glad to change the subject. "Pierre have say one thing more. Maybe it too could be good for us. When Pierre come back here from Detroit, Alexander McKee come with him. He is here now."

Abel snorted at the mention of the Tory renegade who had crossed the frontier not only to take service with the English but to become their Deputy Indian Commissioner. "What good can he do us?"

"Maybe not much. But maybe some. We will see. You Americans think McKee is all bad. Nobody, my friend, is all bad."

Abel scowled out at the Indian town. "Which house she in?"

"Better you not know. You will set foot in the house of Pierre—and the house of Chicatommo—but at no other house will you even look, no matter what."

"Which house?" persisted Abel.

"The one by the rock—with the two horses behind."

Abel looked at the miserable bark hovel. An Indian sat on his heels in the doorway, cleaning and oiling a rifle. Lounging on the ground around him were half a dozen other Indians chattering and laughing unconcernedly. Taking a second look, Abel realized with a start that the Indian with the rifle was Spencer.

"When do we see Chicatommo and find out what he has to say?"

243

"When he send for us. McKee is with him now."

Abel tried hard to sit still on the bench. With so many watchful eyes upon him he had need to put up as calm a front as Spencer was managing. Their first encounter when he had undertaken to restore a slave to his master had ended in disaster for Spencer. Now a second duel had begun. Spencer must know that. Surely by now he must have sensed the threat that was gathering. In coming up from the canoe they had passed immediately before his door. He must have recognized Gamelin's white companion and realized that something threatening his grasp on his captive might be under way. But if so he still give no sign. He went on joking and gossiping with his cronies as though there were nothing on his mind. He had had experience all his life with the need to hide whatever he was thinking. No doubt that had made it easier for him so soon to begin acting so much like an Indian.

Abel was endeavoring, without much success, to bring his own thinking into some sort of order. It did not seem possible even now that Philippa could be in that bark shack not two hundred feet away. Unless she was tied up under a blanket she must have had a chance to see enough through a crack or around the edge of the elkskin hanging in the doorway to guess that something of possible importance to her was happening. Even if at that distance she could not see who he was, she must be wondering if the presence of a strange white man might not have something to do with her. There was the other chance, of course, that her mind had really been touched by so many troubles. She might not remember him. People sometimes became so distraught that they even forgot their own names.

"Here come McKee," said Gamelin.

The notorious partisan was not set apart from other men by horns and a tail or even by the wearing of the King's uniform. In dress, manner, and speech he seemed an ordinary trader. He shook hands with Gamelin and Pierre and came directly to the point.

"You're offerin' a good price. Old Chic wants the money. I'd like to see him get it. He's got more gumption than most Indians and he wants more guns that I can afford to give him. Could be you'll bring it off. I hope so. We encourage 'em to take prisoners 'cause we figger a captive's still got some chance and a scalped corpse ain't got none. But we hate to see 'em get hold of a woman like Mrs. Baynton. And makin' her live with the nigger makes it worse."

"Was that why you came down from Detroit?" asked Abel. "To straighten that out?"

244

"No. I try to steer clear of a place when there's something like this goin' on. Indians is trouble enough to get along with without stirrin' 'em up extra. But I had to see Old Chic and long's I was here I been smellin' around some. He wants them guns bad. But could be this Tawik wants the woman the same way. If he does, he might have the whip hand. I can't afford to shove Old Chic and I ain't sure how much of a shove he'll feel like giving the nigger. Since the nigger's turned Indian, Old Chic don't set near so much store by him as at first, but he still might not want to raise too big a stink. Only piece of advice I got for you is this: this Tawik's got a good many friends here. If you do work out a deal with Old Chic and start off for the Ohio with her, they'll follow and take her away from you again. Better for the two of you to go along with me back to Detroit. Old Chic likes to keep his word and I like to keep mine, and if he tells me he's sold her to you, I'll back him up by seein' to it nobody takes her away from you between here and Detroit. From there we'll figger a way to get you out through Canada and the Iroquois country to Albany."

"That makes sense," acknowledged Abel. "I have to think about her and agree I'm obliged to you."

"Another thing, Old Chic likes his own way," said McKee. "He's bound to have some trick or other up his sleeve. You and Tony'd best go along now and try to make out what it is."

Spencer, still idly conversing with his friends, did not look up as they passed. Chicatommo's house was small but built solidly of logs and loopholed for defense. The doorway was framed by a fringe of stretched and dried white scalps. The white visitors ducked under these dangling mementos of Chicatommo's martial ardor and went in. The old chief was seated on the ground by his cooking fire. He regarded Abel impassively and gestured toward places on either side of him. The two white men sat down. Nothing was said while the pipe was passed nor, as the ritual of Indian hospitality continued, while Onaya, his wrinkled old wife, passed trays of meat. After a warning glance from Gamelin, Abel forced himself to taste the food. Still nothing was said. Gamelin waited as impassively as the Shawnee.

"What we hung on?" demanded Abel finally.

"Be quiet," said Gamelin.

Spencer entered and stood just inside the doorway, his arms folded. Abel was again struck by how complete the Negro had, during so short a residence among the Indians, been able to assume the appearance, manner, carriage, even the expression, of an Indian. Chicatommo spoke briefly.

Spencer replied as briefly. Abel guessed by the intent way Gamelin listened that the suggestion that Philippa be sold had been brought into the open. But if so, Spencer betrayed no hint of emotion. He looked at Abel gravely.

"I understand you have come here to buy a captive. Since she is my property my consent has been asked. And since the proceeds are to be devoted not to my private gain but to the purchase of rifles, which we very much need, I have agreed. My agreement has been subject to one reservation. She is not to be taken away against her will."

Abel started to his feet. "Whatever makes you think she might not want to go?"

"I did not say that was what I thought. I said it is a possibility we must investigate."

"Is she really crazy?"

"That is a conclusion you must draw for yourself. After you have talked to her. If you will, come with me."

Abel followed him out. Spencer paused before Chicatommo's door and pointed.

"That is my house. She is expecting you."

"No use my talking to her unless we can talk alone."

"You will be able to. I shall not eavesdrop. And no one else around understands English."

Abel walked to the bark hut. The Indians who had been sitting about the door with Spencer had disappeared. A stocky young squaw came out, scowled at him, and walked away. He drew aside the elkskin doorflap and went in. Philippa was bent over a clay pot of water, frantically washing her hands and face. She straightened and turned toward him. Her face was still damp, her hair hanging in a tangle down her back, her feet were bare, and her one-piece doeskin dress was frayed and stained. She was pale and thin and there were dark circles around her eyes. There was about her none of the gleam and sparkle that he remembered so well aboard *Naiad*. And yet no matter how marred by misery and squalor, she was still beautiful. And the first words that she gasped out implied an apology for her appearance that was still feminine.

"I only heard five minutes ago that you were here."

"Took me long enough to get here," said Abel. "I was in New Orleans when I first heard what had happened to you."

She was not listening to what he was saying. She seemed conscious only of the need to get on quickly and mechanically with what she must say to him.

"It was magnificent of you to try to help me. But you mustn't stay in this town another minute. He has so many friends. They'll surely kill you."

"We don't have to stay another minute. All we have to do is start out."

"You don't understand. He'll never let me go."

"He already has."

Her eyes widened incredulously. "But that's impossible."

"He wants the money as much as Old Chic."

"Did you hear him say that? Or did someone tell you?"

"He told me himself. Only he's got some notion you might not want to go. He said I better make sure of that first."

"Oh," moaned Philippa.

She sank to the edge of the bed, appearing so confused and bewildered that for a moment Abel thought her mind must indeed have been affected. Yet when she looked up at him her eyes were lucid and painfully perceptive.

"He's right. I can't go."

"You can't stay here. You don't belong here. You belong among your own people."

"Not any more. I can never face my kind of people again."

"That's nonsense. You're not the first woman that's been kicked around by Indians. Hundreds have got back and folks have been glad to take them back."

"My case is worse. You cannot conceive how much worse. Things have happened to me that are—irreparable."

"I know all about that. And there's no use talking about it or thinking about it. You had no more to do with it than you might have had to with the wood on the fire if they'd started in to burn you. Once you get back it'll seem like something that happened so far off and so long ago that it could have happened to somebody else."

"No. I can never forget that it happened to me. No one could. No one will. I am finished. So entirely finished that I have not left even the will to kill myself."

"Maybe you've got some call to worry about what people may say about you. That's something that can make it bad for a woman, for a fact. But nothing's so bad it can't be helped some. The man who brought you out of the Indian country would know all about everything you'd been through If you showed up married to him, there wouldn't be very much people could say."

She came slowly to her feet, staring at him as incredulously as when he had said Spencer had no objection to her ransom. "You're proposing to stand between me and—and everything else—as only a husband can? Is that what you're saying?"

"That's right."

The pinched, defiant look passed from her face. Her dry, hot eyes softened mistily.

"I remember you on the deck of *Naiad*—and in the cabin.

247

I didn't pay much attention then, but I have thought of it since. You were in love with me then, weren't you?"

"On sight."

"Are you still?"

"No use talking about me. We're here to get you figgered out."

Her eyes again were dry and burning. She stiffened with resolution. Her voice remained low but became harsh and decisive.

"That is the truth. And you have left me no room for twisting and turning—no recourse but to tell you the whole truth. I owe you that so that you will give up all thought of saving me. I am beyond saving. You have not heard all that happened to me that first night of my captivity. No one knows—no one but I. I have tried to deny that it could have happened, but I cannot. I can never forget a moment of it. And what I can least forget is that it was like one of those revolting dreams we sometimes have in which we take delight in the most unspeakable impulses."

She paused to watch the effect of her confession. But no flicker of expression passed over Abel's grim set face.

"We all have a streak of that in us."

"But mine is more than a streak. It is a taint—a contamination. I must make you understand so that you will see that you must abandon hope for me, so that you will go away while you still can. Once I was able to imagine myself a conventionally chaste woman. But in my heart I must have known better—and been afraid. I must have been driven by that secret fear when I chose a husband who was cold and intellectual. But that did not save me. It led instead to that contemptible dallying with poor Heber Fortiner. I should have known then. I do know now. I am lost. There is no hope for me."

"There must be some. Look at the way you keep on fighting him off so hard that he has to beat you all the time."

Philippa flinched as though at last a blow had been struck against which she could no longer stand. But she braced herself and replied steadily.

"That is only a deeper part of the taint. I despise myself so much that I feel I can never suffer enough. I embrace punishment because I know I can never be punished as much as I deserve." She faltered. In her eyes there was the desperate glaze of the wild animal when it has ceased to struggle against the jaws of the trap. "For there is something else which I have never before admitted—even to myself. Underneath it all is the horrible cunning thought that if I can anger him enough he may again take me by force."

248

Abel's dreadful outward calm remained unbroken. He nodded thoughtfully.

"But that's not what he wants. He's turned Indian and has to behave like an Indian."

"No. It's not so simple as that. He burns with wanting. He's trapped too. But he's stronger than I." The words suddenly were pouring from her as freely as blood may spurt from a wound. "He's forcing me to make the decision. He is determined to wait until I offer myself. He is waiting for me to consent to adoption into the tribe. That will be the signal that I have yielded. I have been as resolved that I never will. But I know myself too well. Sooner or later I will—and find peace."

"You'll never find peace that way."

"I suppose not. Because I am the most abhorrent in that I am not even honest. I yearn in secret for him to take me and still because he is a Negro I will not let myself accept him as a man. Yet he is a good man. A better man than Rodney —or Heber—or maybe even than you."

For the first time since he had come in Abel's gaze left her pale, tormented face. He looked thoughtfully about the miserable hut, at the gourds and skins hanging from the low ceiling, at the ash-strewn cooking place, at the three rawhide beds. At length his glance returned to meet and grip hers.

"Looks like we've said about all there is to say about you. So now let's talk about me. I'm in a fix too. I got you into this and one way or another—whether you want it or not— by God, I'm going to get you out. I can't go back either until I do."

She sank again to the edge of her bed and bowed her head. But when she looked up she, too, was resolute.

"I can understand the awful responsibility you must feel. But no matter how well I understand, that's your problem. I cannot help you with it any more than you can help me with mine."

Abel turned and went out. Spencer had been rejoined by his companions. All were squatted on the ground, halfway between his house and Chicatommo's, noisily absorbed in a plumstone game. With the eyes of his Indian fellows upon him he did not trouble even to look up at Abel's passing. But a second later he sprang up and overtook Abel.

"There is one thing more I should tell you," he said. "For her sake—so that you, and her people when you tell them, will not utterly condemn her. That first night she was taken I hated Heber Fortiner so much that I was glad to injure the woman who had shown him favor. No punishment you could wish me could equal the remorse I have felt since. She knows, I think, how I feel about that."

"What difference how you feel, if she's taken away from you?"

"None, of course. But I saw in your face as you came out that she had decided to stay. Do not deplore her choice too much. Indian life is harsh. But it has many compensations. We live in honesty and freedom. Those are very great blessings. She is beginning to sense that. And you may tell her people that I will care for her with as much care as any man could."

"Is that all you want to say?"

"Yes."

Abel returned to his seat by Chicatommo's fire.

"She says she doesn't want to go back," he told Gamelin.

Gamelin nodded. "That is why Chicatommo want you to come here. He think maybe when you talk to her she change her mind."

"She's ashamed ever to face white folks again and that makes her think she might's well stick with Spencer."

Gamelin nodded again. "That is what Pierre tell me. I do not tell you, because I know you will not believe. What will you say to Chicatommo now?"

"Say to him I'll pay him a thousand to see her safe in Detroit—whether she wants it that way or not."

Gamelin had some difficulty clinging to the composure required by Indian diplomacy. A gleam of astonished approval, almost of awe, crossed his face. He addressed Chicatommo. The old chief considered the proposal for some minutes. Then he nodded.

Gamelin looked at Abel again. "You have pointed for him to the trail ahead. Many Indians from far away come here to go with Chicatommo to kill white people on the river. Nobody here see them before. Sometimes nobody here ever see them again. Chicatommo have only to make the wink at such a one and before morning Tawik will have the stab in the back. Then all will be easy."

"That's the way I figgered."

Gamelin wagged his head, marveling. "Pierre have live thirty-seven year among Indians. For twenty-three year I have trade with Indians. But in one day you have learned as much."

He began removing silver pieces from his belt. Chicatommo spoke up.

"He say, where is the other five hundred."

"I haven't got it with me," said Abel. "Tell him tomorrow McKee will take her to Detroit with him. And you will take with you to Vincennes a letter to send on to my people in Kentucky. Chicatommo can be sure they'll send the other five hundred because he'll still have me here."

"I do not like this part," said Gamelin. "Chicatommo will have you where the hair is the most short. Suppose something happen. Suppose the wolf bite me before I get to Vincennes. Or the bear hug me. Suppose the letter to Kentucky is lost. Suppose the money is slow to come. It will be the most bad for you."

"Not so bad as anything else I could do," said Abel. "Go ahead and tell him. Tell him this is the way it has to be."

Reluctantly Gamelin explained to Chicatommo. He took a longer time to consider this amendment to Abel's offer. Then once more he nodded. Pierre came over from his place with writing materials. The box containing them was moldering, the paper yellowed with age, the dried ink required much moistening with water, but he was proud of his ability to produce the wherewithal to write a letter. There was even a faint glint of interest in Chicatommo's cold eyes as he covertly watched this mysterious process by which white people at a remote distance might be made aware of every detail of the most involved message.

"Be sure your people understand well the need for much hurry with the money," Gamelin counselled earnestly. "Chicatommo always keep his word, but he will not want to wait too long. If the money do not come soon, you will not die so easy as Tawik."

Abel wrote steadily:

Dear Jasper:
I have ransomed Mrs. Baynton. She is going home to Philadelphia by way of Detroit. It will take me longer to get back to Louisville than I had figured. So if you are able to travel when you get this look for me in Pittsburgh. If you happen to run across Tom and Tim and get some of my money back, send five hundred dollars to Gamelin in Vincennes. I would like to see him paid this much more, but if you haven't got the money yet, don't fret about it.

Abel.

He read it over and decided that he had covered the ground adequately. There was no use agitating Jasper with a full report on his situation since there was nothing that Jasper could possibly do about it unless he had the money. That was a hundred-to-one shot, but if he did then all would work out. If he did not, there was still the chance that he might escape—perhaps not a very good one on account of the value Chicatommo set on him, but still a chance. Other men had escaped Indian captivity. He realized well enough that he could not have staked anything, let alone his life, on two more doubtful chances, but he did not feel heroic. He resented the necessity and the senselessly unlucky course of events that had led to it. But he had paid his other debts, with interest, and he was now paying this final one.

Spencer came in and there ensued another brief exchange between him and Chicatommo. He went out and a one-eyed Cherokee came in. Gamelin nodded to Abel, they rose, shook hands with Chicatommo, and returned to Pierre's bench. Nacawah was saddling and bridling Spencer's two horses. The one-eyed Cherokee came out of Chicatommo's house and he and Spencer mounted. When Nacawah saw that the Cherokee was going with him, she began reminding her husband at the top of her voice that all Cherokee were thieves and that he must look sharp to their horses while he was away. Abel watched Spencer until the two horsemen had disappeared into the swamp.

"What did Chicatommo tell him?" he asked. "We were there. You heard it."

"He tell him to go to the Cherokee camp on Mad River," said Gamelin. "He tell him next week he go again to the Ohio to burn boats and he must know how many Cherokee will go with him. He tell him that he, Tawik, must be the one to go to ask the Cherokee because all Indians know he have the eye that see more than what is in sight and so they will not dare to lie to him."

"I mean, what was it Chicatommo told him to get him to go wandering off while we were still here."

"Chicatommo never say what is not so. He tell Tawik the woman stay with him so long as Chicatommo live—and Tawik live."

Abel shifted restlessly on the bench. "I'd begun to get the idea Spencer was some smarter than not to see through that."

"It is Chicatommo who see most plain. This Tawik is good. He feel friends with all Indians. He think all Indians are good." Gamelin rubbed his chin thoughtfully and sighed. "It is too bad for Tawik. But maybe the only way for him. And surely the only way for her."

"Or for me," said Abel.

Onaya came to Chicatommo's door and yelled at Nacawah. Nacawah turned with a start. Onaya beckoned. Nacawah joined her. The two women spoke briefly and, Nacawah's shoulders drooping, went into the chief's house. Abel crossed to Spencer's house, drew aside the doorflap, and looked in.

Philippa was at the loom. She looked only to see who it was and turned back to her work.

"There is no good your talking more about it."

"I didn't come to talk. I came to tell you McKee is taking you to Detroit. The English will see that you get to Montreal and then back to the United States."

"But I have decided not to go, I've already tried to make you understand that."

"You are a captive. Chicatommo is head man of this town. McKee is Indian Commissioner. They're the ones that do the deciding."

She rose and faced him. After all that had happened to her there was spirit left in her.

"If this is your doing, then you're making a number of mistakes. Spencer will be back tomorrow. He and his friends will follow and McKee, who never crosses Indians, will hand me over to him."

"Spencer won't be back tomorrow—or ever."

"I don't believe you."

"You will by night. I'm telling you now so that you can start in getting some things straightened out in your mind. He's dead."

She showed no more feeling than had he in making the announcement.

"I can see I have to believe you because I can feel it must be true. He was born doomed—doomed never to know justice. Who did it? You? Chicatommo? Those French traders?"

"What difference? What counts is the whole business is over and done with."

"Only for Spencer. Not for me. And perhaps not for you. You are quicker than was Heber to make decisions for other people, and you cannot always escape the consequences."

"That could be. McKee will be starting first thing in the morning."

She sank on the edge of her bed. He dropped the curtain. The next morning he stood in the doorway of Chicatommo's house watching McKee and Philippa riding off along the northbound trail that led to Detroit. Across the river Pierre was shaking hands with Gamelin after ferrying him to the other bank and Gamelin was turning westward toward Vincennes.

Fingers plucked at Abel's sleeve and he re-entered Chicatommo's house. Oosak, Chicatommo's Cherokee lieutenant, and two bigger-than-average Shawnee warriors were standing, waiting, beside the seated chief. The two Shawnee took

Abel by the arms and forced him down on Chicatommo's bed. Oosak pushed a block of wood under Abel's extended legs. While the Shawnee held Abel in their firm grasp, Oosak lifted a club and struck each leg above the ankle just hard enough to snap the shinbone. Having broken each leg, he next proceeded deliberately to set them and bind them with splints.

Chicatommo watched this performance with unblinking calm. He was a man whose word was good. He had agreed to keep his captive alive and whole until the rest of the money arrived, provided it arrived within a reasonable time. He had taken care not to cripple his hostage permanently. But he had also taken care that his prisoner should entertain no foolish ideas about saving his money by escaping before it arrived.

13

Job lay in his bed, watching for daylight. As the autumn nights lengthened, his impatience with their length grew upon him. For him the day could not begin until he could begin to see. In the darkness meanwhile he could only listen and smell, as his senses, sharpened by a lifetime in the wilderness, struggled to free him from the clutch of his bedridden body. He could smell the frosty night air slipping under the door in among the warmer odors that filled the kitchen, the pleasant, sharp tang from the three barrels of cider ranged in the open along the north wall of the blockhouse awaiting the first hard freeze, the churned-up mud of the riverbank about the ferry landing, the newly sawn lumber on the skidway. His hearing had a wider range. He could hear the successive creaks of the two doors as Selina, the only early riser among the Traners, left their house and went out to the shed to milk their cow, the whimpering of a baby in the newest movers' camp the other side of Donovan's, even the groan of the ungreased wheel in Jim Butler's grist mill five miles away over the hills beyond the river.

Then he knew that the first gray of dawn must have come into the sky behind the mountains, though he could see no glint of it yet on the kitchen window, for he heard the scratch of their claws as his dogs came up the outside stairway that had replaced the onetime ladder. Since he had been unable longer to go down to chain them up in the morning, they had been taught to come to him at the first streak of daylight. One after another the great beasts pushed through the blanket flap over the hole in the wall beside the kitchen doorway and were around his bed in the darkness, sniffing and nuzzling at him.

He felt around for his hickory staff, which had an iron spike in one end and a boat hook at the other, and rapped on the floor. Judah jumped from his couch in the storeroom below, ran up the stairs, stirred coals out of the ashes in the fireplace, and lighted a candle. Job reached behind his bed for the bucket of meat that had been put there ready for him the night before, and began tossing chunks to the dogs. When they were fully occupied with the meat, Judah stepped around them and edged toward the bed. Job had recovered the use of his arms, but he was still paralyzed from his ribs down. He resented being helped and his temper was at its worst in the morning, which brought that moment of the day when he was the most dependent upon help.

"Well, goddammit, git at it," he snarled. "Git at it and git it over with."

Judah stripped back the blankets and, rolling Job about like a baby, hastily dressed him. Then, breathing as fast with relief as was Job with annoyance, he drew alongside the bed the squat four-wheeled cart with a basketwork armchair nailed to the platform, and deposited Job in the conveyance in which he would spend the rest of the day. The instant that he was in his chair Job shoved Judah away and grasped his hooked and pointed hickory staff. Pulling and pushing with it, he was now master of his own movements. Judah laid his rifle in his lap and opened the kitchen door. Job thrust with his pike and drove his cart along the rails which extended across the floor from beside his bed out and along the new balcony that Judah had constructed for him. The maple tracks ran all the way around this balcony, which encircled the second story of the blockhouse. Judah had copied the device of cart and rails after the trainway designed by Basil Allen, Job's new English bookkeeper, to move timbers from the mill along the skidway where the flatboats were built.

Traner's Station, beginning to take shape in the gray early light, looked less like a frontier settlement each month that passed. The boatyard now extended both ways from the sawmill; there was a general store and two taverns; and the original settlers had given up planting crops in order to rent their cleared land to movers for campsites. The great summer rush of movers was over, but there were still so many coming, hoping still to get downriver before it froze, that flatboats were sold the day they were finished, even though Silas Mapes now had four under way at a time and a gang of fourteen carpenters working on them. Job's first disgruntled glance was to see if there was yet any stir of life in the carpenter's bunkhouse and his next, more interested, was at the brushy slope above the flume where buckwheat from one of the Traners' untended fields had run wild up the hillside. In the growing light the big doe with the two half-grown fawns snatched a last mouthful and began to drift toward the shadow of the woods above. She was all of a hundred and eighty yards away, but there was no wind. Job waited until she had stopped again to sniff and look around. The dogs, watching him, whined eagerly. The shot echoed among the silent hills. All three deer rose in long, sailing leaps as though on springs. But after those first prodigious jumps there were only two continuing to bound on into the edge of the timber.

"Got her," muttered Job. "Go fetch her."

Judah ran down the stairway. Job reloaded his rifle and picked up his staff. At every time of day, as he looked out from his restless circling of the balcony, the rifle was in his hands or his lap. Since the use of the cart had enabled him to be always on the move and on the lookout, he had shot three wildcats, any number of rabbits, muskrats, and weasels, so many ducks and geese that Abbie had lost count, and even, occasionally, a surfacing fish, but this had been his first deer. The achievement greatly improved his humor as he resumed his survey of the settlement's awakening.

Luke Price, the night watchman at the mill, must have been reminded of the hour by the sound of the shot for he was running to wake the hands. Selina, her baby wrapped in a shawl, was hurrying along the path from the Traners' house to the kitchen in the end of the bunkhouse. She had taken Abel's place as the one Traner willing to work regularly. It had been her own idea that with so many carpenters working in the boatyard it was worth Job's while to save their time by hiring someone to cook for them. Basil, muffled in a greatcoat, came out of his office in the other end of the bunkhouse to take his invariable early-morning walk. As always he looked first of all to see if any new movers had come in during the night. By day he always dropped whatever he was doing whenever new parties of movers showed up and ran out to take a quick look at them. By the time they had got their stock fed and watered and their cooking fires started and had got around to asking about the price of boats, he was generally able to make a close guess at what they were able to pay. For a man who when he first came had not intended to stay longer than overnight, Basil was beginning to take a tolerable interest in the business.

Ham was starting to sizzle in Abbie's skillet in the kitchen. Job rapped on the wall to remind Esther that it was time to get up to have breakfast with him. Silas came out of his shack beside the mill and started up the hill along the flume to open the head gate. In this weather it was kept closed at night lest a sudden freeze crack the planking. Job seized his staff and propelled his cart around the balcony to the further corner from which he could watch Silas. In the few weeks that he had had the cart he had learned to get around in it so fast that his dogs had to run to keep up.

Esther slowly combed and braided her hair. She had worn it in two braids down her back ever since she could remember and it had never occurred to her to do it any other way. Her dress was half on before she decided, it having turned so much colder during the night, that the time had come to change to her winter dress. It was of the same butternut brown homespun and also hung shapelessly from her shoulders to her ankles, but it was of wool instead of cotton. It had been hanging all summer from the same peg to which the mirror was hung and in snatching it down a button caught and snapped off. She slipped on the dress and knelt to feel around on the floor for it. With the sun so far around to the south the light from her one small window was too dim to see under the bed. She jerked back the muslin curtain that had never been drawn aside since the new glass window had been put in, and, turning, caught sight in this suddenly clear light of her face in the little mirror.

There had been a time the winter before when she had never passed that mirror without pausing, sometimes for minutes at a stretch, to study herself in it. But not in all the months that the winter dress had been hanging over it had she once moved it aside to look again. Now she had to stoop a little to see into the glass. She must have grown two or three inches during the summer. The young girl's plumpness had gone from her cheeks, the chin was oddly pointed, the eyes larger, the neck longer. She looked down at herself. All along she had been half aware that her arms and legs were beginning to seem thinner, her waist narrower, her breasts more rounded, but in her continuing listlessness had taken no interest in a change so gradual. She seized a handful of the woolen gown and drew it tighter about her.

"Abbie," she called.

Abbie came in, grumbling. "What's takin' yuh so long? If'n yer paw doan git his brekfus real quick he's a-gonna bite my head off."

"Can't you take this in?" said Esther. "It hangs on me like a sack."

Abbie's frown was wiped away. "Bless Gawd," she declared. "I jus' bin a-waitin' fer yuh to ketch on yuh ain't so chubby no more. I surely kin take it in. Afore noon I'll fix it."

Esther pulled off the dress and reached for the cotton one, but Abbie snatched up both homespun gowns and tucked them under her arm.

"Might's well do 'em both tuh once," she said. "Whilst I'm at it yuh kin jus' wear this one."

She took from its peg one of the Philadelphia dresses, a green serge, and, overriding Esther's reluctance, slipped it on over her head.

"I already done tuk in this here one—so's it 'ud be ready fer yuh. Now yuh kin see fer yerself yuh got no call to go 'round lookin' like a bag o' corn shucks."

Stepping back with her head on one side, Abbie surveyed Esther with a criticial satisfaction that led to new dissatisfaction. Dropping the homespun dresses on the floor, she climbed wheezily up on the stool, groped about on a high shelf, and clumped down again with a paper packet clutched in her hand. From the packet she shook a dozen hairpins. Esther was smoothing the serge over her slim hips and, standing on tiptoe, trying to see the effect in the mirror. Abbie pushed her to a seat on the edge of the bed and, again ignoring her protests, gathered up her braids. With the practiced touch of some remembered experience out of her long and varied past, she wound the braids into a crown on Esther's head, thrusting each pin in firmly to punctuate her remarks.

"I ain't said nothin' 'cause all summer yuh's bin too mopey to listen to nothin' from nobody. But maybe now yuh kin see fer yerself yuh is a growed-up young lady and might's well start in makin' out to act like one."

Even the dogs lifted their heads when Esther came out to join her father at the table that had been set beside his cart. Job stared.

"Like I bin tellin' yuh right along," he proclaimed, "yuh never eat enuff to keep a mouse a-kickin'. Yuh keep on yuh'll be nothin' but skin and bones." He bent over his plate again and then, struck by a new thought, peered at the green dress. "Real foxy get-up fer a work day," he said. "Yuh couldn't be aimin' to ketch the Britisher's eye?"

Esther slipped into her place at the table.

"Be a waste of time. He'll be pulling out for Kentucky most any day now."

"What makes yuh think that? Did he tell yuh so?"

"No. But he never intended to stop here like he has. You real set on having him stay?"

Job grunted irritably. "Yer even gittin' so's yuh talk like him."

"Suppose he did start in taking some notice of me," persisted Esther. "You want him to stay that bad?"

"What's got into yuh this mornin'? Don't go to gittin' uppity with me jest because yuh got thet Philadelphy dress on. Yuh know right well why I've kept him on here. He comes from a place in England where they make iron and he claims he knows how they go about it. I got me a hill full o' iron ore and it could turn out to be worth more'n eight boatyards."

"You ain't answered me, Paw."

"Ain't no use. Yuh never lissen no matter whut I say."

"Mostly you say—'less she's got something wrong with her a woman needs a man."

"And I say it agin. No question it's time yuh had yuh one. But I ain't never set out to pick him fer yuh. Pick him yerself. It won't be me thet has to go to bed with him."

"If I married Basil then he'd stay and help you make iron. Is that what you're getting at, Paw?"

"No call to come at me with a knife. Yuh ain't bin carryin' on with him like yuh counted him a one-eyed Pottawattomie with the shakes and the small pox. Yuh spend more'n half yer time cooped up with him over there in thet hole he calls the office."

"That's because he's been teaching me to read and write and cipher."

"Whut the hell good is thet to a woman?"

"It'd be some good to you to have somebody in the family able to add up your accounts and read your letters to you."

"So thet's whut yer aimin' at? Yer countin' on spendin' the rest o' yer life hung around my neck. Well, I'm a-tellin' yuh I don't want no dried-up old maid under my roof—no matter kin she read all the fine print in Holy Writ upside down."

"Then it is Basil. He's the one you want under your roof. Is that it?"

Job roared with anger. "This is whut I git fer bunkin' up thet winter with a furrin woman. Yuh is jest as contrary as yer French maw." He seized his rifle and staff and began propelling his cart toward the balcony, his dogs crowding after him. In the doorway he came to a stop and glared back at her, his rage baffled by the urgency of his need to make her understand. "They's only one thing I want. When yuh git yuh a man I want yuh should git yuh one thet's man enough to look after yuh."

With a jerk of his hook Job slammed the door. Abbie wagged her head.

"He keeps takin' on like he don't expect to live out the week. But the way he scoots up and down on them wheels, he's got the go in him to last another forty year." Looking around from the door to Esther, she parted her pursed lips slowly into an approving grin. "Yuh see? Yuh try to make out it doan make no difference how yuh look. But the minute yuh fix yerself up even a mite it gives yuh so much spunk yuh even talk back to yer paw."

Esther listened to the violent thuds of her father's staff as he drove his cart impatiently along the balcony and, taking up her slate and the three tattered copies of the *Pittsburgh Gazette* which served her as reading texts, set out for the mill office with a brisker step than usual. Basil Allen looked up from his ledgers as she entered. Though still in the middle twenties he wore a full brown beard which so masked his expression that she was seldom sure whether he was actually commending or covertly ridiculing her efforts. He sprang up from his desk and came forward to meet her. This morning, as he bowed over her hand, there seemed no slightest glint of amusement in his quizzically alert, pale brown eyes. And he did not release her hand, even after conducting her to her chair beside his, until she pulled it away.

"If I may be so bold as to say so," he said, "you are looking remarkably well this morning."

His beard continued to hide the possibly mocking curl of his lips, but his eyes were taking in her hair and her dress with as much attention as though, after all the hours she had spent in this room these last three months, he were noticing her for the first time. She glanced down at the green dress and lifted her eyes to meet his glance. He looked away, cleared his throat, and took up her slate. But then, instead of examining the exercise she had written upon it, he laid it down again.

"And if I may say something more," he said, "at even more risk of seeming personal? I have been amazed by how fast you learn."

"I had to. The river's likely to freeze up most any day now. Somebody was bound to tell you that then you'd be stuck here 'til spring and you'd light out right sudden."

"Suppose I were to say that I've already thought of that—that I might not so much mind—staying here until spring?"

He spread his hands out on the desk and smilingly waited for the effect of this significant announcement.

"My father'd be mighty glad to hear it."

"He would?"

"He thinks you've been taking hold of things here right well."

"Would you be glad, too?"

"I ought to be. I reckon I've got plenty more to learn."

He was leaning forward now, speaking more and more eagerly.

"Perhaps then I should advise your father of my intentions—I mean my intention to stay on. Would you advise that?"

A tinge of color had come into Esther's pale face. Silas thrust his head in at the door. Basil swung around, scowling.

"Ain't seen Luke Price anywhere's about, have yuh?" asked Silas.

"Not since he built my fire this morning."

"If yuh happen to see him, tell him Hugh Garret's here."

Silas paused only long enough to spit carefully beyond the box of sawdust on the floor before withdrawing and slamming the door behind him.

"At least once a day the old fool makes some excuse to stick his head in that door just so he can spit on my floor," grumbled Basil. "Who's Hugh Garret?"

"The sheriff from Pittsburgh," said Esther. "There was some talk Luke got drunk there last summer and bit a constable's nose off. Still, I wouldn't reckon the sheriff would come all this way looking for him."

Basil had already sprung up and was opening the door a crack to peer out.

"Is that the sheriff getting out of his canoe at the ferry landing?"

Esther joined him at the door, but he only opened it another inch as she stepped around him to look out. Sheriff Garret was exchanging shouted greetings with her father on the blockhouse balcony and then starting up the stairway to join him.

"Yes, that's him. I mean—that's he. Why can't you say him? It sounds better."

She turned to discover Basil struggling into his greatcoat.

"I'm going to look for Luke," he explained, speaking very fast. "The sheriff just might be after him and Silas doesn't like Luke much and I've an idea would as soon the sheriff took him. Luke said something this morning when he finished work about fishing off the rocks down by the point. I'm going to slip down there and tell him to look out."

Without waiting to see how she received his involved explanation, Basil brushed past her, ran around the corner of the bunkhouse and then the corner of the mill, and was lost to view among the willows along the river bank. Esther closed the door and returned to her chair. Now that she was alone her eyes were dancing and her lips on the verge of smiling. She picked up one of the *Pittsburgh Gazettes*, but the vision of Basil's eager face hovered between her and the printed lines. This morning had brought the first faint stirs of comfort she had known since that other morning so many months ago when she and her father had been felled by the same stunning blow.

Her pleasant reverie was disrupted by Selina's stormy entrance. As usual she was clutching her baby, and as usual she looked harassed.

"I knowed yuh was in here by yerself," she said. "I seen Basil run off. And I jest got to talk to yuh."

Selina looked more than harassed. She looked desperate.

"What's happened now?"

"Kate jest this minute run over to tell me. And Eben jest got through tellin' her—over in the Donovan cow shed. He told her not to tell nobody. But she couldn't wait to tell me. Is it so, Esther? Is yer paw aimin' to buy Traner Mountain?"

Selina's complaints were many and vocal and often shared with Esther, for whom she felt a species of fellow feeling in that they were each so often put upon. But she ordinarily had more foundation for her laments.

"Whatever for?" asked Esther. "Most of the timber's been cut off. It's all rock and grown up to brush. It's not worth anything to Paw or anybody."

"Basil says it is. He says the mountain's full of coal. He says that makes it worth plenty to yer paw on account of the iron ore he's got on his place right alongside. Basil told Eben he might git yer paw to pay a good price fer it."

"Nobody can get him to do anything. But if he does buy it, I should think you'd be glad. Don't you need the money?"

"We surely do. The worst way. But I've heared how Caleb and Micah and Eben talk. Was they to git their hands on any money, they'd take straight off fer Kentucky. Or this new country folks talk about this year north of the Ohio. Then where would we be? In a far country without a roof over our heads—where we knowed nobody—and the three of them more worthless than they are here. Soon's the money was gone we'd be ten times worse off than we are here." Selina's voice rose to a shriller pitch. "I couldn't stand it. I couldn't stand no more than I have to stand here. Driftin' off down thet river on a raft spillin' over with young uns and with no idea where we're goin' to end up or the next meal's comin' from." She shifted the baby to her other arm. "And this one peaked as he is—and another one a-comin' already. I couldn't stand it, I tell yuh. Yuh got to talk to yer paw."

"I'll talk to him, Selina. Though it won't be much use. Talking to him only makes him the more set on whatever he's of a mind to do. But I'll try."

Selina flung open the door and turned angrily on the step. "Yuh'd best try hard. Abel's bound to turn up one day to see his folks. Miserable as they is, he sets some store by 'em. But if'n they ain't here no more, then he'll never be back."

Through the door Selina had left open Esther saw the sheriff when at length he returned to the landing, got in his canoe, and started back downriver. Suddenly she sprang up. But once in the open she slowed her homeward walk to a meandering amble, pausing to notice the work in progress on the flatboats under construction on the skidway, to answer the endless questions of a mover's family, and to chat with Susie Donovan, who had just crossed on the ferry after visiting her sister on the other bank. Only then did she saunter on to the blockhouse. Her father did not look up even when she stood beside him. All of his attention was upon the new rifle lying in his lap. It was no longer than his other one, but the stock was heavier and the barrel much thicker. It had that look of ugliness and brutality that went with unnecessary power. Job was fondly stroking the lock.

"The piece Ike Schob up in Pitt has been a-makin' fer me," he announced. "Hugh Garret he stopped past Ike's shop and brung it along with him. It throws a two-ounce ball 'stead of a half ounce like the common run o' rifles. Ike he tried her out while Hugh was there a-watchin'. Hugh says it don't drop off more'n a half-inch at four hunnert yards."

Esther looked from the gun out over the settlement. There was not a spot this side of Donovan's that would not now be within range of Job's marksmanship. The sheriff was rounding the bend past the willows into which Basil had followed Luke.

"Did Hugh Garret come all this way just to bring you the rifle?"

"Nope. Hugh he wanted to see me and he brung the piece along jest as a favor."

"You think he was looking around for runaway redemptioners? Silas says this year they been coming over the mountains with every bunch of movers."

"Hugh he's got more to do than fool around with thet kind o' trash."

"Silas says they offer twenty shillings reward for catching one. If Hugh rounded up enough of them it would be worth something to him."

Job was still fondling the rifle.

"If'n yer bound to know whut brung Hugh, I'll tell yuh. Whut he come to ask about was whut I knowed about Fortiner. Hugh says Fortiner never showed up at Limestone nor Louisville. He didn't stop off at that new Yankee place at the mouth of the Muskingum on the north bank and he never come back as far as Wheeling. His folks back in Maryland

264

ain't never heard a word from him and they've tuk to frettin'. They writ Hugh a letter askin' whut he kin find out."

"But why should we know anything about it?"

"Hugh he figgered when Fortiner took over his boat from me he might of talked some about where he was headin' fer downriver. But them days I wasn't in no shape to talk to nobody nor notice nothin'. Abbie, though, she don't miss much. She figgered whut Fortiner had most on his mind was havin' him some fun and from whut she says about thet yellow-haired woman he had fixed up the cabin fer yuh'd have to guess he was on a warm track."

"She was real pretty," said Esther. "Abbie's always throwing it up to me how she dressed and how she fixed her hair. Do you reckon the Indians got 'em, Paw?"

"Mebbe. Anyhow, his folks back in Maryland is mighty upset. Accordin' to whut they writ Hugh, they'll pay five hunert dollars fer certain word of whut happened to him. Nosin' off downriver lookin' fer sign 'ud be a good winter's job fer some footloose young sprout. Chances like thet never come along when I was young and had two legs."

"She was a real nice boat," said Esther, looking over the balcony rail at the empty shipway where it had been built. "When you going to set Judah to making you another one?"

"Whut fer? More money in flatboats."

"Now that Judah's all done with your balcony and cart he's got time on his hands."

"He ain't got half time enough fer whut he's doin." Job looked up from the gun long enough to scowl at her. "Yuh keep yer nose so close to thet slate yuh don't notice nothin'. S'pose yuh didn't even see thet bargeload o' brick when it come down from Pitt last week? Judah's right over there in thet shed buildin' me a furnace."

"You going to put in a still?" Esther giggled foolishly, deliberately stirring her father's temper.

"No. Nor it ain't a lime kiln neither—nor a tannin' vat— nor a Dutch oven—nor a sugar kettle—nor a salt pan. Don't yuh pay no attention to nothin' around here? It a-gonna be a furance to smelt iron ore. I bin lissenin' fer months to how much Basil claims to know about makin' iron and now I aim to find out how much."

Job caught sight of a mover's dog trotting along the path between Donovan's and Traner's. He lifted the new rifle, casually took aim, and lowered it again, balancing it approvingly in his hands.

"She's got a real handy feel," he exulted.

Again he lifted the rifle, this time taking more careful aim.

Esther, watching the heavy black barrel steady as Job sighted along it, forgot all the carefully planned craftiness of her approach.

"Are you fixing to buy Traner Mountain, Paw?"

Job lowered the rifle and glared at her suspiciously.

"Whut fer? It ain't worth half o' nothin'. Yuh got some idee I'm crippled in the head 'stead of the legs?"

"It's full of coal. And you need coal to make iron."

Job became convulsed with a greater rage than could, even with his temper, have been accounted for by her unseemly curiosity. Then as suddenly the gust passed and he became immensely cunning. "Yuh bin talkin' to Basil. Basil he's bright some ways, but he's got mebbe a mite more to learn afore he gits real good sense. We uns got timber around here to last a hunert years and long's we got all thet charcoal there won't be no use fer coal. I ain't got no more idee o' buyin' Traner Mountain'n I have o' jumpin' up and dancin' a jig."

Esther leaned over him. "Stop fooling with that gun and look at me. The only reason you're saying you don't want Traner Mountain is because there's something you want more. You want it worse than you want coal or iron—or maybe me. You know if the Traners get any money they'll take off downriver and then the last chance that Abel will ever come back here will be gone. That's what you're after. You want him back within gunshot. That's all you've had on your mind since the day he left."

Before she had finished she was shaking him. He pushed her away roughly.

"Ever since yuh showed up this mornin' in thet goddam dress yuh bin meaner'n a weasel. Why'n goddam hell would I have Abel on my mind? Will yuh tell me thet? If'n he hung around last spring I'd surely laid lead to him soon's I could set up. But he's gone down thet river and nobody don't mostly ever come back up it. By now he could be a thousand mile down it or forty feet under it or feedin' the buzzards anywheres along it. Thinkin' about his ever turnin' up here agin is the furthest from all I got me to think on. And if'n yuh was even half a woman yuh'd never speak his name—not to me nor to nobody. He got up out of yer bed and walked off. A man can't do a woman no more dirt than thet. Yuh'd best git hold o' yerself and go to gaggin' on thet some more."

Job grasped his staff and drove his cart furiously around the corner and out of the sight of her. Esther steadied herself against the rail. Abbie came out with a basket of clothes, but after one look at Esther's face held her peace and kept on down the stairs. There were times when Abbie stood more in awe of daughter than of father.

266

Suddenly Esther ran down the stairway and on past the ferry landing to the path that led south along the riverbank. After the path passed through the sugar bush it narrowed between tangles of yellowing raspberry vines. She ran on, heedless of the briers tearing at the green serge dress. Not until she had caught sight of the curl of smoke from Ish's campfire did she slow to a walk and endeavor to control her panting. He had not been around much this summer, but if he were using his camp at all he would almost certainly be somewhere near in the middle of the day, for it was his way to do his hunting and fishing in the early morning or the late evening. Next she could see his bark lean-to, and his smoldering fire, and the rack over it on which he was smoking jerky, and his beached canoe, and the other bark shelter over his racks for stretching and drying pelts, but no sign of Ish. Then she saw him sitting right there by the fire, his buckskin and his own skin so much the color of the earth and the dead leaves, and he all the time holding so still, that her first glance had passed right over him. He pretended that he had not noticed her approach and jumped up with a great show of surprise when she stood beside him.

"You recollect that man from Philadelphia that bought the keelboat last spring?" she asked.

Ish began to nod and grin, every wrinkle in his weatherbeaten, toothless face taking its own part in his foolish beaming. Already he had guessed that she had come to ask him to do something for her.

"Well, they never showed up at Limestone or Louisville. After they passed Wheeling nobody's seen hide nor hair of them. I want you to take your canoe and go downriver looking for sign until you figure out what might have happened to them."

Ish's grin faded and he looked more foolish than ever. When he sighted a panther on a distant rock or the track of a buffalo in the edge of a swamp, his face became as keen and knowing as ever did Job's. But when he looked at another person his jaw dropped and his eyes clouded, which did as much as the occasional fits he had to make him appear the imbecile so many people considered him. He was willing to help her and wanted to please her but he was utterly mystified.

"That yellow-haired woman he had along with him," she tried to explain. "She was right good to me. I can't sleep from wondering about her."

Ish was more bewildered than before.

"You're always going off on long hunts," she said. "Last spring you were off for two months somewhere back in the mountains. Paw thinks you worked your way clear down to Cherokee country. You used to take to the river most every summer. You've been up and down it twenty times. I should think you'd be glad of an excuse to take another trip. Winter's coming on, but so much the better. There won't be so many movers cluttering up the water."

Ish brightened a trifle. She was on slightly firmer ground with him now.

"Yer paw want me to go?" he asked.

She shook her head. "Paw doesn't know anything about it. But you take off in the night and he won't need to know where you've gone. Nobody will know—but me."

Ish's face began to clear. He picked up a stick, drew his knife, and began to whittle. He was thinking hard, if slowly, and with each long, delicate shaving that curled from his blade, his thinking was leading him nearer the track which at last he had glimpsed.

"S'pose," he asked, "I was to run acrost Abel somewhere's down-river? Want me to tell him to come back?"

Esther's cheeks burned. "No. Tell him nothing from me. I don't ever want to lay eyes on him again. All the same, people—that is, all of them except Paw—have got to be reasonable. A man's got some right to visit his own folks if he's a mind to. So maybe there is something you better tell him, if you just happen to run across him. Specially since you've always been more partial to Abel than to anybody—even Paw. If you should happen to see him, you might tell him about how Paw gets around up on that porch of his where he can see every which way and about that new gun of his that will carry all the way to the Traner doorstep. You might tell Abel that, so if he does happen to come back to see his folks he'll know how far off Paw could get at him."

Ish was grinning foolishly again. Now that he fully understood his mission he was captivated by it. There was nothing he enjoyed so much as doing favors for friends.

He had no feeling that the task he had undertaken presented enormous perplexities. To him there seemed no more insurmountable difficulty in combing hundreds of miles of desolate riverbank for traces of a man who might have passed in a canoe nearly a year before than might seem to face a city dweller going along a street knocking on doors. Inquiry at settlements along the river would be simple, for they were so few and small. And in the wilderness stretching between them he had the equivalent of a pack of hunting dogs to assist him in picking up the trail. He knew of fifteen or twenty spots along the Ohio where there were hidden camps like his own on the Monongahela, inhabited by other solitary old woodsmen who had elected, as had he, to live out the remainder of their years in comfort, hunting, fishing, and seeing people only when they chose. They survived in their solitude because it had become second nature to them to be constantly aware of whatever moved in the woods behind them or the river before them. Such watchers as these might take little note of a three-family flatboat overflowing with children and livestock, but would take as personal an interest in a single man paddling past as they might in a canoe load of Indians. So he had no slightest doubt that, were Abel still alive, sooner or later he would find him. The one problem that did disturb him was the lateness of the season. If the river froze, as it was likely to do any day, his search could be delayed for weeks, possibly months. He decided to make as fast a run as he could as far as he could, all the way to Louisville if he could make it, and then to work back up the river as the weather warmed in the spring.

He had scarcely passed Wheeling when a wave of zero temperature rolled out of the northwest. Ice formed along the margins of the Ohio and choked the tributary streams. The main river continued to flow, the sweep of its current breaking the marginal ice into cakes and carrying them along. He knew from experience with many other winters that in a day or two the drifting ice would make travel by canoe impossible. He paddled furiously, resting no more than an occasional hour at a time, to keep ahead of the ice pack.

He was still ahead of it when he sighted Limestone. No more than a moment after his first glimpse of the waterfront his view was cut off by a snow squall, but in that moment he had also caught a glimpse of the anchored keelboat a hundred yards off the beach. She had, even at that distance, the distinct look of the boat Abel had built. He straightened his stiff back, dug deep with the paddle, and, when at length the outline of the keelboat loomed immediately before him through the slanting snow, muttered with satisfaction that he had so well estimated the current and his bearings. Then his jaw dropped slackly, but his eyes became sharp as a ferret's. Now that he could see every structural detail, there could be no question that this was the keelboat that he had watched Abel build and in which the missing Fortiner had set sail downriver. The impressions beating upon his senses were as tangible as a covey of partridges whirring up from a thicket. Wherever he looked—at the curve of the hull, at the tilt of the bowsprit, at the rake of the mast—he could see Abel at work. Abel had made himself so much a part of his ship that it was not easy to think of him as separated

269

from her. By the green scum on the line the boat had been anchored here for at least two weeks, more likely three. Were Abel anywhere around Limestone, he would have visited her. Then Ish saw the iron ring rimming the hawsehole to protect the wood from the wear of the anchor line. That had not been there when Abel had finished his original job back at Traner's Station. It had been an afterthought, added some time in the last six months. And whoever had wielded the hammer to shape it had taken the trouble to finish it as smoothly as though with a whetstone. Abel's ironwork was like that. The feeling grew upon Ish that Abel was near, that he might even be aboard.

He backed water alongside. There was no stir of anyone moving on deck or in the cabin and no one answered his calls. But someone had been on board not long before. He could smell the fire in the little iron stove in the cabin. The swirl of falling snow still shut off the town. He swung over the rail, pulled his canoe up after him, and opened the cabin door. His first glance set him back. Someone had been living aboard the keelboat. But it was not Abel. The place was filthy, littered with empty whisky jugs, and smelled of burned bacon and dried vomit. In the fading light Ish made a rapid inspection of the craft. There was nothing left to connect her with Fortiner's fancy setup. She had been stripped bare of everything movable such as personal effects or baggage. The man who cooked and slept in the cabin was the only one who had been aboard for days. He could have gone ashore and had his return cut off by the snowstorm.

The hold smelled faintly of tobacco and ginseng and Negroes. Ish lighted the lantern and went down the ladder. At some stage the keelboat had come to grief and had required extensive repairs. The new planking had been laid in so well that except for the freshness of the timber it could scarcely be told from Abel's original work. Like the ring, it looked as though it had been. Then, turning over the pile of mildewed mattresses stacked against the side, Ish saw the rusted trap that had been lying under them. It was one of his own beaver traps, one of the pair he had given Abel. He went back on deck, propped up the canoe, spread his blanket under it, and went peacefully to sleep. The next step in looking for Abel was to wait right here for the man who lived here to come back.

He was awakened toward morning by the bumping of ice against the hull. He could see campfires ashore and hear the shouting of movers as they worked with teams of horses and oxen to drag their flatboats farther up the beach out of danger. The keelboat was shivering under the bombardment of drifting ice. Anchored here in the open river, she was likely to take a harder pounding than was good for her, and if the anchor line parted and she drifted ashore she would surely break up. She was the same as Abel's boat and the bridge that might lead him to Abel and she had to be saved.

He pulled up the anchor. The bumping ceased as the boat drifted with the ice. The tiller was no help, but with a sweep oar he was able to keep her off the beach and out in the current. He knew this stretch of the Ohio as well as he did the Monongahela. Three miles below there was a point sheltering a little cove. Drifting past the point in the first streaks of daylight, he worked hard with the oar, caught the upstream eddy below the point, beached the prow of the boat, and moored her to a tree. Here, sheltered by the point from the full pressure of the ice pack, she was safe. He went back to his blanket under the canoe and resumed catching up on his sleep.

Jasper, that morning, awoke to the same glow of contentment to which he had awakened in each of their riverbank camps since they had left Louisville. Hagar was not in her blanket beside his, but his first realization was that she was not far away. The fire was built up, the perch that she had caught the night before was spitted over it, and he could hear the chop of her hatchet as she gathered more wood. He stretched luxuriously and took a deep breath to remind himself that the pain in his chest had quite gone. The brush-thatched lean-to, faced away from the wind and toward the fire, had been made the more weatherproof by the night's snowfall. The silence of the snow made him aware of the low, grinding rumble in the distance. Leaning on his elbow, he looked out at the river to see that during the night it had filled with floating ice which in midcurrent was heaving and tossing like a released log jam. The canoe was well up on the beach and safe, but could manifestly not for the present carry them any farther. They were stormbound. This was one morning that they could not leap up and rush on. They could only compose themselves comfortably in this snug, snow-blanketed, fire-warmed nook, and wait, perhaps for days. He lay back, sighing with new contentment.

Hagar appeared beside the fire with a bundle of wood the size of small logs. He turned over to watch her. The lines of her classically perfect figure seemed to flow into an endless succession of sculptured poses. Even when he had been at his sickest he had doted on that store of grace and strength upon which she drew to serve him. Her hatchet flashed up and down as she trimmed the branches from two six-foot spruce poles. Since the moment that they had embarked on their upriver journey she had done all the physical work, all the paddling, all the shelter-making, all the fire-building, all the cooking. He had protested mildly that he was no longer sick, and had continued to bask happily in the fierce devotion of her solicitude. She did not look up at him. But she knew he was watching her. After a while she spoke.

"How yuh feel?" she asked, beginning to split the spruce poles into long, thin panels.

"Good as new," he said. "What's that you're making?"

Her face lighted up when he addressed her. She no longer struggled to hide from him what she was thinking or feeling. The play of expression over it was as quick as the movements of her hands.

"River's full of ice," she said. "We can't go no further by canoe. But we got to git us to Limestone right now. So I'm makin' us a sledge."

"Why a sledge?"

"To pull yuh in."

"Preposterous. If press on we must, I can walk."

"Yuh ain't gonna. Recollect how the doc said yuh might stand the trip if'n yuh tuk it real easy."

"Keeping that excellent advice in mind, what better way to heed it than to linger here in this admirable camp for a day or two? The weather might change."

Hagar's hatchet was still for a moment. His lightness seemed to have caused her to pause to reassess her own earnestness, to re-examine each reason for disagreeing with him.

"Thet hole back of our old Salt River cabin couldn't o' meant nothin' else," she said. "Like I keep tellin' yuh, they'd dug it real careful and then dug it up again real fast. When Tom and Tim they buried the money there, they figgered on waitin' around Louisville fer me to show up. But not more'n a week before I went out there to look around they'd dug it up again. It stands to reason thet when thet redhead all of a sudden tuk off fer Limestone with Todd Barklit, they run back to git it and tuk off after her. We ain't got one day to waste. Tom and Tim they headed fer Limestone lookin' fer trouble and they always kin find it faster'n yuh could gut a rabbit."

"As I have repeatedly agreed, your reasoning is unassailable—up to a point. Obviously they changed their minds about remaining in Louisville. But what leads you to so long a leap as the conclusion they followed Magda?"

"Back in New Madrid I lissened many a time to 'em talk. When a man gits thet anxious to pull up a petticoat and is as bullheaded as them two, he don't let nothin' stand in his way."

She resumed her chopping. Jasper sat up in his blankets, his arms wrapped about his knees, and waited to catch her eye. But she refused to look at him.

"With so fixed a conviction of man's impetuosity, I am astonished you take so little heed of mine."

She looked at him then, her eyes glowing under the visor of the black bonnet that protected her treasured black curls. When her eyes met his she was transfigured. The scar became as nothing. Beautiful was too weak a word. She was like a flame bending toward him. But what she said was:

"First I got to git them two boys straightened out."

Jasper hugged his knees in delight at his success in having tricked her into so near an approach to an admission.

"Then hope, as the poet so well said, 'like the gleaming taper's light, adorns and cheers my way.' "

Hagar's laugh was infrequent but when it came it rang with the gusto of a man's.

"Yuh go to eatin' thet perch whilst I finish riggin' this sledge. We git us the rest o' the way to Limestone and could be the hope part'll be over with sooner'n yuh think."

The snow, except where drifted, was not more than a foot deep and it was just cold enough to offer the least friction to the sledge's runners. Hagar was able to pull her burden with ease and, whenever the going was at all open, to make good time. In stretches of unavoidable brush, she encountered more difficulty and at times was forced to cut a trail with the hatchet. Jasper's ventures to offer assistance were met with the most violent objection.

"Yuh stay in thet there sledge," she threatened finally, "less'n yuh want me to tie yuh in it."

He retreated to his place. Working farther from the river, Hagar found more open woodland and, free of the brush, was able to pick up speed, frequently to a run. The labor of pulling up a slope was rewarded by the occasional chance to coast down the other side, with Hagar racing beside the sledge, steering with a hand on Jasper's shoulder. She seemed almost to welcome the steeper climbs, to exult in her efforts as much as did Jasper in contemplating them. She laughed when the sledge overturned. When one smooth incline permitted her to ride with her feet on the runners she even sang a half-remembered snatch of a French boatman's song. Never, reflected Jasper, his complacency beginning to fail him, had a man been thus served by his beloved. Their roles were completely reversed. He, the man, was the protected and pampered one being sustained by the strength of the woman. It was she, not he, who was giving jubilant voice to these crows of exuberance. Then his relieved laugh rang with all the vigor of hers when he further reflected upon how thoroughly, in that moment to come, perhaps no longer distant, their roles were destined to be reversed.

Hagar, pulling to the top of a hill toward noon, came to a stop with a gasp of surprise. Jasper sprang up beside her. Through the snow-wreathed trees they could catch one narrowed glimpse down the next long slope of a keelboat grounded in an icebound cove.

"*Naiad*," cried Jasper, seizing her hand and starting to run down toward the river.

Ish never fell into so deep a sleep that he was unable to detect the faintest untoward sound. He was out from under the canoe, rifle in hand, and, from a loophole in the cabin, was inspecting the approaching man and woman long before they had reached the beach. The man, he decided, was a fool, running into the open like that with whatever weapons he might own left out of reach under the blanket back in that sledge. But the woman had more sense. She had her rifle ready and she was looking sharply from one end of the boat to the other instead of just standing there waving her arms and talking.

"She must have been carried away from her Limestone anchorage by the ice," Jasper was saying. "How fortunate we stumbled upon her before she started to break up."

"Somebody had a fire in the cabin last night," said Hagar. "See how the snow's melted on the roof."

"Abel would never have gone off without leaving somebody to watch *Naiad*," said Jasper. "The Negroes, undoubtedly. They've never seen ice. It must have frightened them out of their wits. Probably the moment the ship grounded they jumped to shore and made off."

"No tracks but our'n on this here beach," said Hagar.

Ish's ears had twitched at the mention of Abel's name. Just as he had guessed, he had been on the right track from the moment he had climbed over the keelboat's rail. All he had had to do was stay aboard until somebody showed up who knew about Abel. There was nothing he liked so little as palavering with strangers, but this was a time there was no getting out of it. He stepped across the snow-covered deck to the rail, his rifle held loosely in the crook of his arm.

"Who are you?" demanded Jasper.

"Name's Flourish Hyd," said Ish.

"Ish," cried Jasper, giving Hagar a hug. "Abel's oldest friend. I've heard him mention Ish a thousand times."

Ish beamed. If the tall man knew Abel that well he could not be quite the fool he seemed. And now he was beginning to look at the mooring line and the soft, muddy beach in which the keelboat's prow was grounded with the manner of a man possibly able to size up what he was looking at.

"She appears to be quite snug here," Jasper pronounced.

Ish never liked using an extra word but some accounting was called for. "Ice was a-poundin' her some where she was hitched off Limestone. So I turned her loose and pushed her in here."

"Masterly seamanship," said Jasper.

He reached for the rail to pull himself aboard but Hagar remained by the sledge.

"How far's Limestone?" she asked.

"Mebbe three mile," said Ish.

Jasper turned back to Hagar, grinning in rueful acknowledgment of having in his excitement over the combined encounter with *Naiad* and Ish momentarily forgotten the urgency of their principal mission.

"We'll be back in a trice," he said to Ish. "Tommorow at the latest. You'll stand by the ship?"

Ish nodded emphatically. If the keelboat had become Abel's property he would most assuredly stand watch until Abel himself appeared. His mouth opened several times to voice an inquiry concerning Abel's present whereabouts and welfare. But he found no opportunity to get in a word on account of the immediate and violent altercation in which the man and the woman had become involved. The altercation resulted in the man getting into the sledge and the woman towing the sledge off up the hill. Ish stared. It had become apparent that he had never been so wrong in his life as when he had guessed at first sight that the odd-looking, tall, skinny man with the big nose was a fool.

At the edge of the clearing around Limestone, Hagar came to a stop. Jasper stood up to make a preliminary survey. For the last mile he had ceased to enjoy his view of Hagar's supple figure taut against the weight of the sledge and had begun to dwell instead upon the various risks toward which they were hurrying. Barklit, the twins, Evan Branch, and the miller all were presumably here and they had one trait in common. All had sufficient reason to wish him ill. But his first look was partially reassuring. Limestone was no longer a more than commonly uncouth little backwoods settlement. It had taken on some of the aspects of a town. A dozen new houses had sprung up. Many people moved about the streets. Movers' camps stretched for more than a mile along the waterfront. Wherever so many people had congregated, the more simple and primitive forms of violence were frowned upon. There was even a small encampment of federal soldiers. Obviously the beginnings of law and order had come to Limestone. There was some reason to hope that here he was very nearly as free to give rein to his wits as he might in any genuine city. Upon Hagar, however, the scene had an opposite effect.

"Tom and Tim they'll be layin' real low," she said. "They know some about sheriffs and constables but they ain't never seen soljers before."

"We'll find them if they're here," said Jasper, beginning to face their task with more spirit. "Whoever's caught a glimpse of that pair will remember them. First off, I think we should separate and make independent inquiries. You take a gossipy stroll among the movers' camps and I'll hang around the store to see what I can pick up. Meet me there in the lumberyard in an hour."

When Jasper reached the lumberyard he was bulging with news.

"Catastrophe, no less. Before Abel left here for the Indian country he'd lost ship, slaves, and the rest of his money. By the most fearful mischance he encountered Magda's onetime master, who is also the man who once owned the trade goods. This confounded Neave has bought the inn with the proceeds and has become generally so prosperous that Magda has shaken off Barklit and is going to marry him tomorrow."

"Then we got to find Tom and Tim real quick," said Hagar. "They bin here in Limestone more'n a week. Skads o' movers has seen 'em and, like yuh say, nobody that sees 'em misses takin' notice. They bin keepin' clear o' soljers and folks that live here, but they bin spendin' their time nosin' among the movers' camps, and along the waterfront and specially around the inn. We got to find 'em right now."

Her vehemence distracted Jasper from his preoccupation with Abel's misfortune.

"I recall all too vividly my own several experiences with their excitability. And I can only assume you know it even better. But can it be that we may actually anticipate some overt attempt to abduct the bride?"

"Long's they come this far, they won't back off without tryin' somethin' miserable. They're too used to bein' so big and strong and they got no sense to go with it."

"Just to satisfy a passing curiosity—suppose they were to make off into the woods with their prize? What then? They share so many undertakings, but here would seem to be one on the verge of baffling."

"They'll figger out what to do about that when the time comes. Fight, most likely. When they fight it's a caution. What we got to figger is how to find 'em first."

"Quite so. For their sakes, your sake, and my sake—not to speak of Abel's, for whom the recovery of any part of his money would prove now of vastly more moment than before. But to dwell upon our problem we must first dwell upon theirs. Their situation as well as ours is somewhat more complex than you have so far noted. There are, for example, other suitors who may be in their several ways as determined as your brothers. Barklit withdrew from the English service on her account. And young Evan Branch has likewise cast discretion to the winds. Evan's case is particularly interesting inasmuch as it has appeared at times that she looks upon him with more personal favor than she does the others."

"We jus' stand here a-gabbin'," said Hagar, " 'stead o' doin' somethin'."

"We also stand here thinking—a process which upon occasion proves useful." Jasper's eyes began suddenly to sparkle, his mustaches to quiver, and the whole length of him to squirm as though every inch of his skin were tingling. "A number of thoughts occur to me. The other suitors—all the suitors, singly and in combination—most certainly invite our attention. Either Barklit or Evan may have excited more of your brothers' displeasure than has Neave himself. On the other hand all four may have formed a temporary alliance against the innkeeper. Our first object must be to pick up enough of these tangled strands to gain some idea of their probable pattern. It is better for you to make the approach to Barklit and Evan, for you have been friendly with the one and are to the other unknown, while both hold me in low esteem. I understand that while not on speaking terms, either with each other or the miller, each is in residence at the mill in order to keep the other under surveillance. In view of your former association it would seem perfectly natural for you to go directly to Barklit and equally natural to ask him point-blank about your brothers. Your search may end then and there. If it does not, draw young Evan aside and instruct him to meet us—discreetly—here in the lumberyard. While you are thus occupied I shall pry a bit about the center of the web at the tavern."

Jasper selected a table in a corner and waited. It was mid-afternoon and the inn's common room was deserted except for a man asleep at another table and two absorbed and silent drinkers at the end of the bar. Neave was not in evidence

277

but presently Edna approached his table, eying him with frank curiosity.

"A tankard of stout, if you please, Miss," said Jasper.

"You must be Irish," said Edna. "Or maybe English?"

"Does that mean you have no stout?"

"We have Kentucky whisky and Pittsburgh beer. But the beer isn't very good."

"Then, by all means, let's say a glass of whisky. And would you be kind enough to inform Mr. Neave that I should like a word with him?"

"My father's very much occupied just now. You must have come from Lexington. Nobody could have got in by river this morning."

"Your father doesn't know me," persisted Jasper. "But I am certain he would be interested in making my acquaintance. Particularly if you were to announce me as a man here to inquire about his keelboat."

"But he hasn't got a keelboat any more. The ice carried it away last night."

Jasper fixed upon her his most indulgent smile.

"Would you nevertheless do him the great favor of giving him the message?"

Edna returned the smile with one even more indulgent.

"You talk like a scholar, dress worse than a mover, and have mustaches like an Italian."

"Have you then been acquainted with so many Italians?"

"No. But we have a book with a picture of an Italian cardinal with mustaches just like yours."

"An ancestor, conceivably, though I myself was born in Connecticut, the son of a Congregational minister. Attendance at Yale College may account in part for my speech and much hard travel altogether for my dress. I am prepared to discuss the subject of my past more exhaustively if only I might first have a moment of your father's attention."

Edna laughed forgivingly.

"I'll bring you your whisky and go look for him."

Neave came out from some inner room with the air of a very busy man with very little time to spare. But at his first glimpse of Jasper his step slowed and he gave him a sharp second look. Many strangers came daily to his tavern but seldom one so outwardly remarkable.

"Mr. Neave?" said Jasper, rising and bowing. "I understand you have a keelboat for sale."

"I did have," said Neave. "But due to the negligence of a drunken rascal of a watchman it was carried away by the ice last night."

"Which would suggest that she may by now be piled on

some wild shore," said Jasper. "Perhaps the next island—perhaps against the Indian bank a hundred miles down. Long experience with this river would lead me to conclude that there is something like one chance in ten of her being located and recovered in anything like seaworthy condition. You are a busy man so I shall not beat about the bush. I will give you twenty-five dollars for her—where is and as is."

"Ah," said Neave. "An extraordinary offer. The more extraordinary the more one considers it."

"Am I to understand you have no interest in it?"

"A very faint one. In proposing this pittance you seem to be overlooking your own rule of a one-in-ten risk. She is an exceptional craft and if whole worth twice two hundred and fifty dollars."

"You have made a point," acknowledged Jasper. "And I will stand by mine. I will give you fifty dollars. That is my last offer. Please take it or leave it."

"Your assurance might lead to the assumption you are already informed of her location and condition."

"As a publican you are no doubt accustomed to indict the integrity of strangers. But your impeachment falls of its own weight. If such were the case, why am I here—when it would be so much simpler merely to wait for the ice to clear and slip the craft off downriver beyond your reach?"

"Unless she has stranded so near I was sure to get word of it before you could make off with her."

Jasper rose haughtily. "I am making you an offer of fifty dollars for what you must have considered, until a moment ago, a total loss. Do you take it? Yes or no?"

Neave gestured to Edna, who had been lingering, intensely interested, within earshot. She dashed to the bar and brought writing materials. Jasper sat down again and began drumming impatiently on the table. Neave took up the pen, examining its point as though in doubt that it was in a condition to write and then turning it over and over in his fingers as though in greater doubt that he had any wish to write. But at last he looked up.

"To whom have I the honor of making out the bill of sale?"

"You are selling the keelboat *Naiad* to Abel Traner."

Neave threw down the pen.

"I knew there was some trick. I'll have no part of it."

"Do not let passion becloud your judgment," said Jasper. "Mr. Traner has been beset by many difficulties, with some of which you are acquainted. He is at the moment in a far country. He is personally much attached to the ship, having built her himself. He is my good friend. If, while he is away, I can by any exertion of mine recover his ship for him, I should

279

be happy to do so. That accounts for my entire interest in the matter." He took out his purse. "I don't know that I made it clear that I am prepared to pay in silver."

Neave watched, wetting his lips, as Jasper counted out the Spanish silver pieces, then, raking the coins to his side of the table, picked up the pen.

"You might as well have held a pistol to my head," he said, signing the document with an angry flourish.

"Instead of forcing fifty dollars into your pocket," said Jasper.

He examined the bill of sale, put it in his pocket, and began to sip his whisky. The moment her father had withdrawn, Edna came flying back to the table.

"I know now who you are. You're Jasper Hedges."

"What leads you to that conclusion?"

"Evan has told me all about you."

"So? Is young Branch then a friend of yours?"

"Of course. He saved us from the island. I like him. So does Johnny. Of course, Father doesn't."

"Could that be because Magda also likes him?"

"Father can't forget that time she ran away with him."

"An episode somewhat difficult to forget. Still, one might imagine the proof to be in the pudding. Is there not some rumor that among her several suitors your father is the one she is marrying?"

"That's more than a rumor. She is. Tomorrow. But that's only because she's finally decided it's safer. Magda thinks all the time about being safe. And even after he's lost the boat and the slaves ran away, Father's still got the inn and it's doing very well. While she doesn't think Evan will ever amount to much. She doesn't think he knows where he's going." Edna's eyes grew dreamily large. "But if I were Magda I'd climb up behind Evan on his horse and not care where the horse galloped."

Jasper took another sip. "That reminds me. I, too, am an old friend of Magda's. A sort of old family friend, as it were. Before I leave I'd like to pay my respects to her. I suppose it would have to be without your father's knowing. Do you think you could arrange it?"

"I don't see how. That is, not for quite a little while. She's in the back parlor with Father and Eli Cramp right now. Eli's the notary. Father's canceling the rest of her contract. That's so she'll be a free woman when she marries him tomorrow."

Jasper's eyes glittered strangely. "Perhaps it'll do as well for you to take her my message. I agree with you that she's fond of Evan and it's too bad to have her going to the altar oppressed by anxieties about the estimable young man's future. You can tell her that as a matter of fact she need have no concern for his prospects. Explain to her that a rather unusual business opportunity has come to him. Mr. Traner and I are shortly embarking upon another New Orleans venture that gives promise of proving even more profitable than the last. Evan has some money he is in a position to invest and we are taking him in as a partner. So, though he may grieve for her for a time, he will presently be consoled by a voyage to New Orleans and all the novel as well as prosperous experiences awaiting him there. Will you tell her that so that her compunction for him may be allayed?"

Edna gasped, entranced by the vista opening before her. "I can't wait to tell her, Mr. Hedges."

Evan, waiting in the lumberyard with Hagar, was glowering. He had the appearance of one who was present at all only because he had been brought almost by main force. When Jasper turned the corner of a lumber pile and stood before them, the young man bristled indignantly. Jasper looked first at Hagar.

"Todd Barklit ain't seen hide nor hair of 'em," she reported.

Evan took a threatening step toward Jasper.

"I have nothing whatever to say to you, Mr. Hedges," he announced. "Certainly nothing you would like to hear."

"Granted, Mr. Branch. And it is of no consequence, since you happen to be here only to listen. So pay close attention. Soon after dark—sooner, possibly, if she can slip away from the inn—Magda will come to the mill looking for you. She will appeal to you for advice. She will say that now that the time is so nearly upon her she does not see how she can go through with the wedding tomorrow."

Evan grasped two handfuls of Jasper's coat. "How do you know that? Who told you? Did she tell you?"

Jasper released himself. "We are not discussing what I am saying or what anybody has said to me. We are concerned only with what, presently, Magda will say to you."

"So she's finally beginning to come to," exclaimed Evan. "I've been trying all along to tell her she was crazy. Only she wouldn't listen. Every day for the past two weeks I've been trying to tell her."

"Good for you. I'm sure when she comes to you you'll continue to give her the best of advice. And if you are of a mind to help her completely to escape her predicament, you will have horses ready so that before morning you may both be as far away as Lexington."

281

"We'll stop at Lexington only long enough to find a preacher," declared Evan. "Then we'll go home to Louisville where she should have stayed in the first place."

In his happy excitement he would already have been bolting off had not Hagar's firm hand closed over his arm.

"A capital solution to her dilemma," said Jasper. "But there remain one or two practical details. So pray continue to listen. You must realize that when Magda disappears from the inn and you from the mill, Neave may bitterly bemoan his misfortune, but Barklit will be on your trail in an hour, breathing fire and brimstone."

"I can handle Barklit."

"I'm sure you can. Nevertheless, his companionship might not prove altogether an asset to your honeymoon. So consider how simply his rude pursuit may be avoided. On your way back to the mill, stop at the store and tell a story with that relish which people will understand on account of your known dislike of Neave. Say that the keelboat I bought from him for fifty dollars is safe and whole in a cove not three miles downriver, that I have taken you in as partner, and that you are going to join me aboard tonight so that the moment the ice clears we can set out on our next New Orleans trading voyage."

"But I don't want to go to New Orleans. I'm taking Magda home to Louisville."

"Quite so. And you are not my partner. Nor am I immediately off for New Orleans. But still spread the story. In your youthful exuberance impart it to all who will listen. Reflect. As you ride through the night toward Lexington, how much better to know that the vengeful Barklit is floundering through the snow toward the keelboat."

An appreciation of the various facets of the stratagem was rapidly dawning on Evan. "It won't be because I'm afraid of Todd Barklit."

"Your disdain of him needs no proving. But this would seem an occasion you might better reserve your energies for the bride."

Hagar released her grip. After one plunging stride away Evan stopped and grinned back at them.

"A thousand thanks, Jasper. And as many apologies for all I have said against you." His glance, with a sudden flicker of passing interest, went from Jasper to Hagar and back to Jasper. "And your own share of luck too."

When they had returned to the sledge Jasper decined to get into it. Instead, he walked beside Hagar, whistling his satisfaction over the turn which he had been able to give to events. She drew his arm against her.

"Yer so smart—sometimes it gives me the shivers. The minute thet story gits to Tom and Tim and they see she's gone from the inn they'll come a-tearin' fer the boat."

Jasper's whistle died away. "Which brings up the unavoidable flaw in an otherwise impeccable design. Unhappily, so will Todd Barklit."

"Whut difference," said Hagar placidly. "If'n Tom and Tim don't git there first, then Ish and me I reckon kin take care o' him."

As they sighted the keelboat from the crest of the low ridge that stretched from the hills bordering the river out to the point, Ish's rifle cracked. Jasper ducked but Hagar looked up. A headless turkey tumbled from his roost in the lightning-torn top of a pine overhead and fell with a thud in the snow at their feet. Hagar picked it up and they went on. Ish, waiting apologetically at the rail, was stirred to a burst of loquacity.

"Had my eye on him fer quite a spell but didn't want to leave the boat to fetch him whilst yuh was away."

There was a fire going in the galley as well as the cabin. Hagar swiftly cleaned, plucked, and split the turkey. The halves were browning over the fire; she had had time to get well along with a furious scrubbing of the cabin; and the shadows of night were gathering before Ish made another remark.

"Bin somebody a-watchin' from them willows out on the point since long in the afternoon."

Hagar sprang up and walked deliberately into the bow. The surface of the snow along the nearer face of the point was unmarked except by the tracks left by a rabbit and a pair of partridges. From Hagar's lips burst the sudden, sharp attention-demanding call of a quail cock on lookout. There was silence for a moment and then she began to cluck and twitter and scold after the fashion of a mother quail giving firm and explicit directions to her ranging brood. Again she was silent. This time there came a single low cheep out of the willows. She resumed clucking and scolding. The directions were now more emphatic. There came another subdued cheep. She turned back to Jasper.

"It's them, all right. I told 'em to git on in here."

Jasper's face became a study in chagrin.

"But if they've been there in those willows the most of the afternoon, then——"

"Thet's right. They must o' bin here all the time yuh was fixin' it fer thet boy to make off with the redhead. The minute they seen me in town they must o' back-tracked here to see where I come from. They was scared to show themselves—

they got good reason to be—so they kept away from the sledge tracks and was a-layin' over there back o' the point waitin' fer a chance to let me know they was around." She looked up at Jasper. "All the same, thet scheme o' your'n was still right smart."

"After the fashion of one of Don Quixote's more inspired exploits."

The allusion was lost on her. But after going into the galley to turn over the turkey halves she came back to him.

"It didn't all go fer nothin', Jasper. It done me a world o' good. Yuh was thinkin' real fast—fer Tom and Tim—and fer me."

"And for myself," said Jasper, beginning wanly to smile. The smile became a chuckle. "And the two innocents en route to Lexington—they, too, have their respective rewards."

The last light faded. Hagar set the lantern on deck half-way between the cabin door and the beached prow and one of the broiled turkey halves beside it. Obeying her abrupt gesture, Jasper and Ish followed her up to the roof of the cabin. Sitting there overlooking the lantern-lighted foredeck but themselves hidden from sight in the darkness, they began eating the other half-turkey and waited. An hour passed.

"You're certain they're coming?" whispered Jasper.

"Might take 'em a spell to work up their nerve," said Hagar. "But they're a-comin'."

Ish lowered his section of the turkey carcass and lifted his head. Hagar, too, listened. Jasper had heard nothing. Then he saw two blurred shadows becoming detached from the greater shadow of the woods. The two shadows, faintly visible against the paleness of the snow on the open beach, advanced upon the keelboat until they were lost to view under the curve of the bow. More minutes passed. Hagar remained silent and motionless.

Suddenly Tom and Tim swung together over the rail and stood on the deck, blinking in the light.

"Set down," directed Hagar coldly. "There by the lantern."

The two young giants come shambling nearer and sat down, laying their rifles carefully on the deck beside them. They did not look up into the darkness in the direction from which Hagar's voice had come. Their sheepish eyes were fixed on the sodden and bedraggled moccasins at the end of their long outthrust legs. Two guilt-ridden children could not have seemed to cower in greater awe of the sternest parent. Wriggling in the extremity of his uneasiness, Tom's hand brushed the turkey half beside the lantern. The hand, seemingly of its own volition, fumbled at it.

"Put it down," said Hagar. "Nobody's ast yuh to eat with us."

Tom dropped it. Another several minutes of silence ensued before Hagar's icy voice came again out of the darkness.

"Where's the money?"

Each twin reached convulsively inside his shirt and each laid on the deck between the turkey and the lantern a crumpled banknote or two and half a dozen silver dollars.

"Where's the rest?"

Tom and Tim looked unhappily at each other and hung their heads lower.

"Let Tim do the talkin'," said Hagar. "Where's the rest?"

Tim began to shake. Finally, in a choked voice, he brought out his admission of the forever-damning depth of their ignominy.

"Old Sol Trexler dug it up."

Jasper could hear the breath go out of Hagar as though she had been hit.

"I might of guessed," she muttered after a moment. "I was thet sure they'd come back fer it I never looked close."

But when she again addressed the culprits her voice was as unsympathetic as before.

"Are yuh a-tryin' to tell me yuh so simple yuh follered the red-head all the way here to Limestone even after yuh'd already lost all the money?"

For the first time the twins looked up. They were shocked by this attack from a quarter to them so unexpected. The frenzy of his attempt fully to comprehend the enormity of the charge held Tim speechless. It was Tom who first found words.

"We never follered her nowhere. We bin lookin' fer old Sol."

"Don't lie to me," threatened Hagar.

The sting of injustice restored Tim's voice.

"Don't yuh recollect how he was all the time gabbin' about when he was a boy back in Berks County, Pennsylvania?"

Both twins were talking now, gasping with relief that at last the time had come to reveal and share their many troubles.

"We figgered oncet he got hold o' all thet money he'd head fer back East to show off to his home folks."

"So we got us to Limestone faster'n we figgered he could, and bin watchin' fer him to come through."

"Whether he come by Lexington or the river he'd o' had to come through Limestone."

"But he never showed up."

285

"Mebbe he beat us here. Mebbe he circled 'round."

"So what Tom and me is a-goin' to do next is make fer Pittsburgh. We're a-keepin' after him 'til we ketch him."

Tim's voice had gathered strength during the delivery of this final announcement. The spirits of both twins were rising. Their faces were turned up more bravely toward the invisible and inexorable Hagar in the darkness above the cabin door. But she had fallen strangely silent.

"Whutever got into yuh," demanded Tim with a sudden curiosity shading toward counteraccusation, "to set yuh to thinkin' we uns could turn thet simple over a wench? Yuh uster have better sense'n thet. Yuh gone soft in the head?"

Jasper spoke up hastily.

"To err is human—as you, my friends, have been so abundantly demonstrating. However, the reasoning that has so far guided your pursuit of the thief is, in my judgment, unimpeachable. By a happy coincidence, we now have the use of this very staunch craft, which can ride out river weather any mere canoe must shun. Were we to join forces, with a ship and crew so sturdy we might be certain of reaching Pittsburgh ahead of the quarry. What do you say?"

"Tom and Tim they think thet's a right good idee," said Hagar promptly.

"Then so soon as the worst of this present ice has cleared we will sail."

"Yuh won't have to wait past daylight. It's rainin' upriver."

"Do you mean that as a statement of fact—or a wish?"

"All I mean is thet it's rainin' up there. Mebbe yuh didn't see—jest afore dark—how the spots were showin' up on the ice floatin' past. If'n yuh didn't, ask Ish. He seen 'em."

Jasper, with a slight start, turned to peer through the darkness toward Ish, sitting with his back against the mast.

"Ah, Ish, to be sure. So many surprises must have scattered my wits. How extremely fortunate, Ish, that you, too, are one of us. Your presence rounds out our company. You will wait in Limestone for Abel, tell him where we have gone, and accompany him to Pittsburgh."

The dry rasp of Ish's reply came out of the darkness that shrouded him.

"Whereat's Abel?"

"You mean you didn't know?" exclaimed Jasper. "And have not troubled to ask? Small wonder that you may have concluded we are all quite demented. Abel is in the Shawnee country—attending to the ransom of Mrs. Baynton—a captive taken with the unfortunate Fortiner party."

By the sound Ish had pulled up his leather shirt and was

286

thoughtfully scratching himself. The result of his meditation was a casual announcement that seemed of no greater moment to him than his immediate preoccupation.

"Mebbe I better jest take me a look at how he's makin' out."

"Evidently you did not catch what I said. Abel's not merely skulking about on the Indian side of the river. He's deep in Shawnee country. As a matter of fact, he's there in the character of an ambassador—at one of their towns called Amaquah—negotiating with a chief called Chicatommo."

Ish let out a slight grunt that might almost have indicated pleasure as well as surprise. "Old Chic." He chuckled. "He's real mean—Old Chic is."

All instances of irrationality irritated Jasper.

"You have obviously had much experience with the savages. Enough surely to lead you to realize no purpose can be served by any attempt of yours to interfere. You may even disrupt Abel's mediation, which is of the most delicate nature. And you are almost certain to miss meeting him here. I know his plans well. Before I left Louisville I had a letter from him written from here on the very eve of his entering the Indian country. He went in from here and planned to come out again here. You will encounter him the sooner by awaiting him here. Moreover, he went in the custody of Anthony Gamelin, a French trader familiar for years with the Indians and one who has had many former dealings with Chicatommo. Gamelin would never have taken Abel if he had had the slighest doubt that it was safe."

Ish left off his scratching and pulled down his shirt.

"Mebbe so. But mebbe I better just smell around some."

"Nobody," said Hagar suddenly, "not Tony Gamelin nor nobody, kin ever be real sure about Injuns. Abel's hide counts fer more than Abel's money." She leaned forward into the light and stared down at the twins. "And you two will go along with Ish—if'n he'll take yuh."

With the sudden ease and grace of two great cats they were immediately on their feet, rifles in hand.

"Look at them," marveled Jasper. "Faces instantly as bright as though they had been invited to a carnival. And, if you could but see it, my face would be shining too. I permitted the worthy Gamelin to convince me that my many fears for Abel were to be ascribed to my ignorance of the ways of the savages. But you, my darling, are wise with the wisdom of the ages. How much better to be sure." He sprang up, his voice ringing with eagerness. "All, then, is decided. We will anchor off the north shore, at whatever point, Ish, you wish to disembark. We will await you there so that when Abel emerges from the wilds his first sight will be of the ship he imagined lost to him." His impatience grew. "If the ice is thinning as you say, perhaps we can cast off now."

"Best wait fer daylight," said Hagar.

She dropped to the deck and advanced into the light before her brothers. At sight of the black curls framing the serene face under the poke bonnet they stared and violently nudged one another. Jasper slid down and edged out into the light beside her.

"We heared back in Louisville yuh'd tuk up with him," said Tom.

"Ain't no skin off'n us," said Tim.

"Have yerself some turkey," said Hagar, sealing the reconciliation.

Relieved of one apprehension, Jasper leaped to the next. He joggled Hagar's arm.

"While all unfolds with so much promise, it more than ever behooves us to take no single unnecessary chance. You say wait for daylight, but have you forgotten? Barklit can be here before then."

"Todd'll do the fergettin'—oncet he takes him a look at who-all's here."

"How can you be certain he will come alone? He could be accompanied by a throng of townspeople."

Tom spoke up over his quarter of the turkey.

"Yuh don't need to fret none about Todd's gittin' here afore daylight. Jest at dark, when Tim and me was a-headin' fer the boat, we seen him nosin' along yer sledge tracks. We kotched him and tied him up."

Tim completed the accounting. "Less'n he wants to lay there and freeze, right now he's a-rollin' through the snow back to town. Thet'll take him 'til some past daylight."

For Abel the December blizzard reinstituted time as a conception with which lapse and passage and period might be connected. Autumn obviously had gone and winter had come. He had long since given up the attempt to count the days of his captivity. It had been different at first when Chicatommo had sat by the fire, contemplating him unblinkingly, sometimes for hours at a stretch. Then there had been the constant possibility that at any moment he might, as he continued to brood over the matter, come to the conclusion that he had been swindled. Then, too, with the old chief around, there had been a frequent coming and going of his lieutenants, a sense that the conduct of affairs was centered here, that decisions were in the course of being taken, any one of which might vitally affect a captive. But toward noon one day of the second week Chicatommo had, without seeming warning, risen from his place and stalked out the door. Oosak had lingered only long enough to tie Abel's wrists and splinted ankles to the corners of the bed before hurrying after him. Thereafter, though by the sounds all went as usual in the town outside, there had been nobody in the cabin except the two women. Onaya had watched him at night, Nacawah by day. No moment passed during which the implacable stare of one or the other was not fixed upon him. While prudently refraining from mistreatment which might leave marks upon him, they indulged themselves by putting filth in his food, keeping his bed water-soaked on cold nights, spending amused hours catching and transferring lice from their persons to his, and generally subjecting him to every sort of minor indignity suggested by his helplessness. His dislike of the women took on the proportions of a mania.

The blizzard, Abel surmised, foreshadowed Chicatommo's imminent return. Whatever the miserable project that accounted for his absence, whether attacking boats on the Ohio or outlying farms along the frontier, the weather would bring him back. Indian depredations always ceased when the first snowfall made tracking easy. And with his return the hour of reckoning would be at hand, for ample time had elasped for Gamelin's dispatch of Abel's letter on to Louisville and the delivery of the money, if it were ever to take place, either by way of Vincennes or the Miami to Amaquah. Abel had eaten but little of the messes the women had daily offered him. He now ceased to eat anything at all. The weaker he became, he decided, the less prolonged could be the processes of that reckoning.

The morning of the fourth day after the blizzard Onaya filled the larger of her two brass kettles with water, swung it over the fire, threw in nearly an armful of dried venison and dried pumpkin, and then dug even deeper into her store of winter food. This presage of the master's return was, toward noon, confirmed by a sudden stir in the town. Next, the blanket in the doorway was whisked aside and the old chief strode in to take his accustomed place by the fire. The gloomy cabin which for so long had known but the desolate presence of the two women was suddenly thronged. Chicatommo was followed in by Oosak, the two big Shawnee, and, at the end of the file, Pierre. The old trader remained standing by the door. Each of the Indians took one passing glance at Abel and paid him no further attention.

After an interval to indicate by how much he was outranked by the others present, Pierre was summoned to join the circle seated about the fire. The pipe was passed. The women moved in with bowls of the venison and pumpkin stew on the surface of which floated, as special delicacies to celebrate the chief's home-coming, the broiled carcasses of frogs and field mice. Chicatommo ate sparingly, while his younger companions gorged. The eating finally gave way to belching and, after another wait, Pierre's presence was revealed as an answer to the need for an interpreter. Without preamble or looking around from the fire he addressed Abel.

"Old Cheek have been at Lac Sainte Marie. He buy from Jeem Girtee ze guns wiz ze first five hundred dollar. Eet take much time. Jeem is ver' stingee. Old Cheek want many guns. Now he come back for the next five hundred dollar. When will eet come?"

"How would I know?" said Abel.

Pierre continued as though he had not heard. "I have ze word from Tonee in Vincennes. I cannot tell you before. Ze meeserable squaws nevair let me see you. Ze word ees zat ze seester of Tonee have die. Tonee have go to New Madrid. *Mais* he have leave his bosseman in Vincennes. When ze monee from Louisville come to Vincennes, he weel come here wiz eet *immediatement*. When weel eet come?"

Abel considered Pierre's news with a kind of detached interest. So long as Gamelin was in Vincennes, there had remained the possibility that, even after it had become apparent that no more funds were forthcoming, the worthy Frenchman might still hit upon some way to delay matters. Now even this faint chance was gone.

"There'll be no money," he said. "Tell Old Chic that and let's get it over with."

"No, I weel nevair tell heem zat," said Pierre. "Always eet ees bettair to live one day longer. Maybe Old Cheek wait. He have ze grand desire for more guns."

He spoke to Chicatommo in Shawnee at some length. The chief gave a curt gesture of dismissal. In the doorway Pierre turned for one more remark to Abel.

"I have hear from McKee too. Madame Bay ees on ze boat to Montreal."

The doorflap dropped behind Pierre. Abel turned his head until he could see Chicatommo. His retainers and the two women were more covertly watching him, waiting with varying degrees of interest and anticipation for him to indicate the nature of the next development. The old chief continued to stare straight before him while he pondered his decision. In the background the impatient women came to their own conclusion regarding the outcome. Nacawah went out and returned with a basket of pine splinters. Their dour faces brightened as they busied themselves with daubing each splinter with pitch. The first stage in burning a captive was a privilege usually reserved for the women and children. The insertion and ignition, one at a time, of such splinters was one of their more favored devices. Onaya's and Nacawah's splinters were very many and very small.

Abel shifted ever so slightly on his rawhide bed. It had probably been a mistake to starve himself. Otherwise when they untied him he might have put up a sudden fight with a chance of drawing upon himself some angry knife thrust or tomahawk swing. But he had let himself get too weak for any such effort. The silence in the cabin continued, except for an occasional snap of the fire. Oosak and the two Shawnee stared sedately at nothing, but the two women were almost leaning toward Chicatommo, watching him like hunting dogs waiting for their master's first sign the chase might commence.

Abel's mind drifted to Philippa on the deck of the lake schooner. Soon she would be in Montreal, then New York, then home among her own people. The gleam would return to her hair, the brightness to her eyes, the bloom to her skin. The memory of the shame of her captivity would fade. Presently she could again face living. He was so accustomed to the idea that his own life was over that the price he had paid did not seem a great one.

One livelier spark struck through the dusk of his weakness and apathy, for he had been closer to Jasper than ever to anyone except Ish. Jasper must be well again by now. Hagar would have seen to that. With luck they might one day even get hold of some of the money the twins had taken.

Chicatommo lifted his head. The women reached eagerly for their basket. From the chief's bloodless lips came a guttural command. Oosak and the two Shawnee stood up. For Abel the walls of the cabin seemed momentarily to dissolve. As though revealed by a flash of lightning, he caught a panoramic glimpse of his long river voyage. He saw the free, open sweep of river, and forest, and sky, felt the lift of *Naiad* under his feet and, for one instant, recalled what it had been like to know that no matter what was happening even more than that was always about to happen. The smoke-blackened walls of the cabin closed in about him again. The voyage that had seemed to lead on and on had led finally to this.

The two Shawnee bent over him, the stench of their oiled bodies for the moment stronger than the other smells in the cabin. They loosed his wrists and ankles and jerked him upright on the edge of the rawhide bed. Oosak stripped off the splints and moved aside so that Chicatommo could see how successfully the bones had set. Each limb was straight and smooth. Chicatommo grunted his approval. He had kept the letter of his word. His prisoner was still whole. He grunted another command. Oosak reached for a log of wood. The two Chawnee clutched Abel's shoulders. Oosak lifted a stick and broke each shinbone again. There swept upon Abel the realization that he was not, after all, about to die. Chicatommo, in the bitterness of his avarice, was still determined to imagine there might yet be more money. A groan of protest burst through Abel's clenched teeth. The Shawnee tightened their grip while Oosak set the bones. Abel's weakness seemed but to make the pain the sharper.

During the night it became perceptibly warmer and the next day there began a second and heavier snowfall. The inhabitants of Amaquah withdrew into their huts, staked down the doorflaps, and devoted themselves happily to making heedless inroads upon their diminishing food supply. Late winter invariably brought the time of starving and therefore, according to Indian reasoning, there was the more occasion to enjoy eating while they still had plenty to eat.

Onaya and Nacawah, balked of their immediate entertainment, reluctantly laid aside their basket of splinters. But they were partially mollified by Chicatommo's direction that the prisoner must not be allowed to waste away from lack of eating. Abel's refusal to open his mouth make the task of feeding him an increasingly diverting pastime for them. They held his nose, pried his teeth apart with a knife blade, kneaded his stomach, and choked spoonfuls of corn mush and venison scraps down his gasping gullet.

The next afternoon the sun returned and with it another cold wave. Abel could hear the shouts of the Indian children as they cleared snow from the ice on the stream to make room for skating. Suddenly the gay clamor dissolved into shrieks of terror. Every dog in town set up a frantic barking. The children scattered toward their homes, their screams trailing behind them. New adult shouts of astonishment and perturbation were mixed in the bedlam. And through it all came the thin wail of a song on the order of an Indian sorcerer's chant. The words were but gibberish intoned with an eerie rising and falling inflection that resembled neither Shawnee nor English and were being mouthed in an odd, gobbling way that might easily suggest these were not sounds intended for earthly ears. The singer kept on into the center of the town and, ramblingly, toward Chicatommo's house.

In the cabin the women cowered against the wall and looked beseechingly toward Chicatommo. According to their immediate interpretation of the cries of alarm and the weird singsong something entirely unnatural was occurring. Oosak, sitting by the fire, trembled and likewise looked to the gnarled old figure who in every crisis must bear the brunt of decision. The chief himself was not totally unaffected. Instinctively he lifted his pipe, making the ceremonial gesture in the four directions to summon the aid of those several supernatural powers, among the multitude infesting the universe, who were deemed more friendly to man. Then, recovering his scowling aplomb, he harshly commanded Onaya to draw aside the doorflap so that he could see out. Instead of obeying, she crept across the floor nearer to him. He snatched a stick from the fire and clapped the burning end against the patch of bare skin above her leggings. Moaning, she crept on across the floor to pull and hold open the doorflap, though she, afraid herself to look, buried her face in its folds.

Through the open doorway the people of Amaquah could be seen emerging, some shamefaced, the most still deeply agitated, from their houses to take a second look at the spectacle that had caused their initial fright. In the open space before Chicatommo's house Ish, his buckskins smeared with snow and festooned with bits of evergreen, his long, grizzled hair streaming in the wind, his wrinkled face completely without any sign of human intelligence, was wandering about in meandering circles, chirping that uncanny chant in his high-pitched, cracked voice. His knife and tomahawk were still in his belt, but he had no rifle and his empty hands were stretched out before him as though he were blind as well as witless.

Abel began to comprehend. By some extraordinary chance, due to his roaming so widely through the wilderness, Ish must have picked up some word of his captivity. This grotesque entry into the town was to further some special idea of his own. Few white men knew Indians as did Ish. Aside from having spent a lifetime hunting them, as he had elk and buffalo and bear, he had been friends with them at times during the years between the wars, had lived an occasional winter with Mingo and Cherokee, and, Job had always maintained, had once taken a Wyandot wife. He knew Indians well enough, at any rate, to risk this trading on their implicit belief in witchcraft and their peculiar awe of insanity.

Chicatommo's eyes, fixed on the circling intruder, narrowed with a suspicion that hardened swiftly into a sense of outrage. The more unexpected the situation, the more incumbent upon him to deal with it. His people were looking past Ish to see what he would do. He lifted his rifle into his lap, but for all his seasoned ferocity hesitated to use it. A single shot would settle the matter for him but enormously increase their alarm. He snapped a sharp command to Oosak. Oosak reluctantly obeyed insofar as going out in front of the cabin and venturing to beckon and call, placatingly, to Ish. For a time Ish took no notice. With the fascinated children peering between their legs the townspeople, still fearful but driven by curiosity, were edging nearer.

Ish's next circle brought him before Chicatommo's doorway. Abel raised his head. Ish's wandering, apparently sightless glance passed over him. Chicatommo gestured peremptorily to Oosak to bring the mad visitor in where, shut off from the view of the crowd, he could be dealt with in the privacy of the cabin. Oosak reached out diffidently to pluck at Ish's sleeve. At the touch Ish's singsong ended in a piercing scream and he fell to the ground in convulsions. Abel had twice seen Ish have one of his fits. Each time the seizure had consisted of no more than a few squints and grimaces and had had no noticeable effect other than to leave Ish looking sleepy. But this one was a far more portentous performance, with Ish flopping about like a fish out of water, his eyes rolling, his lips foaming, his breath whistling, which ended, after a final unearthly screech, in his becoming as rigid as a man of stone. Oosak leaped away. The townspeople, howling in dismay, fled to their houses.

Abel looked at Chicatommo. It was as easy to follow the course of his thinking as though he were pantomiming it in the clearest sign language. He was not shaken by the superstitious dread that had scattered his followers. His shaking was with rage. His hand groped for the handle of his tomahawk. His strongest impulse was to split the skull of the witless wanderer whose arrival had so disorganized the community. But discretion overcame his fury. The others, like most Indians, were persuaded that the spirits of the insane invariably returned to haunt the scene of their death. Were the stranger to die here, most of them would likely abandon the town, preferring winter camps in the forest to a place under so threatening a curse. The old chief coped with his problem with the cunning with which he had coped with so many others. He sent for Pierre. Oosak, with a gasp of relief, rushed off to summon the trader.

Pierre came. Chicatommo gestured his desire that the stranger whether dead, sick, asleep, or bewitched, be taken off into the woods and left at least a day's journey from the town. Pierre was none too pleased with his assignment but was compelled to acquiesce by the insistence in Chicatommo's

294

scowl. He brought his horse but was unable, unaided, to lift Ish's stiffened body into the pack saddle. The two women and Oosak were for once more afraid of something else than they were afraid of Chicatommo. The old chief was obliged to come out himself to assist in arranging the pack horse's load. Pierre trudged morosely off into the forest. The townspeople peered from their doorways. The shadows of night were gathering.

Abel lay back and considered the remarkable change in his situation. There had been shrewd and definite purpose in Ish's simple-minded stumbling into the Indian town. That purpose he had achieved. He had located Abel's exact position. He had probably not foreseen being packed off by Pierre, but he would shake off the old trader at a moment of his choice. Sometime during the night he would come back into the town. Precisely what he might then have in mind no other mind could possibly guess. To carry off from Chicatommo's house in the middle of his own town a captive who could not walk would seem to pose a problem to confound even Ish's peculiar approach to problems.

The town was as silent as though it were long after midnight instead of that noisily sociable evening hour when neighbors exchanged visits, suitors sang their pleas, and old men told their stories. There had been one brief commotion as people caught their dogs and tied them up inside their houses. All had a livid picture of the madman's spirit returning in the darkness, and no one wanted a yipping dog before the door attracting ghostly attention to his particular domicile. After that one burst of activity the town had fallen into an uneasy quiet. In the far distance a wolf pack howled and then even the forest became silent.

Oosak appeared in Chicatommo's doorway and, as a reprimand for his pusillanimity of the afternoon, was contemptuously sent away. Onaya and Nacawah huddled on the ground behind Chicatommo, edging as close to him as they dared. Their eyes were wide and staring. Constantly they listened. The faintest whisper of the night wind along the roof set them to shivering. Chicatommo rose, kicked them out of his way, and got into his bed. Further to show his scorn of the women's foolishness, he pulled the blanket to his chin and appeared at once to fall asleep. Onaya crawled, an inch at a time, to the doorway and fastened the lower edge of the doorflap more securely to its corner stakes.

Abel tugged, uselessly, at the rawhide thongs and waited. Ish might return early in order to gain the advantage of more hours of darkness, or he might come late when he could expect more people might have fallen asleep. Suddenly Abel could tell by the women's breathing that they conceived that they had heard something. In the adjoining house a child whimpered once. In the next house a dog got out half a bark. The effort ended in a gurgle as someone in the house throttled him. There were no other sounds. But the women were clutching each other and staring at the doorflap. It bellied inward slightly as though something no more tangible than a puff of wind were pressing gently against it. With low moans of anguish the two women groveled forward on the ground, burying their faces in their arms.

Chicatommo rolled from his bed, tomahawk in hand, and went to the door to listen. From without, so near that the burst of sound seemed to shake the blanket, there came the harsh, shrieking call that a raven makes when diving through the air. It was the dread cry of the Raven-Mocker, the wizard of Indian superstitition whose visit to a house means someone in it is about to die. The women groaned. With a growl of rage Chicatommo tore aside the doorflap. The blow that felled him came so immediately that it seemed a part of his own rash gesture. He staggered backward into the fire, his head split to the ears. Ish sprang in to stand astride the women who were pressing their faces the more convulsively into the ground. His bloody hatchet descended again and then once again. Abel, observing the triple execution, felt no more compunction than did Ish in perpetrating it. Born on the frontier, he felt there was nothing to distinguish the killing of Indian animals from the killing of other animals.

Ish's knife blade sliced across Abel's bonds. His one passing glance of the afternoon must not have missed the splints on Abel's legs, for the discovery that Abel could not walk brought from him no faintest grunt of surprise or dismay. He crouched, drew Abel's arms over his shoulders, and started out with him pickaback.

The town was still as silent as though by now every Indian in it was holding his breath. In the boldest warrior who might have peered out from the refuge of his house any impulse to interfere was suppressed by his glimpse of the shadowed figure of the Raven-Mocker setting out from the chief's house with his shadowy burden.

Ish trotted to the stream and turned down its bed, taking advantage of the thinner wind-blown snow on the ice. But even here there were thigh-deep drifts at intervals and at best his progress away from Amaquah was a slow, hard struggle. A mile down the stream he turned off into the deeper snow of the forest. After floundering another hundred yards he came upon the tracks he had made that afternoon when approaching the town. Here he set Abel in a snowbank and straightened his back.

"Come daylight," said Abel, "they'll go to looking around. Indians can think good enough once they go to thinking. They'll figger out spirits don't leave tracks and with all this snow you have to wallow through they'll be up with us in an hour."

Ish pulled up a drooping hemlock bough. Under the bough was the end of a hollow log. From the log he drew his rifle and a pair of snowshoes. The rifle he handed to Abel. The snowshoes he began to tie on.

"Come daylight," he said, "we'll be forty mile from here."

"You're crazier'n you made them think you are," said Abel, "if you think you can pack me ten miles by noon tomorrow."

Ish bent over, backed into Abel, grasped his thighs, and set off again. There was never any use trying to carry on an argument with him. He just stopped answering. A man might as well argue with himself. The snowshoes were a considerable help, but the snow was soft and powdery and with so heavy a load they still sank into it. With each step Ish had to lift his foot before sliding it forward. It made walking twice the trouble. He was tough and had done a lot of hard traveling in his day, but he was no longer young. With going as bad as this, he would do well to stand it for seven or eight miles. If he kept on at as fast a pace as he had kept to this far, he might not make five. Already he was panting. Long before noon tomorrow and more likely some time before daylight they would be looking around for a place to stand off the Shawnee with their one rifle.

Ish's second stop was beside a snow-covered log beyond which was a cedar thicket. He slid Abel to a seat on the log. The cedar thicket began to shake and two enormous shadows emerged from it. It was too dark to make out their faces, but two such gigantic and identical outlines could only belong to the Crohon twins. Abel began to feel lightheaded. To look out through Chicatommo's doorway and see Ish doing a cakewalk through the middle of Amaquah had been unbelievable enough. But now to find this pair waiting for him here in the night in the middle of the Ohio wilderness was altogether beyond the borders of reason.

"So yuh got him right off?" said Tim. He sounded disappointed.

"We was jest aimin' to push on in and have us a look at how yuh was a-makin' out," said Tom.

"Where'd you two come from?" demanded Abel weakly.

"Hagar and Jasper they sent us," explained Tim.

Ish saw this as no occasion for idle talk.

"His legs is broke," he said. "We have to pack him."

Tom handed his rifle to Tim and, bending, pulled Abel up on his back. Ish, now free of his burden, started off at once with the swift, lunging stride of the experienced snowshoer. Tim, carrying the rifles, came next. Tom, with the trail broken for him, kept at his heels. Every mile or so the twins swung Abel from one broad back to the other. Ish, noting how well all was going, stepped up his pace. The alternating burden-bearers kept up with apparent ease. As they plunged on, Abel's dangling legs were snagged and buffeted by outthrust low branches. At first the pain in his recently set shinbones was like bands of fire, then the fire spread to his knees and his thighs and finally became an agony that he was certain he could not bear if he were to be whipped by one more branch.

When he came to the sun was glaring in his eyes. His dangling legs were still catching in the underbrush, but they were numb and might as well have belonged to somebody else. Ish was still lunging on ahead. Tom was carrying him. From behind Tim gave a low whistle. Tom stopped and Abel was swung over to Tim's back. Both were breathing hard but when they saw his eyes were open they grinned at him cheerfully. They were too tireless to be human. The sun was two hours up. If they had kept up this pace all night they had made Ish's forty miles and more. Their Shawnee trackers, running over the snow without any extra weight to bear them down, had a real job on their hands. Abel, who had had nothing at all to do, was so worn out that he could not hold up his head. His chin kept bobbing against Tim's shoulder. It was like bumping against a rock. You could look a long time without ever finding one other man, let alone two, able to pack so heavy a load through deep snow for twelve hours on end and be still grinning at the end of it. Just like nobody in the world but Ish could have walked off with him out of the middle of a Shawnee town. It was surely luck that Ish had happened to run across the Crohon boys or Jasper had come across Ish or however it had happened that the whole pack of them had got their heads together. But even with all that luck and this forty-mile run piled on top of it, there still was not enough to save it all from going to waste. They could make maybe fifty or sixty miles, which was twice what anybody else could, but they could not keep going through snow like this all the hundred and twenty or thirty miles to the Ohio. Sooner or later they would have to stop and the Indians would catch up with them.

Then he saw that Ish had already stopped. He was on the bank of a flowing stream. It must be Mad River, for the current was fast enough to keep it free of ice. And Ish was digging a canoe out of a snowdrift. They had got away after all.

Sheriff Garret got out the letter from Baltimore and read it again. It was the third letter he had received from Fortiner's people. This one informed him that a cousin of Heber Fortiner's, residing in Alexandria, had received by the last packet from New Orleans a letter from his wife's brother in Louisville mentioning in passing that last spring a keelboat named *Naiad* had taken on a cargo of tobacco there. A man named Abel Traner was understood to be the owner. This report was being passed on to the Pittsburgh sheriff on the chance that it might assist the inquiries it was the writer's fervent hope were being pressed. The sheriff looked up from the letter and out the window at the keelboat tied up at the foot of Chancery Street. The morning's sighting of the keelboat beating her way upriver had stirred considerable interest in Pittsburgh, particularly among the boatmen along the waterfront. No other craft had managed to get up the Ohio since the unusual winter storms had set in four weeks before. He folded the letter and put it back in his pocket.

His deputy, Omar Hicks, was coming up the street from the landing, walking as fast as his dignity permitted. He came in, sat on the bench against the wall, clasped his knee in his hands to show how unexcited he was, and made his report.

"She's named the *Naiad*. Just like Pete Mole said. I seen the name right on her bow. Nobody's tried to paint it out. And Abel Traner's on her. I seen him too. I kept far enough off so's I wouldn't have to speak to Abel. Figgered I better talk to you first. They was four more people on the boat when she first got in. They come ashore near an hour ago. That's what took me so long—gettin' me a look at them. Soon's they hit the dock they went different ways. They're all a-nosin' around town like they might be lookin' for somebody. Two o' them you can hardly tell apart—a pair o' backwoodsy young sprouts but real big and handy-lookin'. The third is a gal. She's big, too—a fine, strappin' wench, except for a scar on one side of her face. The fourth is the same tall talker from the East who done Barny out of two weeks' keep at his tavern last winter."

The sheriff listened attentively, put on his hat, and set out for the waterfront. Omar, keeping at his elbow, enlarged upon his observations. At the landing the sheriff paused and looked at him.

"Maybe you better sidle around town and see what them other four are up to by now," he suggested.

"You're the boss," said Omar, crestfallen that he was not to be privileged to witness the imminent demonstration of authority on the deck of the keelboat.

"Don't do no extra talking to nobody," counseled the sheriff gently. "Just drift around like and keep your eyes open."

Omar moved off, his feet dragging. The sheriff mounted the gangplank with astep as unhurried. On deck he came upon Ish rolled up in his blanket asleep against one rail and Abel seated in a chair with his splinted legs stretched out and his crutches propped against another.

"Hello, Abel," said the sheriff.

"Hello, Mr. Garret," said Abel.

The sheriff looked about him with appraising interest at the mast, the rigging, and the array of worn boat poles and sweep oars. "You must have had yourself quite a time getting up-river."

"Not too bad. The water was real high and most the time there was plenty of wind so we could sail a good bit. Have a chair."

Abel moved his crutches out of the way. The sheriff politely took no notice either of them or of the splints on Abel's legs. There was still plenty of wind. He moved the chair around so that he could sit with his back to it. He had the air of a man who had come aboard merely to pay a social call on an old acquaintance.

"I mind me the January of seventeen-eighty. I was coming up from Wheeling with a bargeload of buffalo jerky. Folks was right hungry in Pitt that winter and I figgered on getting me a real good price for it. Well, it turned cold so quick and froze so hard that barge was froze in right out in the river before we could pole her to shore. It was too cold to hunt and the ice was too thick to cut a hole through so's we could fish, and we had to eat up that jerky to stay alive. When the ice did start to go out, the cake we was froze in the middle of was near a quarter of a mile across. We was carried all the way down to the falls at Louisville before enough of it melted so's we could get the barge pried loose. The climate's changing, for a fact. We don't have winters like that no more."

"People in Pitt were hungry that winter, all right," agreed Abel. "That was the year the schoolmaster came down to stay with us."

Jasper came running up the gangplank and to an abrupt halt at the head of it.

"Hear anything?" asked Abel.

"Not as yet. But it occurred to me to return when I heard you were being honored by a visit from the sheriff."

"This is my friend, Jasper Hedges," said Abel.

The sheriff twisted in his chair to survey Jasper. Jasper walked over and stood behind Abel's chair. His presence seemed slightly to dampen the sheriff's sociability. He reached into his pocket.

"Long's I'm here I might's well ask you about this—same's I have been everybody else that's come up the river. I have a letter here asking about Fortiner's boat—the one you built. Where you been—did you happen to see anything of her?"

"Some. This is her."

The sheriff digested this statement.

"What you figger on doing with her?"

"Whatever I like. She's mine."

The sheriff seemed relieved that they had so soon got to the nub of the matter. He put the letter back in his pocket.

"You don't have to tell me, but I have to ask. Where'd you get her?"

"From Fortiner first. Then I sold her to a man named Neave. Then I bought her from him again."

"He's got the bill of sale," said Jasper.

The sheriff ignored Jasper. "Was that at Louisville?"

"No, at Limestone. After I got back from New Orleans."

The sheriff rubbed his jaw reflectively. "Sounds like you done quite a piece of traveling. Running up and down the river so much—did you ever hear any more about Fortiner —I mean, after you got the boat from him?"

"Yes, I did. He drowned."

"Where'd you hear that?"

"In New Orleans—from his boatmen, Fred Burd and Ben Taafe. If you haven't heard about it yet maybe I better tell you."

"Maybe you better had."

"The whole party that left here in the keelboat was in a skiff. Fortiner had whipped Spencer, one of his niggers, and Spencer saw a chance to sink the skiff. They all got ashore except Fortiner. Shawnee—Od Chick's pack—grabbed them on the bank. Spencer took up with them, they axed Baynton and Buck, the other nigger, and took Fred and Ben and Mrs. Baynton captive. A Vincennes trader, Anthony Gamelin, bought Fred and Ben to work on one of his boats. That's the story they told me, when I saw them in New Orleans."

"It's quite a story," said the sheriff.

"The two boatmen are undoubtedly known in Pittsburgh," put in Jasper, "and will return in time. They will vouch for it."

The sheriff looked at Jasper and then back at Abel.

"If Fortiner made over the keelboat to you, he must have done it before he took off in the skiff."

301

"He did. The keelboat was stuck on a mudbank just across from the mouth of the Scioto. It was night and there were Shawnee in the woods on the shore. That's why he took to the skiff. He made the keelboat over to me if Jasper and me would stay and keep the Indians thinking everybody was still aboard while the skiff was making off. It looked like a good chance to me because the river was rising and I figgered it might keep coming up. It did and floated us off before morning. We kept on downriver."

The sheriff tipped back in his chair and considered these several technical circumstances.

"So that's all there was to it?"

"Yes. That's all there was to it."

"By no means," said Jasper. "There's much more to the story. When Abel eventually heard Mrs. Baynton was a captive, he went in person into the Indian country and gave himself up to get her off. That was when his legs were broken—twice. He'd have been burned if Ish hadn't come along just in time to snatch him away."

The sheriff peered around at the sleeping Ish. "That Ish, he surely does get around."

"You persist in missing the point," said Jasper. "Mrs. Baynton is on her way back to this country. More than possibly she is already at home by now. She, too, can vouch for Abel's story."

The forelegs of the sheriff's chair descended to the deck. He looked at Jasper in wild wonderment.

"Beats me how you Easterners can all the time keep getting yourselves so mixed up. When you can tell a man's telling you the way something happened, what's the good of wanting somebody else to tell you the same thing?" The sheriff fished the letter out of his pocket again. "I've got maybe a mite more to tack on to the story myself. Fortiner's folks back in Maryland, they're offering a reward for certain word of what happened to him. Looks to me, Abel, like you've won it."

"I don't want it," said Abel.

"It's quite a piece of money."

"No," said Abel.

The sheriff sighed resignedly. "Puts me in kind of a bind. They say for me to whack up this money between me and whoever brung me reasonable proof. No way I can take my share except after I've found somebody to hand the other half over to."

"Hand it to Jasper. He knows as much as I do about what happened."

302

"An excellent solution," said Jasper.

The sheriff rose. "Then that's settled. If old Ish there ever wakes up, tell him for me he's getting too old to go rampsing around the way he does. Be seeing you, Abel. And—Mr. Hedges, if you'll come over to my place—at your convenience—we'll have in a notary and take your deposition."

Abel watched the sheriff go down the gangplank, and turned to look at Jasper.

"Find yourselves a place to stay while you're laying for old Sol?"

Jasper's pleasure over the outcome of the interview with the sheriff was immediately clouded. "Not as yet."

"What I'm getting at is—this north wind is picking up right along. Ish and me could get us upriver to Traner's Station before dark if we got any sort of a start—while if we fool around we might not make it for another two months. The river can freeze up tonight."

Jasper panted with sudden anger. "Fantastic," he declared.

"What is?"

"Your stupidity. From the most painful experiences you have learned nothing. Less than nothing. Last year at this time you showed far more intelligence. What fancied call of duty summons you now? Then—at Limestone and at Louisville—you did not stammer and blush even when duty to your country was cited."

"Maybe I haven't learned much," said Abel wryly, "but I surely paid for the lessons."

"Was it then some obscure sense of guilt that impelled you to cast your wealth to the winds? Can that also account for your now rushing back to replace your neck under the yoke from which you once escaped? If this is not true, then what does draw you back?"

"Nothing. But there's nothing to keep me away either."

"Ridiculous," said Jasper.

"Not so ridiculous as to get within four hours of the place I was born and then to back off like I was scared to show my face among my own folks. If you're bound to argue, that's no way to prove I'm my own man. And I'll leave the boat here so that you and the Crohons can stay on her. Ish and I can go by canoe."

Jasper's anger grew upon him.

"If sail you must, sail in your own ship. We will never deprive you of her."

"Suit yourself. Anyway, you don't have to worry too much about finding you a roof. Hagar and the boys can run you up a half-faced camp in no time. Only best get them at it. Could

303

be we could have us some real winter by dark. If the river don't freeze right off you can start looking for me back here day after tomorrow."

Jasper began to shout. "Do you imagine that only you are capable of forming plans? Hagar and her brothers are at this moment engaging horses. We, too, are aware of the weather. We are anxious to be off while the road over the mountains is still open."

Forgetting his legs, Abel started up from his chair and fell back into it.

"Now you're coming up with something that is really ridiculous. They've got no more real chance to get back that money than I have of sailing this boat over Laurel Mountain. And if they're keeping at it mainly because they think they owe me something—that's still more ridiculous. After the way those boys packed me through the snow, they don't owe me anything. It's the other way around."

"That may be your view." Jasper was continuing to shout. "But there chance to be other views than yours in this world. Theirs, for example. They are proud. They are determined. They will never give up. Not until they have turned every stone in Berks County."

"I don't know the old mossback that robbed 'em, but I'd guess he'd be no more apt to go back to wherever he came from than Ish there might be. If you've had this up your sleeve all along, why didn't you say something about it before?"

"Because we could not be sure before. Not until we had tried Wheeling and here. It is only now that we have been forced to realize that he may have come East overland by way of the Wilderness Road and the Valley of Virginia."

"Or headed for Mexico or Cuba or Canada or Timbuktu. Well, if that's that—then that's that. So get going so that you can get back here good and early in the spring. It's the boats that are ready to shove off early that always get the best cracks at the best-paying cargoes."

For all the icy wind perspiration stood out on Jasper's forehead.

"We're not," he stammered, his voice suddenly weak, "we're not coming back."

Abel stared. "For God's sakes. What's got into you?"

Jasper walked away to the rail, blew his nose, and walked slowly back. His face was red and he was looking at everything in sight except at Abel.

"That I cannot sufficiently describe. But it is what has gotten into Hagar that matters. She is convinced that the one

304

hope for her brothers is to keep them away from the frontier."

"So she won't marry you unless you live in the East?"

"Precisely."

Abel began to laugh.

"You may well laugh," said Jasper. "You are recalling by how far my past has missed preparing me for the responsibilities of a domestic establishment. You are thinking that I was not intended by nature to sit soberly every night by the same fireside. And you are perhaps unable to imagine me in the sedate and fatherly curb upon the wayward inclinations of two such as Tom and Tim. But my condition is yet more abject than you can conceive. To persuade her to marry me I would serve longer than did Jacob for Rachel, I would swim the Hellespont, I would tilt at any dragon. I would even strive to become a moral influence."

"I ain't laughing much," said Abel. "But I ain't crying at all. You ain't coming out so bad. Soon's you get yourself settled somewhere, be sure you let me know where you're at. Before I start back downriver I surely want to come take me a look."

The north wind howled around the corners of the blockhouse. Esther leaned from her bed, groped under it, and drew the other buffalo robe up over her. All afternoon it had kept getting colder and just before dark the first flecks of snow had started to fly. By now the blowing snow sounded less like snow than pellets of ice. They were hitting the window like buckshot. From the kitchen came an even more uncommon sound. Job whistled. Only once before had it ever got so cold that he had let his dogs come in at night. Their claws scratching eagerly, all five came bounding up the stairway, wormed their way through their blanketed doorway, and fell to snuffling happily about Job's bed.

"Git down," yelled Job. "Git down, yuh goddam doughheads. Lay down and be quiet."

The dogs, sighing, composed themselves on the floor. Esther snuggled deeper under her buffalo robes. Two of the dogs were already snoring. The flames of the fire Judah had built up the last thing before he had gone to bed sent flickering gleams dancing across the elkskin door-hanging. The sounds that came from beyond it were so distinct that it seemed almost as if she could see through it. Three of the dogs were snoring now. The oldest, Pete, had pre-empted his place nearest the fire and was busy biting at fleas. Then, suddenly, the biting and the snoring stopped. Old Pete began to whine. Joe grunted angrily. One of the younger dogs barked and the next second all were barking. Job bellowed with rage and laid about him with his staff as far as he could reach from his bed. But for once they paid no slightest heed either to his commands or his threats. One after the other they plunged out through their doorway, on down the stairs, and gathered on the ferry landing, barking more furiously than ever. Someone or something out on the river had excited them beyond endurance. Job held his swearing and listened. Every slightest whimper from the dogs meant as much to him as though they were talking to him. He began to beat on the floor with his staff and to yell for Judah.

Judah came running up the stairs. He bundled Job into his cart and held the kitchen door open while Job drove himself out on the balcony. Esther sat up in bed to listen. The dogs broke off their frenzied barking.

"Ish," bellowed Job. "Be thet you, Ish?"

The reply from out in the river came indistinctly to Esther inside the log walls of the blockhouse. But the dogs' feeling for Ish was second only to their regard for Job. Their uproar had been excited, not threatening. The possibility that Ish might have returned filled her with consternation. She sprang from the bed and began frantically to dress.

"Judah," roared Job. "Git over to the mill and git Silas over here—and every man along with him—and every team in the barn. Abbie, you fat tub o' lard, roll out o' thet nest o' your'n and git up here. I want every bucket and kettle yuh got and I want 'em full o' water."

As she dressed, Esther could see through the frosted window the glimmer of lanterns as men ran from the mill. Job was yelling from the far corner of his balcony. This time the response was clearer. It was Ish. He had got back. Esther was running out, fumbling at the last button of her dress, when, both shouldering aside the elkskin hanging, she collided with Abbie, laden with empty buckets.

"Git up on thet stool," wheezed Abbie. "Yer paw wants more water."

Esther stood on the stool and ladled water from the fire keg on the shelf. Abbie started out with the first two filled buckets.

"Fill them other two," said Abbie. "And then git the big kettle and fill it."

Job's cart was darting back and forth along the balcony outside, while he shouted a torrent of meaningless commands, which Silas on the ground below was echoing as he directed his crew. Judah came running in to carry out the kettle and then Abbie was back with her buckets. Judah returned and swung the keg, now half empty, to his shoulder. Esther followed him out.

Night and the blizzard had shut out all of the outer world except for the one narrow lantern-lit area beside the block-house stretching down to a glimpse of the dark water at the river's edge. Men and horses were swarming like ants out of a disturbed anthill over and around the shipway on which the keelboat had been built. The snow had already been shoveled off it and now the meaning of Job's demand for water became apparent to her. The water had been dashed over the timbers of the cradle and the slide where it had instantly frozen into a hard sheathing. That glittering, ice-smooth runway stretched down to the river and under the slowly rising prow of the keelboat. She remembered the day of the launching when she had watched the boat slide slowly backward into the river. It was as though time had stood still. Again the keelboat was half in, half out of the water. The same men held the same ropes stretched taut against the weight of the same boat, only now the craft was being drawn up instead of being let down. The dripping prow was inching nearer along the iced timbers, each second more of the curve of the hull was emerging from the darkness into the gleam of the lanterns.

Esther ran to her father. The unreasoning fear that had been with her since the first dog had barked tightened into a sharp, hard knot of certainty when she saw his face. There was the same set to his mouth, the same gleam in his eyes, as when he had raised the new rifle to take a sight at the dog, only now it was as though he were looking along the barrel at a whole herd of buffalo. He had been possessed by no such elation since the day he had set out with his dogs to run down Ish's Indian. Again something to be hunted was in view, and again he was about to close in upon his prey. She gripped his shoulder.

"What you pulling that boat up here for?" she demanded. "Will you tell me that?"

He grinned up at her, shamelessly pleased with himself.

"Ain't yuh got eyes to see with? Or skin to feel how cold it's turned? Was we to leave her out in the river tonight, she'd be froze in and a goner by mornin'. Wouldn't want to see a boat as good as her crack up like an eggshell, would yuh?"

She caught sight of Ish. He was still on the keelboat and had come out of the cabin to peer over the rail through the driving snow. Those of Silas' men not pulling along with the horses had set their shoulders against the hull to rock it back and forth to keep it from binding against the iced timbers. Already the boat was within a few feet of completing the return to the cradle in which she had been born. Esther ran down the stairway. Alongside the hull she could not see over the rail and Ish was no longer in sight.

"Whoa," yelled Silas. "That's done it, boys."

Men and horses eased on the ropes. *Naiad's* journey had ended where it had started. Esther clutched Silas' arm.

"Where's Ish?"

"In the cabin a-holdin' Abel from rollin' out o' bed."

"Abel's in there?"

"That's whut Ish says. I ain't seen him myself."

A thread of wood smoke was blowing out flat from the chimney in the cabin roof. She remembered the little iron stove—the day she had watched from her window while Abel hammered it into shape—the night she had stood in the doorway, the buffalo robe in her arms, and caught sight of Abel's startled face in the glow from the grate. Silas was suddenly remembering something too. He turned to spit downwind and turned back to lift his lantern higher so that he could look into her face. She gave him a hard push toward the keelboat.

"Go tell him to get up out of bed. No matter if he's sick—or what's wrong with him. Tell him to get home—as fast as he can."

Silas chuckled. His crew's success in rising so well to the sudden, extraordinary demand in the night had left him in high spirits.

"He can't, 'cause he can't walk—even with his crutches."

"Crutches! What's happened to him?"

"His legs is busted. And accordin' to Ish, on top o' thet he set so still hangin' to the tiller all afternoon, his feet, they's frostbitten."

She saw Ish then. He was crossing the plank that someone had already placed between the rail of the keelboat and the middle of the stairway. He had a pair of crutches under his arm and he was heading for her father on the balcony. She ran up the stairs after him, but she did not follow him to the cart. She no longer wanted to talk to him. After knowing Ish so long and so well, she would never have dreamed, if she were not seeing it with her own eyes, that he, of all people, would betray Abel. He was sticking the crutches in the cart back of Job's chair.

She ran on into the kitchen. Both of her father's rifles were leaning against the wall at the head of his bed. She snatched them up and hid them under the mattress in her room. Then she remembered his horse pistol. She ran back into the kitchen and got it down from its hook over the fireplace. She was just turning when the door bumped open and her father's cart burst in. She tried to hide the pistol behind her, but he had seen it in her hand. He grinned. Like Silas, and with more reason, he was mightily pleased with himself. Things had come out better for him than he could ever have expected.

"I ain't going to let you shoot him, Paw," she said.

He went on grinning. "I ain't never shot a man yet in his bed."

Job backed his cart into the doorway and yelled down the stairs.

"Abbie, git yerself a pan o' snow and git in there and help Ish rub his feet."

Esther pushed past the cart and ran down the stairs and along the path past the mill. The wind was so strong and the blizzard so thick that for a while she was afraid she might not be able to find the Traner house. She turned back and began counting the standing palisade poles and working her way from one to the next. The Traners were hard sleepers and slow to waken, but when at last they realized who was beating on the door they were all up at once.

"Abel's back," she told him. "He's hurt. You'd best get over there and look after him."

She was indifferent to their excitement. They could have been made no more hysterical by an announcement of the Angel Gabriel's appearance. They had been lost when he went away and now, like children, they had been found again. She stumbled back through the storm, up to her room, and got into her bed. There was no hope of sleeping and seemed none of ever getting warm again. She huddled, shivering, under the buffalo robes and dreaded the coming of daylight.

But daylight came, inexorably. The wind was letting up, but there was no let up in the continuous gabble of the Traners crowded into the cabin below her window. It was scarcely more than full light when there came a scratching at the elkskin hanging. Selina sidled in and sat down on the edge of the bed. For once her face was bright and for once she hugged the shawl-swathed baby against her as though she was glad she had it in her arms.

"Somethin' I had to tell yuh right off," she whispered. "It's all right now if yuh let yer paw buy Traner Mountain. With Abel back to take hold, it don't matter none to me whether we make off fer Kentucky tomorrer."

"Is that what he's going to do—take all of you to Kentucky?"

"It stands to reason. He won't want to stay here long's he don't git along with you and your paw no better'n he does."

309

Selina rose and edged toward the door, her eyes feverish with the excitement of the night's events. " 'Course, we can't take off nohow 'til the weather breaks." She turned in the doorway for one final item. "He's bin to Wheeling and Limestone and Louisville and all the way to New Orleans."

"What brought him back?"

"All he said was he happened to be comin' this way."

Selina dropped the curtain. Esther braided her hair, wound the braids into a crown on her head, and drew on the green dress. Each successive movement was slow, methodical, deliberate. She went into the kitchen, stepped over the dogs, and sat down at the table across from her father. Abbie, bent over the fire, looked around but after one brooding glance turned back to her skillet. Job, whose appetite since his fall had been undependable, this morning was eating with gusto.

"I've made up my mind, Paw," said Esther, "that there ain't no real good reason I shouldn't marry Basil."

Job continued mopping up the gravey on his plate.

"When?"

"Whenever you say. And once you tell him, then he'll stay on here. That's what you want, ain't it?"

"And once folks hear about it the Traners, they won't have so much to snicker about. Thet's whut you want, ain't it?"

"What difference do they make? They're taking off for Kentucky."

"Yuh figgerin' on marryin' up with Basil before they get away?"

"If you say so. Only you'll have to build us a house first. There's no room for us in this one."

Job reached down to wipe his hands on the nearest dog.

"Only trouble with marryin' up with Basil is ketchin' up with him to tell him about it."

"Why? What have you done now? Where is he?"

"Ought to be about halfway to Pittsburgh by now, if'n he ain't got off the road in the blizzard."

"You do some terrible things, Paw—but mostly they make some sense. What made you run him off in the middle of the night? Couldn't you wait 'til morning?"

"I don't want no runaway redemptioners hangin' around my place. When I told him thet he started in runnin' right thet same minute."

"So you knew that's what he was—all the time."

"Same's yuh did. Only yuh was savin' it to bring up jest afore the weddin'."

Esther's eyes were burning in her pale face.

"While you kept him around and even let him think he could have me—because you had use for him. But then last night all of a sudden you had more use for something else. You had to make sure of nothing standing between you and Abel."

"Abel," Job snorted. "Everything begins and ends with Abel—fer you."

"That was it, wasn't it, Paw?"

Job looked around from the dogs and for the first time directly at her.

"Nothin' nor nobody kin stand between me and Abel. Nobody but you."

Esther rose and leaned across the table toward him. The dogs were climbing over him, endeavoring to lick his hands and face. He pushed them away and grinned up at her placatingly as might an indulgent husband at a scolding wife.

"Set down. It's harder to keep yuh put then these here dogs."

She was trembling but her voice was not.

"Is there nobody wearing pants you're not ready to shove me at? It's a wonder it ain't been Silas or Judah, while you're at it. Abel Traner lamed you and, like you said, made the most fool of me a man can make of a woman. But he can work iron. Is that what it's come around to?"

"Yer always bound to twist things up no matter be they straight's a string. Nothin's come around to nothin' it ain't always bin. Oncet yuh wanted him. Mebbe yuh don't want him no more. Either way, all yuh got to do is walk across thet plank and tell him."

"I'd sooner see you go ahead and shoot him. Or set your dogs on him—if that's the chance you're itching for."

Job's glance went past her to Abbie.

"Wut's thet yuh got there?"

Abbie had a tray in her hands. On it was a covered dish, a slab of hot cornbread on which a lump of butter was melting, and a mug of coffee.

"Seliny she done packed all the Traners off home," explained Abbie. "She said Abel needed some rest. But none o' thet no-'count lot never done nothin' 'bout feedin' him. A man so worn down as him needs rest—fer sure—but he needs somethin' to eat, too."

Job looked back at Esther.

"Yer maw was a mite mean, some o' the time. But there wasn't no time thet she was ever skeered—not o' nothin' nor nobody."

Esther met the challenge in his fierce, hard little eyes. Her chin came up and she ceased to tremble. Turning, she took the tray from Abbie and started out.

In the cabin Ish got up, put more wood in the stove, lay

down on the floor again, and went back to sleep. Abel, lying in the bunk, wriggled his toes. The way they were beginning to burn, there was not much chance of his losing them. He could thank Abbie for that. And Job himself had saved the keelboat.

From where he lay on the bunk he could see the nearer wall of the blockhouse, again only the length of a plank away. Except for the new balcony nothing much had changed there. Through the opposite porthole he could see, across the snow-covered fields and movers' camps, smoke curling from the Traner chimney. Nothing there had changed at all. He was still, as much as he had been before, his brothers' keeper. And beholden to Ish, even some to Job, besides. Now that he was back, there was nothing so very different about him either. All he had brought back with him were a pair of broken legs and frostbitten feet. Everything else that had come to him while he was away had been taken away from him again. Even Jasper. The boat, of course, had come back with him. But that night before he left when first he had stretched out on this bunk the boat had already seemed the same as his.

The kitchen door creaked. And then he was taken the rest of the way back to the other night. Again Esther was coming across the plank. She was carrying a tray instead of an armful of buffalo robe, but again she was making straight for the cabin door. The door opened and she stood in it.

The clouds had thinned and there was a good light on her. The open door let in a puff of clean, sweet air into the hot cabin. She looked more different than anything else had and yet strangely the same. She had grown up. She was taller and thinner, and with her hair done up and a dress that fitted she carried herself like a woman. But she was still Esther. She had the same little-girl look of holding nothing back and yet holding everything back.

"Thought you might do with some ham and eggs and pone," she said.

It was a relief to hear no more edge to her tone than as though she was passing a plate down the table to a stranger. She might have been expected to come at him with every claw out.

"I'd be much obliged," he said.

She shoved the stool over next to the bunk and bent to arrange the tray on it. He raised on one elbow, watching her. During his year away he had begun to take the trouble to notice the real differences among women. He thought of all the others he had watched in this same cabin. Philippa. Magda. Hagar. Félicie. She was not in the least like any of them. But the comparison was not all in their favor. No one of them had a trimmer shape or a smoother complexion. And there was something about her, something oddly disturbing.

Ish sat up, yawned, stretched, appeared to become suddenly aware of Esther's presence, and beamed at her foolishly. She turned and looked at him as though she had never seen him before. His mouth dropped open. The atmosphere in the cabin became electric with many difficulties too complicated for Ish's command of words. Abel made haste to fend off at least one of them.

"Never any use trying to figger out what Ish has been up to. What he told me was he was just poking downriver with some idea of maybe stopping off to see Simon Kenton when he came across my boat anchored off Limestone. When he found out my legs were busted he brought me home."

Ish was edging toward the door.

"Reckon yuh could do with a mite more wood," he said and bolted out.

Esther rose and looked steadily down at Abel.

"Is that all he told you?"

"Ish ain't much of a talker and most of the time he was right busy—what with the weather and me no good to anybody. He said your pa was laid up. He said my folks were about the same. He said you'd been well. He said you had a young English bookkeeper. And that was about all."

"Then maybe I'd better tell you—straight off—long's you can't get around to find out for yourself—how things are here. When he first broke his back Paw took it real hard. But he's got over part of that now. Once you finally did show up—and hurt, besides—he backed off some from the idea of shooting you the minute he sighed you. Next to that, the main thing is that he'll buy Traner Mountain. He could use the coal to go with his iron ore. That ought to bring you enough to give you and your folks a right good start in Kentucky."

"Yur pa's a good man," said Abel. "And I owe him a good turn. But I wouldn't say—not straight off—that I'd want to sell."

He was speaking with great care but paying more attention to the discovery that he could study her in the mirror without her noticing. The more closely he looked the more he could see in how many ways she was different from any of the others who had been, at one time and another, reflected in it. Except for one. Madame Marillac. Esther had the same eyes and hair and skin, the same way of holding herself. He went on speaking carefully.

"What I mean is—I figger I better sit around and think

313

things over for a spell—before I make up my mind. I mean about Traner Mountain."

She turned partly away from him. The sun, edging above the shoulder of Traner Mountain, brightened the cabin, making her white skin seem whiter and her black hair blacker. Framed in the porthole behind her the smoke from his brothers' chimney was now rising directly upward. Suddenly the sense of expectancy was with him again. And as suddenly her calm broke. She dropped to her knees beside the bunk. The strength of her fingers struck through the blanket into his shoulder as she shook him. Her eyes were bright with tears.

"This is no place for you to sit around and think. Go away —and take your boat with you—as soon as the ice will let you. And stay away."

"You think your pa wouldn't stand for my waiting 'til—say spring?"

"Not only him. Nobody could."

"Eben thinks that before too long he might get used to seeing me around and that if there was any sign of you and me happening to pick up where we left off, he might begin to figger on letting me run his new furnace."

She released her clutch on him and hid her face in her hands. He reached out, tentatively, and touched her hair. She jerked away.

"Don't pat me—like I was a dog."

His fingers slipped from her bowed head down along her tear-wet cheek and under her chin to lift her face. Her eyes were fiercely closed against the sight of him.

"What makes you think I'm so sure to take to the river again?"

"You did before. And you're twice as apt now—after all you've seen and done."

"Maybe from all that I learned something."

Her eyes flew open.

"What?"

"Maybe that what a man wants most is a place for himself. Maybe that this is mine."

What had started in her throat as a sob came out as something very like a little girl's giggle.

"Everything's maybe. So maybe I better tell Paw not to shoot you—that is—not right straight off."